Before the Snow Flies

MISSION POINT PRESS

Published by Mission Point Press
and Chandler Lakes Books
2554 Chandler Rd.
Traverse City, MI 49696
(231) 421-9513
www.MissionPointPress.com

Cover photo courtesy of Crescent Rose Photography.

ISBN: 978-1-943338-17-7
Library of Congress Control Number: 2019934695

Printed in the United States of America.

JOHN WEMLINGER

BEFORE the SNOW FLIES

MISSION POINT PRESS

To my wife, Diane,
A woman of keen insight into people ...
   a woman of caring and compassion ...
and
a licensed professional counselor.
The world is desperate for more
   people like you!

★ ★ ★ ★ PRELUDE ★ ★ ★ ★

The wars in Iraq and Afghanistan are like the progress of an inchworm moving through time. It surges and then it flattens out, it surges again, and then flattens out. But in combat, the concept of time can be meaningless. Months and years are like millennia compared to the mere fractions of a second in which lives can be lost or momentously changed forever.

This book, though it deals with the difficult subject of suicide in the face of wartime catastrophes, is meant to be hopeful. When I first started to write it, my focus was on military suicides, but the deeper I got into it, the more I thought, *it isn't only military suicides.* The root causes of suicide are the same regardless if you are a male or a female, black or white, gay or straight, military or civilian. It respects no race or religion.

The book's hero is a member of the military. Why? Because that's a culture I know. I was a professional soldier for a long time ... twenty-seven years ... and I write best when I write about things I know.

Major David Keller, at war for a long time, survives a life-altering injury inflicted by a roadside improvised explosive device in Afghanistan, but, mentally, he falls into a deep abyss. You are about to share several emotional journeys: Major Keller's, his family's, and his friends', both old and new.

I write novels because I enjoy the challenge of turning out a good story that captures readers' imaginations. However, I also like to think that in some small way, after the reader closes the book and reflects, even if only for the briefest of moments, on what they've read, there is a message of optimism, a message of *what might be* if we treat one another with caring and compassion. So, turn the page. I hope you enjoy the read.

1.

FALLING

No one saw it coming. The road had been swept twice this day. The improvised explosive device, IED in military parlance, should have been detected and cleared. What was about to happen shouldn't have, but, this day, Murphy's Law was about to be implemented: *If something can go wrong, it will go wrong, and at the worst possible time.*

1435 hours: During the final week of his combat tour, Major David Keller was looking down at his handheld GPS to see exactly where they were. He was traveling with his battalion's operations officer, its command sergeant major and the sergeant major's driver on their way back from a meeting with a local village leader when the explosion ripped into their Humvee. He sat on the side of the vehicle closest to the bomb and, at that short distance, the thunderous noise, the blinding light, and the blast of heat all came at them at once. The only one of the four not wearing a seat belt, that lapse of safety was likely what saved his life. The blast's force literally blew him out of the fireball that their vehicle suddenly became.

★ ★ ★ ★

1437 hours: It's a dream, that's all, just a dream. He'd dreamed it a thousand times before: the one where you're falling. He expected to hear the wind whistling past him, but he couldn't hear anything. The miserable sandy grit that had been the Afghan desert but now was a byproduct of the explosion swirled around him even at the fifty or sixty feet he'd been thrown clear of the burning vehicle. He couldn't see anything, but then again, he was so out of it, the line between conscious and unconscious was razor thin.

★ ★ ★ ★

1505 hours: The pilot deftly settled the Blackhawk helicopter onto the Maltese cross that marked the center of the concrete helipad and quickly rolled the throttles back to idle. A medic in an olive-green flight suit jumped out as soon as the aircraft touched down. Two corpsmen waited at either end of a gurney positioned well outside the slowing orbit of the rotor blades. A nurse hunkered down under the rotors and approached the helicopter's medic. They stood close to one another, the medic bending down to speak into her ear in order to be heard over the shrill turbine-whine of the helicopter's twin engines. "This one's pretty bad, ma'am. IED. He took the brunt of the blast. Killed everyone else in the vehicle." He threw a thumb over one shoulder, pointing to three stretchers inside the helicopter, each holding a body, concealed in a thick black plastic body bag. After taking care of the living, the helicopter would reposition onto another helipad in the same complex to unload those less fortunate at the hospital's morgue. "No idea how he survived," the medic continued. "One leg's fully severed. We looked, but couldn't find it. The other is just hanging there by a thread. He's lost a lot of blood. He started to come to a few minutes out, so I started a morphine drip. He just went under. Thought it best ... you know ... I wouldn't want to wake up to something like that." The medic pointed to the patient's missing and nearly missing legs.

★ ★ ★ ★

1507 hours: David's mind reeled. The only sense that seemed to be working was his sense of smell and it wasn't like anything he could ever remember: an odd combination of cordite, blood, and the antiseptic scent of freshly opened sterile bandages.

★ ★ ★ ★

1508 hours: The nurse motioned for the two corpsmen to come forward. She patted the helicopter's medic on the shoulder: "OK, we got it from here. Good job." Turning to the corpsmen, who were leaning in to hear her, she said, "OK, the docs are waiting. Let's get him prepped for OR." They slid the stretcher out of the helicopter and lifted it onto the gurney while the nurse took the IV drip from the medic. She gave the pilots a thumbs-up with her one free hand and hustled away from the helicopter blades, which were already starting to turn faster as the engines throttled up.

★ ★ ★ ★

1510 hours: The falling sensation lingered. Nothing made any sense to him. *What? Where am I? What the hell ...* His mind's eye captured a bird's eye view of a snow-covered field. *How did I?* He recognized where he was, but could not comprehend how he got here. This field was just outside his hometown of Onekama. Inwardly he laughed. No one except folks from there ever could figure out how to say that name. *One comma* was the typical mispronunciation. He always corrected them: "It's pronounced Oh-neck-ah-ma." Even then, they'd have to say it a few times before they got it right. The field grew nearer and nearer. It was as familiar to him as his own name. He recalled trudging through it, rifle slung over his shoulder, on his way to his father's deer blind. He remembered tearing across it on his snowmobile with Maggie holding onto him for dear life as she screamed for him to slow down. *Maggie ... How long ago has it been?* He couldn't focus sufficiently to come up with the answer exactly, so he settled on *fifteen years ... give or take ...* He felt himself settle into the snow.

"Don't you just love the snow when it's fresh like this?" Her voice was clear and familiar. He struggled to turn his head. Lying there in the snow next to him was Maggie, just as he remembered her from his senior year of high school. "Let's make snow angels," she said.

He watched her raise her arms from her side to above her head while sweeping her legs from side to side. She was giggling.

How? It isn't possible.

"It's your turn, David. Make your snow angel," she urged him.

Her smile had always dazzled him. *No, it can't be. You can't be here ... I can't be here.*

"Go ahead, David. You're never too old to make snow angels," she chided him.

He could feel himself raising his arms from his side to over his head and then back down to his side. But when he tried to move his legs, there was no equivalent sensation.

★ ★ ★ ★

1511 hours: The patient spasmed on the stainless-steel operating table. The doctor looked across at the surgical nurse. She shook her head. He looked at the nurse anesthetist who nodded and said, "OK, he's out. He won't move again. BP's a little low, but heart rate is stable. He's all yours, Doctor."

"Let's stabilize this left leg first as best we can. We'll let the docs at Landsthul see if maybe there's some miracle they can perform on him. I've got a friend in orthopedics there ... I'll call him when we're through here." The nurse nodded and immediately began gathering surgical instruments she knew he would need. The doctor turned to a technician behind him who was working at a computer station: "Notify scheduling that Major David Keller here will require an ICU spot on the next C-9 headed for Landsthul ... highest priority."

2

MAGGIE MCCALL

M-22 is one of America's most scenic byways. It meanders in a series of lazy curves through open fields, dense forests, and across spectacular inland lakes as it makes its way from Manistee all the way to Northport along the eastern shore of Lake Michigan, a distance of about eighty-five miles. The first village along that route, as one drives north, is the village of Onekama, an expandable resort town that boasts a year-round population of about four hundred, but swells to fifteen thousand summertime visitors who crave its mild weather and lake accesses between Memorial and Labor Days. It is imbued with all the pleasures of small-town life and all of its tribulations as well.

As locals in Onekama go, Maggie McCall was a relative newcomer. She'd been in town a little over sixteen years. But today, she wished she was anywhere else in the world. She wasn't going to answer the knock at the front door, but, as she peeked out the kitchen window, she could see her friend Emily Weber's car in the driveway. Still holding the ice pack against her right eye, she opened the door.

"Oh, God! He hit you?" Emily swore an expletive under her breath.

"Not exactly," Maggie replied.

As the two settled over fresh cups of coffee, Emily gently took her best friend's hand in hers and asked, "You all right, Mags?"

"Yeah ... I am ... just damn glad it's Tuesday and I don't have to open the Yellow Dog today."

"Well, the coffee shop and its patrons can just wait a while," Emily opined. She stirred cream into her coffee, took a sip, and then proceeded, "It's all over town already. I've heard a couple of versions, but the only thing they had in common is that the sheriff's office was here last night. What the hell happened?"

"Ray showed up here about seven o'clock. He still has a key. I was out here in the kitchen. I didn't hear him until he was right there in the doorway." She pointed to the kitchen entry from the living room. "He scared the bejesus out of me."

"We've got to get these locks changed," Emily offered, realizing that the suggestion was a nickel late and a dollar short. "Was he drunk?"

"He was, and you know what he's like when he's like that."

"Oh, Maggie."

"Yeah, well he starts yellin' at me about the Yellow Dog being more important to me than him ... " Tears came to the corners of her eyes. Maggie dabbed at them and continued. "I guess Mrs. Burney across the street could hear him yellin' and swearin'. She's the one that called the sheriff's office, and me and Jack are just lucky there was a deputy close by that could take the call. He got here quick."

"Jack was here?" Without waiting on the answer, Emily repeated, "Oh, Maggie."

"He came in the middle of it, just before the deputy got here. Ray was swearin' at me, calling me all kinds of foul names. Jack told him to stop. I told Ray to get out. He made a move toward me and Jack moved in front of him. Ray grabbed him and when he did that, Jasmine lunged at Ray. Ray gave her an awful kick to the belly ... bounced that poor dog halfway across the kitchen. Ray still had a hold on

Jack, so I tried to get him to let go. That's when I caught Ray's elbow in the eye."

"Quite a shiner you got there, kiddo!"

It was the way she'd said that. Maggie chuckled, "Yeah, well I wish I could say 'you should see the other guy,' but truth is Ray didn't even get a scratch. The deputy got here just before things really started to get out of hand. He made sure Jack, Jasmine, and I were OK, then he took Ray home to his dad's. At least, that's where I think they took him. I think Ray's dad has the sheriff's office trained to just bring him to his place. Honestly, I don't know, and I don't really care. I just know I don't want to ever see him again. I'm thinking about going to Chicago for a while."

"You think he won't follow you there?"

Maggie shrugged. "I don't know."

"He will, you know. He's crazy like that. It won't matter to him that he's a nobody in Chicago. He thinks his daddy will protect him, no matter where he is, no matter what he's done. No, Maggie, you need to stand up to this asshole once and for all and you need to do it right now. You can stay with me and Chuck until you can get the locks changed on the house. We can get a restraining order that keeps him away from you. And, you can file for divorce and full custody of Jack."

That was a lot for Maggie to digest and it all seemed so overwhelming to her. "Chicago would be a lot easier."

"Would it? Take a minute and think about it, Maggie. The court would have to be on your side right now, especially since the sheriff's office had to come out last night. Hell, I'll go to court and testify that he's been an asshole ever since you married the guy. But if you leave and take Jack with you, who knows what Ray and his father might do? I wouldn't put it past them to accuse you of kidnapping Jack and running away to Chicago."

Maggie sat at the kitchen table with her head cradled in her hands, the ice pack still jammed against her right eye.

Jasmine, her five-year-old golden retriever, got up and walked over to her and laid her head gently in Maggie's lap.

"He kicked that sweet dog last night?" Emily asked disdainfully.

Maggie nodded and added, "Doc Wickern checked her over this morning. He said she's OK. Maybe a bruised rib or two, but nothing broken. He took some X-rays. She seems OK." She smiled down at the dog and rubbed her head with her unencumbered hand.

"How's Jack?"

"I dunno," she said shaking her head. "He says he's OK, but no son should hear his parents fight like we were last night, and, certainly, no son should ever have to step in front of his father because he thinks he's about to hit his mother."

"Jack's a good kid, Maggie. You've done a good job with him, no thanks to Ray. Besides, Ray isn't ... "

Maggie sat bolt upright and put her hand up toward Emily. "Stop right there, Em. Ray's the only father the boy's ever known. That isn't going to change." The kitchen fell silent. Emily looked away from her best friend. Then Maggie offered, "Besides, Ray wasn't always like this, Em."

"I know, Maggie, but he's like this now and you, Jack, and Jasmine deserve better." The dog lifted her head when she heard her name, but then put it back down again on Maggie's lap.

Maggie looked at her friend and said, "I'm more afraid of Clipper than I am of Ray."

Paul "Clipper" McCall, Maggie's father-in-law, started out as a barber in Onekama back in the early 70s, hence the nickname "Clipper" which had stuck with him to this day. His foray into politics began as a member of the village of Onekama's city council. It was difficult to tell what he liked best about politics, the exposure or the power, but it wasn't long before he'd set his sights on higher office. In the late 80s he was elected as state representative. By 1990 he'd become the speaker of Michigan's House of Representatives. Then in 1992, the state of Michigan imposed term limits on their state legislators and Clipper decided it was time to run for the US House of Representatives, where he served until 2005. His political career ended with his defeat in a Republican gubernatorial primary race. But Clipper had kept careful track of his friends over the years and he was not bashful about calling in markers, especially when his son needed bailing out of "unfortunate misunderstandings," as Clipper preferred to call Ray's not infrequent brushes with the law.

Emily waved her hand dismissively. "That ol' bag of wind. He's pushed people around long enough. It's time someone stood up to him, Maggie, and there's no better reason I can think of than Jack."

3

LANDSTUHL

D r. Philomena Goldstein, at only thirty-five years of age, had risen rapidly to become the director of the Department of Psychiatric Care at the miitary facility, Landstuhl Regional Medical Center in Landstuhl, Germany. She was, by ten years, the youngest department head at the hospital, but everyone on the staff loved and respected her. Most of the other department heads were damned glad she was there so they didn't have to deal with all of the mental and emotional trauma associated with war wounds. Yet, she knew she was nonetheless a disappointment to her father, Dr. William Goldstein, head of neurosurgery at the University of Chicago Medical Center. When she had decided to enter psychiatry upon graduation from Harvard Medical School, he had said to her, "Philomena, you have a gift: the hands of a concert pianist. You are called to be a surgeon."

"Surgery is too routine," she'd said to him. "I want my days to begin with me having no idea how they will end." Five years ago, she'd arrived at Landstuhl. With combat-wounded service members arriving almost daily, her work there had lived up to her every expectation and then some. There had been two docs in the department then, an army lieutenant colonel and herself. Though she was not in the military, her contract was through the Pentagon and so she had to learn how to function within that new and very different milieu. The lieutenant colonel turned out to be more of a mentor than a boss, but he'd retired two years ago and was not replaced. Dr. Goldstein's contract was rewritten, her salary increased marginally, and she was promoted to department head. Within her department, she was the only one with a medical degree. The other five practitioners were licensed professional counselors, or LPCs, for short. All had received formal training in the nuances of dealing with combat-wounded service members. But the real test was working in the crucible that was Landsthul Regional Medical Center. Her least experienced LPC had over five years' experience, all of it right here, working almost exclusively with wounded service members who'd been evacuated to Landstuhl from either Iraq or Afghanistan. Their job, one of the hospital's most difficult, was to interview every one of them and assess, as best they could, the mental health care needs of each patient and make sure that assessment was well documented in their medical records. It was an impossible task, not because the department wasn't fully dedicated to their mission, or because its practitioners weren't skilled at what they did. There simply wasn't enough time. The average length of stay for a wounded service member at Landstuhl was a mere two weeks. Landstuhl was where recovery began, not where it was completed.

It was, indeed, very rare for Major David Keller to have been here for six weeks, four of which found him in a medically induced coma. A week ago, David's surgeons made the decision to lift him out of the coma. Two days ago, two of Philomena's LPCs began talking to him. Now, on this early January morning, it was Philomena's turn after both of her LPCs came to her indicating their concern for this particular patient's mental health.

David, from his bed, turned his head toward the door when it opened and then went back to blankly staring out the window at the opposite end of the room. Dr. Goldstein had been warned that he was not very responsive to visitors, especially doctors, and her knee-length white clinic coat was a dead giveaway. "Major Keller, I'm Dr. Philomena Goldstein. How are you feeling today?"

David turned back toward her. His expression was one of disdain. "How am I feeling? You've got to be kidding me, Doc. Look down here," and he pointed to the lower half of his hospital bed. "See anything there? No, you don't, because both my legs are gone. So, how the hell do you think I feel?"

She opened her laptop and David's medical records were there in front of her. She glanced through them to see if he was on any type of medication that might heighten his anxiety as a side effect.

"What kind of a doc are you?"

She looked up from the computer. "I'm a psychiatrist."

His face lit up in a sarcastic sneer. Dr. Goldstein could see it coming.

"Well, dammit, if I had a thigh, I'd slap it," he chortled.

Dr. Goldstein steeled herself.

"Dr. Phil, as I live and breathe! Where am I? I thought I was in Landstuhl, but it must be Hollywood if you're here. Where's the studio audience, Doc? I know you probably have millions of bored housewives looking in." Keller faked combing his hair. "How do I look, Doc? Is this good enough for TV? Yeah, OK, go ahead and save me in the next hour, will ya?"

She'd been here before. When she first arrived at Landstuhl some of her professional colleagues had made the same joke. She'd shot them down with a piercing stare, and then the comment, "Is that the best you've got? I've heard that since my first day of residency ... so no points for originality." The word quickly got around not to ever call Dr. Goldstein *Dr. Phil*.

She closed the lid on her laptop and shot Keller a look.

"Oops, touched a nerve did I, Doc?"

She smiled at him. "You did, Major."

The smile faded from his face and he turned back toward the window. Barely audible, but sufficiently loud enough for her to hear, David said, "Yeah, well, at least you still have your legs."

"They are doing some incredible things with prosthesis these days, Major."

David continued to stare wordlessly out of the window. Dr. Goldstein didn't pursue the thought any further because she really had no idea if prosthesis was possible for him or not. Landsthul didn't have a prosthetics department. When she'd asked the orthopedic surgeon who'd removed the remaining leg about the possibility of prosthesis, he shook his head and said he wasn't sure. All she knew for sure was that whatever recovery he was facing, prosthesis or not, it was going to be long, difficult, and, at times, even torturous.

Dr. Goldstein changed the direction of their conversation. "We've kept your family updated on your condition."

David turned toward her. "I have no family."

Dr. Goldstein was prepared for this. Both of the LPCs who'd talked with him earlier said he denied having any family. So, she decided to press the point. Thumbing through his computerized file, she started to say, "Your DD Form 93 ... "

David shot her a look, "I know what my form says, but I have no family."

"Your father ... "

"Haven't seen him since I graduated from high school."

"Your younger brother ... "

"What about him? I haven't seen him either."

The picture was becoming clearer now for Dr. Goldstein. In David's records she'd read the Report of Casualty Officer Visit. The casualty officer, whose job it was to notify the next-of-kin that Major Keller had been wounded, had gone to the address listed on David's DD Form 93, Record of Emergency Data, looking for Mr. Thomas Paul Keller, who was listed as Major Keller's father. However, at that address he'd found a young couple with a completely different name who explained to him that Mr. Keller no longer lived there. He'd moved in with his son, PJ, and his wife. They gave him the new address, right there in the same town, Onekama, Michigan. At that new address, the casualty officer met PJ, his wife, Natalie, their two sons, Max and Sam, and Major Keller's father, his next-of-kin, Tom Keller.

By regulation, the casualty officer is required to notify that person listed on the DD Form 93 as the next-of-kin, but in this case, there had to be some slight bending of the rules when Tom told the casualty officer that he didn't have a son named David. It was at this point that PJ, short for Paul John, pulled the casualty officer into the adjoining kitchen. "Listen, you're in the right place. My brother, David ... uh, Major David Raymond Keller...that's who we're talking about right?"

The casualty officer confirmed, "Yes, sir."

"Uh, yeah. OK, then. He's my brother. That's our dad in there," he said, pointing to the other room. "But he has his days. Sometimes he can recall David, and sometimes he can't. Today is one of those days when he can't, apparently. It's dementia."

The casualty officer gave the information to Tom because that was what the army required him to do, but he made sure that PJ and Natalie heard everything and when he asked if Mr. Keller had any questions, he looked first at the old man and then to PJ.

David's denial that he had a family was disconcerting to Dr. Goldstein, to say the least. Even though the wounded warriors she saw, *her warriors,* as she liked to think of them, were merely passing through the hospital, she also thought of Landsthul as *her hospital.* Standing now next to David's bed, she said to him, "Your brother, Paul, has asked to be kept apprised of your status. So, you do have people out there that are concerned about you, Major."

"My dad's a handyman and I heard my brother is an attorney ... the county prosecutor, I'm told. They've got their lives, I've got mine," he said, gesturing toward his missing legs, "such as it is. I don't want anything from them, least of all their pity. So just write up whatever you have to write up and tell me where to next, and when."

Dr. Goldstein tried a different approach, one that had worked for her before with people who were service oriented. "Major Keller, you damn near died twice. The first time was from blood loss, the second time was from an infection. That's why the coma was induced, so that your body could concentrate on fighting the infection and not worry about any burdens that the mind might put on it. You're on the right path now, but you are going to need a lot of help going forward. It's quite likely, I think, that your family will want to be a part of that."

"Yeah, well, I don't see much in my future without my legs, so let's just stuff the psychobabble. You aren't going to keep me here in Landsthul to work on my psyche. You need the bed for the next poor sonuvabitch that gets blown to bits. So, just answer the questions. Where to next? When?"

Even Dr. Goldstein's patience was wearing thin at this point, but she stayed on course. "I don't make those calls. You are correct, we aren't going to keep you here to work on your head. But, know this, if I could keep you here, I would. And I will make sure that wherever you go from here, they know you have a family back in Michigan that cares about you. Dammit, Major, you're alive today because a lot of good people cared about you and did their jobs as best they could under some difficult conditions to save your ass. We aren't going to stop now just because you've got a shitty attitude."

David smiled wryly. "So, Dr. Phil, that's it? That's what's wrong with me ... shitty attitude. How about if I just take two aspirins? Then don't call me again, Doc. I'll call you if I need you ... which I won't." He turned back toward the window.

She turned on her heel, and as the door closed behind her, she stopped, lowered her head, and realized that for the first time in a long time, she'd let a patient get to her. She hadn't helped him one little bit with her visit, but she had gained some professional insights into David's psyche. She knew he wouldn't be here much longer. Back at her desk, she resolved that her write-up in Major David Keller's medical records was going to reflect her very deep concern for his mental health. It was her grim assessment that, if left to his own devices, without proper mental health treatment David could become suicidal, and that was an outcome that Dr. Goldstein considered absolutely unacceptable.

4

GOOD NEWS, BAD NEWS

Margaret Lassiter McCall was known for her perkiness, her ever-fresh look. Naturally attractive in a California-girl sort of way, she needed little makeup to make heads turn. Her hair was a mahogany brown, long and wavy, and today she wore it pulled back in a ponytail. Under her apron, she wore a pair of black slacks that hugged her trim frame and a white blouse with the sleeves rolled up to just below the elbow because she didn't want them dragging in a customer's food. At work, the ever-present apron was a habit she'd learned from her mother, who'd been the one that taught Maggie her way around the kitchen, especially when it came to baking.

However, that morning, looking at her reflection in the coffee shop's powder-room mirror, she pulled down on the bags under each eye and let go. The bags returned. "Shit!" she muttered under her breath, stepped back from the mirror, washed her hands, and returned to the front of the Yellow Dog Café. It had been a busy morning. Only one breakfast bagel sandwich remained in the case and she was already halfway through her supply of lunch sandwiches. The construction business was once again robust around Onekama as people of means were building mammoth homes along Lake Michigan or around Portage Lake. Framers, plumbers, electricians, masons, tilers, HVAC mechanics, and laborers of all types stopped at the Yellow Dog on their way to their job sites and stocked up on Maggie's sandwiches for their breakfasts and lunches. She poured herself a steaming cup of dark roast, plunked down in one of the easy chairs in front of the café's expansive glass window, and took a moment to enjoy the warm sun streaming through. Sunny days in January in northern Michigan were a rarity, and she told herself she had earned the break. But she'd no sooner settled into the chair when the door opened and Emily walked in. She took one look at Maggie and said, "Still not sleeping well?"

"It shows that much?"

Reluctantly Emily offered, "Yeah, Mags, it shows. What's the matter, kiddo? Don't tell me that soon-to-be ex of yours is coming around. Just call the cops ... "

"No," Maggie interrupted her, "it's not that. He's abiding by the PPO. He knows all the locks have been changed and I think his father has really cracked down on him after I called the sheriff that day he was parked across the street just staring in here at me."

"What's the attorney telling you about the divorce?"

Maggie got up and got her friend a cup of coffee. As she handed it to her, Maggie sat back down in front of the window and Emily settled into the chair next to her. "I'm losing sleep over this damned divorce," she said.

"It shows," her friend said nonchalantly.

"I've finally managed to get angry about this, Em. Dammit, I've been married to Ray for sixteen years. The attorney says that's considered 'a long-term marriage.' He says I should be able to get what I want out of any settlement we reach."

"OK. So, what's the problem?"

"Clipper."

Emily was a very successful businesswoman in her own right. She owned one of the largest real estate firms in all of Manistee County. In any given year she and her hand-picked group of associates did a volume of business measured in the hundreds of millions of dollars in sales. She knew lots of powerful people in the region. She was in fact considered to be one of them, but when she heard the word *Clipper* she just threw up her hands. "What's he trying to do now?"

"Invoke something his attorney is calling *grandparents' rights,*" Maggie responded.

"Well, where the hell was he when that no-good son of his was slipping further and further into the bottle and leaving you and Jack out on a limb? He's got some nerve. There's no such thing as grandparents' rights, is there? What's your attorney telling you?"

"He says that there really isn't any such thing, but ... "

Emily, shaking her head, chirped, "There's always a *but* with Clipper, isn't there, Mags?"

"Yeah, Em, there is. He's pushing me for a compromise that I'm not sure I should make."

"May I ask what might that be?"

"I want primary custody of Jack. I want the house. The mortgage has a balance of ninety thousand. I want Ray to take that on or he can get Clipper to pay it off. I don't care as long as I still have the house. The Yellow Dog is in my name, so Ray and Clipper, neither of them, can get their hands on my business. And I want five-hundred dollars a month in child support, along with a guarantee from Ray or Clipper, again, I don't care which one, that Jack's college tuition will be paid for."

"Sounds fair to me. You put up with a lot from that jackass for a long damn time. So, what does Ray want?"

"That's just it. So far, the jackass doesn't want anything. It's Clipper that's made the demand for visitation every other weekend."

"I thought Ray was living at Clipper's."

"Now you're seeing my dilemma," Maggie replied.

"But the PPO ... "

"The personal protection order just keeps Ray away from me. It doesn't include Jack."

"Screw that. Let's just go get one for Jack. Ray doesn't deserve to be around that sweet boy." Emily was furious.

"The word from Ray's lawyer, who is actually Clipper's lawyer as well, is that if I try something like that, they will fight me tooth and nail in court, and wouldn't I be better off just allowing Clipper and Ray to see Jack every other weekend."

Emily looked at her old friend. "What's Jack say about all of this, Maggie?"

"We've talked a couple of times about it. Jack's OK with it. He doesn't care for his father at all. He thinks he's treated me rotten for as long as he can remember. But Jack has a soft spot for his grandfather."

"This would be a lot easier for me to swallow if Trudy were still alive," Emily offered.

"Yeah, me too. Truth be known, I think a part of Ray died with his mother. He was always a bit of a hell raiser, but Trudy could always settle him down. After she died, Clipper never tried. All he does is make excuses for Ray. He bails him out whenever he gets sideways with the law."

"So, I guess it comes down to one question, 'Do you think Clipper and Ray can be trusted with Jack every other weekend?'"

Maggie thought for a moment and then answered, "If Jack were younger, I'd say no. But he's sixteen, Em. In two years, he's off to college. Who can I trust then, except Jack, to make good decisions? Maybe this next couple of years with Clipper and Ray will be good experience for him. Jack's the one who said to me the other evening, 'C'mon, Mom. Stop worrying so much about me. I'm a big boy now.' "

"Is he driving yet?"

"He's got his learner's permit and he's chomping at the bit. I expect he'll be ready to take his tests in a month or so. Why do you ask?"

Emily shrugged. "I wouldn't let him go over to Clipper's unless he's got a car. If the cheese should get binding while he's there, Jack would have the good sense to leave and come home, if he's got a car. Don't you think?"

"Yeah, well, where am I going to get a car for him? All I've got is my old pickup."

Emily smiled and gave her good friend a conspiratorial look. "Add it to the list for Ray's lawyer and tell him, while he's at it, to tell Clipper to make it a new car ... maybe a nice Chevy Equinox or a Jeep, so Jack can make it back and forth from college when that time comes."

Maggie smiled at her friend and simply nodded. "No wonder people like the real estate deals you negotiate for them. Thanks, Em."

"You're welcome." There was a rather long pause between the two, then Emily changed the subject. "Have you heard the news about David?"

"David Keller?"

Emily knew her friend knew exactly which David she was talking about. But David Keller lived in a really dark place inside Maggie's memories and she knew Maggie did not like to go there, so she gave her a pass. "He's been hurt, Mags."

Skeptically, Maggie replied, "So what will this be? Purple Heart number five?"

"No, Mags, I mean he's been really hurt this time."

Maggie, who'd moved behind the counter and begun to tidy up, stopped what she was doing and looked at Emily. "What happened?"

"He's lost both legs. A roadside bomb. He's the lucky one. The other three in the vehicle were killed. PJ says he's being transferred to Walter Reed Hospital in Washington."

"PJ told you about this?"

"I'd heard a rumor. I got wind of it from a client of

mine ... the young couple that bought Tom Keller's house after PJ and Natalie took him in ... that an army officer had turned up on their doorstep one night looking for Tom. They gave him PJ's address. You know me, just can't let sleeping dogs lie. So, I had some business in Manistee yesterday afternoon in the courthouse, where I just happened to bump into PJ..."

"Just bumped into him, eh," Maggie smiled at her. "How coincidental."

Emily smiled back, "Well, that is, I bumped into him after his secretary told me he was in courtroom four."

Maggie nodded knowingly.

"Anyway, while I was in there I bumped into PJ. He wasn't going to just volunteer the information about David. You know they don't talk. So, I just up and asked him. He told me old Tom didn't even remember having a son named David when the officer told him what had happened. That dementia is such a terrible thing."

Maggie didn't say a word and for the briefest of moments, Emily felt like she never should have said anything to her.

Then, in a voice gone raspy, Maggie asked, "What's PJ going to do?"

"He doesn't know. Talk about having your hands full. I mean county prosecutor, married, two young sons, Tom living with them ... and now ... this. I tell you my heart goes out to him and Natalie as much as it does to David."

Maggie didn't respond. Emily checked her watch. "Maybe I shouldn't have said anything, but I didn't want you to hear about David from the grapevine ... better, I thought, if it came from me." She gave Maggie a hug and whispered, "You OK?"

Maggie, her voice even more raspy, said, "Thanks, Em. I appreciate it."

"OK. I have to go to an appointment in Pierport in fifteen minutes. I'll call you later." She hated leaving her like this.

Maggie nodded.

When the door closed, Maggie watched her friend slide into her late model Cadillac Escalade and pull from the curb. While Maggie's beauty was wholesome and natural, Emily was the more glamorous one of the two. Her makeup and hair were always perfect. She dripped diamonds, necklaces, earrings, bracelets, and rings, first because her lucrative real estate business let her afford them, and two, because "showy" is what she had to be for the clients she dealt with. They were looking at million-dollar properties along Lake Michigan. She'd said to Maggie, "Hell, Mags, if it's *showy* they want then it's *showy* they will get." But Maggie knew that under that glamorous façade was a true friend. She watched the Cadillac disappear around the curve in M-22 just north of Portage Street, then she turned the deadbolt lock on the door and flipped the *Open* sign to *Closed*. As she headed for the powder room, she put her hands over her face and let the tears she'd been holding back begin to flow.

5

IT'S BEEN A LONG TIME

PJ Keller was not by most measures a pessimist, though no one would have blamed him for being just that given the way this trip had started. Even odder, he'd had a premonition, likely stress induced, that it would not go well. He had only three days to get from Onekama to Washington, DC and back. Two trials awaited him at home. One was a murder trial, the other, a sexual assault case. Both crimes had shaken the quiet, this-can't-be-happening-here community of Manistee when they'd occurred within a couple of weeks of one another. One letter to the editor asked the question, *Was Manistee becoming another murder capitol like Detroit?* He'd chuckled to himself when he read that, but he was careful not to dismiss it altogether. Manistee County, in geographical size, was larger than metropolitan Detroit, but its population was only a fraction of Detroit's. As he'd gotten deeper and deeper into the gruesome details of both crimes, he was stunned at both their violence and their close proximity in both time and location to one another. PJ knew the good people of Manistee, both the town and the county, were looking to him as the county prosecutor to put the two perpetrators away for a good long time and restore the sense of safety that had, at least for the moment, been splintered.

When the first leg of his flight to Detroit out of Traverse City was delayed by over two hours, it set off a chain of events that rippled through his entire day—and night.

Instead of arriving at Reagan National at 12:30 p.m., he landed at Dulles Airport at 1:00 a.m.

The delay had caused him to miss a meeting with Dr. Masters, the head of the psychiatric department at Walter Reed National Military Medical Center. While waiting helplessly at the Detroit airport, he called and rescheduled, but Dr. Masters wouldn't be able to see him until three o'clock the following day. Making matters worse, Dr. Masters had suggested that PJ not see his brother until they'd had a chance to talk. "I am aware that there is an estrangement between the two of you. He has made that abundantly clear to me and some of my staff. I am also aware of your father's dementia. But we don't believe your brother is aware of it and we have not mentioned it to him. So, I think it's a good idea for us to meet so that we can prepare you for what you are walking into and perhaps you can offer us some insight into how we should proceed. From a physical standpoint, your brother's recovery is going as well as can be expected for a man who came as close to death as he did. It's his mental state that has all of us concerned, Mr. Keller."

At about 1:30 a.m., PJ, despite the early hour, called Natalie from the cab on his way to his hotel. "Everything OK there?"

"Fine, PJ. Don't worry. Dad and the boys played Scrabble after they finished their homework. They all watched Monday night football until the boys' bedtime, and then he helped get them settled into bed. He's asked about you. I told him you were on a business trip and would be back in a few days. About ten o'clock he said he was tired and went to bed. I've just been lying here reading and waiting for you to call. Long day, huh?"

PJ chuckled, "That's an understatement. This cab ride is probably going to cost me as much as the airline ticket." He paused for a moment and then asked, "Did Dad mention David?"

"No. I don't think he has any memory of that evening."

There was a fairly long pause. Natalie thought for a moment that the call might have been dropped, but then PJ said, "I'm sorry, Nat. You didn't bargain for any of this ... "

She interrupted him. "PJ, stop it. I love your dad. The boys like having him here. This is where he needs to be until ... " She didn't finish the thought. She didn't need to. The doctors had all told them the dementia would progress to a point where they would need round-the-clock care for him. There was no timeline for them to follow, but PJ, Natalie, and even Sam and Max could see the changes happening. "We just need to enjoy him while there is still some of the old Tom left."

"You're right, of course." He filled her in on the rescheduled meeting with Dr. Masters, told her he still planned on being home as scheduled, and then said, "I love you, Nat. Give the boys a hug for me, will you?"

"Sure will," she said reassuringly. Then she added, "PJ, it's going to be all right ... everything ... your dad being here with us ... David ... it's all going to be OK." As he disconnected the call, he reflected on how lucky he was to have married this woman and that comforting thought stayed with him until the cab pulled up in front of his hotel. It was 2:30 a.m., and it would be a short night followed by a very long day.

★ ★ ★ ★

He had been in Washington, DC before, several times, but most recently he'd attended a national conference for prosecuting attorneys there just about a year ago. He found the city exciting. He'd taken the time to visit national monuments and to tour Arlington National Cemetery. This morning, however, he spent steeling himself for the two meetings he would have at the hospital. The meeting with Dr. Masters he anticipated would be the much easier of the two, but this was the second psychiatrist that had expressed concern over his brother's mental health. Both had commented on David's deep resistance to acknowledging that he had a family.

While this was troubling to PJ, he had not admitted to either of the docs that there might be a grain of truth to what his brother was apparently telling them. PJ was angry at his only sibling. *David was the one that left us,* he often rationalized. And it was true. During his plebe, or freshman, year at the United States Military Academy, David had sent infrequent, short, but effusive letters home about how much he loved West Point. Even then he was talking about the army becoming his career, his life. These letters were sent to their father, Tom, who would share them with PJ, but the old man never commented one way or the other on them. After that first year, the frequency of David's letter writing dried up to nothing, in all likelihood because Tom never wrote back. PJ could recall his father remarking, "Your brother has no idea what he's getting himself into. Mark my words, PJ. Mark my words."

Tom had opposed his son's attendance at West Point from the very beginning of the application process. PJ had sat on the periphery of many arguments and watched them degenerate into shouting matches over the issue. He never took a side, but he understood where his dad was coming from. Tom had been drafted into the army in 1967, and by January 1968 found himself sitting squarely in the middle of the Tet Offensive as a military policeman in Saigon. Viet Cong guerillas had infiltrated the sprawling city by the thousands, killed two of his best friends, and wounded him. It was then that Tom realized that not only the politicians, but the military brass, were pissing in everyone's ear. He'd told David, "We weren't winning the 'hearts and minds' of the Vietnamese people. The enemy's will to resist in South Vietnam knew no limits. They would sacrifice as many men, women, and children as it might take to drive the Americans home, just as they'd done with the French."

Tom's view was that everyone had been cruelly duped. He came home to the US and was one of those veterans who threw their medals away in protest of the war. He had been fooled once. He would not be fooled again. Then, in the wake of the ardent nationalism that followed 9/11, his oldest son, a good athlete and a better student, wanted to throw away his life following some misplaced sense of loyalty to a government full of men that had little or no regard for life. Then there was the glory and tradition of attending the US Military Academy at West Point, New York. Tom would have none of it.

During David's four years at West Point, he'd spent holidays at the homes of his classmates. If he wasn't home, he wouldn't argue with his father. His summers were spent going to army schools, like airborne training and air assault school, or being detailed to an infantry unit in Germany or Italy, anywhere but home. Any connection David ever had to Onekama, Michigan simply faded away to nothing over the years ... until now.

★ ★ ★ ★

Colonel Robert Masters was the epitome of a professional soldier. His Army Class A uniform was immaculately tailored to fit his tall, trim body. Close-cropped, but not white-walled, hair with a hint of silver on the sides gave him an even more distinguished look. But it was the heap of ribbons above his left breast pocket that drew PJ's attention. After they'd introduced themselves, PJ noted, "That's the Silver Star, isn't it," as he pointed to the award that sat at the top of the heap.

Modestly Dr. Masters nodded, "Yes."

"Well, Doctor ... er ... or should I call you Colonel ... "

Dismissively, Dr. Masters waved his hand, "Call me, Bob. All right if I call you PJ? Dr. Goldstein put in her notes that is what you preferred to be called."

PJ nodded and then said, "I'm no expert on the military, but isn't it a bit unusual for a doctor to hold the Silver Star?"

Dr. Masters paused for just a second. This meeting was about a patient, not about him, but he instantly liked PJ, this brother of his patient, who'd come here and was about to walk into a very difficult situation. Smiling, he said, "Yeah, I guess it is, but I haven't been a doc my whole career. I was a Special Forces medic for four years and then went to med school ... courtesy of Uncle Sam. I followed that up with a psychiatry residency at Tripler Army Medical Center in Hawaii ... landed here about ten years ago ... been really busy ever since." Dr. Masters smiled as he added that part to his brief career summary, but, with that out there, PJ did notice a certain weariness in the doctor's eyes.

Nonetheless, his humble, easygoing manner put PJ more at ease than he'd been since leaving home. He liked that Dr. Masters had reduced what had to be at least a twenty-year career into a couple of sentences and never once tried to sound like the hero that he obviously was. He didn't know exactly what Dr. Masters had done to earn the Silver Star, he just knew that it had to have been done under fire and involve exceptional heroism. He'd read his brother's Silver Star citation once online. He knew it wasn't something that the military awarded just for being under fire. One had to distinguish oneself dramatically under unusual circumstances and against seemingly insurmountable odds. In fact, in a lot of cases, what a soldier, sailor, marine, or air force member might have done to earn a Silver Star or Navy Cross read a lot like many of the citations for the Distinguished Service Cross, or even the Medal of Honor.

"Thanks for coming, PJ. We appreciate it."

"Yeah ... well ... my brother can be a bit ... " he paused looking for the word, shrugged his shoulders, and then said, "stubborn, to say the least."

Dr. Masters smiled and acknowledged, "To say the least!" Pausing, he motioned for PJ to sit down in a leather easy chair positioned in front of a huge oak desk cluttered with stacks of books, journals, and folders. Dr. Masters sat down behind the desk. "Dr. Goldstein told us that you have asked to be kept abreast of your brother's progress. That tells me that when David says he doesn't have a family, he's not exactly being honest. The problem is I don't know who he is trying to deceive—my staff and me, himself, maybe all of us. What's your take on that?"

PJ put his hands together on his lap and explained, "It's been a long time since I've seen my brother. It's been a long time since our dad's seen him."

"What's a long time?"

PJ thought and then answered, "At least fifteen years. David hasn't been home since he left for West Point."

Dr. Masters, incredulous, said, "Not once?" He followed that up with, "How do you account for that, PJ?"

PJ explained the reasons for their estrangement.

"OK, I get why your father's upset at him. How do you feel about all of this?"

It was a question PJ knew he would be asked. He decided he would be honest. "I'm angry with my brother. Sure, he and Dad have a beef, but he could have been a bigger man about it. He could have at least tried to understand where Dad was coming from. So, he goes off to school and then into the army and never bothers to look back toward home even once." PJ shook his head, "So, yeah, I'm angry at David."

"And does it upset you that he's basically left you to deal with your father's dementia by yourself?"

PJ had not expected this question and it pissed him off. He steeled his gaze at Dr. Masters and said, "You're a shrink and you're trained to read into things, but you've misread that, Doc. I love my dad. My wife loves him, too. So do his two grandsons. He's where he needs to be until the time comes when he needs round-the-clock care. Don't try to link my anger with my brother to having to take care of our dad."

"Fair enough."

PJ wasn't sure Dr. Masters had bought it, but he frankly didn't care. He'd told the truth. "So, Doc, how long will my brother be here?"

"Fair question, but one that doesn't have a clear answer. Physically, he is recovering from some very traumatic wounds faster than the surgeons thought he would. It's his mental health that is standing in his way at this point. There are some things that you should know before you see your brother. First, our prosthetics people aren't sure he is a candidate for prosthesis. We have the best prosthetics department in the world here at Walter Reed, but they have to have something to work with. So, their first issue is most of both legs are gone, PJ. But the larger problem is that your brother is rejecting their offer to work with him and see what might be done. Please understand, they are one of our busiest departments. They have a backlog of patients a mile long. Some are still here, some have gone home and are waiting on the call to come back and move on with the process. They can't wait for your brother's attitude to become cooperative."

PJ nodded, "Understandable."

"So that brings me to our larger concern." Dr. Masters paused.

"Which is?"

"PJ, I think your brother might be suicidal and I can tell you that as long as we feel that way, we aren't going to let him very far out of our sight."

Dr. Masters hadn't sugarcoated this and it caught PJ up short. "Jesus, Doc ... suicide ... I haven't seen or talked to my brother in a long time, but that ... well ... that just seems so far outside the realm of my understanding of the David Keller I know."

"I understand. You should know that he hasn't used the word *suicide* with either Dr. Goldstein's staff or our staff here at Walter Reed. It is our experience, however, in dealing with serious, debilitating wounds like David's, many service members entertain the idea of suicide. Usually, it is something that is short-lived. As soon as their recovery becomes apparent to them, loved ones rally round them, and they get the idea that there is some hope of returning to an altered but almost normal life, the idea of suicide ends. Frankly, David is long past the point where we would have expected this to have happened. Instead he insists he has no family, he refuses prosthetic care, we have to almost force him to physical therapy, and he isolates himself from other patients, other amputees, who might be able to offer him support and understanding. For me and my staff, just as it was for Dr. Goldstein's staff, the worst part of his recovery is that he refuses to engage with us in any kind of meaningful conversation that could be considered even the least bit therapeutic."

"But you'll keep trying, right?"

"We certainly will."

"So, you will keep him here until you're sure he won't ... ?" PJ couldn't bring himself to complete the sentence.

"Yes, that's correct. There is one last thing before I send you down the hall to his room. Just as we haven't used the word *suicide* around your brother, I would ask that you avoid using it as well. If it seems like a kind of cat and mouse game we are playing, I can understand why you would think that, but we don't feel like we need to give any kind of suggestion to your brother. Are you OK with that?"

"Uh ... yeah ... whatever you say, Doc." PJ was still reeling from the idea that his brother might be seriously considering suicide.

Dr. Masters walked him down the hall to the nurses' station, where he introduced PJ to an army nurse, Captain Amy Reynolds. As she walked him to his brother's room, she said, "Your brother sure knows a lot of generals, or, should I say, a lot of generals know your brother."

PJ thought it was small talk. He didn't respond.

Captain Reynolds continued, "The chief of staff of the army was here the other day just to see him. Before that, a three-star, a couple of two-stars, and a slew of brigadier generals ... "

PJ asked, "How was he with them?"

She stopped in her tracks and looked at him. "Cordial, but despite all of their encouragement, he hasn't changed his attitude. A couple of them told me his injuries are a big loss for the army. They said he was on his way to becoming one of them."

PJ, not steeped in the way of the military, asked, "One of who?"

She chuckled, "One of the most exclusive clubs in the world, Mr. Keller. The thing every member has in common is that they all call themselves *General* and for them to predict that your brother, a major, was already somehow destined to be one of them ... well ... " she paused and shook her head, "that means to me he is a helluva soldier."

She continued a short distance down the hall and pointed to a room door. "This is your brother's room. He's in there by himself—Dr. Masters' orders. We have him on closed-circuit TV, so we can monitor the room at the nurses' station. I won't go in with you. He doesn't care for the medical staff, so it's best if it's just you and him. I'm down the hall. There's a call button on the bedrail; punch it if you should need anything."

"Thanks." PJ pushed the room door open and stepped in.

In spite of the bright sunshine streaming through the room's large window, his brother was asleep. PJ approached the bed cautiously, checking his watch. It was 4:00 p.m. His flight out of Reagan National was scheduled to depart at seven thirty. He sat down in the chair next to the bed and studied his brother's face, which was mostly as he remembered it. David sported some slight graying about the temples, but other than that he hadn't aged much. PJ let his eyes wander toward the foot of the bed where the blanket lay flatly stretched across the mattress. *Jesus,* he thought to himself. He judged that his brother had a scant six inches or so of either leg remaining. His eyes returned to David's face. His color was good, and he watched the rhythmic rise and fall of his chest as he slept. He could not imagine recovering from wounds as devastating as these. Then his brother awoke.

PJ said nothing. David's head turned almost instinctively toward PJ as if he could sense that there was someone else in his room. Recognition was not instant. Perhaps it was the confusion of just awakening, perhaps it was the lack of recognition from such a long separation, maybe it was a combination of the two, but PJ was the first to speak: "It's PJ, David." He wanted to blurt out, *how are you feeling,* but caught himself up short.

"What are you doing here?" It was gruff, tinged with a sense of defiance.

Younger brother or not, PJ was not going to be intimidated, "Nice to see you, too, David."

David turned his head toward the window, but said nothing.

"What's this crap about you not having any family?" If he wanted to be shitty about things, PJ decided that he could be equally as shitty.

David slowly turned back toward his brother. "There's no need for you to get involved ... "

"Stop it, David. I've been involved since the casualty officer showed up on our doorstep ... "

"What was he doing on *your* doorstep? Dad is listed as my next of kin ... "

"Dad lives with me and Natalie now."

David did not respond to this.

PJ continued, "So Natalie and I were right there as he explained to Dad what had happened to you."

The gruffness returned, "Well, I bet the old man can't wait to tell me 'I told you so.' "

PJ bit his tongue. The remark and the way his brother had said it pissed him off so bad that he wanted to grab him by his shoulders and shake him. Instead, he composed himself and simply said, "Truth is, David, I don't think Dad even remembers the casualty officer being there."

"Yeah, well, he didn't want me in the army, so I can see where he would block ... "

PJ couldn't help it. His voice raised an octave in pitch and the next level in volume. "You pompous ass. If you had even bothered to call us once in a while ... send a Christmas card ... something, David, to let us know you cared about anything else except you and your illustrious career, you would know how ridiculously stupid that remark really is." David looked like he wanted to shoot back at his brother, but PJ had no intention of letting him get a word in edgewise. "Dad has dementia. There are moments when he doesn't even know who I am, who Natalie is, who Max and Sam are, and we are with him every day. Why in the hell should he remember his oldest son who went off to join the army fifteen years ago and hasn't bothered to come home even once in all those years. He's not blocking anything, David. He's slowly losing his mind."

David just laid there, staring at the ceiling.

PJ couldn't read any reaction. Standing next to the bed, he checked his watch. He had plenty of time to catch a cab and get to the airport. But his rising anger made him want to get the hell out of this room before he said or did something that he'd regret. As his brother continued to just lie there, showing no reaction to the news about their father, PJ said, "I have a flight to catch. I came here because Dr. Masters asked me to come. He thought it was important.

I'm not sorry I came, but I am sorry that you don't recognize when people care enough about you to go out of their way to help you. You do what you want to, David, but here's what I know. Dr. Masters isn't going to let you out of here until he sees your mental health improving, and I couldn't agree more. In the meantime, I will stay in touch with him. He will have my number. If and when you feel like it, you can give me a call. But don't bother if all you want to do is feel sorry for yourself. When you're ready to get better, maybe even come home, then call. Believe it or not, David, you do have a family that cares." He turned on his heel and left.

At the nurses' station, Captain Reynolds, somewhat surprised to see him so quickly after leaving him at the door to his brother's room, asked, "How did it go?"

PJ shook his head and reiterated to her what he'd told Dr. Masters: "My brother is stubborn."

She smiled and nodded in agreement.

Then PJ added, "But, Captain Reynolds, don't ever let him tell you he doesn't have a family that cares about him. That's pure bullshit, and I just told him so!"

6

OBSESSION

Ray McCall sat in a corner of Shirley's Restaurant as far away from the crowded bar area as he could get. He wished it were darker, but it was late March and the days were getting longer. He stared out the window and impatiently fidgeted. He was ten minutes late for this meeting, but the person he was to meet wasn't here yet and it pissed him off. He was paying this guy good money. He shouldn't keep him waiting like this. A waitress appeared. "What can I get you, Ray?"

"Beer ... a Budweiser." Like everything about Ray, he was gruff, almost surly. He didn't even look up at her from his phone, where he was looking for a message from his tardy employee.

Sensing his foul mood, she asked, the friendly tone to her voice now gone, "Want a menu?"

Without looking up, he shook his head.

Asshole, she thought as she walked away from the table.

Ray was about six feet two inches tall, still young enough to have good muscle tone to go along with an athletic look. He'd played football on the only district championship football team the Onekama Portagers had ever produced. He'd been a junior that year and as good a running back as he was, he'd played the entire year in the shadow of David Keller, a senior, who was eventually selected to the Michigan High School Athletic Association's Class D All-District and All-State teams. Touted as the next senior sensation, Ray's football career ended the second game of his senior year when a 275-pound tackle from Buckley High School had smothered him in a vicious tackle that broke his collarbone and separated his right shoulder. That shoulder still bothered him when the weather turned cold and damp. But Ray still had a reputation around town as a tough guy with a short temper, and that had only gotten worse since his breakup with Maggie. He was not above using his physical size to intimidate. Ray didn't care what people thought about him, because equally common knowledge around town was that his father could and would bail him out of any situation.

By the time the guy he was waiting for finally arrived, he'd finished the first beer. "Where the hell have you been?" It was loud enough for their waitress to hear as she approached their table.

"Uh, yeah, sorry, Ray. There were a couple of customers in the store at closing time ... contractors ... really good customers and they needed to order some supplies. I couldn't just throw them out."

Lowering his voice, but not notching down his surliness, Ray scolded, "Listen, Charley, I'm a good customer, too. When we have a meeting scheduled, I don't expect to be kept waiting. Got it?" It was a sneer clearly meant to intimidate the diminutive little man he'd been waiting on. It didn't matter to Ray that had Charley been on time, Charley would have been the one kept waiting. That's not how the narcissistic Ray McCall operated.

The waitress came over and before Charley could say anything else, Ray ordered another beer, told her his friend wouldn't be staying very long, and shooed her away with a brush of his hand, further confirming her previous opinion of him. As she walked away, Ray turned his attention to Charley. "So, what's she been up to?"

Charley Sharp was not what his last name implied. Thirty years old, divorced, over his head in debt, dodging child-support payments, and an addicted gambler, he was every woman's worst nightmare. For the past six months he'd been living in a small apartment above the hardware store in Onekama where he held down a part-time job. Ray had chosen Charley for this particular job, not because he had any confidence in the man, but because both his place of employment and his place of residence were directly across the street from the Yellow Dog and he knew Charley would do anything to earn a few extra bucks. And, if being quiet about what he was doing was a job requirement, Ray knew he had already sufficiently scared Charley by threatening him within an inch of his life if he told anyone what he was doing for him. Of course, Ray also knew that Charley was spending every dollar he paid him at the casino, so he would not risk losing this newfound source of gambling cash.

★ ★ ★ ★

Charley's job working for Ray was to keep an eye on Maggie, a job that Ray would have preferred to do himself, but the restraining order Maggie had filed made that difficult to impossible. Charley was to keep track of who was coming and going from Maggie's place of business. Ray hated this expense which detracted from his own gambling habit, but an ultimatum from his father necessitated it. A couple of weeks ago, the Manistee County sheriff himself had stopped by Clipper's house after dispatch had received a complaint from Maggie at the Yellow Dog. Ray was parked in his truck across the street from the coffee shop, just staring into the shop's front window. His presence there was a clear violation of the personal protection order Maggie had filed against her soon-to-be-ex-husband. The sheriff advised Clipper that a deputy had found Ray exactly where Maggie had said he would be and that he was well inside the five-hundred-foot separation distance required by the PPO. Ray had moved on begrudgingly, after giving the deputy some lip, but the sheriff made it clear that he wasn't going to keep on tolerating Ray's disregard for the law. "Listen, Clipper, if that had been anybody but Ray, we would have hauled his ass into the county lockup and he could have cooled his jets there until a lawyer bailed him out. But ... well ... Ray is your kid and we all know how he can be, so the deputy just took Ray's bullshit on the chin. Good for Ray, though. He did move on. If he wouldn't have done that," the sheriff paused for effect, "let's just say you and I would be having a different conversation right now."

Clipper thanked the sheriff for his courtesy. When Ray wasn't home by six o'clock, Clipper drove to a nearby diner for a bite of dinner. When he returned home about eight o'clock, he found Ray sitting at the kitchen table eating a piece of cold fried chicken. Clipper approached him from the rear and, with the flat of his hand, smacked his only child solidly across the back of his head. Ray jumped up ready to fight, but as soon as he saw his father standing there, he backed off. "What the hell was that for?" he hollered.

"Listen to me, Ray. I'm only going to say this once. Maggie's got a restraining order against you. The sheriff came by this afternoon and told me you were parked across the street from the Yellow Dog. I don't know what kind of game you're playing, but if you violate that PPO again, I'm going to ask the sheriff to lock you up and keep you in jail until your divorce is final. You keep fucking around like you are, and you will lose all custody of Jack. Let me make this clear to you. I don't want that to happen. That boy's got the potential to be everything you aren't, and if you fuck up the deal, the lawyers and I are working with Maggie. I will disown you." He gave that a minute to sink in and then said, "You won't get a penny from me for the rest of my life, and you sure as hell won't get anything after I'm gone. You understand me, Ray? I'm done foolin' around with you."

★ ★ ★ ★

And that was when Charley entered the picture. Despite Ray's rudeness, Charley was genuinely pleased that tonight he finally had something to report. "Ray, there's this one guy. Don't know who he is. Stranger in town. Got Illinois license plates on his car...a BMW ... one of them fancy ones, 700 and something ... I don't know. But he's been at the Yellow Dog every morning and every afternoon for the last four or five days. He and Maggie talk every time. He's in there for a lot longer than it should take for someone to buy a coffee and a sandwich."

"Ummm, Illinois plate. BMW. What color is it?"

"Black."

"Anything else I should know about?"

Charley brushed his index finger along his chin thoughtfully, shrugged, and said, "No. That's it for this week. You still want me to watch the place?" There was an eager anticipation in Charley's squeaky voice. This was easy money and they both knew it.

Ray hated this little shit, but he had no choice. Maggie still belonged to him. She had belonged to him ever since David had left town at the end of the summer before his and Maggie's senior year of high school. David hadn't been gone off to West Point more than two weeks before he and Maggie first hooked up. Ray had always had a thing for her, but it had been pointless as long as David was around. Mr. Football, Mr. Basketball, Mr. Baseball, Mr. Class President, Mr. Fucking Everything. Ray never had liked the guy. But David had no sooner gone than Maggie had practically thrown herself at him. They'd run into one another out at the end of Portage Lake's north pier. She was out there with a few of her girlfriends. He was out there with a couple of his teammates. She was wearing a bikini. He was afraid his erection would show through his wet trunks. Before he even knew what was happening, Maggie was leading him down the pier and into a small valley between two sand dunes. They spread their towels on the sand and in a few minutes, he was kissing her. When she unashamedly removed her top, he took his trunks off and the sex with her, as it had always been, was rough and tumble. He sometimes had the thought that Maggie was trying to hurt him, but it didn't matter. Ray liked it that way and so, apparently, did she. Ray believed that it was this first encounter on the beach that had gotten Maggie pregnant. That pregnancy had seriously complicated their senior years, what with his football injuries and all, but they'd gotten through it. They married the week after graduation. Life had been good then. It could be just as good again, but not if Maggie was fooling around with some guy from Chicago. *That bitch whore.* Ray stared out the window at Shirley's Restaurant into the ever-darkening evening.

'Ray, you got my money?"

Charley's question snapped him back to reality. "Uh, yeah, I got it." He dug in his pocket and produced a roll of twenty-dollar bills. After peeling off ten of them, he started to slide them over the table top to Charley. Behind him the waitress approached. Ray abruptly pulled the money back and then shooed her away. When she was gone, he looked around to see who else might be looking and then slid the money across to Charley. He then instructed, "Meet me here next Friday night. I'll check on this Illinois guy. In the meantime, you keep an eye on Maggie ... " he paused and then added, "and don't keep me waiting again, Charley."

7

THE COMMITTEE

The Yellow Dog was in its second year of operation and one of the things that Maggie was most happy about was her ability to make her business profitable the year round. Yes, the summer months, from Memorial Day to Labor Day, were by far her very best months, but she'd given it a try and found that January through April, and October through December, she could also squeeze out a small profit. It seemed that the Yellow Dog had somehow become a meeting place, and so it wasn't uncommon to walk in at breakfast or lunch and find a group of three or four people huddled around a table talking about all sorts of things. Most times no one even bothered to tell Maggie they were meeting there. This morning in early March was different. Henry Hanratty had called two days ago and asked if Maggie would set up and reserve a table for ten people for a meeting scheduled at 9:00 a.m. Maggie of course agreed and made a note to increase the number of breakfast meals she'd prepare that morning. Eight people had already arrived and Maggie was working on their breakfast orders when Emily walked in. "Mornin', Mags. Big crowd today, huh." Behind her, John DeKuyper walked through the door and joined the larger group.

Maggie looked over her shoulder while standing at the panini press and cheerfully replied, "Mornin', Em. You a part of this?"

Emily replied, "Sure am. Henry called me a couple of days ago and asked if I could be here. Told him I wouldn't miss it for anything."

"So, what's going on?"

Henry was signaling for her to come over and sit by him. Emily held up a finger and said, "Just a sec, Henry. Be right there." She asked Maggie for a to-go cup.

"Want something for breakfast?"

"No, thanks. Just coffee this morning."

Maggie handed her a sturdy paper cup with a hot sleeve on it, smiled, and said, "So, you're not going to tell me what this meeting is all about?"

Henry was standing up, waiting on Emily to take her seat. "Listen, Mags. I've got to get over there before ol' Henry has a stroke. But keep an ear open, you might find this interesting." Emily turned on her heel, filled her cup with dark roast, and then joined the group of nine others.

There were no introductions. Onekama was a small town, especially during this time of year, in the early spring before the weather turned predictably good and the out-of-towners returned. Everyone around the table knew everyone else, and as Maggie took an inventory of this group of who's who in Onekama, it didn't take her long to realize that it was actually quite a powerful group of folks. Henry Hanratty was rumored to be worth a lot of money, all made off the stock market and some very wise investing on his part. There were two medical doctors, both retired out of lucrative practices, one in Detroit and the other in Indianapolis. John DeKuyper was a retired attorney who specialized in criminal defense. Besides Emily, there were three other women attending, and, while Maggie didn't know their stories well at all, she knew that each lived in a beautiful home overlooking Lake Michigan. Oddly, she thought, the chief of the Onekama Township Volunteer Fire Department and the Manistee County sheriff filled out the rest of the group. Henry gently called them to order. "Good morning to all, and thanks for taking time out of your very busy schedules to meet this morning. As most of you know, I am a marine." The saying 'once a marine, always a marine' embodied Henry Hanratty. He had served two tours in Vietnam and had received both a Purple Heart and the Bronze Star Medal with a "V" device for his actions there in combat. At age seventy-five he still looked the part, lean and tan after spending January and February at his estate in Englewood, Florida. He'd come back to Onekama a month or two ahead of when he usually would just for this meeting. He exuded an air of self-confidence, and, if Henry Hanratty called and asked you to meet with him, you were a fool if you didn't find the time to do just that. "As a veteran, I feel like I owe a responsibility to other veterans. So, let me ask, how many of you know Major David Keller?"

Maggie was cleaning up around the coffee pots and when she heard this, her heart moved to her throat.

Every hand around the table went up. Henry continued, "How many of you have heard of the tragedy that has befallen him?" At this point, five of the hands went down. "Let me take just a moment to bring you up to date. A little over three months ago, he and three other members of his unit were the victims of an improvised explosive device. David was the only survivor, but he has lost both of his legs. I spoke to PJ Keller yesterday so I could have the latest information. David will be discharged from Walter Reed hospital in Washington, DC soon. From there his rehabilitation will continue at the Veterans Hospital in Ann Arbor, Michigan where he is expected to be for at least a month. At this point, he is wheelchair bound and is currently not being considered for prosthesis."

Maggie kept wiping the same area around the coffee pots, over and over. She was fighting back the tears.

One of the women asked, "Is he coming home?"

"That's a good question, Anna. PJ doesn't know. He tells me that David's mental state right now is ... " Henry paused, searching for the right word. "Fragile, I think, is probably the best word to describe it. I think that is perfectly understandable after what he's been through."

The sheriff prefaced the most piercing question up to this point with, "I've known David since he was a little boy. What happened to him is a pure tragedy." Every head around the table nodded in agreement. "So, what is it that you think we can do, Henry?"

"I'd like us to form ourselves into the 'Welcome Home, Major David Keller Committee'." He gave that a moment to register with all of them and then continued, "We all know that Tom Keller's mental faculties are failing. PJ and Natalie are doing everything they can to make him comfortable. Now David's injuries are just one more thing on their plate. This is David's hometown. He grew up here. This is where his family is, and so this is where he should come home to and I propose we do our part to honor David's personal sacrifice and help make that homecoming as easy as possible for both David and his family."

"Henry, have you talked this over with PJ?" John DeKuyper asked.

"Not yet. I wanted to meet with all of you and see what kind of support I have. I have an idea, actually a whole series of ideas, that I'd like to discuss with all of you. I wouldn't bother any of you if I thought I could do everything by myself, but, if we really want to honor David's service and his sacrifice, I'm going to need help. That's why I've called you here today."

Emily asked him, "What do you think we might do, Henry?"

He looked over at her and smiled. "Well, Emily, I'm reaching for the stars, I know, but if there was ever a group that could make that reach, it's this bunch. The easy stuff is greeting him. You know, a parade down Main Street, fire engine ladders forming an arch with an American flag waving between them, the Scottville Clown Band hammering out a rousing Sousa march, a dinner to honor David's service out at the Portage Point Inn ... all of that kind of stuff." He looked around the table and didn't see much reaction. "But what I think we really need to have waiting for him is a house."

This time there was a reaction. He could feel every eye at the table on him now. He had their full attention. "I've taken the liberty of contacting an architect in Traverse City. One of his specialties is designing complete homes with everything fully accessible to someone with a disability. He actually customizes the accommodations to fit the specific disability of the home owner. I've told him about David and what happened to him. He said he'd do the design work for us for two grand even. I asked him if he could redesign an existing home, or would we have to do a completely new build and he said he was flexible. So, Emily, here's where you come in. What's out there that we might be able to purchase?"

Out of the corner of her eye, Emily saw Maggie disappear into the powder room. She was sorry she hadn't been able to prep her friend on what this meeting was about, although Henry had not been nearly this specific when they had talked on the phone. She chided herself for being so thoughtless. Coming back to Henry, she asked, "Why not redesign PJ and Natalie's house? Don't you think it's a possibility that David will move in there with them?"

Henry said, "Umm, that's a possibility I suppose, something I guess I should talk over with PJ. But, in the meantime, am I to assume that I have all of your support on this?"

DeKuyper, always the attorney, asked, "Money, Henry, where's it all going to come from?"

Henry put his palms on the table top, bent forward over

them, looked around the table, and said, "To start with, from us. I'm putting in the first hundred thousand." The fire chief and the sheriff whistled. Then Henry lifted his hands up with palms facing them. "But I don't expect all of you to be that generous. What I propose is a Go Fund Me page. The Kellers are an old family around these parts, and David's story is one that will speak to people around the country. My bet is we can raise more than enough to pay for whatever might be required, whether it's a new build or renovation. So, what do you say? Are we a committee? Raise your hand if you are in." There was no reluctance on anyone's part; nine hands joined Henry's. "Great. How about we meet in two weeks? I'll talk with PJ and bring some answers back to the table. Emily, in the event we need to find a house or build a house, could you do a little investigation of available real estate?"

Emily, her eyes fixed on the powder-room door, looking for Maggie to emerge, merely nodded and, without making eye contact, said, "Uh, yeah, sure, Henry."

"OK, thanks to each of you. I truly appreciate your support. Let's do this again in two weeks, same time, same place. Don't leave without signing the sign-in sheet. I'll put together a roster with everyone's contact information on it and email it to all of you. If you can't make the meeting, just let me know. I'll provide minutes to keep everyone abreast of the plans."

Maggie emerged from the powder room, red rims around her eyes, just as the group was breaking up. Emily stayed back until everyone was out the front door and it was just her and Maggie. "I'm sorry. I guess I should have clued you in ... "

Maggie held up her hand, "It's OK, Em. It's just that he's been gone so long. Do you really think he'll come back to Onekama?"

8

PLAYING THE GAME

The ambulance service contracted by the government to transport David Keller from Walter Reed National Military Medical Center to the Veterans Administration Hospital in Ann Arbor had been the low bidder on the government's request for a bid. Under the provisions of their contract, transports of a non-emergency nature that were in excess of five hundred miles could be conducted at the ambulance service's convenience rather than the government's, and certainly not David's. Consequently, he arrived in Ann Arbor in the middle of the night. He was housed in a ward with four other patients, three of whom woke up complaining about the lights and the noise at this early morning hour. David didn't blame them. The orderlies moving him along didn't seem to care.

This move was neither something that he wanted, nor that he felt he needed. He had become somewhat acclimated to life in his wheelchair. During his last week at Walter Reed, he'd mastered how to get in and out of bed without assistance and, though considerably more challenging, he'd been able to get himself on and off of the toilet, although his skill in this regard right now was limited to bathrooms that were specially equipped with proper grab bars and railings and sufficient room for him to maneuver his wheelchair into exactly the right position. He wasn't stupid. He could figure these things out for himself, he thought. *Why am I here? I don't need this. What's the point?*

However, his doctors had insisted on this move to Ann Arbor to further his rehabilitation. One of those doctors was Colonel Robert Masters, who wanted this time to be a transition, a kind of halfway house, for his patient. Dr. Masters had forwarded massive amounts of clinical information gathered by his staff, all of which he had carefully reviewed. David seemed to be coming around, but Dr. Masters had added plenty of cautionary notes into David's medical records because he wasn't sure if he was, in fact, "coming around," or, instead, had learned how to "play the game." Dr. Masters and PJ Keller had been in contact via email just prior to David's move to Ann Arbor. PJ had asked if his brother had indicated any interest in coming home to Onekama. So, Dr. Masters had asked his patient point blank, "Are you planning on going home after Ann Arbor?"

The answer had surprised Dr. Masters for two reasons. First was the quickness of it. Second was its pessimism. "Yes, sir. Where the hell else can I go?" None of it had set well with Dr. Masters, and he conveyed this to PJ in an email:

PJ,

I have spoken to your brother and put the question you asked me directly to him. While he indicates he is coming home, I detect a certain fatalism, if you will, that leads me to not completely rule out that he might still be contemplating something more drastic. My professional opinion is that we should not rule out the possibility that he still may be considering suicide. There remains the possibility that he believes he can throw us off track by telling us what he thinks we want to hear. Thus, I am convinced that this month or more at the VA Hospital in Ann Arbor is more necessary than ever. He will be working with a psychiatrist there, Dr. Jill Hightower. Her number is 248-776-8493. May

I suggest you contact her directly. I have alerted her that you will call. May I also suggest that you try and visit your brother again. You know him better than any of us, PJ, despite the long absence. Any insights you can give Dr. Hightower would be very welcome. I am also at your disposal. You have my number and email. Don't hesitate to call or write. All of us here at Walter Reed wish you the very best. Your brother is a hero and all of us here honor his sacrifice.
Sincerely,
Bob

The VA Hospital was very different from Walter Reed. Things here seemed to David to be less organized. Ann Arbor lacked the sense of urgency he'd noticed among the staff at Walter Reed. His first day, he'd been fifteen minutes late to a physical therapy appointment. No one came looking for him. When he did manage to get there, his therapist noted that he was late, and when David had apologized and told the white lie that he'd gotten lost on the way, nothing else was said. At Walter Reed, first of all, he'd never been allowed to get to physical therapy by himself. An orderly had always shown up five or ten minutes before his scheduled time and taken him to where he needed to be. And had he not been where the orderly was to pick him up, an immediate search of the hospital would have been conducted until he was found, and an ass-chewing of monumental proportions would have ensued to ensure that he didn't ever disrupt the hospital's schedule again. This place was a lot more laid back. He had a daily physical therapy session that lasted two, sometimes three hours. Every day he saw Dr. Hightower or one of her staff. While frequent, these meetings varied in their duration, sometimes an hour or more, other days just a few minutes. He enjoyed the positive reinforcement from the staff at physical therapy. He didn't like that he couldn't tell exactly what Dr. Hightower or her staff were thinking about his progress.

When he was not at physical therapy, or talking with a shrink, he was free to move at will around the sprawling hospital's campus. It was early March, so the temps outside were unpredictable, but there were more and more days when the sun was out and he was able to get outside and move around. As one would expect, the hospital's campus was very accommodating to people with disabilities. Every entry door had a ramp and a push-button door opener. Concrete paths crisscrossed the campus, and they were kept snow- and ice-free. He spent little time on his ward, didn't even know the names of those housed there with him, nor did he care to know them. Since his devastating injuries, he preferred to be alone. He spent time in the hospital's library almost every day. He read until he became drowsy and often dozed off while sitting in front of a large window that magnified the heating effects of a chilly spring sun. The hospital also operated a bus service to places downtown, but to get on the bus one had to have the proper credential provided by the patient's primary physician. In his case, that was Dr. Hightower, and, thus far, she had not indicated any willingness to give him the bus pass. If she did not offer it to him this week, he was going to ask her for it. While he wanted to avoid appearing overly anxious to get away from her or the hospital, he'd seen a commercial on television for a gun show in downtown Ann Arbor weekend after next and he had an interest in attending it.

Two important things had stuck with him from his brother's visit to Walter Reed. First, that his father was suffering from dementia and had apparently reached a point where he wasn't able to live on his own anymore. And, second, that the doctors were concerned about his mental health and that he wasn't going to be left alone until they saw improvement.

David had carefully developed a plan since then. He

needed to go home and see his father and brother. There were some fences there that needed mending. Once that was done, with any luck, before the snow flew, he would take the ultimate step to end his confinement to this miserable life some unknown bomber in Afghanistan had committed him to. If he needed to suck up to a bunch of shrinks in order to put his plan in motion, then so be it. That was what he would do.

9

BROTHERLY LOVE

Henry Hanratty had been fairly insistent when he'd called, and so PJ's secretary had booked him into a vacant time slot in her boss's busy schedule. PJ was due in court. He would have liked the time to do some preparation, but this was Henry Hanratty and even though PJ really couldn't spare the time, he was an important constituent in Manistee County and particularly important in Onekama. PJ hoped this would not take more than fifteen minutes or so. The two shook hands as Henry said, "PJ, nice work on those two convictions a couple of weeks ago. Murder and rape ... you don't expect that sort of thing to happen in small-town America. I'm glad to see that these guys are going to be locked away."

PJ nodded and thanked him. Henry sat down in the big leather easy chair in front of PJ's desk, a sign that this meeting was not going to be quickly over. Inwardly PJ shrugged, and then asked Henry if he'd like a cup of coffee or some water. He declined and then surprised PJ by asking, "How's David doing?"

PJ knew the rumors were flying around Onekama. He'd heard a lot of them. *"PJ, sorry to hear of David's death,"* was the worst one, but there was another one out there that was equally false. *"PJ, I heard David's being fitted with two artificial legs and will soon be walking around on them. Isn't it amazing what they can do with prosthetics these days!"* If he tried to set everyone straight on his brother's status, that's all he'd have time to do. Perhaps he should be thankful that Henry was here asking him. If anybody could get the straight skinny out to help calm the rumor mill, it was him. "He's recovering well, Henry. Thanks for asking. He's just been moved from Walter Reed. He's at the VA Hospital in Ann Arbor. He'll be there at least a month ... more physical therapy." PJ saw no need to mention his brother's mental state.

Henry's piercing blue eyes brightened as he asked, "Any idea what he's going to do when he's done there?"

PJ shrugged, "No. It's kind of one step at a time, Henry."

"I can understand." There was a pause and then Henry continued, "PJ, the reason I wanted to talk to you is ... well, there's a committee ... " He paused again. "We're all volunteers. We want David to know that he's welcome to come back home to Onekama and we want to make his homecoming the best it can be."

PJ at first thought they were talking about a ceremony, maybe a parade, a few speeches and he knew, in David's current state of mind, he would not want any of this. But, then, the conversation took a whole new twist when Henry added, " ... and we've managed to collect about a quarter of a million dollars so far."

PJ leaned forward and put his hands on the edge of his desk. Wide-eyed, he said, "Henry, what the hell?"

Henry smiled, "Well, we want to build him a living space, a home, if you will, that can accommodate whatever disability he is left with after all of his rehabilitation is complete. The committee ... "

PJ held up his hands, "Whoa, Henry. That's too much to ask ... "

Henry was shaking his head and interrupted him, "How many tours of duty did your brother serve in Afghanistan and Iraq?"

PJ had lost track of the actual count, but responded, "I dunno, five or six altogether, I believe."

"Then it's not too much to ask and besides, you haven't asked. We are a grassroots organization. The committee has only ten members, but we have a Go Fund Me page for David's homecoming." Modestly, he continued, "The committee members have anteed up one hundred twenty-five thousand. The rest has come from people across the country. Your brother's a hero, PJ, and people want to honor him."

"I ... I don't know what to say."

"Well, we do need some information ... " And with that Henry laid out a series of questions, taking careful notes as PJ tried to answer them. Some of the questions PJ could not answer, and so this meeting concluded with him saying, "Listen, Henry, I'm still stunned by this. What you're doing ... well, it's over the top."

Henry shook his head and offered, "We are happy we can help, PJ."

Offering his hand, PJ said, "David's doctor in Ann Arbor has asked me to give him this week to acclimate to his schedule there, then she wants me to schedule a visit the following week. I intend to do that. I want to share all of this with him. It's the kind of thing that I think would buoy up anyone's spirits after experiencing a loss as big as David's. Of course, Natalie and I will talk about it. He knows we have Dad at home with us. I know for sure that David doesn't want to be considered a burden. He's really stubborn about that." PJ shrugged resignedly. "So I really have no idea what he's thinking."

Henry nodded, "You've got your hands full, that's for sure."

"But Natalie, David, and I will talk about it," PJ repeated. "I will let you know."

Henry moved toward the door. "Thanks for your time."

PJ immediately felt guilty about begrudging the man this time. "No, Henry, that's nothing. I still don't know what to say except *thanks*. You didn't have to do this ... the committee, the fund raising ... it's all so much."

Henry glanced back over his shoulder and said, "This country owes your brother a debt of gratitude. This is just one small installment in an effort to make good on what we owe him."

★ ★ ★ ★

That evening, after the boys were asleep and Tom had headed upstairs to his bedroom, PJ told Natalie about the meeting with Henry and she broke down and cried. It was the first time she'd done that in over two years. The last time was when they'd gotten the news that Tom Keller's mind was falling victim to the terrible effects of dementia and he probably should not be left to live alone. PJ held her close to him. Her head nestled against his chest, she said, "We can move the boys into one bedroom. David can have the master down here. We can have the bathroom in there adapted to whatever meets his needs. We'll take the bedroom upstairs."

He held her tighter, "OK ... OK ... let's not get too far ahead of ourselves here. I'm going to call Dr. Hightower tomorrow and schedule a visit next week with her and David. If he's decided to come home, then it's time I start pressing him for some answers to the same questions that Henry asked me today. Let's see what David's got in mind before we disrupt everything here."

Natalie looked up and kissed him tenderly on the cheek. "OK," she said, and the two of them headed off to bed.

★ ★ ★ ★

PJ's trip to Ann Arbor was punctuated by a series of phone calls. The first was from his office over a filing that was due to the court that day, then a couple of defense attorneys were looking for a plea deal for their clients, and the final one was from a judge who was particularly rankled by a plea deal for a robbery suspect that the judge felt was simply too light, given the seriousness of the crime and the fact that the guy was a repeat offender. It had been negotiated by an aggressive defense attorney and an inexperienced assistant prosecutor. PJ agreed with the judge and told him that he was busy today, but first thing in the morning he would get with his young assistant, who would renegotiate the deal or take the defendant to court if his attorney wouldn't listen to reason. The judge had said to him, "PJ, please let David know that Denise and I think of him often and we wish him a speedy recovery." PJ had thanked him, but then, a few miles down the road, pessimism crept in and he had the thought that with wounds like David's, there would be no such thing as a *speedy* recovery.

★ ★ ★ ★

Dr. Hightower, true to her name, was at least six feet, four inches tall. If she had been wearing high heels, she would have come close to six-six. On the wall in her office, PJ saw a picture of the Notre Dame women's basketball team and stenciled across the bottom was NCAA Runner Up, 2010-11. He pointed to the picture, "You were on that team?" It was as much a statement as a question.

She said, "Yes, it was some of the best times of my life."

"I watched that national championship game on TV. It was a real dog fight, as I recall."

She smiled at him and said, "A really tough one to lose, that's for sure, but Coach McGraw, in the locker room after the game, told all of us that as tough as this loss would be to absorb, in the long run, it would build our character, make us better people. Looking back on all of it now, I think she was absolutely right. It taught me to get back up, to set new goals, to keep on moving forward."

PJ nodded. "All good lessons."

Dr. Hightower segued, "Speaking of 'moving forward,' I am happy to report that I think I have seen some real progress with your brother."

The comment both relieved and alarmed PJ. Cautiously he said, "Glad to hear it. The last time I saw him at Walter Reed he was pretty down. Do you really think he could get better this fast?"

"Yes, I do, but I share your concern. Dr. Masters and I have stayed in close touch. He has cautioned me to avoid being too optimistic. He thinks your brother just might be trying to play us." It was the way she inflected the word *play* that caught his attention.

"And you don't think that he is?"

"Mr. Keller ... "

"PJ, please."

"PJ, this is a really tough call for any mental health professional. We all know it happens. We all guard against it. But, at the end of the day, all any of us can do is gradually give our patients greater and greater latitude. We have to let them go out into the world." She shrugged. "And then we watch how they respond. Dr. Masters agrees. Thus far, my observation of your brother is that he is physically recovering from his devastating wounds remarkably well. I keep in close contact with his physical therapist. His attendance has been quite regular and they report he is cooperative. Perhaps equally important, however, are the open and honest conversations he and I have had about the idea of suicide. He tells me he has considered it ... something that Dr. Masters reports he could never get David to admit while he was at Walter Reed."

PJ thought, *Well, at least it's not the elephant in the room anymore.*

"Please understand that this is not uncommon for someone who has suffered the loss that your brother has. Not only has he lost both of his legs, he also suffers from a guilt complex because he was the only survivor of the IED. It is only human nature for him to ask himself, 'Why me? Why was I chosen to live? Why didn't I die alongside the others?' The good news is that he and I are working on the difficult answers to these questions. In the meantime, I am encouraged that he has asked me if I would give him a bus pass."

PJ looked puzzled.

"We have a bus service that runs between the hospital here and some interesting locations downtown. It provides our ambulatory patients a way of overcoming the isolation that can accompany a long-term stay in the hospital."

PJ thought it interesting that she referred to his brother, who was without legs, as *ambulatory,* but the more he thought about it, the more he decided that this was, in fact, real progress.

"For the past several weeks he has enjoyed more freedom than he had at Walter Reed. Dr. Masters agreed on this strategy. He has been able to get about the campus. Now, with the bus pass," she held it up, "which I will give to you to give to him, he can become acclimated to moving about in the real world. This is going to be very new to him. For example, he's going to have to use ramps, handicapped accessible doors, and public restrooms. Here at the hospital, everything is handicap accessible, but now, his challenge will be to learn to live with his disability in the real world where they may or may not have accommodations. I am encouraged that he has asked me for the pass. We have talked about some of the challenges he might face and I believe he's ready for this next step."

"Has he mentioned us ... his family, I mean? Has he said anything about coming home?"

She became more serious. "We have talked about both subjects. He doesn't talk freely about either, but, listen, PJ, I think the reluctance on his part is because he doesn't want to become a burden on anyone."

A burden, PJ thought. *Yeah, that's David, all right.*

"We have talked about his long absence from the home front. I have even gotten him to open up about the rift with your father. Dr. Masters and I believe this is significant progress. He wouldn't discuss his family at all at Walter Reed."

"My visit there was less than encouraging," PJ said, but then had the thought that this wasn't very flattering to Dr. Masters. He added, "Don't get me wrong, Dr. Hightower ... "

She smiled at him, "Jill, please."

He returned her smile, "Yes, OK, Jill. Dr. Masters could not have been more honest or forthcoming. I hadn't expected things to go well, but from what you are telling me, there is definite improvement and for that I am thankful to you both."

"Thanks, but we still have some ways to go. I'd like to talk with you again, after you've spent some time with David. He knows you are coming." She glanced at her watch. "He should be waiting in the cafeteria. From there you and he can go wherever you'd like." She handed him the pass. "He will have to sign out at the security window at the main entrance. Then the two of you can go anywhere off the hospital's campus that you'd like ... maybe to a restaurant for lunch. Zingerman's is hard to beat."

"Do we have to take the bus?"

"You may, but it's not necessary. Take as long as you'd like, as long as he is back by midnight." She handed him her card. "Here's my cell phone. Give me a call at your convenience after you've met with him. I'd like your impressions of the brother you saw at Walter Reed and the brother you will see today."

★ ★ ★ ★

By contrast, PJ's greeting from his brother in the VA Hospital cafeteria could not have been more different than their first meeting at Walter Reed. This time David greeted him with a smile and an extended hand, not at all what PJ had been expecting. "PJ, good to see you," he said, smiling. "Thanks for coming down." Physically, he looked like a completely different person than he'd seen in that hospital bed at Walter Reed. His color was good, his hair was combed, he was clean-shaven, and neatly dressed in a bright yellow, button-down collar dress shirt with a white tee shirt underneath. Over that he had on a University of Michigan windbreaker, loosely zipped up. He wore jeans with the legs turned under as he sat comfortably upright in the unpowered wheelchair. After they'd shook hands, David spread his arms wide and said, "What do you think of my new ride?"

To be honest, the fact that it was unpowered surprised and perplexed PJ. He smiled at his brother and simply said, "Great, but where's the ... " he paused awkwardly looking for the right word. *What the hell would you call it ... engine ... motor.* He said, "Where's the engine?"

"You're lookin' at it. Me. I'm the engine."

"I thought ... "

David interrupted him, " ... that I'd have one of those little sportsters. They offered to outfit me with one of those, but I turned them down. The learning curve was a lot smaller with this model. I've gotten quite good at maneuvering this baby around." With that he pushed back a few feet from his brother, locked one wheel with a left-handed grip, and, with the other hand, spun the wheelchair three hundred sixty degrees in practically the blink of an eye. "See what I mean?" Betcha can't do that in your La-Z-Boy!"

PJ smiled at him. "You are amazing!" He heard himself say that. It had been a long time since he'd had a positive thought about his long-absent brother, but he truly meant it. The person in the wheelchair in front of him was not the same person he'd turned his back on at Walter Reed nearly a month ago now. He held up the pass. "I've got a get-out-of-jail-free card here. Want to go get some lunch?" PJ saw a sparkle come to his brother's eyes. He stepped behind the wheelchair and said, "I'll push, you guide. Which way to the main entrance? You have to sign out first."

David's first encounter with the real world came as PJ wheeled him up to the front-seat passenger door of his Chevy Tahoe. The butt-high seats were at least six inches, maybe as much as a foot higher, than the practice car seats he moved into and out of during his physical therapy sessions. He said to PJ, "OK, bro, give me a second to figure this out." He made sure the door was open to its maximum, then glanced up to see if there was a handle above the door opening that he could grasp onto. There was, but it was just out of his reach.

Behind him, he heard PJ say, "Let me help you."

Immediately, David responded, "No, don't. I've got to learn to do this myself."

PJ thought, *Burden!* But in that instant, he watched his brother reposition the wheelchair just a few inches closer to the door, muscularly boost himself up with his right hand on the armrest of the wheelchair, and grasp the handhold above the door with his left hand. For just a split second, David hung there in mid-air until he pulled his body up with his left hand and pushed himself into the car's front passenger seat with his right hand. Triumphantly, he looked over at PJ and announced, "There. How was that?" He grabbed the seat belt, hooked it up, and said, "OK, let's go. I'm starving."

"Zingerman's OK?" PJ asked.

"Don't know. This is my first jail break from this place."

PJ laughed, "Dr. Hightower recommended it."

"Then let's go. You met Dr. Hightower?" David didn't wait for an answer. "She's one very tall lady, huh?"

PJ laughed. He had never met a woman as tall as her. "You know she played basketball at Notre Dame?"

Mischievously, David looked over at his brother behind the steering wheel and said, "For the men's team? She's tall enough!" There was a pause in their conversation for a chuckle and then David asked, "What's she saying about me, PJ? Any idea when I can get out of here?"

He glanced sideways. "She tells me you are making good progress."

David shook his head. "Yeah, that's what she tells me too, so, no, she didn't give you an idea of when?"

PJ simply shook his head. The rest of the short trip to Zingerman's was small talk. The restaurant's parking lot was packed, so both concentrated on trying to find a spot. Handicapped places were available near the entrance, but PJ had neither a placard to hang in the windshield nor the appropriate license plate. He apologized to David, who told him not to worry. "I could drop you at the door."

"Naw, don't do that." Just then David eyeballed a space. It was about as far away from the entrance as was possible. While David requested that PJ let him maneuver from the car into the wheelchair, he was fine with PJ pushing him into the restaurant. After placing their order, they found a table at the back of the dining room. PJ removed one of the chairs and David rolled his wheelchair into the spot until he was well clear of the aisle. As they waited for their order, PJ asked, "Given any thought to where you are going to go when they do throw you out of the hospital?"

David nodded, "Yeah, I have."

When the pause became awkwardly long, PJ said, "And?"

"Look, PJ, I don't want to become a burden ... "

Burden! Again, the burden! PJ interrupted him, "Stop with the burden thing, David. You've given your entire professional life in service to this country. You've been badly wounded in that effort. You are not a burden to the country, you are not a burden to the doctors and nurses that care for you, and you certainly are not a burden to your family." His delivery was direct, confident, and uncompromising, but another awkward silence ensued, during which their meals arrived.

"I think I'd like to come home, at least for a little while."

PJ took a bite of his sandwich. David watched him, but could not read any reaction to his announcement. "Doesn't that surprise you even a little?" he asked.

"What surprises me, David, is that you think it would surprise me. There are a lot of people in Onekama that are looking forward to seeing you."

"Yeah, but I'll bet Dad isn't one of them."

"Do you want to see him?"

"Will he even know who I am?"

"I expect so. What you need to be prepared for is that his recognition will come and go. This dementia he has is unpredictable. Like I told you at Walter Reed, there are days when he doesn't even know who I am, who Natalie is, who Sam and Max are, and he sees all of us every day."

David changed the subject. "How many years have you and Natalie been married now?"

"Ten this October."

"Oh, wow, sorry PJ."

PJ knew he didn't mean that the way it sounded, but he decided to pull his brother's leg a little bit. "No need to be sorry, David. Natalie and I love one another ... "

"No, PJ, I didn't mean ... "

PJ chuckled and smiled at his brother, "No, I know you didn't."

"I meant I'm sorry that I wasn't at your wedding. I was in Iraq then ... "

His brother owed him no apology. Perhaps he owed their father one, but PJ, since finding out about the seriousness of his brother's wounds, had stopped feeling like one who was owed an apology. "Listen, David, there's no need for anyone to apologize to anyone else. You left Onekama to pursue a calling. It kept you away from us. I'm glad that you are thinking you want to come home, and I've got some news for you." Over the next hour or so, they talked about

Henry Hanratty's committee, which had officially been dubbed The Welcome Home, Major David Keller Committee.

At first David balked at their efforts. "I don't want that, none of it. They aren't the reason I am coming home."

"Why are you coming home?"

He had to be careful here. He suspected Dr. Hightower and his brother would talk about this lunch and what was discussed. "I ... I'm coming home to see you and Dad."

"And then what?" PJ pushed.

"I want to get to know you again. I want to get to know Natalie and my two nephews. I want to see if I can right the ship with Dad. I've been gone a long time. I know that. So, I don't expect any of these things to happen overnight."

It was an answer that sat well with him, but PJ harkened back to Dr. Hightower's use of the word *play*. Was his brother *playing* him right now? So, he pushed back at him. "You were a bit of an asshole when I last saw you at Walter Reed. Do you recall that?"

His brother said nothing, but nodded.

"Do you recall me telling you that there were a lot of people on your side working to pull you through this crisis?"

Sheepishly, David again nodded.

"Then, like it or not, David, you are going to have to accept that you have many people in your court, many of whom you don't even know at all. Henry tells me that over four thousand people have made contributions to the committee's Go Fund Me page on your behalf. You can't stop them from caring. You can't stop them from contributing and, in my humble opinion, you can't walk away from Henry's committee. You are now officially 'A Favorite Son of Onekama' and you have a responsibility to accept that and be gracious."

Much of the rest of their lunch was in silence. PJ felt he had touched a nerve with David, but he wasn't sure until after he'd signed his brother back in at the security window at the sprawling hospital's main entrance. David extended his hand and said, "Thanks, PJ, it was good to get out of this place for a little while. Older brothers are supposed to be teachers to their younger brothers, but today it was the other way around. You've given me some things to think about. Do you have the bus pass?"

PJ reached in his inside coat pocket and pulled out the bus pass. "Compliments of Dr. Hightower."

"Yeah, well, one of my first stops will be at a cellular phone store. May I call you?"

"I'll be disappointed if you don't."

They said their goodbyes. As David rolled his wheelchair to a nearby recreation room he felt a pang of conscience. All of it today had been deceitful. He knew what Dr. Hightower and his brother expected of him and he'd delivered. Inside the recreation room he rolled up next to a display rack holding brochures. Each outlined different cellular service plans. As he backed away from it, he banged into a table next to a sofa and a lamp came crashing down. A staff volunteer rushed to his side. "Are you all right?"

He wasn't, but said he was. *Dammit! You clumsy ox! This fucking chair.* She proceeded to clean up the debris. He apologized profusely to her. She said it was all right, that it didn't matter as long as he was OK. He apologized again and thanked her for cleaning up his mess. He forgave himself for his deceitfulness. He had little choice. He had a plan and he would proceed with it. He rolled his wheelchair over to the poster on a bulletin board near the entry to the recreation room. It advertised the Ann Arbor Gun and Knife Show this coming Saturday. He planned on being there early.

10

THE ACCIDENT

Peter Wagner was beginning to enjoy the more relaxed small-town life he'd found in Onekama. The managing partner of a high-powered, high-priced Chicago law firm specializing in construction and environmental law, he was a certified civil engineer and licensed to practice law in Illinois, Ohio, Wisconsin, Indiana, and Michigan. The firm also had offices in New York City, Atlanta, Miami, Dallas, San Francisco, and Los Angeles. About three weeks ago, he'd decided that it made sense to simply rent someplace near Manistee, Michigan rather than make the ten-hour round-trip drive back and forth from Chicago over and over again while he worked on behalf of a contractor who was planning to build a fifty-room boutique hotel replete with full amenities, including a restaurant, on the shores of Lake Michigan. The contractor's progress had been quickly hamstrung by a series of lawsuits filed on behalf of neighbors whose properties either directly adjoined the construction site or were nearby and who objected to the encroachment of such a commercial operation practically in their backyards. A quick check of Airbnb had netted Wagner an entire house at the top of Portage Street, square in the middle of the village of Onekama. It was way more than he needed for himself, but the thousand dollars monthly rental charge was too good to pass up. The owners, in Florida until the end of May, were just thankful to have someone living there, keeping an eye on the place. He thought that perhaps his brother and his family, an environmental attorney in the same firm, or his girlfriend, a Chicago school teacher, might like to join him on the weekends to enjoy this resort area even though the April weather could be quite unpredictable. In the first two weeks of his stay, they had not yet made the trip, but one was planned for the upcoming weekend and he was looking forward to all of them being there. The weather forecast was for unseasonably high temperatures that held the promise of some walks on nearby Lake Michigan beaches. As he backed out of the garage in his sleek, black 2016 BMW 750 IL, his stomach rumbled and he looked forward to one of Maggie's breakfast burritos. As far as he was concerned, the Yellow Dog had been a great find. Maggie's food was some of the freshest he'd found. In fact, he'd complimented her by telling her that her food was as fresh as that at the Whole Foods store in his posh Chicago neighborhood. His habit was to stop at the Yellow Dog on his way to work in the morning for one of her breakfast sandwiches and then again on his way home in the late afternoon for something for dinner. The burrito was squarely on his mind as he let the Beamer's big V-8 engine effortlessly move the car down the hill toward Main Street. As he crossed Spring Street, a street with a prominent stop sign at Portage Street, he never even saw the red pickup truck that T-boned him, causing every air bag in the luxury car to deploy. The impact pushed him into and through a chain-link fence and well into the yard of the home located at the southwest corner of the intersection. The suddenness of it all, the force of the airbags, and the force of the pickup's impact rendered him unconscious.

Ray McCall's pickup truck was stalled and steaming in the middle of the intersection. He was stunned, but because he was ready for what had just happened ... the airbags, the impact ... he was conscious. Groggily he pushed against the driver's side door and, with more pushing, he finally got it open to the point where he could step down to the street.

Reaching into the pocket of his hooded sweatshirt, he pulled out his phone and punched in 911. Trying to sound as if he were more injured than he really was, he stammered into the phone, "There's been an accident at the corner of Portage and Spring in the village of Onekama. I think we are going to need an ambulance."

The 911 operator asked, "Can you tell me how many cars are involved?"

"Two."

"And how many people are involved?"

"Two. Me and the driver of the other car. I think he might be dead. He's not moving."

"All right, sir. A sheriff's deputy and a state trooper are both responding. They should be there in just a few minutes. An ambulance will be right behind them. May I have your name?"

"Uh, yeah, sure. It's McCall. Ray McCall. My father's Clipper McCall." Adding that little tidbit of information about his father was something that Ray had learned through experience always seemed to help his cause.

The 911 operator knew Ray, both personally and by reputation. *You probably want me to call Daddy, don't you?* she thought, but instead said, "OK, Ray." In the background she could hear the sirens. "That's them coming now." *But I'll be damned if I'm going to call your daddy. That'll be up to you.*

Ray walked over to the BMW. "The guy's still not moving. I think he's dead."

"All right. Just stay on the phone with me until the police get there."

"Uh, yeah, sure." He bent over and peered through the shattered web of cracks that had been the driver's side window. He put his hand over the mouthpiece and whispered, "Now, stay the fuck away from my wife, you asshole." He straightened back up just as the sheriff's car pulled to a stop.

Peter Wagner wasn't dead, but he was listed in serious condition at Munson's West Shore Medical Center in Manistee, where he'd been transported by ambulance. He was undergoing a concussion protocol; his left arm was broken in two places and he had three cracked ribs which accounted for much of his pain. His brother had been notified and was on his way from Chicago along with Peter's girlfriend. His insurance company had also been contacted.

Ray had been taken to the hospital by the sheriff's deputy. A blood sample was taken to determine if he had been driving while impaired. Ray had at first objected to this, but the deputy had coolly and calmly advised him that it would be best if he cooperated, not necessarily because of any threat from law enforcement, but: "Ray, do you really want to tell your father you refused a blood-alcohol test? Think about it. That's like admitting that you're on something." For once, he wasn't. He'd needed all his wits about him to time his high-speed entrance into that intersection at exactly the right split second to T-bone that big BMW, so, he quieted down and submitted. It came back negative for anything that might have impaired his driving ability.

Ray had not bothered to call his father and tell him what had happened. However, by the time he arrived home, courtesy of the Manistee sheriff's office, a bit banged up, but otherwise none the worse for wear, Clipper was waiting on him. Wagner's insurance company had already been in contact with Clipper's insurance company, and they in turn had called Clipper, who was listed as the authorized administrator on Ray's auto policy because Clipper was the one paying the premium. Yes, the accident was covered. Yes, he was aware that this was the second accident in less than two years while Ray had been operating the vehicle. They informed him that the vehicle had already been deemed a total loss by the good folks at Linke's Auto Body and they would be issuing a check minus the five-thousand-dollar deductible Clipper had been forced to carry on the vehicle in

Ray ignored him. "So, I get my stamps and as I'm turning onto Spring Street, the damned coffee cup tips over in the cup holder. I bend over the console to pick it up off the passenger side floor and forget about the stop sign at Spring and Portage."

"How fast were you going? The sheriff's office tells me you really plowed into the other guy."

"I dunno, thirty-five, maybe forty. It all happened so fast."

"Well, you're in a helluva mess. The guy you hit is a lawyer from Chicago ...

Ray thought, *I knew it! Rich prick!*

"You better hope he isn't permanently disabled from this or ... "

"Or what, Dad?" Ray was taunting him now. "I'm going to look for a new truck tomorrow. Don't worry, I'll find a nice used one to keep the price down. I'll give you the info for the insurance company from the dealer and you can call them ... "

"Don't be so damned sure ... "

Ray glared at him, "That's the thing, Dad, I *am* sure. I know you don't want me around here anymore than I have to be, and that's just fine with me. But the price you pay for it is a new truck and the insurance." With that Ray, turned on his heel and said, "I'm going downstairs. There's a ball game on." Sarcasm dripping, he mocked Clipper, "Don't worry, I'm all right, Dad. Nothing broken." Ray disappeared down the basement steps. Clipper just stood there with his teeth clinched. He was about to explode, but, in the end, he knew his son was exactly right. He didn't want him around here anymore than he had to be and Clipper was willing to pay for his son's transportation in order to facilitate his absence.

11

GIRLS' WEEKEND

Maggie closed the Yellow Dog at the usual time, 4:30 p.m., and headed straight home. It had been a beautiful day reaching a high of nearly sixty degrees, really quite warm for an early spring day during the third week of April. It would make for a lovely drive to start a weekend that she had been looking forward to ever since Emily had proposed it last Monday. But it turned out that Maggie wasn't the only one eagerly looking forward to the weekend. At home, she found Jack impatiently waiting with his overnight bag next to him. Maggie wasn't so sure about this part of the weekend. Cautiously, she asked, "OK, do you have everything? Toothbrush? Toothpaste?" She knew she was just grasping at anything that came to mind in a mother's protective attempt to calm her own apprehensions.

He looked at her, puzzled, "Mom, I'm going to Grandpa's, not California. He's got all that stuff there."

She knew she was being ridiculous. Clipper was not her favorite person, and her ex-husband, who lived at Clipper's house, was perhaps her least favorite person, but Jack had already told her, without a hint of disappointment in his voice, that his father was not going to be home that weekend. He was in Detroit, going to Opening Day at Tiger Stadium. If anything, Jack had sounded slightly envious, but Maggie knew Jack held a certain disdain for his father which overshadowed any envy. In fact, she suspected, though Jack had never said it out loud, that he preferred for his dad not to be there. Jack, however, was blind when it came to Clipper, who doted on the boy. Maggie chalked it up to 'that's just what grandparents do,' and since Jack had virtually no relationship with her mother or father, who were separated by both divorce and geographical distance, he in Chicago and she in Sarasota, she gave into it. And then, of course, there were also the terms of her divorce, which allowed Ray and Clipper to have custody of Jack every other weekend. Clipper's home on the shore of Lake Michigan was expansive and included an indoor pool. "Got your trunks?"

"Grandpa's taking me shopping. He says he wants me to have a wardrobe there at his house, so I don't have to worry about packing a bag all the time." Then Jack gave her a huge smile, "He also said we might go look at some new cars this weekend."

Maggie thought, *I should have known.* She smiled at Jack, "OK." She handed him the keys to her old pickup truck. "All right. You know the limits on your driver's license, right?"

He shrugged, his youthful impatience once again showing, having answered this question for what seemed to him to be the thousandth time in the two weeks since he'd passed the tests. "Yes, Mom, I know the rules. You want me to go through them, again?"

His emphasis on the word *again* told her it was time to release him into the stream that was called *real life.* She put up a hand and said, "No. Just be careful. Have a good time." Jack gave her a peck on the cheek and scuttled out the door. She heard the old truck's noisy engine turn over and listened to the roar of the holey muffler as Jack headed out of the drive. Maggie glanced at her watch and saw she had exactly one hour to pack a weekend bag and get showered and changed to be ready for Emily, who was picking her up at six. Emily would be on time or even a little early. She was never late.

★ ★ ★ ★

Maggie had just dragged her overnight bag downstairs and into the kitchen when she saw Emily pull into her driveway. She glanced at her watch and smiled. It was 5:55 p.m. *Good ol' Em.* She met her at the door, bag at her side. "What took you so long?"

Emily smiled at her, "If I didn't know better, I'd say you were looking forward to this weekend."

"Who, me? Whatever gave you that idea?" And off they went for the hour-long trip to Traverse City. The drive was consumed with small talk mostly about who was watching the Yellow Dog in Maggie's absence, who was buying and selling homes in and around Manistee and Onekama, and the magnificent sunset over Grand Traverse Bay as it came into view directly in front of them.

Emily had reserved a suite at the Park Place Hotel and as they stood at the front desk checking in, Maggie offered to give her half of the cost, but Emily adamantly refused. On their way to their suite they settled the matter, agreeing that Maggie could cover dinner and drinks at Georgina's, an upscale restaurant on Front Street specializing in a unique Asian/Cuban cuisine. Emily had made the dinner reservation earlier that afternoon, but, because it was Friday night and the restaurant was busy, the first available seating was at nine. *What the hell,* Emily had thought. *This is a girls' weekend. We hardly ever do this and we didn't come up here to turn in early.* Just glad that she'd called when she did, she'd taken it.

They took just a few minutes to enjoy the twilight view of Grand Traverse Bay from the huge picture window of their suite's sitting room on the hotel's top floor. But it didn't take long for Emily to suggest that, with a little time on their hands, they should head down to the bar at Minerva's, the hotel's main restaurant, and have a libation to celebrate their liberation from their daily lives back in

Onekama, albeit only for a couple of days. The restaurant was crowded, but they managed to find two seats next to one another at the bar and they settled in and began to enjoy the vibe of Traverse City, one of Michigan's fastest-growing urban centers. After drinks came and they toasted to their freedom, Emily could bite her tongue no longer. "What did you think of Ray's latest screwup?"

"Terrible. Poor Peter."

"Peter?" Emily said somewhat incredulously. "You know the guy Ray hit."

"Yes. He'd become a regular customer. Peter Wagner. He's a lawyer out of Chicago. He's working on settling that hotel dustup just south of Manistee."

Emily was familiar with it. The construction, which had already started before a court injunction stopped everything in its tracks, had cost her at least two sales in the area. No one wanted to buy around there until they knew how things were going to be settled. If the neighbors won, property values would be secure. If the builder won, there would be a lot of homes going on the market and their prices would plummet. People came to this part of Michigan because they were looking to buy Lake Michigan homes offering quiet solitude, serenity, and lake views, not because they wanted a bunch of yuppies staying in a boutique hotel at inflated prices mucking any of that up. "Oh, wow. I just knew Ray had plowed into someone not far from the Yellow Dog. Isn't the corner of Spring and Portage Streets pretty close to the limit of his PPO?"

"Damn close ... maybe a little inside of it if you drew a straight line between the Yellow Dog and that intersection, but the good news is, I haven't seen hide nor hair of him since I called the sheriff's office back before the divorce. If he's been inside that five hundred feet he's required to keep between me and him, then he's been damned careful about not letting me see him, and that's exactly the way I want it to be."

"Well, that's good." Ray was a bastard as far as Emily was concerned, but her curiosity still had the best of her. "So, how's the guy he hit?"

"I asked a doc from the hospital that stops in every now and then. He told me he'd recover, but I haven't seen Peter since the day before the accident. I suspect he's gone home to Chicago to rest and recuperate."

"Was Ray drunk?" Emily asked, and then added her opinion. "Probably so, huh. I heard he didn't have a scratch on him. That's how it works, you know. The innocent guy gets all beat up and the drunk driver comes out of it unscathed."

Maggie took a sip of her drink and shook her head. "No, I asked the doc about that. He said Ray was sober as a church mouse." She giggled, "I had to pry that much out of him. I don't think he was supposed to tell me ... you know hospital privacy rules, doctor-client relationship ... all of that legal mumbo-jumbo. I told him about Jack and the legal visitation arrangement with Clipper and Ray because I wanted to know if Ray was drunk at eight o'clock in the morning. If he was, I was going to go straight to my lawyer and ask him to drag the two of them back into court. Grandparent or not, father or not, I will not have Jack hanging around with someone that's drunk at that time of day."

Emily, thrilled to see her friend so fired up, said, "That's the Maggie I want to see. You go, girl." Both women laughed and took a sip of their drinks. A couple of guys in suits walked over and asked if they could buy them a round. It was flattering, but an unwanted intrusion. Emily flashed her wedding ring, which until now had apparently been unseen by their new admirers, a huge rock that sparkled brightly even in the low light of the bar. "No, thanks. That's just not a good idea. My husband's the jealous type. He'll be down here in a minute," she said, telling one of those little white lies that are quite useful sometimes.

She flashed a toothy grin at Maggie, who added, "Well, I'm just divorced, and it makes me feel good to know that you two decided to come over here and give it a try, but here's the thing ... my ex is a real sonuvabitch." She glanced at Emily, whose head was bobbing up and down like a bobblehead. Maggie could hardly repress the laughter. "He's the jealous type ... and if he ever got wind ... " she paused again. Already they were backing away. When they'd disappeared from the bar, Emily and Maggie high-fived one another, breaking out into school-girl laughter.

A light breeze blew off of the bay and chilled them as they walked the few blocks to Georgina's, and, though they were fifteen minutes early for their reservation, a youthful hostess escorted them directly to a table for two. As they waited for drinks, they both took some pleasure from the fact that they had been able to attract the two younger men over to them at Minerva's. When the drinks arrived, they clinked glasses as Emily announced, "Here's to two women, who, apparently, still have what it takes and are on the loose in Traverse City."

Their dinner was amazing. They started with an appetizer of Spanish fried calamari and then decided to split an order of *tallarines y chorizo*, chosen from the restaurant's expansive menu because it seemed to best combine the Latin and Asian flavors that both of them loved so much. The chorizo was homemade by Chef Anthony, laid over a bed of lo mein noodles and covered in a queso-fresco sauce that both of them thought was to die for. Emily chose a delightful chardonnay from the wine list, which they had their waitress recork and bag for them before they left the restaurant. Feeling stuffed as they left Georgina's, they were looking forward to their short, brisk walk back to the hotel.

Once in their suite, both women kicked off their high heels. Emily poured two glasses of the remaining chardonnay and then they got down to the real reason she'd wanted Maggie to come with her on this girls' weekend. "Mags ... " Maggie immediately noticed the more serious bent to her friend's voice, "I've got some news."

Maggie set the wine glass down on the coffee table in front of the sofa she was sitting on. "Sounds serious. What is it?"

All Emily said was, "David."

The thick, pile carpet covering the floor had the best pad money could buy under it, and you could still hear a pin drop. Maggie turned her head from her friend and stared out of the large picture window into the darkness that was Grand Traverse Bay. She wanted to ask, *What about him?,* but the lump in her throat kept her quiet.

"Mags?"

Silence.

"You OK?" Emily knew the nerve she was touching, so she stopped right where she was and gave her friend some time.

Finally, Maggie asked, "What have you heard?"

Emily sensed both anticipation and apprehension in Maggie's voice. "I don't know exactly where to start, but here goes. I had a meeting about a week ago with Henry Hanratty and PJ Keller. We wanted to update PJ on where the committee was ... the committee working on David's homecoming."

Maggie nodded.

"We've raised an unprecedented amount of money, Mags." Maggie remained impassive. "Almost four hundred thousand dollars."

That got Maggie's attention. "My, God. What are you guys planning?" Since its inception, the Welcome Home, Major David Keller committee had met regularly at the Yellow Dog. Maggie had eavesdropped on bits and pieces, but she'd completely missed any details about fundraising.

Emily was still trying to sense where her friend was emotionally, so she tried to proceed cautiously, but that was difficult. The news was big. "Well, it's turned out to be a lot more than just a parade down Main Street and a rubber-chicken dinner for a bunch of stuffed-shirt politicians who want their picture in the paper next to a war hero. The committee is going to buy a house, have it renovated to meet his disabilities, and now, with the contributions exceeding even our wildest dreams, it looks like we are going to have enough money to buy him a van that he will be able to drive." Emily watched the first tears come to Maggie's eyes.

"So, he's coming back to Onekama to live?"

Emily gave this time before answering, because the answer was more complex than a simple *yes* or *no.* "We are hoping for that to be the case, but PJ was very honest with us. We had told PJ about what we were planning based on the contributions we'd received. He said he'd communicated that to his brother. He also told us that while David had expressed surprise and gratitude, he'd also expressed some regret because he couldn't be sure Onekama was where he would want to stay."

"Oh."

Again, Emily tried to read her friend, but Maggie was a blank page. "So, we had a decision to make. Should we proceed with the real-estate purchase and the renovation or just go with the van? We took a vote of committee members. It was unanimous that we should proceed as planned and that perhaps our efforts would convince David that Onekama was really where he should stay. I've found a place; that was, as you might expect, my job."

"Where?"

"Yeah, well, that's another reason why I wanted to be the one to tell you all of this. You know that house just behind Papa J's?"

Maggie, quite familiar with where Emily was talking about, answered apprehensively, "Yes."

"The owners, the Dentons, have agreed to sell it to the committee."

Maggie squirmed a little in her seat.

"They had heard about what happened to David. I ran into Shirley Denton at the EZ Market and she told me that they wanted to sell it to us. The price she quoted was at least fifty thousand below market value. I took their offer to the committee and we decided that it would be perfect for David. Our architect, who specializes in renovations to accommodate specific disabilities, has been down to take a look at the cottage and he's drawing up plans now."

"But, that's right ... "

"Yeah, Mags, I know," Emily interrupted, "it's practically across the street from the Yellow Dog." Again, if a pin would have dropped, it would have sounded like a clatter. A hush consumed the suite as if the air had been sucked out of it. Then Emily looked Maggie squarely in the eye. "You didn't expect for David to come back to town and for you never to see him ... never to have to talk to him, did you?"

Tears ran down both of Maggie's cheeks now. She wiped them away, but new ones formed almost immediately. The lump in her throat felt the size of a golf ball. *Why can't I talk?* She and Emily had been best friends since Maggie had first come to Onekama. They had shared everything. She managed to squeak out, "I ... I don't know what I expected. He's been gone so long. Nothing from him in all that time ... and now ... "

"Do you want to hear what PJ says about him?" It was a question that hung in the air for a long time.

Finally, Maggie nodded. "Yes."

"He says his brother is still fiercely proud ... doesn't want a bunch of people feeling sorry for him. PJ believes David hates what has happened to him and is still reeling from the extent of his wounds. He also thinks he has some deep guilt that he hasn't properly dealt with because he was the only one that survived the explosion that killed three others. But PJ has some trust in David's doctors, who have apparently expressed cautious optimism about his acceptance of the new circumstances of his life. He flatly told PJ he was not going to move in with them. He told PJ, if he can't live independently in Onekama, he will go somewhere else to live where he can do that. That was when I got busy trying to find the right place. I was lucky to have run into Shirley when I did."

"Can't they fit him with ... " She didn't know what. She'd seen some soldiers on the news with terrible injuries who were now using artificial limbs and doing things almost as easily as they had done them before. "I don't know ... artificial legs ... something ... anything."

"Henry asked PJ that very question. PJ said he didn't know. Some of what is apparently holding up any progress in that regard is David himself. He has it in his mind that there isn't any hope, so he won't even talk to the people who might be able to help him. Instead, he seems to have consigned himself to a wheelchair, an unpowered one at that. Again, PJ is hoping that if we can get David back here and settled into a community that is grateful and caring, that it might change David's attitude, but he says he can't guarantee anything at this point."

"When?"

Emily appeared confused. *When what? When is he coming home? When can he guarantee something?*

Maggie sensed the confusion and clarified, "When is he coming home?"

"The committee wants the house and van to be ready by the first of June."

"That's just six weeks. You can't get ... "

"Emily interrupted, "We think we can. My question is, 'Will you be ready?'"

12

IN THE NRA WE TRUST

The ward was noisy this morning. Two patients were being moved out. Two others waited in wheelchairs in the hallway for their beds to be readied. David was more than glad he had plans. He looked out the window only to see that it was still pouring down rain. He could only hope that things would dry out sooner rather than later. It was Saturday, the Ann Arbor Gun and Knife Show opened at nine o'clock, and his plan was to be there early. Shifting from his bed to his wheelchair, a process that had by now become quite routine for him, he grabbed his wallet off the nightstand and rolled himself toward the hospital's main entrance and the security window where he would sign himself out. The bus stop was right outside the main door and a portico provided shelter while he waited on the bus. The rain continued its relentless downpour.

On the bus, he locked his wheelchair into one of the specially designed stalls near the ramp that had just lifted him up and watched the rain pelt against the window. If this kept up, he would be soaked within minutes of getting off. For the moment he was regretting his decision not to bring an umbrella, but, he'd thought, *Who the hell can push a wheelchair and hold an umbrella at the same time?* He could have asked for assistance. The hospital had plenty of volunteers that would gladly accompany wheelchair-bound patients and assist them as they navigated stores, shopping malls, restaurants, etc. But he never even considered asking for help. He was going to buy a gun today and some ammo, neither of which were permitted on hospital grounds. Signage throughout the hospital complex advised that this was a gun-free zone and he didn't dare risk trying to sneak a gun into the place. The last person in the world he wanted to know he had bought a gun was Dr. Hightower; after that, it was his brother, PJ.

He caught his first break of the day when the rain relented just as the bus pulled to a halt at his stop. He released the locks on his wheelchair, rolled it onto the ramp that would lower him through the bus's door, relocked the wheels into place, and then the driver pushed the hydraulic lever that smoothly lowered the ramp the two or three feet down to the ground level. He unlocked the wheelchair, pushed himself backward until he was clear of the ramp, and gave the driver a thumbs-up. By the time he'd gone a half mile, the rain had stopped altogether.

As he got closer to the convention hall the sidewalks became more and more crowded. He assumed they were all headed to the same place he was. *Apparently,* he thought, *the rumors are true.* He'd done a little research on the internet earlier in the week, but had given up after just a few minutes. It was too confusing. Supposedly, the "rules" for purchasing a handgun at a gun show were different from those regarding a purchase at a gun shop or sporting goods store. As he understood them, he would need to find a dealer that was considered a private dealer rather than a federally licensed gun dealer. If he found one of them, he wouldn't need a purchase permit, the background check would not be necessary, and there would be no reporting of his purchase. He'd read on the internet that this was known as "the gun-show loophole."

As he neared the convention center's main entrance, the sidewalk became quite congested, but people obligingly moved out of his way as he maneuvered toward the handicapped ramp. When he got up to the entrance level, there was a long queue of patrons waiting to purchase tickets. He rolled his way to the end of that line and fell in place. It was a quarter to nine. He was early, the rain continued to hold off, but he had not anticipated the crowd. It was a quarter after nine before he pushed the button on the handicapped accessible door, rolled himself into the lobby, and presented his ticket to the attendant who directed him to a handicapped accessible entrance in order to avoid the turnstile in front of him.

The floor was a teeming mass of vendors and buyers. As he surveyed the narrow aisles between the booths and the crowds that were clogging them, he only hoped that people would be as courteous as they had been on the sidewalk. Undaunted, he rolled forward into their midst.

He stopped at the first booth he could find where a sign on the front of the gun-covered table announced, Private Vendor. There were two other customers talking with the seller over two different handguns, one of which he immediately recognized as a Beretta M9, 9mm pistol, the very same pistol that had been his personal weapon during his years of service. He waited patiently for his turn and when neither sale was consummated and the two potential buyers wondered off to an adjoining booth, he rolled up next to the table and asked, "May I take a look at that M9?"

The guy gave David the onceover, noticing his close-cropped hair, broad shoulders, and missing legs, and noting that he'd called the weapon by its military nomenclature, began to put two and two together. "It's a fine handgun ... but then I expect you know that, eh, son?"

David, slid the action back and let it slide forward. He momentarily flashed back to that fateful day in Afghanistan and the explosion that took his legs away from him. "Yeah, I know the weapon well. How much?"

"We'll need to get a background check done."

That caught David up short. "Didn't think I needed one if you are a private vendor."

The man rubbed his chin and looked at David. "Yeah, it used to be that way and still is in most states. But the boys and girls in Lansing changed the law a few years back. If you're buyin' a handgun, got to have a background check, no matter who you're buyin' it from. Don't make a helluva lot of sense to me. Don't have to have one if you're buyin' a long gun ... only handguns. These assholes shootin' things up ... that kid at Sandy Hook used a long gun ... that man in Vegas ... a long gun ... nope ... just don't make sense to me. But then, again, I'm not one of those overeducated lawyers that gets elected and goes to Lansing."

David handed the M9 back to the man. "How long does it take to get a background check?"

"Not long. I got a laptop right here. I can give it to you, you fill out the info, submit it, and a couple of minutes later I know if I can sell you the gun."

David didn't like it. A computer, questions, his answers, submit ... *there's a record that I bought a gun.* He frowned at the gun's seller.

"It's pretty painless, really," the man tried to reassure him.

David leaned toward him. "Yeah, I'm not worried about the background check showing anything that wouldn't allow you to sell me the gun. It's ... It's just that I don't like the idea of an electronic record existing that I bought the gun ... know what I mean. It's like Big Brother's watchin', too close."

The man nodded as if he knew exactly what David was talking about. "What happened to you, son?" He pointed to David's missing legs. "That happen in combat?"

David didn't like talking about this to anyone, including Dr. Hightower, who was constantly trying to engage him to talk about his injury, but he especially didn't like having to talk to some old guy selling guns at a gun and knife show. However, he had the thought that maybe he could strike a sympathetic note with this old bird. "Afghanistan. IED. About five months ago. Rehabbing over at the VA hospital."

"You know you can't take a gun in there, right?"

"Yeah, sure do. Signs all over the place. But I'm going home soon ... up north ... little town called Onekama. Know where it is?" He had a plan to stash the gun and ammo, but he didn't feel the need to share it. He was trying to change the subject.

The gun seller shook his head.

"About ten miles north of Manistee on M-22."

He nodded, "OK, right there close to the casino?"

"Yep, you got it." They were bonding, David thought. "I was in the army for ten years ... Special Forces ... carried an M9 all those years. Just feel safer with one close to me."

"Special Forces, eh. That must have been some real shit duty. How many tours did you do?"

"Three in Iraq. I was on my third one in Afghanistan when this happened." He pointed to his missing legs.

The man rubbed his chin again. "I was a bush marine in Vietnam. Two tours. Fuckin' sorry-ass war ... " The conversation just hung there for a long while. Then he looked at David and said, "Promise me you ain't gonna do nothin' stupid with this if I sell it to you?"

"It's ridiculous, I know, but it will just give me comfort to know it's beside me." David pointed to a pouch mounted under the right-side handle of his wheelchair. "I'll just use it every now and then for target practice ... was a pretty good shot with one of these once."

He stared hard at David. "How about two hundred dollars?"

"I heard you tell that other guy that was ahead of me that you wanted five hundred for it."

He smiled at David, "He weren't no vet and he damned sure ain't given to this country near as much as you and I have, son." He handed the M9 back to David. "She's all yours."

David took it and put it in the pouch before pulling out his wallet. Almost as an afterthought he asked, "Got a couple of boxes of ammo for it?"

"You bet." He rummaged around for a minute in a foot-locker he had stored under the table and produced the ammo.

"What do I owe you?"

"Two hundred. The ammo's on me."

David peeled off ten twenty-dollar bills. After he handed it to the man he asked, "What's your name?"

"Ernie ... Ernie Etherton."

"Pleasure, Ernie, and thanks for your service."

"Pleasure's all mine, son, and thank you, too."

By ten o'clock, David was out of the convention center and waiting at a bus stop. He'd done his research and he knew the bus he needed to catch was handicapped accessible; not all of them were. He had plenty of time to get to the Greyhound bus station on Huron Street in Ann Arbor. He rented a locker there and stashed the M9 and the ammo in it.

The rain continued to hold off until he'd gotten back to the hospital and then the skies opened back up. He rolled himself to the cafeteria and got his dinner. As he sat picking at his food, he thought, *Hightower's going to let me out of this place soon ... she's got to.* At the bus station, after he'd stashed the weapon and ammo, he gathered up a copy of the bus line's most current schedule. Greyhound had twice-weekly service to Traverse City and the schedule indicated that the bus serving that route would be handicapped accessible. He could get the gun out of the locker just before boarding. The plan was coming together. He was not going to live like this any longer than he needed to after patching things up with his father and brother.

13

FURTHER INTO THE ABYSS

After the ball game on Opening Day, Ray McCall made his way over to the Greektown Casino where he'd gotten lucky at a blackjack table. Cashing out twenty-five hundred dollars in chips, he'd gotten himself a room, called a dating service, and spent the night with somebody named Jody. Sunday morning, he awoke to find her gone. A quick check of things and he breathed a sigh of relief to find his wallet, credit cards, and the fifteen hundred dollars cash he had left after giving Jody a grand for her services were all there. It took him about half an hour to lose a thousand dollars of it at the same blackjack table that had been so generous to him the day before. *Oh, well. Nothing ventured, nothing gained.* He located his truck, a lightly used 2014 Chevy Silverado, in the casino's parking garage and headed home. He arrived there still smelling of cigarette smoke, stale beer, and cheap perfume. He'd noticed the brand-new Chevy Equinox sitting in the driveway next to Maggie's old beater pickup. Clipper and Jack sat at the kitchen table engrossed in a game of dominoes. Ignoring his father, Ray said, "Hey, Jackson, how's it going?"

Jack hated it when his dad called him Jackson; that wasn't his name. It was *Jack*; just plain *Jack*. The boy looked up from the lineup of dominoes in front of him and said, "Fine." It was flat, emotionless. Clipper looked past Ray's ignoring him and smiled at his grandson, rather enjoying his sense that Jack felt like his father's arrival was an intrusion.

"You drivin' that old heap of your mom's?" Ray asked him. "I'm surprised she'd let you on the road in that beater."

Jack looked up at his father and then smiled at Clipper. "I'm only drivin' it home. After that, I'm drivin' that new Equinox sitting next to it. Did you see it? Grandpa bought it for me yesterday."

It was a gut punch, but Ray was damned if he was going to let his father see it. *I get a used truck and my kid gets a new damned car!* Ray glanced sideways at his father and then said to Jack, "Nice. Be damned careful with it, though. Insurance is so damned expensive in this state."

Jack saw the disdain build in his grandfather's face. All Ray was doing was sticking a knife in Clipper and twisting it.

"Hey, Jackson, the Tigers are on TV. Want to go downstairs and watch the game?"

Jack looked up at his father. "No, thanks. I've got to go as soon as Grandpa and I finish this."

Clipper glared at his son. Ray still had a bit of a hangover from the night before, so he wasn't in the mood to engage. Instead he turned on his heel, muttered over his shoulder, "Whatever," and headed downstairs. Thirty minutes later he heard the front door close, and then Maggie's truck cranked up. He'd been fuming ever since leaving the two in the kitchen, so, spoiling for a fight now, he headed back upstairs to have it out with his father over the new car for Jack. But Clipper wasn't there.

Jack drove his mom's old pickup home. Clipper, in the Equinox, was in trail behind him. Jack would drive him back home in the Equinox. Clipper thought his grandson had exceptionally good driving skills ... certainly better than his father's.

Still fuming, Ray slammed the front door behind him, roared out of the gravel driveway spewing rocks and dust behind him, and headed for Rosie's on US 31 between Bear Lake and Onekama. There was a cute little waitress there that he'd flirted with the last time he'd been in. The fact that she was half his age had no bearing on his thinking. What he was really looking for was cold beer and lots of it, but maybe she was working tonight. That would be a bonus.

★ ★ ★ ★

As happenstance would have it, she had been working and he had flirted with her and she'd invited him to her place for a beer. They'd spent Monday and Tuesday together. Ray had taken her to the casino and dropped the remaining five hundred dollars trying to impress her with his skills at blackjack, then they'd gone back to her place. She was a sexual dynamo and by the time Wednesday morning rolled around he was worn out in more ways than one. He'd already had too much to drink and was brooding over losing all his available cash. He was trying to think of what excuse he'd offer to his father for being so broke. As he walked in the door, he heard the answering machine beep. He pushed play and listened:

Clipper, it's Henry Hanratty. I just wanted to update you. David Keller is coming home to Onekama after he completes his physical therapy in Ann Arbor. We expect him sometime around the first of June, but I will confirm with you as soon as I know for sure. I thought that since you were the one who gave David his appointment to West Point that you might like to say a few words at a banquet we are planning ... again, date and time to be confirmed, but we will for sure hold it at the Portage Point Inn. Anyway, give me a call when you get this message.

Ray toyed with the idea of deleting it, but decided not to do that. Hanratty would certainly follow up with his dad and Clipper would certainly suspect Ray of messing around with his messages; that's just how he was. And Ray needed to hit his father up for more money.

★ ★ ★ ★

On Friday night Ray entered Shirley's Restaurant, looked toward the back at the table where he and Charley usually met, and found him waiting. This was their first meeting in over a month. Charley was nursing a beer. "You want somethin', Ray?" he asked.

Charley was an employee, and a marginal one at that, in Ray's opinion. Their regular waitress showed up at their table. With the flick of his hand he said, "No, nothing," dismissing her quite abruptly.

Asshole! She thought as she walked away.

Charley, too loudly in Ray's estimation, said, "Wow, you really took care of that guy in the BMW!"

Ray wanted to punch him, but couldn't; not here, not now, not in this public place. Whispering, but with a daunting fierceness in his voice, Ray snarled at him, "Jesus Christ, Charley, why don't you just stand up there on that chair and announce to the whole place that I rammed that fuckin' lawyer. Lower your damned voice."

"Uh ... er ... yeah ... " he whispered, "OK, Ray, but you sure took care of him."

Ray looked across the table with a broad smile and said, "The sonuvabitch should have died; I hit him so hard."

"Well, I sure ain't seen hide nor hair of him since that morning, Ray. I guess you accomplished what you set out to."

A party of two sat down at a nearby table, and Ray didn't want to talk about the lawyer. Lowering his voice, he looked at Charley and said, "I've got a new assignment for you. There's someone else I want you to keep an eye out for and let me know if he comes sniffin' around Maggie." He slid an envelope across the table to Charley, who peeked inside. It contained two hundred dollars and a picture.

Standing at the end of the bar, Rose Davenport, their waitress, curiously witnessed this transaction.

"Who is it?"

"Name's David Keller. Used to live around here. I went to school with him. He thinks he's a real hot shit. My dad got him into West Point. Sucker got his legs blown off over in one of them godforsaken places we got troops getting killed now ... Afghanistan or Iraq ... not sure and it don't matter. News is he's comin' home. Not sure when, but soon ... next month or so. I want you to keep an eye out for him. Let me know if he and Maggie start seein' one another."

"What makes you so sure he's going to see Maggie?"

He glared across the table at Charley, "None of your fuckin' business, Charley. You just keep an eye out for him and let me know when you see him. I want to know ASAP. Got it?"

Charley nodded. "Uh ... yeah, sure, Ray. I'll be watchin' for him."

"Don't forget, Charley," Ray sounded equal parts diabolical and menacing, "no one else knows about this except you and me?"

"Right, Ray. No one else knows."

Ray got up and left. Charley finished his beer and thought Ray McCall was one truly crazy sonuvabitch.

14

HOMECOMING

June 1—Emily's husband, Chuck Weber, was a much-sought-after general contractor who specialized in constructing large, custom-designed lakeshore homes for wealthy clients who could afford such a luxury. In the overall scope of things, David's cottage renovation would not have been a job he would have even looked at except for one dynamic force in his life: Emily. "Fit it in. I need you on this. It has to be quick, correct, and I don't know of anyone else I can make these demands on and also ask that you get it done under budget."

He loved her to the moon and back. Two days ago, Henry and Emily had walked through with a beaming Chuck leading them. The architect's plans for David's handicapped accessible home were very precise. The renovation had gone off without a hitch. Chuck had brought it in nearly ten-thousand dollars under budget, thanks to a fifteen-percent discount on all of the building supplies that had been provided by Onekama Hardware. It seemed everyone wanted to be a part of the war hero's homecoming, including Maggie, who had provided breakfast and lunch to the workers during the renovation.

★ ★ ★ ★

June 2—The night before David's long-awaited arrival home, Maggie and Emily stood in front of the cottage. It was twilight, the evening temperature hovered just above fifty degrees, and a soft, reddish-orange light, the fading remnant of a brilliant sunset, filtered through the leaves of the towering oak trees that stood in the town park just across the street. Maggie said to her friend without taking her eyes off of the cottage, "It's beautiful. You and Chuck did a great job."

"Yeah, thanks, Mags." Emily reached over and took her friend's hand in hers. "You going to be OK tomorrow?"

Maggie only shook her head; words were hard because of a rising lump in her throat.

"You're going to sit with Chuck and me at our table tomorrow night at the banquet." Emily could feel her friend's hand tighten slightly around hers.

"Em, I don't know ... "

Firmly Emily cut her off, "Listen, Mags, I've given this a lot of thought. There's a bunch of ways you could do this, but this way, I think, will be the easiest for you. You're going to have to see David at some point. So why not do it tomorrow night at the banquet so I can be there with you and offer you some moral support? He's going to be seated at the dais along with the governor, Clipper, and a few other stuffed shirts. You will be right in front of him at our table."

"Right in front of him!" Maggie lamented.

"I tried to get a table toward the back, but Henry insisted. It's a political thing ... Chuck and I really had no choice. But we will both be there with you. You don't even have to talk to him. Look at it this way, it's an up-close look at a guy who was your first love, a guy you haven't seen in fifteen years, a guy who broke your heart. You will be dressed to the nines. He will likely be very uncomfortable. You don't have to do anything but sit there and look beautiful."

"Why would I want to do that?"

Emily dropped Maggie's hand, moved to a position

directly in front of her, looked her in the eye, and said, "C'mon, Maggie, it's me, Emily, your best friend forever. Don't even try and play that game with me. You've got to see David at some point. Why not do that in a somewhat controlled environment where you are the one mostly in control?"

★ ★ ★ ★

7:30 a.m., June 3—Dr. Hightower rushed to the VA bus stop in front of the hospital and caught David just before the ramp was to move him up and into the bus. "David, sorry I almost missed you."

He was surprised to see her, but he smiled cordially and stretched out his hand. "Yeah, well, Doc, thanks for everything!"

The question nagged at her. *Is he playing me?* "You've done amazing work, David. I just wanted to wish you the very best. You have my number. If you should ever need anything, just call."

He smiled broadly at her, "Can you score me some tickets to Notre Dame women's basketball games?" They both chuckled. His sense of humor gave her some encouragement.

The ramp began to move him up and over to the bus. She waved at him and said, "Good luck."

At the bus station he collected the M9 and the ammo from the locker, placed all of it in the pouch on his wheelchair's arm, and boarded the bus for Traverse City. Just inside, behind the driver's station, was a stall into which he rolled and locked his wheelchair into place. He'd been careful to empty his bladder before boarding, because, while the bus had a ramp and a stall for his wheelchair, he had no idea how he'd negotiate the bathroom if necessary. However, he'd worried needlessly. This was not your typical Greyhound bus. There was a wide aisle down the middle that gave way to a large handicapped-accessible bathroom. They stopped only once in Grand Rapids to board a few more passengers, and then got back on the road again.

12:15 p.m., June 3—PJ met him in Traverse City at the Greyhound station. He and Natalie had talked about her coming along, but decided against it. The hour-long trip to Onekama would give the two brothers a chance to talk about what David could expect. "Am I going to know the old place?" David asked his brother as they made their way out of the city's congestion toward US 31 South.

PJ laughed, "It's Onekama, David. People pay a lot of money to come to a place that hasn't changed very much in the last fifty years." The small talk continued until PJ reached the open road and, when he was comfortable that he could concentrate less on his driving and more on his brother, he said, "Are you ready for today?"

David looked over at him. "Not really. I wish ... "

PJ interrupted him, "A lot of people are rooting for you, David. Wait until you see. There's a parade. I expect they're lining up right now for it. There will be a brief ceremony when we arrive at your cottage. The committee thought there should be a public event since so many people contributed to your homecoming. The banquet tonight is by invitation. The least we can do is honor all of their hard work."

The use of the pronoun *we* angered David a bit. *You're not the one they're all going to be staring at, pointing at ... Oh, look at poor David ... I'm so sorry for poor David.* He wished for a brief moment that he hadn't committed to this, but the time for refusal had long since passed and he knew it. By the time PJ reached Honor, about twenty miles north of Onekama, David had put away his anger and decided he would just have to grin and bear it.

1:30 p.m., June 3—They were met in front of the Blue Slipper Bar, an Onekama landmark, that sat right at a tight curve on M-22 that bends into the village of Onekama. Three sheriff's deputies on gleaming white Harley-Davidsons led a color guard from the Kaleva VFW. They marched in step to a rousing version of John Phillip Sousa's "On Parade" played by the Scottville Clown Band. PJ rolled the windows of his Tahoe down and music filled the car. As David looked down the mile-long stretch of the scenic highway that led through the village, much of his life flashed before him. The familiar beds of petunias that lined the north side of the street were a part of an Onekama tradition that was more than a quarter of a century old. The petunias weren't yet in full bloom, but the red, white, and purplish-blue blossoms at this early point in the season added to the patriotic atmosphere that the committee had hoped to capture. David looked over at his brother and muttered, "You've got to be kidding me."

PJ smiled at him, "I told you you wouldn't believe it."

Just a hundred yards or so in front of them, in front of the Onekama Township volunteer fire department, two ladder trucks, one from Onekama, the other from Bear Lake, were positioned on either side of the road with ladders extended to form a pointed arch. A huge American flag was suspended from them over the center of the roadway and below that a banner that read Welcome Home, Major David Keller. Beyond the ladder trucks were people, thousands of them strung along both sides of the street. They came in all shapes, sizes, and ages. Some of the men had on old field jackets or hats indicating to David that they, too, were veterans. Some moved to attention and saluted him as he and PJ rolled by. Others, men and women alike, tapped their hearts twice and then pointed at him. He tried to acknowledge each and every one of these gestures. Children of all ages were frantically waving small American flags back and forth. There were signs and flags and more flags. By the time they were at the EZ Market, PJ told him to look in the rearview mirror. Behind them were at least fifty motorcycles, all of them with an American flag flying. "They call themselves Rolling Thunder," PJ explained. "Most of them are vets. They do this mostly for veterans' funerals. I'm betting they're glad to be able to do this for once for some-one who's alive."

It was all too much for him. David reached in his pocket and pulled out a wad of Kleenex he kept there. Dabbing his eyes, he choked out a whispered, "I had no idea … "

PJ looked at him and said, "You haven't seen anything yet, David."

Store windows, the electronic gas station sign at the EZ Market, and more banners all along the route continued to hold greetings of Welcome Home, Major David Keller. And then they reached the public park in the center of the vil-lage. The Scottville Clown Band formed a three-row-deep semi-circle facing David's new home. The heavy thrum of the motorcycles' engines fell off as the sheriff's deputies and Rolling Thunder cut their engines. PJ pulled to a stop, got out and retrieved the wheelchair from the back, and rolled it into position for David to exit. As he grabbed the handhold above the door he said to PJ, "I hope I don't fall on my ass. Wouldn't that be a helluva thing!" PJ laughed. David swung himself deftly into the wheelchair's seat. At his side, through the pouch, he could feel the M9.

By now the crowds that had lined either side of M-22 and then followed Rolling Thunder down Main Street moved into the park and gathered under the shade of giant oak trees. From a low stage that the Portage Lake Association provided for groups that performed at the park's free summer concerts, Henry Hanratty announced over a pub-lic-address system, "Major, a few of your friends wanted to welcome you home to Onekama." And with that a roar of shouts, whistles, and applause drowned everything else out. PJ pushed David in Henry's direction.

Maggie had locked the front door of the Yellow Dog and moved to the corner of Portage Street and M-22, just across from the park. She could see PJ maneuvering the wheel-chair through the crowd, but she was too far away to make out any of David's features. It had been his eyes that had first drawn her to him, but she shed that thought, quickly dismissing it as a foolish schoolgirl's memory.

As the crowd settled down, Henry proceeded. "Major Keller, on behalf of everyone here, we want to thank you for your service to this great country of ours and for the great personal sacrifice you have made on our behalf. What we offer to you is our steadfast friendship and our everlasting appreciation. It is our most sincere hope that Onekama, a place that was your hometown, will become exactly that again. To make that so, we have prepared this home for you." The crowd erupted again in applause. When they'd settled back down, he continued, "And we have had this van built," he pointed to the vehicle parked in the driveway of the cottage, "so that you may move about amongst us and enjoy the beauty of this part of the country you have fought so valiantly for. Please accept these things from all of us here in Onekama." The roar and the crowd's applause arose once again. Henry bent down and asked David if he'd like to say a few words.

Thrusting the mic toward him, even though David would have preferred not to speak, he knew Henry expected him to. David took it and began to talk, but the roar and the applause were too much. He waited for the din to settle. People near the speakers' platform, who could see that David had been given a chance to speak to them, turned and quickly passed the word to quiet down. A few seconds later the park was quiet, so quiet, in fact, that birds could be heard calling. David cleared his throat and began, "I ... I don't know what to say. You honor me as if I am someone special. I am not." *Those three guys that died in that Humvee were special,* he thought. The park remained still. "I grew up here. For that I consider myself to be fortunate. I left here to serve my country. It was my privilege to be able to do that. I am humbled by your reception, but it is a bit overwhelming. So, please forgive me if my words are not as carefully chosen as they should be. To simply say, 'Thank you' seems so woefully inadequate." He stopped speaking and the crowd erupted again. Henry reached for the mic. Apparently ... and thankfully ... David thought, he was done.

Henry introduced someone else on the committee, who wanted to thank the other members for their hard work. David took a moment to look around as applause punctuated the list the speaker read from. Standing on the corner a couple of hundred yards away, he thought he could see Maggie Lassiter, but he couldn't be sure. It had been so long, but he recalled with crystal clarity the dream he'd had just after the IED had detonated, the dream where he and Maggie were teenagers again and making snow angels in that field just out of town. He heard Henry announce that this part of the official proceedings had come to an end. He thanked everyone for coming out, with a special thanks to Rolling Thunder, the Kaleva VFW color guard, the Manistee sheriff's office, the Onekama Township and Bear Lake volunteer fire departments, and last but not least, the Scottville Clown Band, which struck up "The Washington Post March." The crowd began to slowly filter out of the park, many coming by to offer a personal greeting to David, PJ, and Henry. When David looked back at the street corner, Maggie was gone.

★ ★ ★ ★

Lingering in the shadows of the picnic pavilion, in the far back reaches of the diminishing crowd, careful to keep obstructions between him and Maggie, Ray watched it all. When she headed back to the Yellow Dog, he slunk back to his pickup truck parked in front of the Glenwood Restaurant, pulled the bottle from under the seat, and took a deep pull from it. *That bitch!*

★ ★ ★ ★

For the next hour, as the crowd broke up and filtered past, Maggie was busy with a packed house at the Yellow Dog, but as the final customer was served their meal, Maggie's thoughts turned to David. She was amazed at the strength and confidence she'd heard in his voice. *My God, he was nearly dead just a few months ago. He sounded today just like he did when he delivered his high-school commencement address.* Suddenly, she found herself rather looking forward to the banquet this evening. Yes, she'd have to endure a bunch of stuffed-shirt politicians ... Clipper being the most stuffed of the bunch ... but Emily and Chuck would be there with her. And David would be there, right in front of her. She would see him up close. She vowed to look her very best tonight.

15

THE BANQUET

Jack laughed, "You realize that you have not sat down or stopped talking since you came downstairs."

She smiled sublimely at her son and asked, "So, how do I look?"

Jack could not recall his mother ever asking him that question. He never thought of her as someone who either sought or needed that kind of approval. He knew she was going out tonight to a banquet to honor a Major Keller who apparently was from Onekama and that his Aunt Em and Uncle Chuck were picking her up, but rarely had he ever seen her this nervous. "Well, Mom, I have to say you clean up really, really good."

Maggie let that sink in. It wasn't the ringing endorsement of her beauty preparations that she had hoped for, but then she quickly realized she had put her son in an unfamiliar and, therefore, somewhat difficult position. Smiling at him she said, "Thanks ... I think."

"So, do you know this guy ... this Major Keller?"

Oh, Jack, if you only knew. With as little emotion in her voice as she could muster, she said, "He and I went to school together."

★ ★ ★ ★

Most cities, even the smallest of towns in America, had some place or something with which people identified. Typically, these iconic things or places had historical significance. For example, the icon in Gettysburg, was, of course, the battleground. On Mackinac Island, lying between Michigan's upper and lower peninsulas and near the confluence of Lake Michigan and Lake Huron, the landmark was the Grand Hotel, and anyone who had ever been there would know how exactly perfect the hotel's name was. In Onekama, the iconic place was the Portage Point Inn. In fact, the inn was designed by the same architects who designed the Grand Hotel. Opened in June 1903, the inn sat perched on the shore of Portage Lake near the channel that gave way to Lake Michigan. In the early 1900s, steamboats brought throngs of visitors to the Portage Point Inn, most of whom were looking to escape the stifling heat of Chicago summers. Many of these visitors eventually bought property and built summer cottages, many of which had been heavily renovated or torn down completely to give way to modern homes. Generations of families returned to Onekama from points all over the US to enjoy delightfully cool summers, spectacular fall colors, magnificent sunsets, and a quieter, calmer way of life. The Portage Point Inn was a closely woven part of the fabric of Onekama and though their mode of transportation to get there may have changed, people still flocked to the place. Over its hundred-plus years of welcoming people to northern Michigan, it was the site of many galas, but none any more festive than the banquet taking place on the evening of June 3.

★ ★ ★ ★

6:15 p.m. — As Chuck Weber guided the white Escalade into the parking spot, Emily turned to Maggie, who sat behind Chuck in the back seat. "You look beautiful, Mags."

Modestly Maggie replied, "Thanks, Em. You, too."

Emily winked at her, "You ready for this?"

The question struck Chuck as odd, but he kept his mouth

shut. Getting out of the car, he opened Maggie's door and helped her out. Emily waited for them. The parking lot was full, and more cars were streaming in. "How many are invited tonight?" Maggie asked.

"The max the old place can seat is one hundred thirty-five and it looks like they are all here." As they approached the white-columned front porch, a Michigan State Police car with a burly trooper behind the wheel sat parked in an obviously reserved spot. "Looks like the governor's already here," Emily remarked as she pointed to the car.

Chuck laughed, "Yeah. Wonder who made that happen? Clipper? Or Henry?"

As he pulled open the door for them, Emily smiled at him and said, "Likely both. Clipper probably called in some long overdue favor and Henry ... well, as you know, Henry is hard to refuse."

★ ★ ★ ★

Ray, wearing sunglasses and a wide-brimmed hat pulled low over his forehead, sat under an umbrella-shaded table on the deck surrounding the swimming pool belonging to the condos immediately next door to the Portage Point Inn. He was perfectly positioned to see who was coming and going to the banquet in honor of David. When he saw Chuck, Emily, and Maggie step from the parking lot onto the sidewalk leading to the inn's front porch, he swore under his breath.

★ ★ ★ ★

Within a few feet of the entrance to the inn's main dining room, the three of them were absorbed into the crowd. The cocktail hour lasted until seven o'clock, so Chuck took their drink orders and headed for the bar. Maggie tugged at Emily's hand. "Don't leave me."

"Don't worry, Mags." The two of them waded deeper

into the crowd. It wasn't long before Henry spotted them. "Emily ... Maggie, you two look absolutely stunning this evening." Emily smiled gently at him, reached up and made a slight adjustment to his tie, and said, "Henry, I'll give you exactly one hour to stop talking like that. And you, good sir, should wear a tux all the time." Maggie watched her friend and smiled at the two of them. Emily was so good at this sort of thing. But schmoozing bigwigs just wasn't Maggie's forte. Emily asked, "So, Henry, where is it exactly that you would like us to sit?"

He pointed to the speaker's dais, which was a three- or four-foot high platform that stretched nearly from one side of the dining room to the other. In the center was a speaker's lectern adorned with the seal of the state of Michigan and flanked on either side by what Emily estimated to be ten to fifteen place settings. Maggie was the one who noticed that the place setting to the left of the lectern did not have a chair behind it. Henry said, "You folks are at that table directly in front of the lectern." Maggie was prepared to be somewhere toward the front, but she felt a jolt of adrenaline ripple through her as she realized that she would be directly in front of David. He couldn't help but see her ... and she could see him.

Mischievously, Emily said, "Henry, don't tell me that everyone sitting at that head table is going to have something to say tonight."

He chuckled. "No, just the governor and Clipper. PJ is convincing David that he should say something. He's hurting, still. Not everyone can see it, but I can. I saw it in a lot of guys that came back from Vietnam. Hell, I was like that and all I got was a bullet through the shoulder. Still, we have a lot of people here tonight who helped us pull this thing off. I hope David will agree to say just a few words of thanks to them. It'll be good for them to hear from him, and, even though he may not know it yet, it will be good for him, too."

Emily laid her hand on Henry's arm and asked, "Have you told him that? Does he know you are a combat vet?"

"No and no. I was just on my way over there to speak to him."

"Then go, Henry," Emily said, "and don't be bashful about your experience. It might help him."

Henry nodded and turned to head in the direction of a knot of people on the other side of the room, but Emily reached out and grabbed his arm. "You know you have my deepest respect for what you've done. I didn't think it was possible to raise the kind of money you did ... "

Henry held up a hand to interrupt her, "*We*, Emily ... I didn't do this by myself. You were a big part of what *we* were able to do for David ... credit where credit's due."

As Maggie's eyes followed Henry to the other side of the room, she saw David. He was facing her, but was surrounded by five or six people, all of whom seemed to want to shake his hand. PJ was behind him with his hands on the wheelchair's handles. Natalie stood next to PJ. Quickly she turned back to Emily. "I'm going to find our table and put my purse down."

"Sure." As they headed for their table, Chuck caught up to them with their drinks and for the next forty-five minutes they schmoozed with other guests seeking their reserved seats, talking about the weather, the upcoming summer season, and, occasionally, commenting about how glad they were David Keller was alive and back home in Onekama. Promptly at seven o'clock, Henry asked everyone to find their seats and remain standing for the invocation.

★ ★ ★ ★

PJ wheeled David to his spot next to the lectern and then he and Natalie stood behind seats next to him. As everyone in the room bowed their heads in prayer, David locked eyes with Maggie for the first time in sixteen years. He recalled his dream and smiled at her. She bowed her head, more thankful than ever for that particular religious custom that provided a good excuse for her to look away.

The food was typical banquet fare and the governor's remarks were thankfully brief, but Clipper's were not, and David, perhaps more than anyone else in the room, was embarrassed by them. But Clipper, who'd been out of the spotlight for so long, decided this would be a good chance to bask in its glow. When he was finished, Henry thanked him and then said, "Now, ladies and gentlemen, it is my privilege to introduce the man we are all here to honor, Major David Keller." And he handed David the mic.

Maggie, as she had since they'd first locked eyes at the beginning of the invocation, avoided eye contact with him. Emily noticed it, and she also noticed that David couldn't seem to take his eyes off of Maggie. In fact, several times during his brief remarks, Emily thought David acted as if he might be speaking directly to Maggie. The evening ended at nine o'clock. David, immediately after the benediction, told PJ he wanted to speak to Maggie Lassiter. PJ nodded, but too many people intervened between the two of them.

Maggie looked at Emily and said, with tears in her eyes, "Why don't I just meet you and Chuck at the car."

Emily wasn't the least bit surprised, but Chuck was. He asked Emily if Maggie was OK. Emily shrugged her shoulders, looked up at him and said, "No, she's not, but this isn't the time or place to explain it to you." The couple made their way over to David and PJ, who were desperately and unsuccessfully trying to make their way toward the table where Maggie, Emily, and Chuck had been sitting. Someplace in the middle ground between them, they met. After pleasantries, David asked, "Where's Maggie?"

Emily offered, "She's waiting on us at the car."

"What ... "

Emily gave him her business card and interrupted, "David, give me a call before you talk to Maggie. She's hurting. I'll explain when you call. OK?"

David nodded and slipped the card into his shirt pocket. As Emily and Chuck moved toward the exit, the next in line moved up to welcome him home and thank him for his service, but all David could really focus on were Emily's words: *she's hurting.*

★ ★ ★ ★

As PJ started the Tahoe and backed out of his parking space, David asked, "So, Maggie Lassiter still lives in Onekama?"

Natalie offered, "It's Maggie McCall, or at least it was. I don't know if she took her maiden name back after the divorce or not."

"McCall?" David asked.

PJ explained, "She married Ray McCall about a year after you left Onekama. They just got a divorce here recently. Ray's not on a good path, I'm afraid. There were some domestic violence calls. Maggie just got fed up with it and divorced him. They've got one son, Jack."

David was quiet for the remainder of the short ride back to his new home.

★ ★ ★ ★

The phone rang three times before Charley answered. "Where are you?" asked Ray.

"I'm at the casino, Ray."

"Stay there. I'm on my way. Got someone else I want you to keep an eye out for."

"Sure, Ray. I'm here." After he disconnected, Charley started doubling his bets at the blackjack table in anticipation of another payday from his benefactor. He was down two hundred and fifty dollars by the time Ray finally found him and the two went to the bar for a talk.

"You know Emily Weber?"

Charley scratched his chin, "The realtor lady?"

"That's the one. So, you know who she is? You could recognize her?"

"Sure."

"Then I want you to let me know if she happens to be coming and going from my wife's shop."

Charley thought, *Hell, Ray. I can answer that one right now. She's in and out of there every day almost.* He'd admired the Escalade from the front door of the hardware store on several occasions, but he'd more admired the well-turned leg he'd watched step down from the huge car. But instead, he replied, "Uh, yeah, sure, Ray. Can I ask you a question?"

Ray didn't answer. Charley kept at it. "I ... I mean it's all over town ... "

"Dammit, Charley, what the fuck is it?"

"I ... I thought you and Maggie were divorced ... "

Ray wanted to hit him. "That's none of your damned business, you sonuvabitch. You gonna do what I need you to do, or you gonna stick your nose in where it doesn't belong?"

Charley knew thin ice when he heard it cracking. "OK ... OK ... take it easy, Ray. No offense intended. Forget I asked."

Ray stood up from the bar stool and moved very close. "Just you keep your mind on what I asked you to do, Charley. Nothing more, nothing less. Call me if you see her with Maggie."

"Uh, yeah, OK, Ray, sure thing." There was a pause and Ray started to move away, but Charley quickly added, "Hey, Ray, listen ... I'm a little down right now. Could you spot me an advance? I mean, now that I'm watchin' for two people ... well, it's a bigger job now, Ray."

"A hundred, Charley ... not a penny more until you produce some information, and, by God, if you tell anybody ... anybody at all ... that I'm payin' you to watch Maggie, I'll fuckin' kill you. Understand?"

"Sure, Ray, I got it. No one else knows. Thanks."

16

PENT UP ANGER

The morning after the banquet, Emily's phone rang at seven thirty. She didn't recognize the number, so the call went to voicemail as she finished preparing her eight-year-old daughter's breakfast. While Cammie picked at her oatmeal, Emily listened to the message:

Emily, it's David Keller. Thought I'd give you a call before your day got started. Could we meet, maybe at the Yellow Dog for coffee. Give me a call back when you get this message.

The audacity of some people, she thought. *You think you can just come and go in and out of her life as you wish. You pompous ass.* Maggie had been a sobbing mess last night when Emily and Chuck dropped her off at her house after the banquet. Emily offered to spend the night, but Maggie had refused. She said she needed to pull her act together. Jack was home and she didn't want him to see her like this. It took Emily an hour to explain to Chuck why Maggie was so upset and in doing so, she left out, purposely, one important detail. Now, David's voicemail left her fuming mad. *You think you can just show up at the Yellow Dog after disappearing sixteen years ago and just pick up where you left off. Not going to happen if I can help it, you narcissistic sonuvabitch.* She was so angry she was tempted to return his call right then and give him a piece of her mind, but at the last instant, she checked her emotions. She knew she needed to cool down. She didn't have any appointments until mid-day, so she figured she'd give him a call back after her daughter headed off to school.

★ ★ ★ ★

Charley saw the white Escalade drive by the hardware store. He stepped outside on the sidewalk and walked to the end of the building. Across the parking lot he could see Emily pull in and park in David's driveway. He pulled out his phone and called Ray.

★ ★ ★ ★

Emily didn't bother to call David back. Instead she'd decided to have it out with him, face-to-face. In the several hours since she'd listened to the voicemail she'd gone through several phases. At first, as she played out in her mind what she'd say to him, she just let her anger boil over. Her thoughts were punctuated with curses so foul that she caught herself wondering where they had come from. Emily rarely swore out loud, much less to herself. She tried to pull it together. Her inner voice became calm, rational, and logical. Chronologically she would lay it out for him: all the pain and hurt he'd caused Maggie over the past sixteen years. But, now, as she stood in front of his door, she really had no idea what would come out of her mouth. She drew in a deep breath and pushed on the doorbell. She let only a few seconds pass before she rang again, impatience fueling her anger. David answered the door as she was about to ring again for the third time.

She couldn't help but be caught short for a moment as she looked at him sitting in the wheelchair, both pants legs neatly folded under him, a smile broadly smeared over his handsome face. She was sympathetic to the tragedy that had befallen him, but her loyalty to her best friend quickly overtook her sympathy. Anger tinging her tone, she said, "David, we need to talk."

He rolled the wheelchair back and Emily stepped in and closed the door behind her. "Emily, I want to ... "

She wasn't here to listen to what he wanted. She was here to tell him how things were, how things were going to be. "David, let's get something straight. Nearly everyone in this town is glad that you are alive and back home—everybody, that is, but one. Maggie's glad you're alive, but she is less than thrilled to see you again."

"I know ... "

"No, you don't know." Her voice was up at least an octave and her volume was increasing. "Let me finish, David. You broke her heart sixteen years ago. Neither she nor I can understand why you did that. Oh, yeah, sure, we get the service-above-self-thing. But you just abandoned her. She wrote you almost every day for the first month you were gone, David. Did you get those letters?" She paused. She wanted to hear his answer.

He nodded, "Yes."

His answer was like gas thrown at an open flame. "So, I suppose there's a good reason you couldn't answer even one of them." She was nearly screaming at him as she remembered the anguish he'd caused Maggie. "If you could have seen her back then, David, in those first days and months after you excommunicated yourself from everyone back here ... " she balled her hands into fists. "She loved you, David. No matter how noble your intentions were when you left Onekama for West Point, no matter how heroic your acts have been since leaving us, it wasn't right for you to do that to her. And now you're back. And she's hurting."

Emily's anger and her words weren't unexpected. But her passion rather stunned him. He sat there for a moment before saying, "I dreamed about her."

"Actions, David, speak louder than dreams. She never

heard from you. We ... none of us here in town ... ever heard from you after you left."

"No ... no ... " he was searching for the words, "I ... I know that I have no right ... that Maggie was right not to count on me ... "

"Count on you?" Emily screamed it back to him. She shook her head and wagged her finger at him like a teacher scolding an insolent student. "You just don't get it, do you, David. She did count on you. Remember who you were in those days around here. You were the football star, the great athlete, the superb student, the class president, the valedictorian. Everybody looked up to you, David ... most of all Maggie. She said you told her you loved her. Did you do that, David? Did you tell Maggie that you loved her?"

He couldn't look at her, but he nodded.

"She counted on that, David. And look where it got her. You left and never looked back while Maggie started her senior year of high school pregnant and without any word from you."

Her words shot through him like lightning. *Pregnant* ... his head swung in her direction and their eyes locked on each other. He could feel hers burning an angry hole in him. "What?" His words couldn't come out fast enough. "But ... But ... I don't understand ... the letters ... she didn't tell me ... "

It had just come out of her. After all of these years of keeping a secret held strictly between her and Maggie, it had just spilled out as easily as water spills over the top of a pail that has run over. Emily wasn't sure where the breach of confidence had come from. It certainly wasn't in any of the scenarios of this moment that she'd played out in her mind before ringing his doorbell. But it was out there now and the cat wasn't going to return to the bag. She suddenly felt a strange sense of relief. She spat the words at him, "I told her she should tell you, but she wouldn't do that.

She said she didn't want your pity or sympathy. She didn't want you back just because you'd knocked her up."

"But PJ told me ... I ... I thought Ray McCall..."

"Oh, she married Ray all right. She practically threw herself at him after you left and cut her loose. My God, I felt so sorry for her. She was heartbroken, pregnant, scared, and alone, except for me. I tried to discourage her with Ray. I tried to be there for her, but she was living alone in her parents' big lake house. They weren't around. They were all wrapped up in their divorce. Maggie grabbed hold of the first thing that she could that would offer her some stability and unfortunately that was Ray."

"But isn't Ray the father ... "

"Not even, David. You don't get off that easy. Everybody thinks he is ... Ray ... Clipper ... PJ ... the whole town, but he's not. Maggie had a hunch when she found out she was pregnant about six weeks after you left. Oh, yeah, sure, she'd slept with Ray before she found out. It was her way of venting her anger for you. But she had some DNA tests done after Jack was born. Ray isn't the father. Maggie told me it was you."

"But how can she be sure ... "

"You bastard!" She shouted it at him. The windows were open. The neighbors would hear them. Emily didn't care. "You think that little of her. Well, if you want to know for sure, let's get some DNA testing done. Or, you can just believe Maggie, like I do, when she tells me that the only one besides Ray that she has ever been with in her entire life is you, David."

"I ... I ... "

Emily didn't want to give him the chance to talk. Not yet. She still had things she needed to get out. "Yeah, I know, you don't know what to say. That's why we needed to have this little talk. So help me God, David, if you hurt Maggie again like you did sixteen years ago, I will ... " her threat trailed off, uncompleted. "She's coming around to a good place. She divorced Ray. Jack's a really good boy. He's finishing up his junior year of high school, talking about college, and he loves his mother. I don't intend to allow your second coming to change any of that. So, let's set some ground rules, shall we? First, I'll be the one to tell Maggie that I told you about Jack. I owe her that much as her best friend. Second, you keep it light with her. Let her bring up Jack and all those bad memories of when you left. Third, you don't tell anybody about you being Jack's father, not even PJ or Natalie. There are three people who know: Maggie, me, and now you. The only person in Onekama who has the right to expand that group is Maggie. You got that?"

David nodded.

"Fourth, you should apologize to her for just leaving like that. I don't know if she'll accept it or not, but you owe it to her to at least try. And, finally, you've got to promise to do whatever she says. If she says she doesn't want to see you or talk to you, then you stay the hell away from her."

"But I have to see her. I have to tell her ... "

"Tell her what, David?"

"About a dream I had."

"What dream is that, David? She's spent years getting you out of her dreams. Now that you're back, do you think you are entitled to tell her about your dreams? Does that seem at all right to you?"

He had to admit it didn't, but he said, "I just want to tell her about when ... "

Emily's anger was unrelenting. Impatience crept into her tone. Holding up a hand, she again interrupted him, "When what, David?"

"Right after the IED hit the vehicle ... " he paused, searching for the words to explain something that he hated to think about, much less talk about, but he couldn't bring up the dream without mentioning the attack that took his legs and nearly his life. "I was unconscious, badly hurt. I heard the medic tell the medevac pilots he'd looked but couldn't find my missing leg ... " This was hard for him. He hadn't talked this much about that day, not even with his shrinks. "He said I was losing a lot of blood and they needed to get me to the docs ASAP. I felt him and the crew chief lift me onto the stretcher and put me in the chopper. It wasn't long before I went blank. But I remember the dream. I dreamed I was falling through this haze and then I was lying in the snow, in that field along M-22 just outside of town. Do you know the one I'm talking about, Em?"

He'd just called her Em, like he'd done back in the day when she, Maggie, and he had hung out almost all the time together. "Yes, I know the one." She didn't, but that wasn't important at this point.

"And as I'm lying there, I hear someone next to me in the snow. It was Maggie. She wanted to make snow angels ... "

Emily was on her way to a showing, a three-million-dollar home on the beach near Pierport. She didn't want her mascara to run, but as the tears started to flow, she knew she was going to need to stop back home and fix her makeup.

★ ★ ★ ★

At approximately two o'clock, after receiving the call from Charley, Ray pulled his truck into the Meijer parking lot at the intersection of US 31 and M-55. He parked and went inside. There was a wide choice, but he thought the two-gallon size would do the job. He went through self-checkout, paying with cash. Once back at his truck he placed the gas can on the seat next to him and headed for the gas station to fill it up.

17

INTENSE

The noon showing of the three-million-dollar lake house in Pierport had not gone well. Emily was fifteen minutes late, something that had never happened before. The Chicago couple to whom she was showing the house, both MDs, weren't happy about her tardiness, and, while they liked the house, the wife did not like that access to it was by way of a two-mile gravel road that was "dusty and horribly rough." Emily knew that the sale would never happen when the lady doc said, "You'd think for three million you'd get a paved road, wouldn't you?" Emily was of a mood to reply, "This isn't Chicago, bitch," but she let the client's comment pass. On her way back to Onekama, she called Maggie. "Hey Mags, whatcha' doin' tonight?"

In fact, Maggie had nothing to do. Jack had just stopped by the Yellow Dog and told her he and his girlfriend were going into Manistee that evening to go to a movie at The Vogue and get a bite to eat afterwards. "Well, your call is right on time. Turns out Jack's out tonight, so I got nothin' goin' on. What did you have in mind?"

"Listen, Mags, I'd love to do dinner, but fact is Chuck and Cammie are counting on me for dinner tonight. How 'bout, though, I come over for coffee after I get them fed?"

Maggie knew from the get-go that something was bothering Emily. These two women knew each other so very well. But she also knew that whatever it was, Emily would tell her about it in her own time. "Sounds good, but sure you wouldn't like to make that wine instead of coffee?"

"Deal ... see you about seven."

"Red or white?" Maggie asked.

"Ummm, I'll have the red," was Emily's rather distracted reply.

★ ★ ★ ★

With wine glasses full, the two settled around the kitchen table. It was one of two places where nearly all of their serious conversations took place. The other was Emily's kitchen table. They began with some small talk about the two doctors Emily had met earlier in the day. Her rendition of the story left Maggie laughing to the point of tears. "You didn't call her a 'bitch,' Em, did you?"

Emily stared into her glass for a moment and then looked up. "No ... but it was a lost opportunity. I sure wanted to." They both loved the small talk, the gossip, but knew it was over when Emily announced, "Mags, I saw David today."

Maggie replied, "You did," and, with caution evident in her voice, asked, "How is he?"

Emily didn't answer the question. It would become evident as she laid it all out for her friend. "Last night, as the banquet was concluding, Chuck and I took a moment to welcome him home. You had already gone to the car. He asked about you. I gave him my card and told him to call me. He did that this morning."

Maggie took a sip of wine, but said nothing.

"I went to see him." She took a moment to steel herself for the tough part of this conversation.

"And?"

"We talked about you, and ... " This was probably the toughest thing she'd ever had to do. "And I was angry at him for thinking he could just come here and walk back into your life."

"Well ... that's OK, Em. You're my best friend. You're just watching out for me."

"And I told him the truth about Jack."

It was as if somehow the air had been sucked from her lungs. She tried to breathe but breath wouldn't come. Faintly, she managed to eke out, "No ... Emily ... no ... you didn't ... how could you? You were the only other person who knew ... " Maggie's anger was instant at what she considered to be this betrayal by her best friend, the last person in the world she would have ever expected to betray her. She sat there, stunned into silence, staring at Emily.

Emily read her friend's anger like a book, but pressed forward. "He wants to see you ... "

Maggie, confusion, anger, and near-panic washing over her, raised her voice. "Oh, hell, yes, he wants to see me now that you've told him. But what about me, Emily? Did you ever think of me when you were shooting your mouth off?" She was in full fury now. "Well, I don't want to see him, ever, and I'm not sure I want to see you for a while." Her words stung. Making it worse, Maggie walked out of the kitchen, leaving Emily just sitting there.

OK, she's angry, she's upset, give her some time. Emily had anticipated Maggie's anger and made up her mind she was not going to leave; she was not going to abandon her friend. She poured herself another glass of wine and waited.

It seemed like an eternity before Maggie returned to the kitchen. "Why are you still here?" Her eyes were red and her cheeks stained with tears.

"I've been here for you since we were kids. I'm here for you now."

"Go home, Emily. I don't want to talk about this anymore."

"No, and we need to talk about this."

Maggie fussed with some dishes in the sink, her back to Emily. Emily never moved from her chair and never took her eyes off of Maggie. After the dishes were done, Maggie left the kitchen, came back, and left again. Another thirty minutes passed. Emily tried to remember a time when Maggie had ever been this angry with her and couldn't. Twilight faded to dark by the time she'd returned to the kitchen and turned on the light over the kitchen table, slumped back into the chair behind her glass of wine which was mostly still there, and asked angrily, "What does he want?"

"Are you ready to talk about this?"

"Dammit, Emily, I don't know. I never thought that you would be the one that ... "

Emily interrupted, "Mags, I'm sorry. I really didn't mean to tell him. I was angry. You know me. When I get angry, I get impatient. Impatience makes me careless and it just slipped out."

Maggie didn't question her friend's sincerity, but her judgment was another matter. Still angry, she didn't acknowledge the apology, but, instead, repeated, "What does he want, Em?"

At least she's not calling me 'Emily' any more. "I don't know exactly. But he told me a story." By the time Emily had finished telling Maggie about David's dream in the wake of the explosion, both women sat at the table clutching one another's hands and crying. Emily concluded, "I know he left you, but, Mags, honest, I don't think he's ever forgotten you." The two talked some more. Maggie's anger abated. What was done was done. David knew. But Jack didn't. And, if Maggie had anything to say about it, he never would. "You don't think he will say anything to Jack, do you?"

"No, I don't. I warned him to keep his mouth shut. But I don't think I really needed to do that. He's not that kind of a guy." Together the two of them batted around a couple of scenarios involving Jack discovering the truth. Neither one of them boded well for Jack or Maggie, but all of it was pure conjecture. At ten thirty, Emily embraced her old friend and whispered one more time, "I'm sorry, Mags."

Maggie replied, "I know, Em. I'll figure it out. Thanks for letting me know that he knows. I wouldn't have wanted to find that out from him."

Emily opened the front door and stepped out into a mild evening, but one marked by a strong wind blowing in off Lake Michigan. She had no sooner gotten out of the driveway than her phone rang. It was Chuck. She thought he was probably just calling to make sure she was OK.

"Emily, the house is on fire. I've called 911, but it's bad ... "

"Cammie," she screamed, "where is she?"

"She's here with me. We're safe. But the house ... it's ... "

She pressed down on the Escalade's accelerator and the big V-8 engine revved up as the car started to hurtle faster and faster down the three miles of road that separated Maggie's house from hers. She could hear sirens. She screamed, "It doesn't matter about the house. Just as long as you and Cammie are OK."

Over the phone she heard, "Mommy, Mommy, we can't find Tabby."

"It's ... it's OK, honey. We'll find Tabby," she said to her eight-year-old, but even as she said it, she doubted they would. "Put Daddy back on the phone."

There was a pause, and then, "Where are you, Emily?"

"Close. I'll be right there. Oh, God, I'm so glad both of you are safe. I don't know what I'd do ... "

She screeched to a halt on the gravel road behind their lakeshore home, making sure that she didn't block the driveway access for the fire trucks. Chuck and Cammie met her. Chuck had a look of terror in his eyes and Cammie was sobbing uncontrollably and kept repeating, "Tabby ... Tabby ... Tabby." The fire department arrived and within a couple of minutes had a steady stream of water fighting the flames, but the strong wind off of the lake made it a losing battle.

★ ★ ★ ★

Maggie's first customer the next morning was the chief of the volunteer fire department. His hair was matted and mangled, his face, arms, and hands were besmirched with black residue, and he reeked of smoke. "Coffee, please, Maggie."

"Long night, Chief?" she asked as she handed him a paper cup.

"Webers' house. Been up there all night ... "

"What? Emily, Chuck, Cammie ... are they OK?"

"Rattled, of course, but OK. Pretty mysterious, though. That's almost a new house. Just goes up in flames. All that wind last night didn't help matters none."

Maggie called Emily, but the call went straight to voice-mail. She left a frantic message and remained beside herself with worry. Somewhere around noon, her phone rang. It was Emily. Frantic, she answered, "Emily, where are you? I'll be right there. Is everyone OK? I've been beside ... "

"Mags ... Mags ... calm down." Emily was prepared for her friend's near panic. Onekama with its small-town grape-vine, she knew, would have already alerted Maggie to last evening's fire. "We're all OK. We're in Grand Rapids with Chuck's folks. They are going to keep an eye on Cammie while Chuck and I wade into it with the insurance companies."

Relief obvious in her voice, Maggie said, "Oh, thank God. I've been so worried. I left a couple of panicked voicemails. Sorry, but I just didn't know ... "

"It's OK, Mags."

"How could something like this have happened?"

"Chuck and I are baffled. I'm going to tell you something, but I don't want anyone else to know, at least, not yet. Chief Riggins told us he told the sheriff that he could smell gas ... "

"Gas ... you mean like natural gas?"

"No, *gasoline*. He said he was walking along the edge of the porch along the lake side and caught a whiff of it. He asked if we had any gas stored back there. We told him, no. So, he's told the sheriff that he'd like an investigation to look into the cause. The sheriff has asked the state police to send out a forensics team. Chief Riggins told me he wants to rule out the possibility of arson."

"Em, who would do such a thing to you and Chuck? This is Onekama for crying out loud, not Detroit. Who would burn your house down?"

"I don't know. It's a mystery to us, but it's also kind of scary. Know what I mean?"

"I absolutely know what you mean. What can I do?"

"Well, I do have one favor."

"What's that? Anything."

"Chuck and I are going to stay down here in GR for a few days. Cammie's pretty rattled. We think her kitty, Tabby, perished in the fire, but she keeps asking if we can go out there and look for her. She's not going to settle down until I either let her go out to the rubble, which neither Chuck nor I think is a good idea, or ... "

"Em, I'll go out first thing after I close up this afternoon and take a look. I'm so sorry. I know how much she loved that cat."

"Thanks, Mags. It's still a crime scene until the state police say differently, but as long as you stay behind the yellow tape barrier, I'd sure appreciate it if you'd take a look and let us know."

"I'll talk to you this evening." There was a pause, but Maggie sensed Emily was still on the line. "Em ... "

"Have you seen David yet?"

The question surprised Maggie. With all of this going on, she didn't need to be worrying about that. "No, but that's no big deal. Don't you worry about the David thing. Get things wrapped up down there and come back home. You, Chuck, and Cammie can stay with Jack and me."

Laughing, she said, "You and Jack don't have room for all of us."

"We'll make room. You and Chuck can have Jack's room and Cammie can sleep on the sofa. Maybe we can take the pillows off and lay them on the floor. I've got an old comforter we can use to make her a little tent. She'll like that. We can tell her she's camping out in the living room. I'll put a cot up in the basement for Jack. We'll make it work."

They had always been there for one another. To the casual observer, it might appear that Emily had been there more for Maggie than the other way around. Maggie herself had had this thought many times over the years. This was an opportunity to help make up the difference, and Emily loved her for it. "OK, Mags, we'll see. Let's talk this evening. OK?"

"You got it, Em. Take care of yourselves."

★ ★ ★ ★

Maggie sat in her old pickup truck and looked at her phone, hoping to see a sufficient number of bars to place a call. The fuzzy little kitten sat on her lap. She stank of smoke and dampness, but other than that was none the worse for wear. She punched Emily's number in on speed dial and didn't even wait for her to say hello.

"I found her. I found Tabby."

"Oh, my God. You've got to be kidding me."

"Nope. I got there and started calling her name. Pretty soon, here she comes out of the dune grass on the lake side of the house. She's sitting right here on my lap in the pickup. She's wet and she stinks, but I'll get her all cleaned up. She'll be at my house just waiting on Cammie to come get her."

"Wait, Mags. Let me put her on the phone. You tell her the good news."

There was a pause, and then Maggie heard a meek, "Hello, Aunt Maggie."

"Cammie, I found Tabby. I have her right here with me. She's safe."

Squeals of delight. "Aunt Maggie, you found her. I can't believe it. Mommy and Daddy thought ... "

"I know, darlin', but she's alive and well. I have her with me. She'll be at my house and waiting for you when you get back to Onekama." More squeals. Maggie delighted in them. She had been stunned when she pulled up to the yellow tape. The house was a charred mess. No part of it that she could see could ever be reclaimed. Emily and Chuck would have to start all over. The possibility that someone had purposely done this to them lingered in her thoughts. Yet somehow the rescue of Cammie's kitten made everything seem less tragic. "Is your mom still there? Could you put her on?"

Emily asked, "Maggie, will Jasmine be OK with a kitten in the house?"

"Hey, Em, you let me worry about that part of it. You, Chuck, and Cammie, come on home as soon as you can. Everything here is under control."

"Mags, I don't know how to thank ... "

"No need, Em. No need. Just happy to have found this little thing safe and sound. See you soon. OK?"

"You bet."

18

THE NOTE

David pulled the wheelchair up to the kitchen table and sat there for a long time staring at the pencil and paper in front of him. Over and over again, he had carefully planned out how he was going to end his life during long sleepless nights in the hospital. He was simply going to lay down in bed, put the gun to his temple, and pull the trigger. *How much can it hurt? How long can the pain last? Can't be any more painful that what I've been through. When it's done, all the pain will go away.*

Originally, he'd thought the exact location of the plan was less important than the how of it. Then, PJ had visited him at Walter Reed. He recalled what his brother had said to him, *There are days when Dad doesn't even know who I am.* David had thought after that, *So, why would you ever expect him to remember you?* Nonetheless, it was difficult for him to imagine his father like that. Their growing-up years had been, for the most part, carefree. The worst thing that had happened to either him or PJ was their mother's passing. He was fourteen and PJ was only about ten. His considered opinion on this had always been that her death had been tougher on PJ than on him. Tom definitely changed after her death, and as David had reflected on this over the last few months, he'd actually decided that Tom became a better father. Both boys saw more of him than they had before their mother's death, and he realized that this must have been hard for his dad to pull off. He was a handyman who served the needs of wealthy homeowners who lived elsewhere most of the time. He did everything from small carpentry, electrical and plumbing repairs, to lawn mowing, snow removal, leaf pickup in the fall, tree and shrub pruning in the spring, boat and dock installation in the spring and removal in the fall—all of the important but mundane chores that these busy absentee homeowners had neither the time nor patience for, but had the money to pay Tom. Tom had been in great demand. Not only was he trustworthy and reliable, he was good and thorough. It was not uncommon for him to get a call on a Thursday that a homeowner was coming up on Friday and wanted this or that done before they got there. His dad, in almost every case, got it done for them. Yet, through it all, he found the time to cook their meals, help with homework, attend parent/teacher conferences, and watch them play sports. It would have been easy for him to have assumed that each son, as they became old enough, could help him. Yet, Tom never asked them, even once, to help him out. And in return, his boys took advantage of the time he gave them by being model students, getting scholarships, graduating from college, and becoming solid citizens. Both boys owed their dad a deep debt and, after PJ's visit to Walter Reed, David knew he'd need to patch things up with his dad before he could complete his plan. And, then, when PJ told him what the community was planning in the way of a homecoming, the question of "where" seemed to have answered itself.

Then yesterday had happened; Emily's visit and all that that had revealed to him. *Pregnant. I'm the father. I abandoned her.* His conscience was, again, getting in the way of his plan. He shook his head, hesitated for a moment, and then picked up the pen:

Dear Maggie,
This is to tell you how very sorry I am for the pain I
have caused you. I left and never came back and for

that I am eternally sorry. But things between me and Dad had hit a low point. He couldn't understand, and I wasn't willing to try and meet him ... even halfway. Instead I chose to focus only on the army. After speaking with Emily, I realize only now how that decision hurt you. I have some savings. I want all of it to go to you and Jack. My attorney will contact you. You didn't know it, but I never really ever forgot you.
Fondly,
David

He glanced at his watch; it was noon. They would be here soon: PJ, Natalie, the boys, and his dad, whom he'd not really seen very much of since arriving home. Since neither PJ nor Natalie could ever predict how Tom might react in any given situation, and, wanting to save him any embarrassing moments, they had shielded him from the crowds that had surrounded David's homecoming. This would be their first chance to be together as just family at a picnic in the park across the street from David's house. Everyone had their fingers crossed, hoping it would go well. Almost anything would be an improvement over the fight that David and his father had gotten into that last night before David left for West Point all those years ago. He folded his note to Maggie in half with the writing on the inside, scrawled her name across one side of the half-page, and laid it in his lap. He rolled himself over to a kitchen drawer. As he placed it inside, another pang of conscience inserted itself into his psyche, *Yeah, that's what Maggie will say she expected of you. Leave a note, but never face things head-on. Some hero you are!* For the briefest of moments, he considered tearing up the note, but instead he closed the drawer, deciding his mind was made up. Not even the news of Jack would change it.

★ ★ ★ ★

Natalie and PJ arrived at the park and found a table under an oak tree. It was a cool, early June day, but the sun was high in a perfectly blue, unblemished sky, and the huge tree provided respite from its powerful rays. The boys, Sam and Max, ran off with sand buckets and plastic shovels in hand to the beach area on the park's northwestern edge with the warning to stay out of the water until either they or Grandpa got down there to watch them. Tom volunteered to head that way and keep an eye on them, but PJ, after exchanging glances with Natalie said, "No, Dad. Stay here; there's somebody coming that wants to see you."

The old man smiled at his youngest son and said, "Who's that?"

It was time to find out where Tom's mind was, so PJ quickly offered, "David's coming. I'm going to get him. He lives right over there now." He pointed to David's cottage.

If Tom understood what he was hearing, there was no visible sign. The old man looked at PJ, nodded, sat down on the picnic bench, and stared off absently after the boys. Natalie looked at PJ and shrugged. PJ trudged off in the direction of the cottage.

"How is he?" David asked, unable to hide an anxious tinge to his voice.

"Well, I told him you were coming to lunch with us ... "

"And?"

"I dunno, David. His reaction ... or lack of it ... the only way we are going to know how he is is to bring you over there and we'll see."

"Do you think he still hates me?"

The question stunned PJ. Their father wasn't the hateful type—opinionated yes, but never hateful. "David, look, Dad never hated you ... "

"Oh, yeah, that's right. You weren't around that last night before I left for the academy. You didn't hear the things he said about me, about my decision. He hated me, PJ. Plain and simple ... he hated me."

PJ couldn't argue with his brother. He hadn't been there that night and what his brother had just told him was a bit of a revelation. Their father had never talked to PJ about that evening. In fact, in the last fourteen or fifteen years or so, PJ could probably count on the fingers of one hand the number of times his father had mentioned David. That, in turn, triggered PJ never to bring him up. David was, for all of these many years, the elephant in the room. "OK. You're right. I wasn't there. I don't know. But I think I know something about people who hate ... it kind of goes with my line of work. My observation is that if someone hates someone else, they generally talk about or in some way act out that hate. So, David, you have to believe me when I tell you that Dad has hardly mentioned you since you left. For me, that smacks of disappointment more than hatred."

Those words hurt David, and their irony was not lost on him. Suddenly he realized it hurt him more to think that his dad was disappointed in him than it had to think he hated him. He'd worked his butt off at West Point. Every day of his service in the army had been honorable. He knew his father understood what honorable service was. Despite his adamant rejection of the Vietnam War after returning home from it, every day of his father's service had been honorable as well. So, how could he possibly be disappointed in him? It didn't make sense. No, it was just easier to think his father hated him. David stared into his brother's eyes and said, "He hated me that night."

PJ just shook his head. "You've got to give him a chance. Come on. Let's go see how he is."

David drew in a deep breath. PJ said, "I'll drive," and stepped behind his brother's wheelchair. David looked up at him over his shoulder and said resignedly, "OK. What's the worst that can happen?"

PJ didn't want to think about the answer to that question.

David held up one hand and pointed to the park across the street. "On to the picnic, PJ."

If old Tom saw them coming across the hundred yards or so that separated their picnic table from David's cottage, he didn't show it.

As PJ pushed the wheelchair next to the picnic table, David, fully expecting his father to look a lot older than he did, was surprised at how little he seemed to have changed. He smiled and said, "Hi, Dad." What surprised him more, however, was the old man's reaction to his greeting after these many years.

Tom extended his weathered right hand to his eldest son without a word. Standing next to one another at the other end of the table and seeing this, Natalie turned to PJ and nuzzled her head against his shoulder. David accepted his father's proffered hand, and then, David placed his other hand over theirs. Getting around the lump in his throat, David said softly, "Good to see you." PJ could feel Natalie lightly sobbing.

But things changed dramatically after this. Tom sat back down on the bench, looked toward the lake, and said, "Let's go down to the beach so the boys can swim. You know, Natalie, they won't go in until one of us gets down there and I can tell they are just dying to get in that water." Then he started to move off in that direction.

"He doesn't know who I am."

While Natalie headed toward the beach, wiping the last of her tears, to join Tom and the boys, who'd already dashed into the still-cold waters of Portage Lake, PJ and David strategized. They decided it best to begin talking about the elephant. During lunch, the two talked about David's choice of West Point over the Air Force Academy. Tom, if he was listening, did not participate in the discussion. When they started to reminisce over PJ's visits to Walter Reed and to the VA Hospital in Ann Arbor, again, Tom seemed to turn a deaf ear. He focused solely on his grandsons and Natalie. David had the distinct impression that he was somehow interfering in a family get-together. Tom feigned tiredness when asked if he'd like to take a tour of David's cottage and showed little interest in the plans that were made for David to come over to PJ and Natalie's for dinner on Saturday. When PJ stepped behind the wheelchair to wheel David home, David held out his hand and said, "Nice to be home, Dad." Again, they shook hands, but Tom merely nodded in reply. At the foot of the cottage's driveway, David looked over his shoulder at his brother, "Yeah, he hates me."

PJ without breaking stride merely replied, "Too soon to tell, David. What did he say to you that makes you think he hates you?"

Expressing his frustration, David said, "Jesus, PJ, you were there. He didn't say anything at all to me."

At the door, PJ stopped pushing him, stepped in front of the wheelchair, and said, "Exactly. He didn't say anything at all. So how do you know he hates you?" Smiling, he concluded, "So, like I said, 'It's too soon to tell.' See you Saturday about five o'clock." PJ pointed in the direction of the driveway behind them and asked, "Are you learning how to drive that van?"

"Lesson yesterday. One hour ... one and done. It's pretty easy."

"So, you'll drive yourself on Saturday, or do you want me to come and get you?"

The brothers shook hands as David said, "I'll drive myself." Smiling, he added, "See you then. Maybe he'll be different."

PJ, much more accustomed to his father's vagaries of memory, actions, and sometimes unexpected words, shrugged. "Maybe ... but, regardless, he doesn't hate you, David. You've got to give it time."

★ ★ ★ ★

That evening the sunset over Lake Michigan and Portage Lake was a spectacular light show of every shade of red, orange, and yellow. David sat in his living room watching it slowly sink into the horizon, and then decided he'd roll himself down toward the lakeshore at the end of the road in front of his house, toward the public boat launch.

★ ★ ★ ★

Charley Sharp sat on the second-floor landing at the top of the rickety steps leading up to his apartment above the hardware store, but nature's magnificence was lost on him. He was out there to have a quick smoke. Through the haze he'd just belched out in front of him, he watched David emerge from the foot of his driveway and make his way down to the public boat launch. An ugly sneer crossed his face and he thought, *sure sucks to be you, soldier boy. Ray's gunnin' for you.*

★ ★ ★ ★

The days were distinctly longer now and the hues lingered on long after the sun had made its way below the horizon. As he sat there, perched just a few feet above the water on the walkway that jutted out along the boat launch, it grew dark as PJ's words lingered in his ear: *You've got to give it time.* He realized, like it or not, that he had time. His plan was to pull the trigger on his life before the snow flew, usually sometime around the middle of October. This was the middle of June. He had four months to patch things up with his dad, and then the thought came to him, *maybe I should try and patch things up with Maggie, too.*

19

AN OLIVE BRANCH?

B y the middle of June, the village of Onekama had finally thrown off the idleness of winter. School was out, families were looking for quaint vacation spots where they could let their children roam the beach and jump off the pier, and where they could stroll downtown for a sweet treat, enjoy a free concert in the park, read a good book, watch the sunset, and sleep late as they escaped the much more hurried days of their lives "back home." With petunias in full bloom and lining the town's Main Street, Onekama was exactly that place, and so her population swelled in the summertime, the crowds flowing into town as if blown in by the breezes off of Lake Michigan.

As he sat on his front porch watching the pickup trucks with boats in tow roll past his cottage to unload their cargo at the public boat launch, David decided he would need to establish a daily routine. In the army, the very first element of that routine had been vigorous exercise. The seeming futility of that, given his ultimate intention, never crossed his mind. A habit engrained over the course of sixteen years wasn't easily broken, even though the ultimate plan would seem to render useless the effects of such a regimen. M-22, just a stone's throw from his cottage, had a bike lane through town and wide shoulders once he got out of town. He decided that he'd take his wheelchair out each morning for a good long roll ... starting tomorrow.

This morning, Maggie was on his mind. After mulling

over the ground rules Emily had laid out for him, he didn't believe that a simple purchase of a cup of coffee violated any of them, although he was pretty sure Emily would disagree. After brushing his teeth, combing his hair, and shaving as closely as a fresh blade would permit, he put on a neat dress shirt with a button-down collar and his best pair of dress slacks. He had no idea what to expect from Maggie even though Emily had warned him. After seeing her at the banquet, he only knew that he had to go see her; he had to try to talk to her. PJ's words reverberated in his head: *Give it time.* But then he had the thought ... *What's the point in waiting?*

Maggie's heart moved into her throat as she saw him roll past the front of the Yellow Dog. The front door, the main door that nearly everyone used, was not handicapped accessible. It required two steps up into the store and the rather narrow sidewalk separating the store front from the curb along M-22 simply wasn't wide enough for a ramp. There was a wooden sidewalk along the shop's side that led to another door which had to be opened manually. Quickly she tried to recall if anyone had ever come into her shop in a wheelchair, but the thought faded as she watched David struggle with the side door that opened outward, into him. As he tried to move through the open door, both wheels of his wheelchair hit the door's jamb. For a moment, it seemed to Maggie as if the Yellow Dog was trying to protect her from coming face-to-face with someone she was trying to avoid. She, heard a faint curse, the door closed gently on its hydraulic piston, and then she watched him roll to a stop in front of the storefront's large glass window. He looked in just as she looked out. Their eyes locked and he motioned for her to come out to him. *Dammit* ... she could feel her heart beating. She couldn't draw a breath. If she'd had to speak right now, she could not have done it, but, though it surprised her, she managed a gentle smile and a nod.

The place was busy, but all customers for the moment

seemed to have their needs cared for, so she smoothed her apron and caught a quick glimpse of herself in a mirror on a wall next to the front door. Nervously she pushed a lock of hair behind an ear and stepped down to the sidewalk.

★ ★ ★ ★

Almost directly across the street, not one hundred feet away from the Yellow Dog, Charley Sharp was already reaching for his phone.

★ ★ ★ ★

"Damn thing is too wide to fit through the door. Sorry, Maggie." Those last two words hung between them like sodden air. He meant them as an apology for her having to come to him, but Maggie seized on their larger ramifications.

Not sure if she could speak or not, she managed a strained, weak, "David, I'm so sorry for what happened to you. I ... I don't know ... "

He had heard these words hundreds ... no, thousands of times since the explosion that had ripped his legs off. Nurses, doctors, other soldiers, friends, thousands of people had said them to him, but somehow when Maggie said them ... her expression, her intonation ... their meaning penetrated to a deeper spot in his heart. He smiled at her, "It's OK, Maggie. It's OK."

She cleared her throat; the ice was breaking, her voice was clearing. "How 'bout I get you a cup of coffee?"

He nodded, the smile still spread across his face, "PJ tells me you make the best scones around."

"Well, that's nice of him. Yeah, I think they're pretty good. I've got chocolate chip and raspberry today. Want one of those, too?"

He thought for just a second. "Make it raspberry."

"You got it. What do you take in your coffee?"

"Just black, thanks."

She held up one finger. "Be right back."

As she scurried off, David called to her, "Maggie ... " She stopped and turned back to him. "It's sure good to see you."

The lump in her throat was back, bigger than ever, strangling her. She felt the first tear form. She didn't want him to see it, so, as she began to turn away, she managed to squeak out, "Good to see you, too, David." As the front door closed behind her, Maggie slipped into the powder room to pat her eyes dry before getting his order together.

The morning crowd was pretty much thinned out. Only one customer remained inside and she was engrossed in something on her laptop. With no good excuse to delay any longer inside, she wrapped a scone in tissue and drew a cup of black, dark roast out of the thermos. She interrupted her customer's concentration long enough to tell her that if she needed anything just to let her know. "I'll be right outside." She'd nodded distractedly as Maggie turned and headed out.

David had positioned his wheelchair next to one of several small round tables that Maggie used in the summer months in front of the store. A chair for her was positioned opposite of him. "Here you go, one raspberry scone and one black coffee."

"Thanks, Maggie," he said. He took a sip, swallowed it, and smiled at her. Motioning to the empty chair, he asked, "Can you sit down for a minute?"

Awkward might be the best word to describe the next few minutes. He complimented her on both the quality of the scone and the coffee. She politely thanked him. He wanted to know how long she'd had the Yellow Dog. Without a lot of elaboration, she gave him a brief history. Maggie asked him if he'd heard about Emily's misfortune, without mentioning the possibility that it could be arson. He had not heard the news, so she filled him in, including the part about her finding Cammie's kitten the day after the fire when everyone else was certain the little thing had died in the fire. Maggie was thrilled that she'd been able to do this for them and as she related some of the details of finding Tabby, some of the awkwardness between them fell away. When she was finished, David smiled at her and said, "Wow, glad everyone got out," and then he added, "you are a good friend, Maggie."

The awkwardness returned more suddenly than it had dissipated. Both knew they had other things to talk about. David picked at the last of his scone. Maggie grabbed his coffee cup and said, "Let me refill this." She scurried away like a frightened fawn.

He used the time to screw up his courage. She was gone only two or three minutes. When she returned, she sat down and he began, "Maggie, I want to apologize ... " He stopped in mid-sentence, as he watched her eyes become watery.

"David," she began, her voice wavering slightly, "Emily told me that she told you about Jack."

He wasn't surprised at Emily's efficiency. He knew the two of them were best of friends in high school and when Emily had visited him the other day, he knew that that friendship had endured over the last decade and a half. "So, I want to apologize for leaving you like that. It was wrong of me. I had no idea ... "

She was crying now. Full blown tears streamed down her cheeks. She wiped them with a napkin, but others replaced them. Yet, she held up her hand and interrupted him, "David, I don't want an apology."

He feared she was becoming angry at him. All he wanted to do was tell her ... what? *You walked away from her once a long time ago ... Why should she forgive that?*

Maggie swallowed hard and recomposed herself, quelling any anger that may have started to rise up in her, and continued, "I have a wonderful son. I named him Jack. He's smart, loving, and kind. He's sixteen now, a junior at Onekama High. He wants to go to college and study criminal science. I think he might want to become a police officer. I'd rather see him go to law school ... like PJ did," she added.

David sat there taking all of this in, filling in the first of many blanks created by his sixteen-year absence from Onekama. "Why didn't you tell me in one of the letters ... "

"You mean one of the letters that you never bothered to answer?"

She hadn't said that to berate him. She had just stated a fact, but it stung. "If I had known ... "

She had regained her composure, but couldn't help but be at least a little miffed at the same time. "If you had known, then what, David? Would you have come back for me? Would you have taken pity on 'poor Maggie Lassiter' and come back to save her from a life of single-parenthood?" She knew she was getting wound up, but she also knew she needed to get some things off her chest; some things that she'd been thinking about ever since she'd heard he was coming back home to Onekama. "I didn't want you coming back to me like that, David. I knew that it wasn't simply a desire to serve your country that made you leave Onekama. I don't know that I ever understood it sufficiently to think that you would turn your back on all of us so completely. But that's just what you did. No one, not even your family, ever heard from you. Now, here we are. You're back. Frankly, my life would be easier right now if you were someplace else, but this isn't about me. This is about you. People around here respect you." She lowered her head and said, "Even me. I respect you for the sacrifices you've made. You deserve everything this town has done for you. But I just have one favor to ask ... no, let's make that one demand to make of you ... and, if you think you owe me anything, let's make it that you will honor my demand."

The lump had moved from Maggie's throat to his. He couldn't speak, so he nodded.

"What Emily told you about Jack the other day has to remain a secret. Until a few days ago, there were only two people who knew. Now there are three. Please, let's limit it to that. OK?"

"What about Ray?"

The question panicked her, but she remained firm. "What about him? We're divorced. I think he's an asshole. Jack is indifferent towards the man he thinks is his father, but he loves Clipper, his grandfather. I have an arrangement with them both and I need to do everything I can to keep that in place. It's important to Jack's future. So, whatever you do, don't rock that boat."

He wasn't exactly sure what she meant by 'don't rock that boat,' but he felt like he had little room to object to anything she had asked of him to this point. Feebly, he said, "I'll keep the secret, Maggie, but..."

Sternly, she looked across the table at him. "Please, David, no 'buts.' You can tell no one." She stood up, smoothed her apron, and offered her hand. He took it gently into his. "I have to get back to work," she said.

"Do you mind if I come by again? I can't come in, but do you mind coming out here and taking my order ... maybe sitting a while and talking to me?"

She let his hand go and smiled at him. "I'd be disappointed if you didn't. The morning crowd thins out about ten thirty. See you tomorrow?"

"Count on it, Maggie."

20

MORE SHARP REPORTING

Ray McCall was playing poker in the High Stakes Room at Firekeepers Casino just outside of Battle Creek, Michigan, when he finally picked up Charley Sharp's message about Maggie and David meeting in front of the Yellow Dog. He didn't call him back, but ordered another double scotch, neat, drank it straight down, and wallowed in his own self-pity and anger. He was already half drunk and getting worse when he decided to switch from poker to blackjack. He sat down at a twenty-five-dollar table because there was an empty seat next to a woman in a short skirt and a tight blouse with a plunging neckline. He won, she lost. He asked her if she'd like to go dinner, his treat. After a rushed dinner at Nibi, the casino's finest restaurant, she took him to her room at the casino's hotel. More liquor, some pills of unknown composition, and his anger fueled a full night of rough sex. It was ten o'clock the following morning as he roamed about looking for his pickup truck that he only vaguely remembered parking somewhere on the sixth level of the attached parking garage when his phone rang again. Charley again. "Yeah, what is it?"

"Did you get my message yesterday?"

"Yeah, I got it. Suppose you want some money?"

"Well, yeah, Ray, that would be nice, but that's not the reason I'm callin' ya."

"What is it, Charley?"

"He's back."

"What the hell ... "

"Yep. I'm standin' here in the door of the hardware store watchin' 'em. Second mornin' in a row, Ray. Don't know whatcha wanna do 'bout it, but they're definitely gettin' together."

Standing now next to his pickup truck, Ray laid the phone on the bed cover, put both hands on the side of the truck, and hung his head between his arms. He knew exactly what he was going to do about it.

"Ray ... Ray ... you there?"

"Yeah, I'm still here," Ray hollered.

"There's somethin' else you might want to know."

"What's that?"

"David goes down to the lake at night. Just sits there on the ramp next to the boat launch. I've watched him do that now for the past two nights. Just thought you might like to know what some of his habits are. It might help you if you are thinkin' of ... well, you know ... doin' somethin' to scare him off like you did with that Chicago lawyer. That'd be a perfect opportunity. Ain't nobody else down there after it gets dark, 'cept him." There was a long pause. Then Charley said, "I was wonderin' if we could meet up at Shirley's tonight and maybe you could give me ... maybe you could pay me for this info I been collectin' for you."

Ray didn't want to talk to this little sonuvabitch anymore. All he ever wanted was money.

"Ray, you still there?"

"Dammit, I'm still here."

"Uh, yeah, well, sorry, Ray, but I'm runnin' ... "

"Yeah, yeah, I know ... you're running a little low."

Charley laughed nervously, then inquired again, "So, can you meet me at Shirley's tonight? Just a couple of hundred should do it, Ray. How 'bout at six?"

Ray's mind was elsewhere, but he said, "OK" just to get rid of Charley. Then he ended the call without another word. Sitting in his truck, Ray opened the glove box and took out the .38 caliber police special he kept there. He unlocked the cylinder, let it fall open, and checked to be sure it was fully loaded. Then he had a thought. He closed the cylinder, put the pistol back in the glove box, and smiled. He had a better way, a way that would make it all look like an accident.

21

LITTLE STEPS, BIG STEPS

There was a "Y" in the road as M-22 emerged northwest out of the village of Onekama. The left fork was flat and wound along the shore of Portage Lake until it ended at Portage Point, dumping travelers onto a magnificent expanse of Lake Michigan beach. The right fork was winding as well, but far from flat. A long grade wound through orchards, farm fields, pines, and hardwoods that lined the highway. David had enjoyed this first morning "roll" along M-22. The sky was cloudless, a stunning blue. There was a light breeze blowing off of Portage Lake and the sun, still low in the morning sky, was warm but not discomforting. At the fork, he'd paused. He knew what each fork held in store for him. The one along Portage Lake would be very consistent with the demands it would place on his upper body. The one up the hill would be extremely arduous on the way out, but he would likely have to brake his speed coming back down the grade into town. He had chosen the flatter option this morning, vowing that tomorrow morning he'd face that tougher uphill grade. By the time he'd gone out and back to Portage Point he found himself in front of the Yellow Dog, sweat glistening off of his face and arms and his workout pants and shirt virtually soaked. As he was toweling himself off, Maggie appeared. Neither had any idea that Charley was already reporting to Ray.

"Well, good morning. Good workout?"

He finished running the towel over his face, smiled at her, and said, "Yeah, it was."

"Coffee?"

He thought for a moment and said, "Maggie, do you have iced coffee?"

A broad smile crossed her face. Actually, she was rather well known for her iced coffee, not because she did something different with the coffee, but rather it was the ice that was different. The Yellow Dog offered frozen-coffee ice cubes that did not dilute the strong coffee flavor of the high-quality roast Maggie offered to her patrons. "You bet. It's a Yellow Dog specialty."

"Great. PJ tells me you make a mean breakfast burrito. How about one of those, too?" He looked through the plate-glass window and saw only a few customers sitting at tables. He checked his watch. It was ten o'clock. "Maybe you could sit a while with me?"

A caution alarm sounded somewhere inside of her. *What's he want? Why is he doing this?* Maggie ignored it. "Umm, sure, David. Let me get your order together."

When she returned, her alarm still sounding but considerably more subdued, she had his order as well as a cup of coffee for herself. She sat down across from him.

"Have you heard any more from Em?"

Hearing David call her "Em" struck a familiar yet sad chord with her. Besides her, he was the only one she'd ever heard call her best friend "Em." "She called me just about an hour ago." In that conversation, Emily had told her that preliminary tests indicated that the fire started on the lake-side porch and that gasoline had been the accelerant that caused the flames to erupt so quickly. The winds that night had made it impossible for the volunteer fire department, once it had arrived at the scene, to catch up to the fire. More tests were taking place and a formal report by the state police forensics department would be filed. The good news was that none of this was going to slow or stop the settlement of their claim with their insurance company. But Emily had asked her to keep the arson thing close to her vest, so Maggie simply said, "Lots of paperwork, but the insurance claim is progressing. She wasn't sure when they'd be coming home. She said Chuck's parents were being very helpful and supportive and then added, "I'm so glad they have them to fall back on at a time like this."

"How are Emily's parents? Are they still around here?"

"They're both fine, but, no, they moved to Florida five or so years ago. Em still misses them, but her real estate company has really taken off. She's so busy that she only gets down to see them once a year or so. She and Chuck try to take Cammie down for Christmas and New Year's."

David took a big bite out of his burrito and washed it down with a swallow of iced coffee. "Wow, Mags, this is really good."

Again, the familiarity of "Mags" struck a chord. He'd been the one that had started calling her that right after they'd started dating that summer when they were both still in high school. Emily had simply picked up on it. "Thanks."

They were getting reacquainted and caught up, and as that process unfolded itself between two people, there were small steps and then there were some big steps. David felt like it was his turn to take a step, and he opted for a big one. After another bite of burrito and swallow of coffee, he began, "Can I tell you something ... " Just then, a customer went into the Yellow Dog.

Maggie's alarm system was going off, but she didn't let it show. The customer provided a convenient escape, and she held up a finger. "Be right back." Glad for the interruption, by the time she'd taken care of the order, she'd recomposed herself. The alarm had quieted as she sat down across from him again. "OK, sorry. Where were we?"

David told her about the morphine-induced dream he'd had about her in the immediate aftermath of the explosion. Maggie had heard this story from Emily that night at her kitchen table, but she made no attempt to tell him that or otherwise stop his rendition of the dream. It was even more heart-wrenching hearing it from him, but, intuitively, Maggie knew it was good for him to talk about it. When he was finished, she had a bunch of damp napkins wadded up in her hand and she was still crying. "Oh, David ... " was all she could manage to choke out. She reached across the table and took one of his hands in hers.

★ ★ ★ ★

Charley Sharp had positioned himself at the hardware store's cash register so he could take care of customers and see what was going on across the street. When he saw Maggie reach across and take David's hand, he knew that was a piece of information Ray would want to know tonight when he saw him at Shirley's. Charley's hope was that the more details he could give Ray about these two, the more he was likely to get paid.

★ ★ ★ ★

"Maggie, I didn't mean to ... "

She shook her head. "No, David, it's OK. I can't imagine all that you've gone through in the past six months." There was a long pause in which neither of them knew exactly what to say next, neither seeming to know what the next step in their reacquaintance should be. So, they just sat there. Suddenly, Maggie realized that she still had hold of his hand. She didn't want to let go, but decided that, in the wake of their mutual silence, that was the appropriate thing to do.

For David's part, he'd been surprised, happy, and comforted, all at the same time, when she'd reached out for him. He didn't want her to let go either, but also felt the awkwardness that this true act of compassion had as its unfortunate afterglow. The silence between them endured for a long minute when David announced, "Mags, I ... I ... don't know if you have any plans for this evening, but I'd like to invite you out."

If this was another big step for him, it was a giant one for Maggie. Caution alarms bombarded her now ... clanging, gonging at her. They were much harder to ignore this time. "David, listen ... I ... I don't know if that's a good idea ... "

His own spontaneity stunned him. Literally it had come out of his mouth, even before he'd given any thought as to how it might just scare her off forever after the way he'd abandoned her once before. *You have no right to ask her such a thing ... not after the way you've treated her.* Somehow, he had to try and retreat gracefully from what he now realized was an egregious overstep. "Mags, I'm sorry ... I don't know where that came from. It's ... it's that last night I rolled myself down to the boat launch just after dark. I sat there for a long, long time and remembered ... " his voice trailing off.

Caution alarms still clanged in her mind, but her curiosity had the best of her and she wanted to hear what he'd remembered.

When David found his voice, he continued, "I don't know how you remember it. But I remember how life had been so simple back then, when we were kids. This place ... we were just so carefree. One season blended into the other and ... we had ... we had one another to talk to. I must have sat there for a couple of hours last night. It was midnight before I even knew it. I just thought that it would be fun to sit there again tonight and talk to somebody about those days. I thought it would be great to talk with you about those days, Mags. Honest, that's all I was suggesting ... I mean look at me ... " he waved his hand over his missing legs. "I didn't mean that it was a date or anything ... " He was smart enough to realize that he was best off to just shut up.

She felt ashamed of herself. He was hurting, just like her. *Maybe, just maybe,* she thought, *we can help each other with the hurt.* "So that's what you'd like to do. Sit with me at the boat launch and talk, like we've talked this morning?"

He nodded.

The alarms were diminishing. Another customer walked into the Yellow Dog. She left to take care of him. When she returned, she smiled and said, "So, what time would you like me to come down?"

His heart pounded as he managed to overcome his surprise and stutter out, "It's dark about ten o'clock. All the boaters are gone by then. It's quiet and peaceful. Is that too late, Mags?"

It was. She was usually in bed by nine o'clock, because she was up at four o'clock baking and getting ready for the next day at the Yellow Dog, but she said, "I'll see you at ten."

Again, he thought his heart was going to leap out of his chest. Broadly, he smiled at her. "Do you like wine, Mags?"

Coyly, she smiled back at him. "I do, David."

"Red or white?"

Thoughtfully, she paused for a moment and then said, "Red ... merlot or pinot noir."

"I'll find a nice bottle for us to have tonight."

It was nearing noon. She turned to follow a lunch customer into the Yellow Dog, but before she let the door close, she leaned back out and said, "See you tonight about ten."

★ ★ ★ ★

At six o'clock, Ray walked into Shirley's, looking for Charley. He found him sitting at their usual table. Their waitress had watched both of them come in. From the bar area she'd watched Ray slide an envelope over the table to Charley. With as much intention to eavesdrop as to get their order, she approached the table but Ray abruptly waved her off. "I don't want nothin'. Come back and get his order after I leave."

Asshole, she said to herself, again. From the bar area, she saw Ray bang his fist against the table, then he got up to leave. *Typical,* she thought, familiar with his surliness. Once he was gone, she strayed back by the table to see if the other guy wanted anything. Instead of placing an order, and with three crisp hundred-dollar bills in his pocket, Charley hit on her. When she said to him, "not even if you were the last man on Earth," he left as well.

★ ★ ★ ★

Ray parked his pickup truck in front of the public restrooms at the park. From where he was he could see the front of David's cottage, the road alongside the park that led to the public boat launch, and the ramp along the launch's western edge. He waited and watched, looking for David to head down there as Charley Sharp had told him he had on the past two evenings. No one was around as the minute hand on his watch approached ten o'clock. It was dark and conditions were shaping up perfectly for him to carry out the plan he'd spent the day devising.

Then he saw Maggie's pickup pull into David's driveway. She got out and David opened his front door and rolled out to meet her. He watched her push the wheelchair down to the ramp. Once there, he saw Maggie open up a folding chair and take a seat next to David. Rage boiled up inside of him. He took the gun from the glove box and ran his hand down the barrel. He wanted to walk over and put a bullet through each of their heads. He could do that. It was pitch black. No one was around. He could get the job done and be out of there before the sheriff's office could respond, even if someone managed to hear the shots and recognize them for what they were, instead of some kid shooting off fire crackers.

He had his hand on the handle of the truck's door before some semblance of sense overcame his rage. He didn't want to kill Maggie. He wanted her back. He wanted to bury his face in her hair again and smell her fragrance. He wanted to make love to her again. In his mind all of these things were still possible if only he could get David out of the picture, just as he had the Chicago lawyer, just as he had Emily and her old man. No, he'd wait. *She can't be with him all the time. I'll find him alone ... maybe even down here at the lake. It'll be easy. He's a gimp ... no legs ... David Keller's not such a tough guy anymore. Wait. Take your time. You'll get this bastard and then Maggie will be all yours again.*

22

A DEADLY ENCOUNTER

An empty Wild Turkey bottle sat next to him on the seat of the pickup. On the morning of July 1, Ray woke to find himself still having the foggy effects of the previous night's binge. His was the only vehicle, for the moment, in the parking lot at the end of 13 Mile Road in Pierport. Spreading out in front of him for as far as the eye could see was Lake Michigan. He could barely recall sitting there last night pounding down the whiskey. His head throbbed and his vision, though clearing, was still blurry. Today was going to be a long day. *Be patient. You know what you have to do. Follow the plan. Don't rush it.* He rubbed his eyes, started the truck, and drove the short distance to his father's house. All he wanted was a hot shower, a couple of Aleve, and some sleep.

Meeting him at the front door, Clipper could smell the booze. "Where you been, Ray?"

Ray lied, "Ran into Bobby Dunbar last night at the casino. Had a few too many, so slept it off in the truck in the parking lot."

"Dammit, Ray. You're spendin' too much time at that casino. I ain't goin' to keep on givin' ... "

Ray tuned his father out, walked past him, and headed to his room. He didn't have the time or the patience to put up with his old man's nagging. He had to shake off the excesses of last night. He needed to be sharp for what would lay ahead of him this evening.

Clipper followed him down the hall, barking after him like an agitated Jack Russell terrier. Ray spun around menacingly and snarled, "Leave me alone. I'm in no mood ... " The old man backed off, knowing he was no match physically for his son. Clipper sensed that Ray was still sufficiently drunk and, therefore, empowered by whatever he had been drinking, to give Clipper the beating of his life. So, Clipper did what Clipper always had done when disgusted with his only child. He threw his hands up in the air and walked away.

At about ten o'clock Ray's phone rang, jolting him out of a solid sleep. "What?"

Charley said in a whisper-like tone, "Just thought you'd want to know he's back at the Yellow Dog ... "

"Let me guess. You lost the money I paid you last night and you're lookin' for another payday. Here's the deal, Charley. You're fired. I don't need you anymore. You're not gettin' another dollar more out of me."

Sharp had, in fact, lost every single dollar Ray had paid him the night before. In the wake of that loss, and as he thought about the flow of money from Ray drying up, Charley had determined that he had something to say about when the money would stop flowing. "Hey, Ray, before you get so fuckin' high and mighty with me, I should remind you that I know what really happened with that Chicago lawyer, and maybe the state police might like to know about who set that fire at the Webers'. So, maybe you should think about paying me to keep my mouth shut."

"You little sonuvabitch! Are you blackmailing me?"

"Ray, you can call it whatever you want to call it, but a couple of hundred dollars a week for my silence doesn't seem like too much to ask."

"Fuck you, Charley." Ray hung up. He was sitting up in the bed and so angry he was clenching his teeth. *So, you want to fuck with me, Charley. A bullet costs a helluva lot less than two hundred a week. I'll be seein' you, you sorry fuck.*

Somewhere around four o'clock Ray got out of bed, showered, dressed, and headed for the kitchen looking for something to eat. As he rounded the corner from the hallway into the kitchen, he saw his father sitting at the table with his back to him. *Shit!* All he wanted was something to eat, but he knew his father was an argument just waiting to happen. He stopped, turned around, and exited the house. Clipper heard the truck start, shook his head, and finished his soup.

Ray drove to the casino, grabbed a burger at the sports bar, washed it down with a beer, and headed to the blackjack tables. At eight o'clock he glanced at his watch and decided that two hundred fifty dollars in the hole was about as much as he wanted to lose tonight. He swigged down another beer at the bar while watching the Detroit Tigers play somebody ... he wasn't interested enough to even determine their exact opponent. Then he left, drove his truck to the parking lot in front of Onekama Park's public bathrooms, and began his vigil.

He'd had enough beer by now that his mind was somewhat addled. As he remembered what he'd seen the night before, he made a decision. If Maggie showed up tonight he was going to kill her, too, and then head to California, Mexico, or someplace as far away from here as he could get. It began to drizzle rain. He feared that would deter David, and, perhaps, Maggie, from venturing to the boat launch ramp. It seemed he'd worried needlessly.

At precisely ten o'clock, David exited his cottage, rolled himself down to the ramp, and just sat there looking out into the lake. It was dark, clouds obscuring what little moonlight there was. The drizzle, for the moment, had stopped, but even if it hadn't, he would have still come down here. Drizzle rather matched his mood. He was thinking about Maggie and their conversation earlier that morning. After his roll along M-22 he'd gone to the Yellow Dog. Maggie had brought him coffee and a burrito. Their conversation had been friendly, light hearted. Then, he'd invited her to join him again tonight at the ramp. Maggie had refused and quite abruptly said no. Then she'd turned on her heel and left him sitting alone in front of the Yellow Dog. But with that one word, "no," he'd since read thousands of words into it. *No, she didn't want to see him. No, she was angry with him for the way he'd left her. No, she wished he'd never come back to Onekama* ... and on and on.

Never taking his eyes off his prey, Ray exited his truck, leaving the gun in the glove box. Had Maggie been there, he'd have taken it. Maggie could swim, but a gimp like Keller, *no way*, Ray had thought. He walked across the dark park, approaching his unsuspecting victim from the rear. "Well, hello there, Mr. David Keller, big war hero."

It surprised David, his mind elsewhere. The adrenalin jolt was sufficient to raise the hair on the back of his neck. In one quick move, he pivoted his wheelchair around to see who it was.

"Wow, smooth move, Mr. War Hero."

The dark only compounded the years that had passed since he'd last seen Ray, so David didn't recognize the person taunting him. Whoever this was, David had an immediate dislike for him. With no fear in his voice, he simply said, "Well, you know who I am. Who the hell are you?"

"Seems like you ought to know the husband of the woman you've been messin' around with ever since you come back to town."

The speech was slurred and difficult to understand, but David took a stab, "Ray ... Ray McCall?"

"The one and only. Surprised to see me, Mr. War Hero?"

"Well, yeah, to be honest, I am."

Ray's rage was building as he came closer and closer to David. "Yeah, I bet you are. You probably think that this little rough patch that me and Maggie have been goin' through has kind of opened the door for you, don't you?"

"I don't know what the hell you're talking about, Ray. All I know is that you and Maggie are divorced ... "

"Oh, yeah, and so you thought that you'd just march back in town with all of your medals and your missin' legs and maybe she'd take pity on a gimp like you ... "

"OK ... OK, Ray. That's enough. What do you want?"

Suddenly Ray lunged at David. "I'll tell you when it's enough, Mr. War Hero. Let's see how well you can tread water with those stumpy legs of yours."

Before David knew it, his wheelchair was tipping to the side. He could feel himself spilling out of it. He extended his left arm out to brace against the inevitable fall to the boat launch's board ramp. He held on to his chair with the right hand and, as he was falling, the pouch on the right-hand arm of the chair flapped against his right arm. Before he rolled clear of the wheelchair onto the ramp he reached his hand down into the pouch and pulled out the M-9 handgun.

Ray stood over him sneering, "Time for you to go for a little swim, Mr. War Hero."

David was no longer in Onekama. He was back in Afghanistan. A man was about to attack him and he knew exactly what to do, what he'd been trained to do in such a situation. Lying flat on his back, clear of the wheelchair, David extended his right arm in the direction of his attacker. Even though the light was low, he could see the surprise in Ray's eyes as Ray realized that David had somehow managed to produce a handgun out of seemingly nowhere. Ray froze for just a second as he made the decision to proceed or relent. He bent down in an attempt to disarm his victim. Shouting at David, he said, "What do you think you're going to do with that?"

David pulled the trigger, the bullet found its mark, and it was deadly, striking Ray in the middle of his forehead. It hit its mark with such force that Ray's head snapped back so quickly and so violently that the coroner would later conclude that the bullet's impact broke his neck. A broken neck, however, was not the cause of death. The bullet created an entry wound about half an inch wide in his forehead. But, as it exited the back of his head, it took out enough skull to leave a gaping three- to four-inch hole. Forensics would later find some of Ray's gray matter splattered as far as twenty feet from where his body lay. The force of the shot had completely stopped Ray's forward momentum as he was advancing on David. He fell dead just in front of his intended victim, who was still in full combat mode. Forgetting for the briefest of moments that he had virtually no legs, David tried to get up. When he realized that wasn't going to happen, he propped himself up on one arm and, with the other arm extended, moved the gun in slow, steady movements from left to right and then back again, looking for more Taliban, more insurgents, more enemy trying to take his life.

Some people staying in the rental cabins near the boat launch heard the shot, but this was Onekama in the summertime. It was dismissed as a firecracker set off by kids, most likely enjoying their time in the summer resort town. No one bothered to even look out a window, much less walk down to the public dock.

★ ★ ★ ★

4:30 a.m.—The sun was not yet up, but its light was just brightening the eastern horizon as Burt Chartwell and his fishing buddy, Al Harkness, swung Burt's pickup and his twenty-six-foot Grady White fishing boat off of M-22 and down the access road that led to the boat ramp. Al got out as they approached the ramp to help Burt back the rig into Portage Lake, and as he walked toward the ramp a shot rang out. He could feel the bullet whiz past his ear and both men heard it hit the pickup. Al sprang back into the truck. Burt hit the gas and headed back toward M-22 as four, maybe five, more rounds impacted the boat. Neither men were hurt, but before they were at the junction of the public access road and M-22, Burt, a retired deputy sheriff, was on the phone to 911.

Five minutes later, two Manistee County sheriff's deputies swung their cars in a blocking position in front of the boat ramp. Two others quickly followed and blocked the park's entrance at M-22. The sky continued to brighten, but it was still dark as the deputies closest to the ramp moved their cars' powerful spotlights onto the shooter. One of them, Deputy Jim Alter who'd contributed to the Welcome Home, David Keller Fund, recognized him and quickly radioed dispatch asking for a patch directly to the sheriff. Two minutes later they were connected. "Hey, boss, we have a real situation here in Onekama at the public boat launch in the middle of the village. David Keller's on the ramp. There's a body lying in front of him and he's just fired on a couple of fishermen. I've hailed him on the loudspeaker, but he's not responding. Here's what I'm thinking: David Keller's in a flashback ... PTSD, boss ... he probably thinks he's back in Afghanistan. He's going to try and kill anyone that comes near him right now, until he snaps out of it. Maybe if you call PJ and get him down here ... I dunno, maybe PJ can talk him down. We've got the park's entrance secured, but maybe you want to get a marine unit out on the water off the public boat launch. I'd hate to see some boater wonder into this mess by accident."

Fifteen minutes later, PJ's Tahoe skidded to a stop behind the two sheriff's cars. One of the deputies put him up on the loudspeaker. "David," he spoke, clearly, calmly, "It's PJ." There was no reaction from David, who sat propped up against a post that supported a handrail along a segment of the boat ramp. The sun was up now. The deputies turned off their spotlights. On the lake, one of the sheriff's department's marine unit officers radioed that he was offshore and would secure the water side of the crime scene. David continued to hold the pistol leveled in their direction.

"David, it's PJ," he repeated. "I'm coming to you. Don't shoot. It's me ... PJ." As the deputies advised him against such a dangerous move, PJ stepped from behind the cars and walked toward his brother. His hands held up, PJ kept repeating, "David, it's me ... PJ ... don't shoot." The deputies kept their long guns trained on David. If he shot PJ, their plan was to end this right here and now by taking out the shooter, war hero or not.

As he approached his brother, PJ could see the terror in David's eyes. "David, it's me ... PJ. Don't shoot me." He was only about twenty feet away from his brother when he realized that the body in front of David was that of Ray. "David, it's me ... PJ. Don't shoot." By the time PJ was standing over Ray's body, David lowered the M-9, lowered his head, and began sobbing. Behind him the deputies lowered their weapons and called for the ambulances to come forward from their positions near the park's entrance. PJ knelt next to his brother and took the weapon out of his hand. "It's OK, David. It's OK. You're all right. No one's going to hurt you now." PJ felt such sorrow for his brother that he could have cared less about Ray's condition. Still wary, the deputies nearest the boat launch remained behind their cars, vigilant, pistols or long guns still in hand. One of them moved away to keep curious onlookers who had now begun to filter into the park at a safe distance. On M-22 other deputies were busy advising fishermen that they would now have to take their boats out to Andy's Point to put into Portage Lake. This ramp was officially closed until the sheriff's department determined it was no longer an active crime scene. PJ flipped David's overturned wheelchair upright. Then he helped his brother get in it and wheeled him out to the sheriff's deputies. He handed them the M-9 and said, "It's Ray McCall. I'm sure he's dead. There's blood everywhere."

"What happened?" the deputy asked.

"I haven't a clue, but he should probably go to the hospital for observation."

David started to argue. PJ put a hand on his shoulder and said, "It's OK, David. You're safe now, but the docs should check you over." David was too exhausted to object too strenuously.

★ ★ ★ ★

Maggie McCall had arrived at the Yellow Dog about 4:45 a.m. to begin preparations for the day's business. She'd heard the sheriff's cars turn into the park area with their sirens blaring. She'd seen the ambulances roll to a stop, one of them directly in front of her shop, but she was much too busy to take time out to see what was going on. It was Onekama. She'd find out soon enough.

Then she'd seen PJ's Tahoe come screaming into the park area, past the sheriff's deputies that had been placed at the park's entrance on M-22 and she began to worry. While her scones baked, she stepped out and walked to the corner and asked the deputy standing there, "What's going on?"

"A shooting, ma'am. The shooter's still down there. Please stay back."

"Who got shot?"

He shook his head, "Dunno." Then he stepped just past her to redirect a pickup with a boat in tow.

Maggie just stood there trying to see what was going on at the ramp, but the distance was too far. Worried, she returned to her shop. Then about quarter past five she heard an ambulance turn on its siren. Through her front window she saw it swing onto M-22 headed south toward Manistee. Then, with no siren, a second ambulance followed the first. She walked back to the corner. Traffic was backing up on M-22 as deputies redirected boaters and curious gawkers slowed to see what was going on. She looked for PJ, but could only see his Tahoe, parked now in a space down by the boat ramp. When she'd talked with the deputy, she happened to notice that there were no lights on at David's cottage and thought that very strange given the level of activity going on just a matter of a few hundred feet from his front door. She noticed again there were still no lights on at David's.

A wave of regret washed over her. She'd treated him very badly yesterday morning, but if her previous experience with him and her failed marriage with Ray had taught her anything, it was to be cautious. No matter how much she'd tried to make herself angry at David since his return to Onekama, she'd rediscovered a soft spot for him and this scared her. When he'd asked her to join him for a second night in a row at the boat ramp, she panicked. Now she was panicking again. *PJ's car is still here. What if he's in one of those ambulances? What if David ... "* Maggie, more worried than ever, turned off her ovens, locked the shop's front door, and drove to Westshore Medical Center, where she expected the ambulances were most likely headed.

23

THE CONFRONTATION

G rimly the doctor told PJ, "We've sedated your brother. He's resting comfortably, but I'm not sure where he thinks he is right now. He's in and out, back and forth ... " The emergency room doc knew he wasn't being very "medical," but he was used to dealing with severe physical injuries. There wasn't a mark on David. What was going on with him right now was all in David's head, which was shifting back and forth between Westshore Medical Center and Afghanistan as quickly as one might shift gears in a car. "Let's see where he is when he wakes up from the sedative we've given him."

"When will that be?"

He looked at his watch and then back to PJ. "He's going to be out of it until mid-afternoon. Come back about three o'clock and we'll see where we are then."

"Is the sheriff's office leaving a deputy to keep an eye on him?"

The doctor nodded affirmatively. So did PJ, who knew the answer to the question before he'd asked it. His brother had killed Ray. There would be charges—likely open murder— filed against David and as the county prosecutor, it would fall to PJ's office to determine exactly what those charges would be. He and the doctor walked together to the main waiting area of the emergency room and as they said goodbye to one another, Maggie walked up to PJ. "I ... I overheard one of the nurses talking. She said Ray was dead ... "

PJ was surprised to see her. "News travels fast, but I guess bad news travels even faster. I'm sorry, Maggie." He'd always liked her. She'd been like a big sister that he'd never had when she and his brother had been dating during David's senior year of high school. Standing there looking into her eyes he suddenly recalled how she'd been the one that included him in trips to the pier, to the beach, to the ice cream shop, even to the movies occasionally. PJ remembered David hadn't liked his younger brother being invited to tag along, but when he'd been the least bit vocal about it, Maggie had always shut him down. Then David left for West Point, Maggie started seeing Ray, something PJ never really understood, and, the next thing he knew, Maggie was pregnant. For sixteen years their lives only meshed occasionally as they'd see one another around town. This morning as they stood facing one another, her eyes were red, her cheeks tear-stained. "They said David shot him. Is that true, PJ? Did David shoot Ray? What the hell happened down there?" The rasp in her voice increased with each question.

PJ reached out, put a hand on each of Maggie's shoulders, and tried to be as calm as possible. "Maggie, Ray is dead. It appears that David shot him. We don't know why or what happened at the boat ramp. At this point we aren't even sure of when it all happened. David fired on a couple of fishermen this morning when they tried to launch their boat. That's when I was called. I was able to get the gun away from him ... "

"Where the hell did he get a gun, PJ?"

He dropped his hands to his side and shook his head, "Maggie, I don't know."

"So, how is he?" She asked that question calmly, but then broke into tears.

Her question surprised him, but the tears were an even bigger surprise. Granted, Ray was her ex, but he was still her son's father. Nonetheless, he answered, "He's asleep.

They've sedated him. He's extremely agitated. We think he had a flashback to Afghanistan. According to the doctor, he's in and out, switching back and forth between thinking he's back in Afghanistan or Iraq and reality. They are hoping he will be more lucid after he's rested, but we won't really know for sure until he wakes up. We can only hope that he is cognizant enough to answer some questions."

"What's going to happen to him, PJ?"

"I ... I don't know, Maggie. There are a lot of questions that need answering, but none of that can happen until David gets back to reality."

They were walking from the hospital's emergency-room waiting area to the main lobby, arriving there just as a sheriff's patrol car pulled to a stop at the front entrance. The passenger door opened and Clipper got out and rushed into the hospital. Maggie looked at PJ and said, "Oh, no. I don't want to deal with him right now."

PJ acknowledged, "Me neither." But they were in the middle of the lobby, it was practically empty, and Clipper locked eyes on them and immediately headed in their direction. "Your brother killed my boy, PJ. Where is he? Have they locked him up yet? I want to know what you are going to do about this? Don't think because he is your brother, that you can ... " He let that sit out there without finishing the thought. Then he continued, "The sheriff told me he thought he was having some kind of flashback ... that PTSD caused this." He shook his finger at PJ, "I don't give a shit, PJ. My boy's dead. I want that sonuvabitch locked up so he can't do this again to somebody else's son." The old man had worked himself up to tears.

PJ knew he could not be reasoned with when he was like this and to get angry at him would be the height of unprofessionalism, so he only responded with, "I'm sorry, Clipper."

"You're sorry ... yeah, I bet you are." Then Clipper turned to Maggie. "What are you doin' here? Didn't expect to see you."

The honest fact of the matter was that Maggie hadn't expected to be here either, but the reason she was here was her concern for David. The fact that her ex-husband had been shot and killed was only a small part of her emotional distress and that distress was more out of concern for her son, rather than any feelings for Ray. She managed a weak, "I'm sorry, Clipper."

"Yeah, well, never mind. I'm glad you're here. I have to identify the body. Since the two of you aren't married any more, that now becomes my responsibility. But after I've done that, you and I can go to the funeral home and ... "

In typical Clipper fashion, this sounded to Maggie more like a demand than a request for help. It sounded as if Clipper expected it of her and she resented him for making that assumption. She looked back and forth between the two of them, and then focused on Clipper. Screwing up her courage, Maggie looked the old man right in the eye and said, "No, Clipper, I'm not going to do that. I've got to get home. I've got to go to the school, get Jack, and let him know what has happened to his father."

Clipper relented a bit, "Yeah, well ... I guess ... " He paused for a moment and then said, "But maybe after that you can help with ... "

"We'll see, Clipper. We'll see. I've got to go. PJ, let me know what you find out, OK?"

PJ nodded. He could see Maggie was really hurting and he had the distinct feeling it was more over David's plight than the death of Ray. Clipper interrupted his thoughts, "Yeah, PJ, my lawyer will be in touch to find out what you've found out. Make sure you keep him informed. I want that crazy brother of yours punished for what he did to my boy."

24

AN UNDESIRABLE DEFENSE

The flashbacks to Afghanistan had stopped, but David had not been able to recall anything that happened that night at the boat launch. That left the authorities with a lot of blanks to fill in surrounding Ray's death, and the forensic evidence collected at the crime scene was damning. The only missing bullet was the one that killed Ray. Fired at very close range, it had entered at his forehead and exited at the back of his head. It had to be around there someplace. Yet, despite the best efforts of a large team of experts who'd scoured every inch of the boat launch and surrounding park area with all the latest tools, including sophisticated metal detectors, the spent bullet had not been found. That bullet would contain trace elements of Ray's brain matter, but without it there was no proof that the bullet that killed Ray had been fired from the gun recovered at the site of the murder. It was a small point to be sure, but without it, all the other evidence was circumstantial.

Four bullet fragments had been recovered from the fishermen's boat and pickup. There was no doubt in PJ's mind that when ballistic tests were completed, it would prove that these were from the 9mm handgun he'd taken from his brother the morning of the shooting. David's fingerprints were all over the M9 that was the presumed murder weapon. Equally as important, David had admitted yesterday to detectives that he was, in fact, the owner of the M9. During further questioning, he conceded that he did not have a concealed-carry permit and that he'd purchased the gun at the Ann Arbor Gun and Knife Show several months earlier. David had not given them Etherton's name, but a computer check of the weapon's serial number by the Manistee sheriff's office revealed that the last official owner of the M9 was one Ernest Etherton, a private gun dealer. Because Etherton listed an Indiana address as home and because the illegal sale was a violation of federal law, the Manistee sheriff's office turned Etherton's prosecution over to the federal Alcohol, Tobacco, and Firearms Department, which tracked the gun dealer down and took him into custody for violation of federal gun laws. He would pay a big fine for what he'd done for David and lose his permit to sell guns for a year, but Etherton was the least of PJ's or David's worries now.

★ ★ ★ ★

Yesterday, PJ had had his first conversation with his brother since the day of the shooting. "You didn't buy that gun to kill Ray, David. I know that. But I am curious. Why did you have that gun?"

David turned his head away and stared out the hospital room's window.

"Were you planning on using it to ... " He was not a mental health expert. He had no idea if he was helping or hurting his brother, but he had to ask the question. "Were you going to use it to kill yourself?"

David continued to stare out the window.

"David, listen to me. You are in some serious trouble here. They are going to move you to the county jail. You'll be arraigned tomorrow or the next day. My hands are tied here. You say you don't remember a thing about what happened and I believe you. I've talked to Dr. Masters at Walter Reed. Do you remember him?"

The blank stare out the window continued.

"He says flashbacks happen to a lot of combat vets. He also says that lapses in memory are pretty common side effects. So, I believe you when you say you can't remember what happened. But, at this point, the circumstantial evidence is incontrovertible. You shot and killed Ray. The only question now is *what were the circumstances around that shooting?* Natalie and I have talked about almost nothing else except how we can help you. I have an idea, but, before I can do anything else, I have to know." He paused to see if any of this was registering with his brother, who still only stared out the window. "David, are you hearing me? Look at me."

Slowly, David turned his head toward PJ.

"Did you buy that gun to commit suicide?"

The first tears brimmed over the edge of David's eyes. He couldn't speak, but nodded almost imperceptibly.

PJ's heart broke for his brother, who was facing a possible life sentence if convicted on an open-murder charge. His eyes filled with tears as well. "OK ... OK ... now that that's out there, we will find a way to deal with it. But, if I'm going to help you fight this, then I need to know ... " He noticed David's stare was now locked on him; his brother's eyes were glassy with tears as, one after the other, they spilled over and ran down his cheeks. "I need to know that you aren't going to try anything like that."

A sheriff's deputy and a nurse with a wheelchair showed up at his hospital-room door. The deputy said, "Sorry, Mr. Keller, but the hospital is ready to discharge your brother. The sheriff sent me over to transport him to ... "

PJ held up a hand, "Yeah, sure." He looked back at David. "So, how 'bout it?"

This time, David shook his head almost imperceptibly, *no*. It wasn't much, but PJ was willing to take it for the time being.

★ ★ ★ ★

PJ had not slept well since the shooting. He rolled his legs over the edge of the bed and rubbed his eyes. David's arraignment hearing was scheduled for 1:00 p.m. in Courtroom Four of the Manistee County Courthouse. The hearing in the 85th District Court would be presided over by The Honorable James P. Hatch. PJ was very familiar with Judge Hatch, having arraigned hundreds of accused felons in front of him over the last decade. He considered him a fair adjudicator. But this was an arraignment hearing, its purpose merely to advise the accused of the charges against them, determine how the accused desired to be represented, advise the accused of their right to a preliminary examination, and, finally, to set bond. Normally, the accused was not represented by counsel at the arraignment, but in this case, PJ was going to be there, standing next to his brother. David was not in his right mind when he'd shot and killed Ray just over seventy-two hours ago. His complete lucidity had only returned twenty-four hours ago and there was a big gap in his memory. And the accused was his brother. PJ showered, shaved, dressed, skipped breakfast, kissed Natalie and the boys goodbye, and by nine o'clock sat at his office's computer writing a letter.

At eleven o'clock his secretary buzzed him on the intercom. "Mr. Keller, I'm sorry. It's Myles Wingate on the phone. He insists on speaking to you before your brother's arraignment hearing. It's the second time he's called. I can take another message if you like, but ... "

Myles Wingate was the senior partner in Wingate, Fogler, and Bush, a well-heeled Lansing, Michigan law firm handling almost exclusively the legal concerns of elected officials, past and present, in the Michigan legislature. In addition to being a graduate of the prestigious Harvard Law School, he was also a trust-fund heir and known to be, in the legal circles that PJ moved in, a big, loud bag of wind. PJ shrugged and told her to put the call through.

"Good morning, Mr. Keller. How is your day going?" PJ

was pretty sure MylesWingate could give a shit how his morning was going, and Wingate proved it when he didn't even give PJ a chance to answer his pro-forma question. "Myles Wingate here, from Wingate, Fogler, and Bush. I'm calling on behalf of my client, Clipper McCall. We would like to know what you are planning to do with the murder case involving your brother?"

PJ knew the answer to the question. He also had known this call was coming. Clipper, in an agitated voicemail, had told him he was going to get Myles personally involved. To be honest, PJ was surprised that Myles had waited this long. He was not required to answer the attorney's question. In fact, the call was rather presumptuous on Myles's part. But *presumptuous* could be not only Myles Wingate's middle name, but Clipper's as well. Brusquely, PJ responded, "The arraignment hearing is this afternoon at one o'clock with Judge Hatch, Counselor."

"Uummph ... you can't be serious. You're going to prose-cute this in Manistee County? You can't do that. You're the prosecuting attorney and the defendant is your brother. You can't possibly ... you must transfer this case to another county's prosecutor ... it's the law ... "

"Excuse me, Counselor." PJ replied. The abrupt inter-ruption shut Myles up. There was a pause and then PJ repeated, "1:00 p.m. today, Judge Hatch's courtroom ... is there another question?"

Myles, frustration evident in his voice, harrumphed again and said, "You know, of course, Mr. Keller, that if the charges are anything less than open murder, Mr. McCall will instruct us ... "

PJ glanced at his watch. He didn't have time for this. He was composing a letter and it had to be done within the next hour if his estimation of the timing of everything he was planning was correct. "Mr. Wingate, I could care less how Clipper spends his money, but this hour that you are likely going to bill to his account is a waste of his money and your time. Tell Clipper that if he wants to know what charges will be proffered against David Keller, he should come to Judge Hatch's courtroom at one o'clock this afternoon. Now, if there's nothing else, I have some work to do before the hearing."

Without another word, Myles hung up. PJ smiled into the telephone's receiver, "And good day to you, sir."

★ ★ ★ ★

At noon, PJ handed his letter of resignation to Judge Walter V. McPeak, the chief judge of the 19th Judicial Circuit Court in Manistee County. This was not the first time a county's prosecuting attorney had resigned in midterm. The process to find the replacement was established legal precedent in Michigan. McPeak and the other judges in the circuit court would appoint his replacement as prosecuting attorney. PJ sat in the chair in front of McPeak's desk for an uncomfortably long minute while the judge read the letter. Finally, McPeak looked across the top of his reading glasses and said, "I'm sorry, PJ, first for what happened with your brother, and, second, for this. But I can't say it's completely unexpected. I suppose I might do the same thing if I was in your shoes."

"Sorry, Judge, but David's the only brother I've got. I know the lurch I'm leaving you in and I hope you don't resent my recommending Sylvia Wheeler to be appointed as my replacement for the remainder of the term."

"Umm ... " McPeak intoned somewhat ominously.

"I know that is a bit presumptuous on my part, but there is a reason."

"What might that be?" McPeak asked.

PJ answered with another question. "Do you know Myles Wingate, senior partner in Wingate, Fogler, and Bush?"

"Heard of them ... litigators to the politically well-connected, aren't they?"

"That's right, Judge. It seems Clipper McCall has hired them to *assist* Sylvia in my brother's prosecution."

"That's a bit unusual."

Ruefully, PJ said, "Yes, sir, it is. Myles Wingate himself called me this morning and wanted to know to which county we would be referring David's case in a change of venue." PJ knew McPeak's record well. In the ten years that he'd been the prosecuting attorney in Manistee County, he could not recall McPeak ever granting a change of venue.

"That so," the judge intoned solemnly.

"So, here's the thing, your honor. I know you don't like changes of venue and I certainly don't want David to be tried anywhere else other than right here in Manistee County. But if it takes two or three months or longer to appoint a new prosecuting attorney to take my place, Myles is going to use that as another reason to push for a change of venue."

Again, peering over the top of his readers, McPeak asked PJ, "Is she ready for this? Does she know about your recommendation?"

PJ told him, "I've briefed her on what I'm doing. She has had time to prepare. Sylvia can represent the county at the arraignment hearing this afternoon. She's more than capable. As far as the overall responsibilities of being the county's prosecuting attorney, she has a year more experience as an assistant prosecuting attorney than I had when I was elected to the job. Again, Judge, she's more than capable."

There was a pause. Judges in general didn't like surprises and PJ knew that was particularly true with McPeak. "Judge, I'm really sorry for springing this on you. I know how busy your docket is ... how busy the other judges are. But Sylvia Wheeler is a good choice. I think you know that."

Again, McPeak nodded, but this time added, "OK, PJ. Got it. Let me see what I can do to speed the process up."

★ ★ ★ ★

At 1:00 p.m., David and his brother sat in front of Judge Hatch in Manistee's 85th District Court. Hatch began the proceedings. "Mr. Keller, for the court record, would you please tell everyone assembled what's happening."

"I've resigned as the Manistee County prosecutor, Your Honor, in order to serve as my brother's defense counsel."

"Let the record reflect that I have conferenced with Chief Judge McPeak of the 19th Judicial Circuit Court here in Manistee County," Hatch said. "He has polled the other circuit-court judges and they have accepted Mr. Keller's resignation. Further, the 19th Judicial Circuit Court has appointed Ms. Sylvia Wheeler as the Manistee County prosecuting attorney for the remainder of Mr. Keller's unexpired term. Turning to Sylvia Wheeler, he asked, "For the record, Ms. Wheeler, did you know about this?"

"Yes, Your Honor. Mr. Keller had advised me of his resignation plans. I am prepared for this arraignment, your honor."

Hatch thanked PJ for his years of service to the county's court system and then turned his attention to the accused, David Keller.

Reading from a prepared charge sheet, Hatch began, "Mr. Keller, you are charged as follows: Count One, open murder; Counts Two and Three, assault with a dangerous weapon with intent to murder." Hatch looked at David. "Do you understand the charges against you?"

David nodded and said, "Yes, Your Honor."

Hatch next asked PJ, "Set for preliminary exam?"

PJ responded, "After conferring with my client, and if there is no objection from the prosecuting attorney, we wish to waive the preliminary exam and be bound over to the circuit court to stand trial on the charges contained in the complaint."

"Very well, then, Mr. Keller, the only remaining matter

is that of bond. Normally when the charge is open murder, bond is not granted ... "

PJ shifted weight from one foot to the other. "Your Honor, the defense respectfully requests an exception to that be made in the case of my client." PJ put a hand on his brother's shoulder in anticipation of his reaction and said, "The defense intends to file with the court and the prosecution an intent to assert the defense of insanity at trial." At the word *insanity* PJ felt his brother's body go stiff. He could feel David's eyes on him. The insanity defense was something they'd talked about. David didn't want it, but PJ felt it was the best thing to do. The word *insane* rankled both of them, but for different reasons; David, because he didn't think he was insane, and PJ, because such a defense ranged from difficult to impossible to prove. He could not remember a case in a Michigan courtroom where it had ever worked before.

Sylvia immediately stood and said, "Your Honor, respectfully, the prosecution asks that bond be denied. The key charge here is open murder. The accused's mental state does not make him a good risk to be walking around in the general population. What is to prevent something like what happened at the Onekama public boat launch from occurring as quickly and inexplicably somewhere else?"

Hatch looked back to PJ and said, "Mr. Keller, I am not inclined to grant bond in any open murder case and the point the prosecution makes is a good one."

"But Your Honor, my client is not your typical detainee. He is wheelchair bound ... "

Hatch interrupted, "The county jail has provisions for the disabled."

Hatch was forcing him to play a card that was, quite honestly, a long shot and he knew David wouldn't like it. "Your Honor, my client has spent much of the last decade engaged in combat operations in Iraq and Afghanistan. He has five Purple Hearts and three awards of the Bronze Star with "V" device, indicating the awards are for Valor. My client also holds the Silver Star, the nation's third-highest award for valor in combat. Yes, he suffers from PTSD, as do many vets that are walking the streets today. Yes, he was involved in some way in this violent event at the Onekama public boat launch a few days ago, but he does not deserve to languish in prison during pretrial preparations. May I offer an alternative solution to the dilemma facing this court?"

Hatch looked first to Sylvia and then back to PJ. "What do you propose, Mr. Keller?"

"Because of my client's insanity defense, the defendant will be examined as required by statute at the Center for Forensic Psychiatry in Ypsilanti. Concurrently, I have arranged for an independent mental examination at the VA Hospital in Ann Arbor by the psychiatrist who treated him during his recent rehabilitation. The Ann Arbor facility is located close to the forensics center. We agree to his restriction to the grounds of the VA Hospital and the forensics center during this process. Admittedly, my brother needs help. This is a way in which he can be both helped and examined at the same time."

Hatch asked both attorneys to approach the bench. "Ms. Wheeler, this seems to me to be a fair proposal. Are there any objections from the prosecution?"

Sylvia looked at PJ and then back to the judge. "No, Your Honor."

"Very well." Turning to PJ, Hatch said, "Mr. Keller, you will make arrangements for your client's secure transport between the forensics center in Ypsilanti and the VA Hospital in Ann Arbor and you will insure that these arrangements are satisfactory with the prosecutor's office?"

PJ nodded, "We will, Your Honor."

"For the record, there are no objections from the prosecution?"

Sylvia was already anticipating a scathing phone call from Clipper. It had become his habit to "check in" with her daily and offer his advice on how he thought she should prosecute the case against David. But she really didn't care. What her former boss was proposing was fair and reasonable. Wheeler replied, "None, Your Honor."

Hatch nodded and then said, "Bond is set at one million dollars."

The number stunned David and PJ. It was a staggering amount. PJ, a pleading tone in his voice, said, "But, Your Honor ... "

Judge Hatch interrupted, "The charge is open murder, Counselor. Bond is one million dollars. If posted, your client will have no contact with the alleged victim's family and your client will be restricted to the Ann Arbor VA Hospital grounds and the forensics center grounds during his time downstate. This case is bound over to the 19th Judicial Circuit Court for trial." He banged his gavel down and said, "Next case, please."

PJ accompanied David out of the courtroom along with the deputy sheriff that would return him to the county's lockup. "Can you give us just a minute, Bill?" he asked the deputy, who nodded and stepped a few paces away.

David asked his brother, "Where the hell are we going to get a million dollars?"

"We don't have to get a million dollars, but we will need to come up with at least a hundred thousand ... a bail bondsman will want at least ten percent ... and we won't get much, if any, of that back."

David whistled through his teeth. "OK ... I've got about half a mil socked away. Just get me out of that jail cell as quick as you can. The walls are closing in on me, PJ."

"I understand." PJ felt he'd achieved two major victories. One was getting David out on bail. The second was getting him housed at the VA Hospital. He and Dr. Hightower had talked. If he had any chance of winning this case with an insanity defense, he would need Dr. Hightower's expert

25

RECONCILING

Emily walked into the Yellow Dog at about ten thirty and didn't see Maggie until she stepped behind the counter and walked over to the kitchen door. Maggie's back was to her as she washed some dishes from the morning's breakfast crowd. "Hi, Mags."

Maggie dropped the dish she was washing into the dishwater and immediately met her best friend in a warm embrace. Softly Maggie spoke into her friend's shoulder, "I have never been so glad to see someone in my entire life."

Holding her close and rubbing her back with one hand, Emily said, "Are you alright?"

Maggie thought, *Just like her. Her house burned to the ground and she's asking me if I'm alright.* She stepped back, wiped both eyes with the backs of her hands, and said, "No. But that's not the important thing right now. How are you, Chuck, and Cammie doing?"

Emily casually flipped one of her hands across her body. "We're fine. Insurance is all settled. I can't stay very long. We are meeting our builder at the site in a couple of minutes. Chuck and Cammie are meeting me there, but I wanted to stop by and see if you were busy tonight. Chuck and Cammie are going back to Grand Rapids after this meeting. Thought maybe I could bunk at your place tonight. We'll have a girl's night in. I'll bring the wine. What d'ya say?"

She smiled at her old friend, "I'd like nothing better. Come hungry. I'll make spaghetti and meatballs."

Emily grabbed her hand and said, "OK, Mags. See you around five?"

"Perfect."

★ ★ ★ ★

At the same time that Maggie and Emily were firming up their plans for the evening, neither PJ nor Natalie could recall the last time they had gone as a family to the beach during the week, but spontaneous trips like this one had become a priority for them since PJ's resignation. They were packing the car when the phone rang. PJ could see it was Sylvia Wheeler calling. Cheerfully, PJ answered, "Good morning, Ms. County Prosecutor."

"Good morning, Mr. Keller."

"Hey, Sylvia, knock off the Mr. Keller stuff. We're just two attorneys now. Call me PJ."

It was awkward calling her boss by his first name for the first time, but she replied, "OK, PJ. I got a call from a Myles Wingate ... some law firm in Lansing ... says he represents Clipper McCall. Wants to help any way he can. Says he has lots of resources. Says I shouldn't hesitate to use them. You know anything about this?"

PJ smiled into the receiver. He liked her refreshing naiveté in that she had not heard of either Myles Wingate or his high-priced law firm. "I guess I should have warned you, but it slipped my mind. Myles Wingate has made a fortune representing legislators on both sides of the law. Clipper is apparently one of his clients. But, if I may, Counselor, allow me to give you a couple of bits of advice. First, don't let him intimidate you. Trust me, he will try this tactic, but always remember he's got no control over you. Never forget that. Second, if you think you can use them, then use them. God knows they've got the money."

OK, Mr. ... .uh ... PJ. Got it. Thanks."

There was a pause and then, "Sure thing, Sylvia. Anything else?"

"Uh, yeah, there is, sir ... uh, I mean, PJ. I got a call from the state's Center for Forensic Psychiatry yesterday. They are ready to move on your brother's evaluation. They told me that Dr. Fredrick Effingham would be their examining psychiatrist. I looked him up, PJ. They use him a lot. Every one of the referrals he's examined has wound up being sentenced. They would like David available to Dr. Effingham week after next."

PJ recalled something one of his law school professors had taught him. *Bad news never gets better with age.* He told Sylvia, "Well, not what I was hoping for. I have a lot of confidence in Dr. Hightower, though. She's promised me she will get started with David as soon as he gets to the VA Hospital. I plan on taking him there on Monday. He will be there when Dr. Effingham is ready to examine him. I'll get busy and set up his transportation arrangements between the VA Hospital and the forensics center." PJ paused for a moment and then added, "Thanks for the heads up, Sylvia."

"You bet, boss. This is a little hard for me. My heart's not exactly into prosecuting this case."

"Yeah, I get it. But let's keep that between you and me. Besides, Myles isn't going to let you slip on anything ... neither will Clipper, for that matter. Just do your job, Sylvia. You'll be fine."

★ ★ ★ ★

Maggie closed the Yellow Dog promptly at four thirty and hurried home. Jack met her at the door. "Mom, since you and Aunt Em are having dinner here tonight, OK if I go to Grandpa's?"

Since Ray's death, Jack had spent a lot of time with Clipper. Maggie was pretty sure he had bad-mouthed David to Jack, but she had expected that. Ray had not treated her well, especially during the last few years of their marriage, as Ray slipped further and further into the bottle, but Ray was still Clipper's only child. Ray had been cremated. Clipper arranged a memorial service that had been lightly attended, mostly by Clipper's old political cronies. Jack never let Clipper get too far away from him during the visitation or the service. Ray's friends, mostly of the more nefarious sort, were few and far between. They could easily be spotted in the crowd. They were the ones not in suits and ties. Maggie had been very proud of the care and concern her son had shown for his grandfather during this difficult period. She put a hand on his shoulder and said, "We haven't talked much about Clipper, honey. How's he doing?"

"He's hurtin', Mom. He's angry ... thinks that army guy that shot Dad should go to jail for the rest of his life. To be honest, I think he wishes Michigan had the death penalty, he's that upset."

Maggie's heart moved into her throat, but she swallowed hard and asked, "What do you think?"

"I dunno. What the heck was Dad doing down at the boat launch at that time of night anyhow? Was he just in the wrong place at the wrong time? Grandpa says that PTSD is a bunch of crap made up to protect crazy people. I'm not sure he's right about that."

The arm on the shoulder transitioned into a hug from his mom. At first, Jack was a nonparticipant, but then he put his arms around his mother and said, "Maybe I shouldn't say this, but I kind of think Dad got what he deserved. I mean ... look at the way he treated you, Mom." Maggie wanted to tell her son the truth so badly at this point, but she knew that would be exactly the wrong thing to do just now. Jack was searching for answers. She held a key one, but it was sealed deep inside her. She squeezed him harder and said, "I know, Jack. I know."

The doorbell rang, and Emily stepped in. Maggie wiped her eyes dry and Jack walked to his Aunt Em. "Hi and bye," he said to her. "You and Mom have a good evening. I'm on my way to Grandpa's."

Emily gave him a quick peck on the cheek and said, "Sweet boy!"

Embarrassed, Jack smiled at her. Over his shoulder, as he stepped through the door, he said, "Love you both. Bye."

Emily blew him a kiss. Jack waved it off with a big smile and a shy, "Aunt Em ... " She turned to Maggie. "He is the sweetest boy!"

Through spaghetti, salad, and two glasses of wine apiece, Emily and Maggie began to catch up on a whirlwind of events that, within the past few weeks, had impacted each of their lives so dramatically.

"So, it was arson?" Maggie asked.

"Appears so. State police have opened a case, but, of course, there are no leads."

"I ... I just can't believe it, Em. This is Onekama. Things like arson simply don't happen around here."

"Believe me, Mags, when I say Chuck and I have both gone back over and over it. You know ... you ask yourself all kinds of questions, like, 'Did either one of us have a client that was dissatisfied?' We've both had disputes with clients, but neither of us can recall any dispute that could make even our craziest client so angry as to burn our house down. Neither of us have an answer."

The conversation shifted when Tabby, Cammie's rescued kitten, walked into the room with Jasmine, Maggie's golden retriever. "Would you look at those two, Mags. They're fast friends."

"Jasmine is going to miss Tabby when she goes home. I was worried for the first twenty-four hours or so. It was like a Mexican standoff. They sat on opposite sides of the kitchen," she said pointing. "Jasmine over here and Tabby over there, and both just glared at each other. Then Jack picked up Tabby and set her on his lap. He called Jasmine over to him. He sat there," she pointed to Jack's usual seat at the dinner table, "for about fifteen minutes, rubbing each of their heads. The two of them were nose to nose. Ever since then, you don't see one without the other. It's absolutely amazing."

"I hate to keep imposing ... "

"Em, stop it. There is no imposition."

"Well, you know I appreciate it. So does Cammie. Chuck's parents have this border collie, Sydney, that absolutely hates cats, so taking Tabby to GR just would never work."

"No problem. Like I say, Jasmine's heart will break when Tabby goes home."

"We'll arrange a lot of play dates." Emily looked at Jasmine and the cat sitting at her feet. "I promise," she said to them.

After dishes were done, the two settled over a glass of wine at the kitchen table. "So, tell me about David."

"Oh ... where do I start?"

"How about from the beginning. You told me he turned up at the Yellow Dog, so go on from there."

Maggie grabbed a handful of Kleenex from the kitchen counter, took a drink, and began. When she came to the part about how abruptly she had treated him the day Ray was shot, Maggie lost it. Emily let her cry it out and when Maggie was finished Emily looked at her and said, "So you don't hate him for what he did to you all those years ago?"

Maggie's head was down and she was shaking it back and forth. When she looked up at Emily, she surprised both of them, "Hate, him? No. I think I may be falling in love with him all over again."

★ ★ ★ ★

At the same time that Maggie and Emily were enjoying their spaghetti dinner at Emily's house, PJ and Natalie settled into a table at Shirley's Restaurant. Tom and the boys were not very far away at the high school, watching a baseball game. PJ thought it was a good time for Natalie and him to get away and talk about next steps. The defense was going to hinge around PJ's ability to prove temporary insanity. It wouldn't absolve David of his crime, but it might reduce any jail time and it might even get him the treatment he needed to deal with the psychological damage that six combat tours and his devastating injuries had created.

They weren't regulars at Shirley's by any means, but they were long-time locals and PJ's picture had been all over the television news and in the newspaper both for his resignation and his representation of his brother. Their waitress stepped up to their table and said, "Mr. and Mrs. Keller, welcome to Shirley's. I'm Rose and I'll be your server tonight. Can I get you anything to drink?"

When she returned, she placed their drinks in front of them and offered, "Mr. Keller, I'm sorry for what happened to your brother. I was in the park the day you brought him home. He's a true hero."

PJ nodded and said, "Thank you, Rose. It's appreciated." He thought she was ready to take their food order, but Rose had something else to say.

"It's really kind of odd that you and Mrs. Keller sat down at this table." The place wasn't very crowded; only one or two other tables were occupied at this rather early dinner hour. He and Natalie were drawn to this spot because it was in the restaurant's far corner. Other tables were likely to fill up well before any close to them would be taken. It was privacy they were looking for. There was lots to talk over, not the least of which was how the family finances were going to work now that PJ no longer had a steady paycheck coming in.

"What's so odd about this table, Rose?" PJ asked, smiling at her.

She suddenly became rather shy. "Well, it's just that ... I'm sorry, Mr. Keller, it's nothing really."

He continued smiling at her, "No, really, Rose, what is it?"

"This table doesn't get much use, but Ray McCall and this other guy would come in here. I guess I saw them in here three or four times. They always sat at this table ... "

His curiosity was piqued. "Really."

"Don't get me wrong, Mr. Keller. I never liked Ray. He was never very nice and the guy he would meet when they came in here was a real creep ... "

"Who was the other guy?"

"Don't know for sure. Saw him at the hardware store once when I was pickin' up somethin'. Real creepy guy, though. He and Ray ... I don't know what they were up to. Ray treated him pretty bad. Never spent much time with him when they met up. I think Ray was payin' him for somethin'. I saw him give him money once, and, then, another time, I watched Ray slide an envelope across the table to him. He snatched it up real quick and stuffed it into his shirt pocket like he didn't want anyone to see. Then, a few minutes later, that same night, I saw Ray hit the table top like he was mad about somethin'. So, it just seemed an odd coincidence to me that you would come in here and pick this table out. I mean, look around, we aren't exactly busy, are we?" She smiled uncomfortably at him. "Now your brother's gone and shot him ... " She stopped talking. That hadn't come out the way she'd wanted it to. She knew she'd crossed a line. Nervously, she began to apologize.

"No, Rose, that's OK. It *is* kind of an odd coincidence."

Over dinner, PJ told Natalie about a conversation he'd had with Dr. Hightower at the VA Hospital earlier in the day. The day after tomorrow, David was to be transported to the hospital's secure ward. His examination at the Center for Forensic Psychiatry was to begin the following day. PJ was going to Ann Arbor with David to make sure his brother was settled in as best he could be. But throughout dinner, he couldn't stop thinking about Ray and this guy from the hardware store. *What was Ray doing at that boat ramp at that time of night? What business did Ray and this guy have going?* Without telling Natalie, PJ made a mental note that tomorrow he was going to stop at the hardware store and try and find the "creepy guy" Rose had described.

26

A "COME TO JESUS" SURPRISE

It was Tuesday and the Yellow Dog was closed for the day. Maggie had spent the day baking a couple of pies, one blueberry, the other, cherry. On a plate wrapped in Saran wrap, she held a slice of each. Somewhere around five o'clock, she tapped on David's front door so quietly that she could hardly hear it herself. It marked her lack of confidence in what she was doing. While she was debating whether she should just walk away or rap again louder, David answered the door. "Maggie ... I ... I wasn't ... I didn't ... " Finally, he gave up trying to express his surprise and said, "It's good to see you."

She shrugged and said, "To be honest, I'm not even sure I should be here, but I had the day off and did some baking. I thought you might like ... "

"Come in, Maggie." He rolled his wheelchair to one side and pushed the screen door open for her. She stepped through. He took the slices of pie from her, rolled into the kitchen, and placed them on the low counter top. His furnishings were spartan. The living room contained one easy chair with a small side table and a rather large flat-screen television, but the cable had not yet been activated, so the dark screen loomed large over the small living room. The Welcome Home, Major David Keller committee had money remaining for furnishings, but hadn't spent much of it, not knowing what David had or what he might need. "Please, sit down, Maggie," and he motioned toward the easy chair.

As Maggie sat down, both inquired exactly at the same time, "So, how are you?" They laughed nervously, then David said, "Maggie, I ... I'm sorry for what happened ... " his voice trailed off.

She looked at him with a certain sadness in her eyes, "PJ tells me you don't remember ... " Her voice trailed off.

David shook his head, "Nothing."

"One of the things that puzzles me is what was he doing down there that time of night. I know why you were there, but why him ... why Ray?"

Again, David shook his head. He didn't like talking about it anymore than she did, so he tried to change the subject. "Would you like something to drink, Mags?" A fond memory of happier times, she liked it when he called her that. "I have beer or wine ... red or white."

Maggie was nervous and sitting only compounded that. "I'll have a beer if you'll have one with me. I'll get it. I'm assuming they are in the refrigerator."

He nodded. "While you do that, I'll put on some music. You still like country and western?" he smiled at her. She smiled back and nodded.

She went to the refrigerator and found two bottles of a locally made beer from Storm Cloud Brewing, a growing craft-beer operation just up the road from Onekama, in Frankfort. She'd been there last summer with Ray, Emily, and Chuck. The evening had been fun until Ray had too much to drink and picked an argument with her. Grasping the bottle, Maggie tried to twist the cap off, but it didn't budge. She turned and opened up a drawer looking for a bottle opener, and, instead, found a folded sheet of paper with her name written on it. She reached for it, then paused. The opener she was looking for lay right next to the note. *Don't,* she thought, but could not resist the temptation. She unfolded it and the contents shook her to the very soul of her being.

"Finding everything?" David called from the other room.

Her voice cracking, "Yes." She refolded the note, placed it back in the drawer, removed the opener, and popped the caps on the bottles. Her hands were shaking as she picked them up. She knew she couldn't let him see her like this. She drew in a couple of deep breaths, tried to settle herself, and then rejoined him in the living room. It was all she could do to keep from shouting at him, *How could you even consider such a thing? So many people have worked so hard to keep you alive, to make your life comfortable. Why, David? Why?* But she didn't. Instead she asked him, "What's PJ say about the trial?"

David snickered, "He thinks I'm crazy."

"David, stop it," Maggie replied, seeing absolutely no humor in his remark.

He clarified, "Sorry, Mags, but that's going to be the defense: not guilty due to temporary insanity caused by post-traumatic stress disorder. Tomorrow PJ's taking me to Ann Arbor. I'll work with my shrink at the VA, Doc Hightower. Then, I'll be examined by one of their shrinks ... "

"Whose?" Maggie interrupted.

"The state's ... some guy named Effingham. I'll be housed at the VA so when Effingham's not trying to break into my head, Hightower will. She will be an expert witness in my defense when this thing goes to trial. PJ says it won't absolve me of killing Ray, but it might reduce the charge from open murder to some lesser offense."

Maggie began to weep. "David, I'm so sorry ... "

"Why, Mags? Why are you sorry? You didn't do anything."

"Ray ... " She couldn't find her voice.

Patiently, David asked, "Yeah, Mags? Tell me about Ray."

Maggie was crying now, almost uncontrollably. David felt ashamed for putting her in this position. "Hey, Mags. It's OK. You don't have to ... " he paused and then his face brightened. "Hey, how about we go for a ride. I'll show you the new van."

"No, David, I can't ... "

He rolled his wheelchair over to her, took her chin in his hand, and lifted her eyes up to meet his gaze. "Sure you can. C'mon. It'll be fun. Just like old times ... "

How could he be contemplating suicide? "I ... I want you to tell me ... " There was a long pause.

"Tell you what, Mags?" She didn't respond. He decided he'd try and strike a bargain with her. "OK, Mags. Take a ride with me and I'll tell you anything you want to know." He was smiling at her now, that infectious, mischievous smile of his, not like any smile she'd ever known.

She nodded.

"OK, then. Let's go. It's beautiful outside now."

They rolled out of Onekama, heading south along M-22 toward Manistee until they came to Miller Road and the field David had told her about in his dream. Maggie remembered it comically, fondly, and now, after reading his note to her, tragically. It was the field where she had clung to him for dear life while blasting across its snow-covered contours on a snowmobile. She had feared the speed they had traveled at, but she loved holding him so close, so tight. She began to weep again as she remembered him telling her about the morphine-induced dream he'd had as he was being evacuated after the IED blast. He made a sharp, obtuse right turn onto Miller Road. The field laid out on their right, its undulating contours stretching back toward the north and the west. In a quarter of a mile or so, David turned onto the broad shoulder facing Lake Michigan and a setting sun that was slowly fading over the field. "Looks like a brilliant sunset tonight. Maybe we should go out to the beach and watch the sunset across the lake." It was small talk. He really didn't want to be anywhere else but right here with her, right now.

He was relieved as Maggie shook her head. "No." She paused for the longest of moments. He knew she had something else to say. She was trying to understand how he could sink to the depths of depression she'd read into his note to her. She looked at him and said, "Tell me, what was it like?"

Her question puzzled him. "What was what like, Mags?"

Sheepishly she hung her head. "The accident ... the IED ... I want you to tell me about what happened. Everything ... " her voice was cracking. "Tell me everything."

If anybody else in the entire world were to ask him a question like that, he would have shut down completely, but not when it came from Maggie, not here in this place where he'd dreamed of her in the blast's immediate aftermath. Still it was hard for him to talk about. He stared out the windshield as he tried to compose himself.

"I ... I'm sorry, David. I didn't mean to ... "

"No, Mags. It's OK. Doc Goldstein, Doc Masters, and Doc Hightower have all told me I need to talk about it ... but it's ... it's real hard." She was sitting in a captain's chair next to him in the front of the van. "If you pull that lever right there," he pointed to it, "you can swivel that seat." She reached down, pulled it, and swiveled toward him. At the same time, he released the locks on his wheelchair's wheels, pushed back from the van's steering wheel, and swiveled toward her. "Now that I think of it, I can't recall any real physical pain. It all happened so fast ... the flash, the bang, the fire. When it first happened the only sense I had that worked was my sense of smell. When I woke up, I was in Landstuhl with both legs gone. Dr. Goldstein, my shrink there ... boy, did I give her a hard time ... was the one that told me I was the only one that survived the explosion. That hurt more than anything else. That still hurts."

She reached over and took his hand.

David began to cry. "Why me, Mags? How the hell did I survive that? The damned thing blew up right outside my door. I took the brunt of the blast, but I was the only one that survived. How do you account for that? How do I live with that?" He wiped the tears from his cheeks with his free hand, cast an awkward smile at her, then turned and looked out the windshield. "Remember when we were kids and would fly across this field on the snowmobile."

He remembers what I remember. How strange is that? she thought and then nodded.

He was still crying. "I'm sorry. I know I should be able to talk about this with you. I owe you that much. I know I've hurt you."

She kept hold of his hand and smiled gently at him. *So much guilt,* she thought. "I was a mess after you left for West Point and it only got worse when I didn't hear from you. Then ... " her voice cracked, "and then, I found out I was pregnant. I knew the baby was yours. Ray isn't the father. I just knew he couldn't be. Jack is your son, David. And for the longest time I really resented that I couldn't tell you. When things got really bad with Ray, I wanted to tell him that Jack wasn't his son. I wanted to hurt him the way he was hurting Jack and me, but I couldn't, more for Jack's sake than anything else. Then a few years ago, maybe about the time Jack turned thirteen or fourteen, I got right with it. I realized how truly lucky I am to have a boy like him. He's such a great kid, David. So, when Ray slipped into the bottle, I decided I couldn't raise two kids, so I concentrated on Jack and tolerated Ray."

"Mags, I ... "

She held up a hand, "No, let me finish this. Ray has been out of my life for the last three or four years. Physically, his touch made me cringe. Emotionally, I was as unavailable to him as he was to me. I don't miss him. I'm sorry that whatever happened at the boat launch happened. I never wished him dead and I certainly never wanted you to be the one involved like you are. When I first heard you were coming back to Onekama, I didn't want it to happen. I didn't want to see you. But now that you're back, I'm glad, David ... I'm very glad." She squeezed his hand for emphasis. "But, I'm not going to let you hurt me again like that, so I have to ask you ... "

There was a long pause. He had no idea what she was about to ask and she wasn't sure she wanted to know the answer to the question. David finally broke the silence. "Ask me what, Mags?"

"Promise me, you're not going to kill yourself."

It was like someone punched him in the stomach and knocked the wind out of him. He just sat there staring at her. "Mags ... I wouldn't ... "

She held up her hand again. "I read the note in the kitchen drawer, David. I know what you are intending to do and if you are still intending to do something like that, then I can tell you right now I don't want anything you are offering ... not your friendship, and certainly not your money." She managed to get all of that out there, firmly, confidently.

In the trouble of the past days, he'd forgotten all about the note he'd penned that day. It all seemed so long ago, but it wasn't. It had been just a few days, really. "Mags, I didn't intend for you ... "

Maggie raised her voice at him. "No, I'm sure you didn't. What were you planning on doing, David ... see me every day at the Yellow Dog, invite me to sit with you at the boat ramp and talk about old times, and then just go off someplace and blow your brains out ... " She was getting angry now, but didn't intend to be that way. "No, David, if you can't promise me right here, right now, that you won't ever do something like that, then I never want to speak to you again." She held his hand even more tightly. She desperately knew what she wanted to hear from him.

They sat there facing one another as the last remnants of that day's sun faded into darkness. Neither of them talked for the longest time until, finally, David said, "I won't."

And with that Maggie took his chin in her hand, lifted his head up, and kissed him, ever so gently. When she withdrew, she still grasped his hand in hers. "David Keller, I've always trusted you. I trust you now and I'm taking your word as a promise. So help me God, you better never break that promise to me."

David reached over and took her other hand in his and repeated, "I won't, Mags. I promise I won't."

27

SEE WHAT YOU CAN TURN UP

PJ had not intended to take so long to get to the hardware store and follow up on what the waitress at Shirley's had told him about Ray McCall's rather strange rendezvous with some unknown someone at the restaurant. But other duties had had to take priority. Sylvia Wheeler had filed a change of venue motion with the court, arguing that she would find it difficult to empanel a jury that was impartial to David Keller, the much-ballyhooed war hero that had come home to Onekama after surviving injuries that should have probably killed him. She had been almost apologetic toward PJ, telling him that the pressure from Myles Wingate and Clipper to file the motion had been unrelenting. PJ, on the other hand, held no ill will against her. It was what he would have done had he been the prosecuting attorney. But he wasn't. He was his brother's defense counsel and, by God, David was going to be tried right here in Manistee County and nowhere else. He'd filed his counter-motion yesterday just as the courthouse was closing.

He and David were leaving for Ann Arbor at ten thirty for a four o'clock appointment with Dr. Hightower. She had already arranged for David's admittance. David, of course, expressed his complete displeasure over all of it, the insanity defense, the examination by Dr. Effingham as the state's expert, and Dr. Hightower as the defense's. But PJ let him know in no uncertain terms that this was absolutely necessary. Without any recall of what had happened that evening, the insanity plea was the only way out of the open-murder charge he faced, and if Dr. Hightower was to appear professional, thorough, and completely credible to the court she would need ready access to him for the purpose of examination and, PJ also hoped, some therapeutic counseling as well.

He glanced at his watch: 8:45 a.m. He thought he had plenty of time to do what he needed to do as he pulled to a stop along the curb in front of the hardware store. *OK, creepy guy. Let's see who you are.* He walked in the front door to find Mike Kruwinski, an older gentleman who'd worked at the store for as long as PJ could remember, and Bill LeVault, who'd purchased the business about ten years ago, working both cash registers with at least half a dozen customers waiting to pay for their goods. Bill was who he wanted to talk to, but PJ decided to roam around and see if anyone else seemed to be working this morning. He wandered past the paint aisles, the electrical supplies, shelves of cleaning supplies, plumbing hardware, hooks, snaps, gadgets, nails, screws, and, finally, through the tool department. If there was someone else working this morning, they weren't in any of those places. As he walked back toward the cash registers, he overheard Bill say to Mike, "OK, holler if you get slammed again. I've got six big orders in the back that I've got to get materials ordered against." And he headed for the office, located at the rear of the store behind the tool section.

PJ intercepted him. "Bill, I know you're busy, but can I ask you a couple of questions?"

Bill knew PJ's father well. Tom had been one of the store's best customers when he was working his handyman's business. "Sure, PJ. C'mon back to the office. Want a cup of coffee?"

PJ declined the coffee, but, as they were walking, he made small talk. "So, looks like business is pretty good, huh."

"Sure is, and it don't help none when one of your guys just walks off the job and don't tell no one about it."

PJ's ears perked up. "Really, what happened?"

Once in the office, Bill poured himself a cup of steaming coffee from the coffee maker on the credenza behind his desk. As he sat down, he began, "Had this guy ... been here maybe not quite a year ... I dunno, maybe I should have expected this ... kind of a drifter type. Anyway, hired him to work here and let him live upstairs, dirt cheap on the rent, if he'd keep an eye on the store after hours. He was pretty dependable. Here on time, balanced his tray every night at closing, got along with the customers. Then a couple of days ago he just ups and disappears ... went upstairs to check on him ... apartment's empty, food's still in the fridge and in the pantry, but no clothes, shoes, nothin'. He's packed up his belongings and gone. No note, no phone call, nothin'."

PJ looked at him and commented, "This is interesting."

"How's that?" Bill asked.

"Well, Rose, one of the waitresses down at Shirley's, was telling Natalie and me about this kind of creepy guy that would come into the restaurant and meet up with Ray McCall. She thought they might be working together ... said she came in one day to get something and recognized him ... no clue as to what they might be up to. She said she saw Ray give him cash one night and another night slip him an envelope."

"Creepy-lookin', huh. Yeah, I guess that could be Charley."

"What can you tell me about him, Bill?"

Bill looked across the desk at PJ and conspiratorially asked, "Why? You think Charley's got something to do with Ray's gettin' shot?"

PJ shrugged. "Don't know, but it's worth looking into.

No one has a good explanation for why Ray was down at the boat ramp. No one knows what happened. David has no memory of any of it."

"Is it that PTSD stuff I keep hearin' about?"

"Likely it is. I'm taking him to Ann Arbor today to meet with a psychiatrist down there."

"It's all a real shame, PJ. Your brother's a real hero to most folks around here ... and ... well, Ray McCall ... well, he ain't nobody's hero."

"Yeah, thanks, Bill. It's my job to make sure David's interests are handled properly in this case, so that's why I came here today. What else can you tell me about this Charley character?"

Bill stroked his chin. "Not much ... " he paused as if really searching for something and then said, "but there is one thing. He spent a lot of time at the casino."

"Really?"

"Yeah, he bragged to me and Mike a lot about how much he won at blackjack. I dunno ... but I think he might have been makin' that up. Twice he asked me for an advance on his salary. I gave 'em to him, but told him the last time there wouldn't be any more advances. He stopped askin' after that. Matter of fact, now that we're talkin' about it, he left with me owin' a week's worth of pay. Now *that* makes his sudden departure even more mysterious, don't it?"

PJ nodded and then asked, "You wouldn't happen to have a picture of this guy, would you, Bill?"

Bill smiled and said, "Got a photocopy of both sides of his driver's license. Will that do?"

"It sure will. Thanks."

★ ★ ★ ★

On the way to Ann Arbor, the conversation was infrequent,

a certain tension lingering between them. PJ did not tell his brother about Charley Sharp because, at this point, there simply wasn't much to tell. At the VA hospital, they were immediately ushered into Dr. Hightower's office. David gave her the same cold shoulder he'd given his brother on the trip down, but by five o'clock she had taken personal charge of him and assured PJ that she would escort him through the admissions process. They all bid one another goodbye and PJ headed for home.

Along the way, he called Natalie. "Hey, I'm going to spend the night in Grand Rapids. Sorry I didn't tell you earlier, but I've got something I have to check out ... " He proceeded to tell her about Charley Sharp and what he'd learned from Bill LeVault. "I'm going to see Maurice and his brother, but I won't be able to do that 'til the morning. Everything there OK?" She assured him it was. She sensed a newfound optimism in her husband's voice. She knew exactly who he was going to see. PJ had used them once before and told her about them. She began to share his optimism.

★ ★ ★ ★

Maurice Jackson grew up in Grand Rapids, Michigan, and in 1985 graduated from Western Michigan University with a degree in education. He was a language-arts teacher and could speak German and Spanish fluently, but he never taught a single day. Through Western's Army Reserve Officer Training Corps program, he'd been commissioned a second lieutenant and launched a twenty-year career as an army intelligence officer. He'd retired from the army as a lieutenant colonel and returned to Grand Rapids and opened Black Ops Private Investigations, Inc. PJ loved the irony and the tongue-in-cheek humor of the company's name. Maurice's one and only business partner was his younger brother, Wallace, a recently retired Navy SEAL.

A little over a year ago, PJ had commissioned them to work on the identity of a confidential informant who had turned on a Manistee police detective and set him up to be murdered as he drew dangerously close to a drug king-pin who was running fentanyl-laced heroin into Manistee County. The rumor was that the informant was hiding out in the black community in Grand Rapids, the very same community in which Maurice and Wallace had been raised. Within a week the informant was in custody and singing like a canary. The only thing PJ regretted about the entire operation was that the informant eventually walked away from all charges and became lost in the government's witness protection program. He would have preferred to see the little sonuvabitch prosecuted right alongside the drug runner he'd colluded with.

When he walked into the office he was met by Doris Mattingway, a huge black woman, whom you had to get past before being able to see either Maurice or Wallace. "Well, good mornin', Mr. Keller. How are you? The boys tell me you bringin' us some more work. So good to see you, Mr. Keller. Can I get you a cup of coffee? Or, maybe somethin' a little stronger," she threw her head back and launched into one of her famous deep, throaty laughs. PJ had come to like Doris very much.

"Coffee, black, Doris, would be much appreciated," PJ said, smiling at the woman.

"Sure thing, Mr. Keller," she said. He'd tried since the first time they'd met to get her to call him PJ, but she would have none of it. "Go on in. Maurice is expecting you."

The two legal road warriors embraced in front of Maurice's desk, which was littered with files and a breakfast sandwich. "Sorry to interrupt breakfast, Mo," PJ said.

Doris appeared at the office doorway with a mug of coffee, handed it to PJ, and said, "Ain't it awful the way that man eats. Just look at that sandwich. And it's probably the healthiest thing he'll have all day." Doris turned on her heel, clucking like a mother trying to shame one of her children. She walked out of the office shaking her head.

PJ and Maurice looked at one another. Maurice shrugged. "No worries, PJ, you ain't interruptin' nothin' except Doris trying to shame me into becomin' some kind of vegan or something." They laughed and Maurice continued, "Wallace sends his regrets. He's down at the police station this mornin' bailin' out a client. The guy says he's not guilty. Me, I'm not so sure, but Wallace says he's made of money and it's worth our time takin' a look at it. So, we will. Doris told me you'd called and you had somethin' you needed us to look after. What you got, PJ?"

PJ laid it out for him and handed over the photocopy of Charley Sharp's driver's license. Maurice laid a big, beefy hand alongside his face and said, "You say he's a gambler, huh? Well, if that's so and we got a picture, it won't take us long to track his sorry ass down. No, sir."

"While you're at it, Mo, can you see if there's anything else on this guy? I don't know if this is going to go anywhere, but I have a hunch and it would sure be nice if we could have a little leverage when the time comes to squeeze him for information ... know what I mean?"

"I do, PJ. Give us a couple of days. We'll be in touch. Who do I invoice this to, since you ain't the prosecutor up there anymore?"

PJ considered Maurice, Wallace, and Doris to be salt-of-the-earth people and his friends, but he also knew that their success in this sometimes unseemly business was all about getting paid for their efforts. He laughed and gave him a newly minted business card.

Mo took it from him and looked it over. "You gonna make a habit out of being a defense lawyer, PJ?"

The two men shook hands as PJ said, "Damn straight, Mo.

Got to make enough money so I can keep payin' your exorbi-
tant fees!" Both men laughed. PJ headed back to Onekama,
knowing that whatever the bill might be, it would be fair
and any information they collected about Charley Sharp
would get to him in its purest, most unvarnished form.

28

FOOL ME ONCE, SHAME ON ME ...

Davidhad not slept well his first night back at the Ann
Arbor VA hospital. Part of it was his frustration with
having to be back there, but part of it was because one of
the other patients on his ward, a young marine just back
from Afghanistan, suffered from night tremors and night-
mares. At least half a dozen times last night he'd awoken
screaming. The night nurse and a couple of orderlies would
come running each time. One of the other patients on the
ward, after an outburst, said to the nurse, "For the love of
God, give him something." David heard her explain that
she was not authorized to administer anything other than
what his attending physician had prescribed and that he
wasn't immediately available to see this patient. "Then
get another doc up here. You can't just let him suffer like
this." The nurse, while sympathetic, said, "Because of our
budget, the only docs on duty at night are in the emergency
room and they are busy. There's nothing I can do."

It was still dark out when he decided that he'd just get up,
shower, shave, get dressed, and read until Dr. Hightower
came to get him. At eight o'clock, he was sitting in his
wheelchair as the ward door swung open and Jill Hightower
walked over to him. David was amused at how his ward
mates stared at the tall, shapely woman who'd come to get
him. "Good mornin', Doc. Glad we're doing this early. The
quicker I can get out of here, the better."

She smiled at him as if she knew something that he didn't, and that bothered him. She asked, "You want to drive, or shall I?"

"Depends on where we're going."

"How 'bout we start at the cafeteria and see where that takes us."

"You lead, Doc. I'll keep up."

At their table, she had a bowl of yogurt and fresh fruit. He went heavier with two eggs, over easy, bacon, hash browns, toast, and coffee. "Well, your attitude may be shitty, but you don't seem to have lost your appetite," she said, pointing to his plate full of food.

"Oh, you must know Doc Goldstein, over at Landstuhl. She gave me the exact same clinical diagnosis ... shitty attitude. Hey, Doc, the two of you haven't been comparing notes, have you?"

She didn't like his flippant attitude, but kept her cool. "As a matter of fact, David, we have been. Dr. Masters, too. We all agree that you have a shitty attitude." She gave that a moment to sink in and then added, "We all three agree on something else as well."

"What's that?"

"That you gamed all of us the last time we saw you and that we aren't going to let you do that again."

He had nothing in response to that. He remembered his conversation with PJ at Walter Reed, who'd told him that Dr. Masters wasn't going to authorize his release from there until he began to show progress. He didn't want to be here. He didn't want any of these doctors trying to pick his brain apart. He'd promised Maggie that he wasn't going to hurt himself. It was a promise he intended to keep, but it was a promise he didn't think needed to be shared with just anyone, especially some shrink. *Besides, you took my gun away. What do you think I'm going to do? Hang myself? You think you can fix the fact that I'm alive and the other three guys that were with me in the vehicle aren't? Well, that can't ever be fixed.* He fumed silently as he finished his breakfast.

When he was done, Dr. Hightower said, "OK, let's go to my office. We can close the door and you can scream your head off at me if you like." She added, "That is what you'd like to do, isn't it, David?"

She was spot on, but he wasn't going to let her know that. "Want me to drive?"

"No. Lead the way. I'll follow you."

She stood up. "I hope you will follow me, David. I can help you, if you'll just let me."

29

GETTING SHARP

Less than twenty-four hours after he'd talked to Maurice Jackson, PJ got a call. It was about six o'clock and he, Natalie, Sam, Max, and Tom had just sat down to dinner. PJ excused himself, stepped outside, and took the call, "Maurice, don't tell me you've found him."

"Haven't laid eyes on him yet, but pretty sure we know where he'll turn up tonight. What are you doing right now?"

"Just sitting down to dinner."

"Sorry to interrupt."

PJ appreciated his thoughtfulness, but his curiosity was eating him up at this particular moment. "No worries. What you got?"

"Well, you said this guy likes to gamble. We've got some connections in nearly all of the casinos ... do a little work for them now and again."

PJ chuckled, "Yeah, Mo, I'll bet you do."

Maurice chuckled back, "Yeah, well, sent around the mug shot you gave us of this guy. These casinos, PJ, they've got some pretty sophisticated facial-recognition software, you know."

"So I've heard."

"We got a hit at Big Bear Casino, just up the road from you in Traverse City. Wallace just phoned and said he'd reviewed the video from last night. It's Charley Sharp all right, without a doubt. Turns out he's been there the last three nights. Gets there about the same time each night. Wallace got the contact at the casino to take a look at how he's done. He's on a bit of winning streak right now ... plays blackjack ... likely he'll be back tonight and likely it will be right around eight o'clock. Wallace wants to know if you'd like to meet him at the casino and the two of you could put the collar on this joker. Turns out, PJ, there's a warrant out on him."

"Oh, really! That's interesting. What's he done?"

"The warrant's in McComb County. Charley is a deadbeat dad."

"Why am I not surprised? Got any details?"

"I do. Six months in arrears on child support to not just one, but two women. He's a bundle behind; about twelve grand to each woman. You wanted some leverage, PJ. Looks to me like you've got about twenty-four thousand little levers you could pull on him. You got Wallace's number?"

"Yep."

"You thinking you want to head on up there and meet up?"

"I'll give Wallace a call. Should be there in about an hour and a half."

"That should be perfect timing, PJ."

"Thanks, Mo. You guys are not only good, you're fast."

"Hope you say that after you see the invoice. We had to put some seed money out there with our contacts at the casinos. They've got all these rules surrounding this software they've got ... all this privacy stuff. They ain't supposed to be sharing it with the likes of me and Wallace, but a little palm greasin' and they willin' to let loose some of the info. What you do with it from here on out, PJ ... well, that's up to you."

"Understand, Mo. Thanks. Let me get on the road."

Tom wanted to know what was so important that he couldn't finish his dinner. PJ shrugged him off, but explained to Natalie what was up as she walked to the car with him. By the time he'd swung onto US 31 and gathered some speed, he was already on the phone to Wallace Jackson letting him know he was on his way to Traverse City.

Wallace met him at the door of the Big Bear Casino at seven thirty. "My guy's watchin' the security monitors. When he gets a hit on Sharp, he'll call me and tell me where he's come to ground. If everything is like it has been, that shouldn't be too long from now. Buy you a drink, PJ?"

The big, burly ex-Navy SEAL was dressed in a meticulously tailored navy-blue suit. Protruding perfectly from each arm was a crisp French cuff with a gold cufflink. The deep red silk tie was perfectly knotted. PJ also noted a massive gold ring on his right ring finger. Without straining at all to see, PJ saw it bore the Navy SEAL insignia. Pointing to it, he said, "That's quite a brass knuckle you got there, Wallace."

Wallace held up his right hand, "PJ, you wouldn't believe the number of bad guys walking around this world today with this ol' Wallace Jackson seal of approval on 'em like a damned tattoo." He laughed heartily, "Yep, it sure does serve its purpose."

They sat at the bar sipping their drinks. Wallace's phone rang. He took the call, listened briefly, said, "Thanks, man. You know I appreciate it. Look for a little something-something in the mail from me and Mo for your good work." He put the phone back in his inside jacket pocket and motioned for PJ to follow him.

The table games were clustered about the center of the casino's main room, surrounded by a couple of thousand slot machines. When they were about ten yards from the tables, Wallace stopped and put his hand up as a motion for PJ to stop as well. Pointing, he said, "There he is at that ten-dollar blackjack table over there. Pretty sure that's him. Let's go around this way and get a good look from the front."

They moved off and as they approached the tables from the new direction, PJ said to him, "Got him!"

Wallace nodded. "If you want to take it from here, Counselor, I'll back you up. Don't worry. If he tries something, I'll be right there."

"Sure." And with that PJ stepped up behind Charley Sharp and said, "Charley, I'm PJ Keller, David Keller's attorney, and I'd like to ask you a few questions."

Without even turning around, Charley started to bolt, but he didn't even get one step away from the table before he bumped into Wallace, bounced back heavily, and flopped down in the chair he'd been occupying. The player on each side of him looked confused. One of them, whom Charley had actually collided with as he was slammed back into his seat, yelled out, "Hey, watch out, man." The dealer looked at Wallace and said, "Hey, don't start anything or I'll call security." The pit boss started in their direction, but then put one hand to his ear briefly, said something into an invisible mouthpiece, told the dealer to relax, and then nodded at Wallace.

Wallace bent close to Charley and whispered something in his ear that PJ could not hear over the bells, whistles, and music coming from the surrounding slot machines. Charley, however, apparently realizing the futility of trying to get away, got up. The three of them, Wallace in the lead, Charley in the middle, and PJ trailing, returned to the bar area and took a table as far away from the hustle and bustle of the busy casino as possible. Wallace sat next to Charley just in case he got the idea to bolt again. PJ sat across the table from them so he could see Charley's face. You didn't become an effective prosecutor without learning how to read people's faces, judge their body language, and note a million other little nuances that could tip you off when they were being less than truthful.

"OK, Charley, as I was sayin', I'm David Keller's attorney ... "

"Don't know no David Keller ... "

"OK, then, well, we'll just end this conversation right now and I'll let Mr. Jackson here escort you on down to McComb County, where you can answer to the county prosecutor on the deadbeat dad warrant they have out for you. Sorry to have inconvenienced you." He nodded at Wallace, who stood up and grabbed Charley under the arm.

Charley was only halfway up out of his seat when he said, "OK ... OK ... wait a minute ... just hold on for a second." Wallace looked at PJ, who nodded. Charley sat back down.

PJ said, "I'm listening."

"It's like this ... um ... uh ... I really don't know no David Keller ... er ... uh ... at least I never met him ... "

"But ... " PJ persisted.

"But ... well ... Ray McCall asked me to keep an eye out on people who his ex-wife was seein ... "

"What do you mean *seein'*, Charley?"

"I mean like men who'd come around and talk to her ... "

"That's all? Just men who would talk to her?" PJ asked with a note of incredulity in his voice.

Charley paused for a moment and then added, "Well, there was this one woman ... "

"Who?"

"Her name's Weber ... you know ... she's that realtor lady got her name all over the place around Manistee sellin' property."

"Who else?" PJ pressed.

"There was this guy from Chicago ... some attorney ... he'd stop at the Yellow Dog all the time, talkin' it up with Ray's ex."

"And you reported to Ray on this guy?"

"Well, I told Ray he was always stoppin' in at her shop, but I didn't exactly ... "

PJ interrupted him, "What about my brother, Charley? Were you keepin' tabs on my brother for Ray?"

"What're you tryin' to do to me? You tryin' to make it

look like I had somethin' to do with Ray gettin' shot. Your brother did that ... read that in the newspaper. You ain't gonna hang nothin' like that on me."

PJ could detect a rising tide of panic in Charley's voice. So he made the conscious decision to become more formal in an attempt to impress upon Charley the seriousness of the legal fix he had gotten himself into. "I'm just curious, Mr. Sharp. How much did Ray pay you for watchin' my brother, the Chicago attorney, and Ms. Weber?" He was careful to phrase this as if he already knew Charley was Ray's employee.

Charley took the bait. "Not enough."

PJ snickered, "I'm sure, Mr. Sharp." But now with the fact established that Charley had been paid by Ray, PJ could move onto a bolder line of questioning. "So why did Ray want to know who was seeing his ex?"

"Hummmph ... why the hell do you think? Ray was so damned jealous of her. Practically anybody that said hello to her became his enemy. Why do you think the Weber house burned ... "

"Ray torched the Weber house?" PJ interrupted him.

Charley clammed up. He'd said too much.

PJ reminded him, "You either be forthcoming with me, or Wallace here is going to take you back to McComb County. It doesn't matter one way or the other to me, Mr. Sharp, but if you are withholding information about Ray's motives, then I'm happy to see you do some time as an accomplice to his crimes as well. Of course, ol' Ray's dead, so it won't be any skin off of his nose. Your nose, however, Mr. Sharp ... well, that's another matter altogether." He gave Charley just a moment to digest this and then asked, "Do I make myself clear?"

Charley just sat there between the proverbial rock and a hard place. Finally, he looked at PJ and said, "Listen, if I tell you everything I know about Ray, will you let me go on the child support rap?"

"No, but your cooperation in this case won't hurt you either. I'll put in a good word for you." Charley wriggled in his chair. PJ continued, "You got an attorney?"

"No."

"Well, you do now, but you've got to come completely clean with me about your working relationship with Ray."

Charley sat there, thinking. PJ gave him some time. Wallace loomed large as he sat close beside him. Finally, Charley said, "OK, here's everything I know. Ray told me he set fire to the Weber house. He never told me why, but I suspect he thought she was helping his ex-meet other men. He was ate up with jealousy. He told me he took care of the Chicago lawyer, so I don't think that accident up on Portage Street was an accident. Ray had it in for the guy because he thought he was puttin' a move on Maggie. And, your brother, well ... I told him about him and Maggie meetin' up at the Yellow Dog and then, again, one night at the boat ramp. Whew! I thought he was going to blow a gasket over that. My guess is he was down there at the dock to have it out with your brother the night he got shot. He never told me exactly what he had planned, but said he'd take care of it."

"So, why did you leave town the way you did? How could you think this wouldn't be relevant at trial?" PJ asked him.

"I ... I ... I got scared, Mr. Keller. That accomplice thing you talked about. Yeah, I saw that comin'. Figured I could get out of town, nobody knew about Ray payin' me for information ... how did you manage to put all that together, anyway?"

"That's confidential, Mr. Sharp."

"So, what happens now?"

PJ looked over at Wallace. "You free tonight, Wallace?"

Wallace smiled at PJ, "I'm never *free*, Mr. Keller, but if you want me to keep an eye on Mr. Sharp here until we can talk to the Manistee prosecutor tomorrow, I am happy to do that."

"Thank you, Wallace. It was a poor choice of words on my part," PJ said with a good-natured laugh. "Tomorrow, Mr. Sharp, you are going to talk to the prosecutor and tell her everything that you have told me tonight. She will likely have a few more questions for you."

"What about the child-support charges?"

"We can talk to her about those. If you cooperate with her and answer all of her questions, I'm sure there will be some accommodation, but you are going to have to take some responsibility for that. As long as you are coming clean, you might just as well come clean on all of it. Don't you agree?" Charley hung his head and nodded.

30

THE TRUTH WILL OUT

"**D**ammit, PJ, what the hell do you think you're tryin' to do? Your brother ... "

As soon as PJ saw Clipper on his caller ID, he knew what was coming. He took a deep breath and spoke very carefully, "Clipper, you best be careful not only what you say to me, but how you say it. My job is to defend my brother and I will not be intimidated by you."

"Well, my attorneys will damned well intimidate you."

"If you mean Myles Wingate and his crew down in Lansing, I wouldn't count on it. This is criminal law you're into now and not just some namby-pamby shuffling of legal briefs to make some legislator look innocent of an ethics violation."

★ ★ ★ ★

Actually, PJ was amazed at how quickly Clipper had found out. It had just been a matter of a few hours since Wallace, Charley, and he had paraded into Sylvia Wheeler's office and told her about the employment arrangements between Ray and his newfound witness. PJ also advised her that he was filing a change of plea based on new information. Instead *of not guilty by reason of insanity*, the new plea would be *not guilty by reason of self-defense*. Sylvia's brows arched noticeably when Charley told her about Ray's admitting to him that he'd burned down the Webers' house and plowed into the Chicago lawyer.

"Ray McCall was down there at the boat launch that night to threaten my brother," PJ told Sylvia.

She'd been particularly interested in the waitress at Shirley's who could apparently offer some corroboration that Charley and Ray met up on more than one occasion. It was PJ who'd suggested that she let Myles's law firm do the tracking down of information about Charley and the waitress. He'd told Sylvia, "Once Clipper finds out about this, he will tell them not to pull any punches or spare any expense. So, let them do the leg work. Charley is no saint. I'm the first to admit that. They'll find out about the dead-beat dad stuff and God knows what else, but I doubt that any of it will ruin his credibility as far as this case is concerned. I have no idea what they might dig up on Rose. I'll warn her that there will be some snooping. But I seriously doubt that there's anything in her background that is going to materially damage her credibility. She saw what she saw, and Charley says he was being paid to spy on Maggie and report whatever he observed to Ray, so there you have it." Sylvia had agreed and wasted no time in calling Myles, who apparently wasted no time in calling Clipper.

★ ★ ★ ★

"So, I'm curious, Clipper," PJ said, "what do you know about your son's arrangement with Mr. Sharp?"

The question infuriated Clipper. "What? How dare you ... "

"C'mon, Clipper, do you expect me to think you had no idea how jealous he was of Maggie? Where was he getting the money to pay Charley? I had some private investigators check on Ray when I found out about all of this. They tell me he wasn't working anywhere in the area six months before he was killed ... "

"You sonuvabitch ... "

"Clipper, you know what? If that's the way you're going to be, maybe we should just stop right now. You aren't used to anybody playing hardball with you, and believe me, Clipper, this is hardball. So, get ready. The fastballs are going to be coming your way real soon. Tell that to your thousand-dollar-an-hour Lansing law firm." There was nothing. PJ waited a few seconds. "Clipper?" A few more seconds passed. "Clipper, you still there?" No response. PJ could not tell if Clipper was still connected or not, but he couldn't resist adding before he disconnected the call, "OK, see you in court."

★ ★ ★ ★

Emily rushed into the Yellow Dog at mid-afternoon. The shop was empty except for one person in the corner with their laptop open and concentrating on something on their screen. "Mags, can you believe it? Ray burned down our house."

Maggie blurted out, "What?" It was loud enough that the person in the corner looked up briefly and then went back to their computer.

"I just got a call from the state police. They got a tip from PJ. He's got a witness who claims Ray bragged to him about burning the place down."

"No, Em. I can't believe that. Ray was crazy, but ... " she was completely dumbfounded, "but he wouldn't do something like that. Chuck and Cammie were both in there. They could have been killed. No ... he couldn't have."

"I know. It's hard for me to believe, too. But the state police said they found an empty gas can in the bed of Ray's truck. They didn't think much of it at the time, but after this witness spilled the beans, they went to the Meijer store in Manistee ... to the gas station. The Meijer price tag was apparently still on the can and it looked pretty new. They reviewed the security tapes and there's Ray buying this gas can the day before the fire and they've got him at the gas station filling it up. It's just circumstantial evidence, but the police believe it corroborates the witness's story that Ray bragged to him about burning our house down."

"Oh, Em, I'm so sorry ... "

"That's not all. PJ also told me that the lawyer who got banged up in that car accident with Ray ... "

"Peter ... Peter Wagner?"

"That's right. Well, this same witness has told PJ that Ray did that on purpose. You know why?"

All of it was just too much. Maggie just stood there, speechless, stunned.

Emily could see her shock, but she went on, "The witness told PJ that he was being paid to spy on you. He was getting paid for information on men you were talking to. The guy worked right over there," she said, pointing to the hardware store. "He lived just above it in the apartment." And again she gestured in the direction of the store across the street. "If he saw a man talk to you, he told Ray about it ... "

"Oh, my God."

"Oh, yeah! Ray also told him to keep an eye on me because he thought I might be trying to hook you up with David once he had returned home. Can you believe that?"

Maggie slumped down in an easy chair in front of the shop's large plate-glass front window and put her head in her hands and began to weep. Emily sat down in the chair closest to her and put her hand on her friend's knee. "Mags, you OK?"

Maggie shook her head. "So, Ray thought that David and I were ... "

Though Maggie couldn't see her, Emily was nodding her head. "That's exactly right, and PJ thinks that Ray might have been down at the boat launch that night to hurt David."

"So, it was self-defense and not a PTSD flashback?"

"Ummm, well, PJ didn't exactly say that, but he has changed the plea from one of insanity to self-defense. David's still down in Ann Arbor and still doesn't have any memory of the evening, but PJ has told his doctor about all that he has uncovered. The doctor thinks that some of this information might be useful in helping David to remember what happened. But no matter what happens, it does look like Ray was up to something no good, and PJ is feeling pretty good about his chances in a jury trial."

★ ★ ★ ★

Maggie did not sleep well at all that night and she was up before dawn. She asked Jack if she could drive his Equinox today. She needed to go on a trip downstate, but would be back home by dinner.

"What's goin' on downstate?" Jack asked rather innocently.

Maggie was ready for the question. She had decided the night before as she lay sleepless that honesty would be her best policy. "I'm going to Ann Arbor to visit David Keller." She waited for her son's reaction.

Jack stared blankly at her. "Uh ... OK ... what's going on with him, Mom?"

She shrugged, walked over to her son, and put a hand on each of his shoulders. "I don't know, Jack. There's some evidence ... "

"Let me guess, Dad was up to something." Maggie thought, *The boy is smart.*

"Possibly. We don't know for sure. It would help if David could recall events ... "

"And you think you're going down there will help that happen?"

She shrugged again, "I ... I don't know, Jack. All I know is

31

SERGEANT FIRST CLASS VASSILIACK

Maggie arrived at the VA Hospital about nine thirty. It was later than she'd wanted it to be, but the first several hours of the trip were in the dark and she had to be mindful of the deer during those hours. As she swung into the visitors' parking lot of the sprawling facility, anticipation shot a jolt of adrenaline through her and her heart seemed to have moved into her throat. She had no idea what she would say to David when she saw him this morning; all she knew was that she had to see him.

A helpful volunteer at the information desk gave her directions to his ward. When she didn't find him there, one of the other patients said he thought he might be in the library. He recalled overhearing David tell the nurse that was where he was heading.

She found him sitting in front of a massive window with a brilliant morning sun shining through. His head was buried in a book. "What are you reading?" she asked with a smile spread across her face.

"Maggie!" She had completely surprised him. "I...I ... What are you doing here?"

Still smiling, she said softly, "I came to see you." She fought back tears. "So what are you reading?"

Still fumbling for words, he finally managed to tell her, "Dr. Hightower gave it to me. She said I should read it. The title is *Tribe*."

Maggie just stood there, somewhat awkwardly, not sure

what to say next, afraid that she would break down into tears. In spite of the awkwardness between them, she sensed that he was glad to see her. "Mind if I sit down and you can tell me what it's about?"

From his wheelchair he reached over to a nearby table and, with one hand, pulled a chair away from it, spun it around so that she would be facing him, and said, "Sorry, Mags. I don't know where my manners are. Here, sit down." When she sat, David reached over, took one of her hands in his, and said, "It's really good to see you. Thanks for coming."

His touch felt so good to her. It always had. She could have sat there just like this for hours, but she didn't have hours. She'd promised Jack that she'd be home this evening and there was much she wanted to talk about, but she opened with, "Dr. Hightower? Is that your psychiatrist?"

He nodded and chuckled, "And color analyst for Notre Dame Women's Basketball."

"Oh?"

"Yeah, you'll see what I mean. She played on their women's team a few years ago. They were runners-up in the national tournament. She's supposed to meet me here in about fifteen minutes."

"Oh, David, I should have called ... "

"No, Mags, it's OK. She and I have talked about you," he paused momentarily and then added, "a lot. You're being here this morning ... well, it's a good thing."

She squeezed his hand, "Oh, so you've been talking about me, huh?"

David blushed slightly. "Yeah, we have," and then he smiled.

Maggie asked, "Have you talked to PJ lately?"

To Maggie's surprise, David replied, "No. Not since he delivered me here three ... maybe it's four days ago. I dunno. You tend to lose track of time around here. Why do you ask?"

Maggie grew cautious. If PJ hadn't talked to his brother

about the revelations regarding Ray, there must be some reason he was holding back. So, she responded, "I was just curious about where your case stood. I haven't seen PJ around town, so I thought I'd just ask you."

David grew quite serious. "Maggie, here's the thing: I shot and killed your ex-husband and for that, I am forever sorry. But the fact is, I have no memory of having done that. Doc Hightower is trying to help me remember, but I will tell you I am ambivalent. Sometimes I really try to remember and sometimes I get a little afraid. I mean, what happens if I just up and shot Ray for no good reason?"

"I understand ... " David could tell she had more to say, so he just sat there, still holding her hand. "To be honest, I don't think you just 'up and shot' him. I think there was a reason why you did what you did, but that isn't what really bothers me."

"What bothers you, Mags?"

"That note in the drawer at your house ... "

He put his hand up, "That's over." She was looking at him, tears forming in her eyes. "Doc Hightower and I have dealt with that." He held up the book. "That's why I'm reading this. It helps me understand some of the emotional stuff I had going on about why I was the only one to survive the explosion. But the thing that has helped me the most is ... " He could feel the tears now coming into his own eyes. "Your kiss the other night ... remember ... in my van. I haven't forgotten it or my promise to you. What I was planning to do before the snow flies is nothing but an unpleasant memory, Maggie ... honest to God!"

Neither of them had noticed her approach. "Sorry to interrupt." Jill Hightower reached out her hand to Maggie and introduced herself. Maggie reciprocated. "I thought that's who you might be. David has told me a lot about you." Conspiratorially she leaned toward Maggie, lowered her voice just enough so that David could hear, and said, "And it's all been quite complimentary, Maggie."

Maggie smiled warmly at her, "Nice to meet you, Dr. Hightower."

"Jill, please."

"OK, Jill." *My God, this woman is tall*, Maggie thought, liking her instantly.

She looked at David and said, "I have something in my office I'd like to show you. It's a video that Dr. Masters has sent from Walter Reed. It's a message for you, David, from another soldier, a patient of Dr. Masters. I think it might be helpful. Since Maggie's here, I think it might be good for her to see it as well, but I'll leave that up to you."

He thought for just a second and looked at Maggie. "If you're OK with it ... "

Maggie nodded, then turned her attention to Dr. Hightower. "Dr. Masters was his doctor at Walter Reed?"

Dr. Hightower nodded and smiled, "One of the best shrinks in the business." The three of them chuckled at the self-deprecating reference to her professional credentials and then they headed off to her office.

The three of them sat abreast, David on one end, Dr. Hightower on the other, and Maggie in between them. The computer screen filled with a hospital bed. The patient's upper torso was elevated, and he peered, smiling, into the camera. On the bed next to him sat a woman holding a young girl, maybe three or four years old. On the other side of the patient was a six- or seven-year old boy. Off screen, a voice that Dr. Hightower and David recognized as Dr. Masters's, could be heard saying, "OK, Family Vassiliack, you're on."

In unison, everyone waved into the camera and said, "Hello, Major Keller." And then the videographer zoomed in on the patient. The close-up shot revealed his distinctly misshapen head. "Sir, I'm going to dispense with normal military courtesy and call you by your first name. David, I am Sergeant First Class Anthony Vassiliack. When we meet sometime in the future, I hope you will call me *Tony*.

That's what my friends call me. My last assignment was with the First Brigade, 101st Air Assault Division. I was part of a joint task force assigned to Kandahar Province, Afghanistan. Dr. Masters has told me about you. Really sorry about you losing your legs." Vassiliack paused for a moment to clear the lump in his throat. "What we have in common is that we were both severely injured in combat." He laughed and then said, "What's different between the two of us is that while you lost your legs, I lost my mind, so to speak." He pointed to his head. "An IED did this. I understand you are as familiar with IEDs as I am." Maggie looked at David, who was nodding. "The damned thing took out part of my brain. Can you believe that? Even more important, can you believe that I am here today talking to you after losing part of my brain? I tell you, David, if it weren't for these doctors and nurses ... " His voice cracked and faded. After a brief pause, Vassiliack found his voice again, "But I don't have to tell you that. You know as well as I do. But here's the thing, David; here's the ironic difference between you and me. You've lost your legs. Doc Masters says prosthesis is a long shot for you, so it's a very real possibility that you'll never walk again. As amazing as it may seem, even with part of my brain gone, they tell me I'll walk out of Walter Reed someday. My issue is that I have no memory of who I am. I mean, if the doctors and nurses hadn't told me that I am Sergeant First Class Anthony Vassiliack, I wouldn't know that. If my friends hadn't told me I like to be called Tony, I wouldn't know that." Vassiliack nodded in the direction of someone out of the camera's field of vision, "Roll it back, will you, Doc?" The field of view expanded, revealing the woman and children again. "This is my wife, Carmen." He reached out and took her hand, "and these are my kids, Anthony, Jr. and Marissa. They are my memory now. I have to trust what they tell me because I can't remember ... "

Dr. Hightower reached over and hit pause as she noticed tears in David's and Maggie's eyes. "Are you both OK? Would you like to stop and talk about this for a minute?"

David looked at Maggie, who took his hand in hers. "It's so very sad," she said to him.

"You OK, Mags?"

She nodded. David said to Dr. Hightower, "No, let's see the rest of it."

The recording picked up right where it had left off: " ... any of my life before the explosion. When they first came to visit me, I didn't believe them. I didn't want to see them. But then Doc Masters made a good point ... a tough point ... he said to me, "Tony, why would these three be here if they didn't love you; if you weren't their husband and their father? Well, I couldn't answer the question. So, we've spent the last three weeks giving me new memories to try and replace the old ones. Those 'old ones,' David, are lost to me forever, the docs think. I'll never get them back. But you know what, it doesn't matter anymore. Carmen and the kids are here now and we are working on it together. Doc Masters tells me you've got an incredible family, an incredible community back where you come from. You've got people who remember you and love you, and the best part is that you can remember who they are. So, here's the bottom line, David: don't take any of that for granted. Please. Give into your memories. Be safe, my friend." The video faded to black.

Dr. Hightower didn't say anything. She got up, turned the computer screen around, and sat down behind her desk. David said, "Dr. Masters doesn't give up, does he?"

Dr. Hightower smiled at both of them and said, "No, he doesn't." She looked at them and leaned forward, placing her palms down on the edge of her desk. "You know what? I think that's about enough for today, and since Maggie's come all this way, why don't I let the two of you have some time together. We'll meet tomorrow morning about ten o'clock, if that's OK with you, David."

He nodded and asked, "OK if I use your restroom, Doc?"

"Sure."

When the bathroom door closed, Maggie leaned in close to Dr. Hightower and asked in a volume barely above a whisper, "Do you know that they think my ex-husband might have been trying to hurt David?"

Dr. Hightower nodded, "I do. PJ called and filled me in. Have you said anything to David?"

"Not a word"

"Can I ask you a favor?"

"Anything."

"Don't say anything to David." She smiled at Maggie. "Sometimes, it's good for us to know something that the patient doesn't. There are no guarantees, mind you. But every now and then we can use bits and pieces of information to stimulate discussion and even memory. I'm hopeful of that with David."

The door to the bathroom opened and David rolled toward them. "Thanks, Doc, for showing us that clip. Do you think if I wrote Sergeant Vassiliack a letter and sent it to Doc Masters, he'd get it to him?" He had a sheepish look on his face. "I guess I need to thank Doc Masters, too. I was pretty shitty with him when I was at Walter Reed."

"I know he would appreciate that, David, and I'm sure Sergeant Vassiliack would, too."

★ ★ ★ ★

As Maggie pushed David back toward the library, she asked, "How can someone survive losing part of their brain?"

David launched into high praise for military docs and the miracles they performed every day. Hearing him talk like that reassured her that he was being truthful about giving up his ideations of suicide. But curiosity was eating away at her. After watching the tape there was no doubt in her mind that she wanted him to remember what happened that night at the boat launch, for her sake and his, too.

They sat in the library, close together while he told her about the book *Tribe* that he was reading. She vowed she would read it as well to help her better understand the deep bond that forms between comrades-in-arms. Then they ate lunch in the hospital cafeteria. Before Maggie knew it, it was one o'clock and she needed to head out for the three-and-a-half-hour trip back to Onekama. She didn't want to. She could have stayed there with him for as long as he wanted her to and she was pretty sure he didn't want her to leave either. He asked if he could "roll" her to her car. She laughed and, of course, said *yes*. She pushed him and they laughed and enjoyed one another's company for these last few minutes together. At the car David said, "Maggie, I've missed you."

Her heart pounded. She didn't know if he was talking about the last three or four days or the last sixteen years, but it didn't really matter in the end. Maggie now knew that she'd never really gotten over David. Before getting in her car she lifted his face up to hers and kissed him deeply. Something inside her was stirring. As for David, he felt himself becoming erect, a sensation he could not remember having occurred since the explosion that took his legs.

32

PARTIAL RECALL

S ince resigning as Manistee County prosecutor, PJ didn't need to keep his phone on twenty-four hours a day, but old habits were hard to break. He'd forgotten to turn it off or at least turn it down, and its ring jolted him out of a solid sleep. As he picked up, he immediately noticed two things. First, it was 3:02 a.m. on July 19 and, second, it was Jill Hightower calling. A surge of adrenaline accompanied his near panic. "Dr. Hightower?"

She could hear and almost feel the urgency in his voice. "Yes, PJ ... "

When a doctor called at this hour of the morning, the automatic assumption was one of bad news. He didn't let her finish what she was about to say before asking, "Is David OK?"

"He is, now. He's resting comfortably, but he's had a rather rough night."

"What happened?" His voice betrayed a rising concern. She tried to reassure him, "David's just fine, PJ. He had another flashback tonight ... "

PJ swung his legs over the side of the bed. Natalie who'd heard the phone ring and could sense her husband's concern, rolled over toward him and asked, "What is it?"

He put his hand over the mouthpiece, "It's David ... he's had another flashback." Returning to the call, he asked, "He didn't harm anyone?"

"No ... no, he didn't harm himself or anyone else. But it's quite remarkable really ... "

"How's that, Jill?"

"He's had a partial recall of what happened that night. I've spent the last hour talking to him. He remembers Ray McCall coming up from behind him. He recalls Ray telling him that he resented him trying to get back with Maggie and he wasn't going to stand for it. Ray dumped him out of his wheelchair and threatened to throw him into the lake. He remembers pulling the gun out of the pouch on the arm of his wheelchair. But after that he goes blank."

PJ was fast coming out of his sleep-addled state, but he repeated a few points back to her, just to be sure he had it all. When she confirmed it, he said, "This is huge."

"Yes, I know. That's why I'm talking to you at this time of the night. She chuckled and then added, "or should I say 'morning.' I knew you'd want to know ASAP. I have an idea and that is the other reason I wanted to call."

"I'm all ears."

"Just so you know, you are the second person I've called about all of this tonight. The first was Dr. Masters. He has so much more experience with these kinds of PTSD-related flashbacks than I do. He agrees with what I am about to suggest to you."

"If you and Dr. Masters agree, then I'm all in, Jill."

"Can you pick up your brother today?"

The suddenness of it stunned him, but he had complete faith in the two of them. "Yeah, sure. I don't know where the prosecutor is going to want to go with this case now that David has recalled at least part of what happened that night. It corroborates the testimony of a key witness. But in the event she still wants to take it to trial, it's important that I ask if you've done everything you need to do as an expert witness testifying on behalf of David?"

"I'm confident that your brother suffers from combat-related PTSD that manifests itself in the form of flashbacks to when he was in combat in Afghanistan and Iraq. Based on his recall tonight, I believe the flashback at the boat ramp could have been caused by Ray McCall's threat to do him bodily harm."

"What about what happened tonight?"

"A nurse was wheeling a cart full of midnight medications. Things were pretty quiet. Most nearly all the patients were asleep, including David. She was directly in front of his ward when a wheel came off the cart and it fell over. The nurse said it made an awful racket. She heard David screaming. She called for help. She and two orderlies managed to restrain him and the floor nurse immediately called me. He was still pretty agitated when I got here, but he kept saying over and over again, 'Maggie. I've got to see Maggie!' Did you know she visited him yesterday here at the hospital?"

"Maggie McCall was there ... to see David?"

"Yes, and here's the thing, PJ; I think Maggie could be the key that unlocks the rest of David's recall on what happened that night. There is something between the two of them, some connection ... "

"Geez, Doc. They were high school sweethearts, but that was a long time ago."

"Has David told you about the dream he had right after the accident?"

"No."

Dr. Hightower recounted it and ended by telling him, "It's very difficult for him to talk about it. He doesn't like to remember anything about that day, but when he talks about that dream, it's like he's a different man. I was really glad when I found her here today visiting with him. We all watched a very powerful video that Dr. Masters sent me. It was another soldier with combat wounds very different than your brother's but still very serious. I watched the two of them as they watched the video together. I have to tell you that David's and Maggie's connection may have languished over many years, but it still exists. He is better when he can talk about her, and today, I would have to say that he is better when she is around him. So, that is why I'd like you to come and get him. Let's get him back home to Onekama where he and Maggie can see one another, where they can be together, and let's see what happens."

"When would you like me there?"

"I'll need the morning to get his discharge arranged. Any time this afternoon will be fine, though."

33

THE TRIAL

PJ sat at the defense table with his brother beside him. As experienced a prosecutor as he was, this was his first time on this side of the courtroom and he could feel a little uneasiness in the pit of his stomach. On the other side were Sylvia Wheeler and the venerable Myles Wingate himself. Wingate's silver hair, thousand-dollar suit, hand-crafted Italian leather shoes, and relaxed, casual manner gave off an aura of experience and wealth beyond anyone else in the room. Before the bailiff called the court to order, Myles spent the time chatting up spectators, mostly reporters, like he was running for office. The case had garnered some national attention. PJ had even heard the rumor that NBC's *Dateline* might be considering the case for one of its shows. Seated in the first row, immediately behind Myles and separated only by a railing, sat Clipper.

PJ gestured across the aisle to Sylvia with his eyebrows and a nod in the direction of Clipper. Sylvia read his gesture, frowned, and simply shrugged. PJ continued to watch Clipper and it didn't take him long to determine that he was an angry man. PJ had him pegged as set on one thing, and only one ... revenge. As he and David waited for the trial to commence, Clipper stared belligerently at the two of them.

Clipper's anger and Myles's cockiness perplexed PJ. He knew Sylvia had no taste for this trial. In fact, she had discussed dismissing the charges after PJ, as part of the discovery process, had told her about David's partial recall of events the night Ray was murdered, an account seemingly corroborated by Charley Sharp. However, she had gotten tremendous pushback from Clipper and Myles, who insisted she take the case to trial. Maybe it was her inexperience, maybe it was the pressure, but there was also a lingering thought that her former boss might just hand these two overconfident windbags a good whoopin'. She felt both honored and humbled that, at the young age of thirty, she had been appointed as the county's prosecuting attorney. She wanted to succeed in the job. But the more she thought about it, the more she realized she would be willing to endure defeat in this case just to see Myles's and Clipper's faces if this trial went the way she thought it might.

They had drawn Judge Walter V. McPeak, the chief judge of the 19th Judicial Circuit Court, as the presiding judge in David's case. PJ had tried many cases in front of McPeak and considered him a fair adjudicator. McPeak had directed the court clerk to empanel a larger than normal *venire,* that pool of possible jurors from whom the jury would be selected. He'd anticipated that *voir dire*, the process where the prosecution and the defense questioned potential jurors to determine which of them would be empaneled, might be a long and drawn-out process. He had already decided that he would be a little more liberal than normal with both sides on their challenges because he had long ago turned down the prosecution's request for a change of venue on the grounds that an impartial jury could not be found. The jury would be composed of fourteen citizens living in Manistee County, two of whom would be empaneled as alternates. McPeak didn't want any appeals to be based on too narrow a jury pool or too restrictive of a *voir dire*.

As it turned out, McPeak had been right. Each side had rapidly ripped through the twelve preemptory challenges allowed in a murder trial. PJ had eliminated another twenty potential jurors on challenges for cause. Sylvia and Myles were near that same number. The fireworks began when

PJ asked the first potential juror if they had ever served in the military. Myles jumped to his feet and objected to the question. PJ countered that his client suffered from PTSD caused by his service in the military. "We will prove that, Your Honor, here in this courtroom." He implored the judge, "I want jurors who understand what my client has been through." McPeak overruled Myles's objection, and the question about military service remained the first question PJ asked each potential juror.

Myles, however, was wily. His first question of the next potential juror was, "Do you consider yourself a Republican or a Democrat?" Of course, PJ immediately objected. McPeak immediately sustained the objection, but Myles wasn't about to give up. "Your Honor, I'll rephrase the question. The father of the victim in this case is a well-known Republican political figure in these parts. Are you familiar with Mr. Clipper McCall's political affiliation and, if so, do you believe that could interfere with any decision you might render in this case?"

Again, PJ was on his feet objecting. McPeak personally hated that politics had to become involved, but Myles's rephrasing of the question made it as valid a point as PJ's about military service. The sword, as they say, cut both ways. He overruled PJ's objection.

They'd been at it almost two days, only seven of the fourteen jurors had been empaneled, and they were just a little over halfway through the pool of potential jurors when Myles asked if the attorneys could approach the bench. "Your Honor, it's quite obvious that we are not going to be able to empanel an impartial jury from Manistee County. I respectively request the court reconsider my earlier petition for a change of venue."

PJ reacted with a strong objection. McPeak, wanting to remain fair and impartial, adjourned court for an hour and took PJ, Sylvia, and Myles to his chambers. Clipper followed Myles like a puppy, but McPeak excluded him from the discussions. "Mr. Wingate, please explain to your client that this is a procedural matter. His presence is neither needed nor appropriate." Clipper retreated after ranting and raving for a brief moment at Myles. When the lawyers completed arguing their points, McPeak advised them he would take matters into consideration and excused them without either side knowing which way the judge would fall on a change of venue.

When he called the courtroom back to order, McPeak soundly dismissed the prosecution's request. "There are still plenty of potential jurors to be examined. I believe there is a jury to be found here, Ms. Wheeler, Mr. Wingate. Let's continue working to find out who they are." He turned to the clerk and directed her to call the next potential juror to the stand.

That decision rattled Myles, who asked that his objection to the judge's decision be made a matter of the trial record. McPeak waved a wary finger at him and responded, "Mr. Wingate, both your pretrial petition and this one are a matter of record. My refusal to grant either is also part of the record. Your stipulation to place your objection to my ruling in the record is redundant and unnecessary. Denied. Now let's move on with jury selection." McPeak briefly considered adding, *unless you choose to try my patience further*, but thought better of it.

Voir dire took nearly a week. When it was all said and done, a jury of five women and seven men was empaneled. Two of them were veterans of military service. One of the women was a minority; two of the men were. Their average age was forty-seven, older than the defendant who was approaching his thirty-sixth birthday. Two were fully retired, eight were missing work to serve on this jury, one was a housewife, and one was currently unemployed. Politically, PJ was pretty sure there was an equal blend of Democrats, Republicans, and Independents. All had answered in the affirmative to PJ's final question, "Do you believe you can form a purely objective opinion of the defendant's guilt or innocence based on information presented to you during this trial?"

On August 15, at ten o'clock, the last juror was empaneled and Sylvia delivered the prosecution's opening remarks, short and to the point:

Ladies and gentlemen of the jury, as unfortunate as the circumstances around the shooting of Ray McCall may be, it will be proven beyond a shadow of a doubt that David Keller, did, on the night of July 1, at the Onekama public boat launch, willfully fire a deadly gunshot into Ray McCall, and later, early in the morning of July 2, fire upon two innocent citizens merely attempting to launch their boat. The defense will attempt to make you believe that other factors were at play: PTSD and self-defense. I ask you to remain objective, even skeptical. The weapon used was illegally obtained, unregistered, and unlicensed. The shooting was fatal to Ray McCall and could have easily been the same for the fishermen. The defendant's valor and service to his country are not the issue facing you. His actions that night and the next morning, and only those, are on trial here.

When Sylvia sat down, PJ observed Myles leaning into her. As he got up to deliver his opening remarks, he could overhear the Lansing lawyer critiquing her delivery and her comments. "What? That's it. Young lady, this was your chance to lay it out for the jury and you've not done that. There's insufficient detail ... " The windbag continued on.

PJ felt sorry for his former protégé. He'd recommended her taking on Myles's help, but he should have foreseen both Myles's and Clipper's narcissism. He should have realized that both of these egotistical sonsuvbitches would want to take over the prosecution's case. While Myles continued to critique Sylvia, PJ began:

Ladies and gentlemen of the jury, I will be as concise as the prosecuting attorney. We admit that my client fired every shot, including the one that killed Ray McCall. Testimony, however, will also prove that while he was doing that my client was flashing back to some combat scenario that he faced in either Afghanistan or Iraq during one of his six combat tours. In the death of Ray McCall, we will prove that my client acted in self-defense, regardless of where his mind may have been at the time of that deadly shot. As to the shots fired at the fishermen, you will hear powerful testimony about the effects of post-traumatic stress disorder, or PTSD as it is often referred to. Your job is to decide if my client is guilty of either charge beyond a shadow of doubt. We will prove to you that there are many shadows to be dealt with for those who suffer from PTSD.

When he was finished, PJ turned away from the jury and looked over at Sylvia, who was still being rated on her performance. His opening remarks had been even shorter than hers and he was glad that he didn't have to listen to Myles's critique of his performance.

McPeak directed, "Very well. The prosecution may call its first witness."

Myles stood and announced in a deep baritone voice, "The prosecution calls Manistee County Sheriff's Deputy Robert Depuy."

McPeak looked at Sylvia, his expression one of confusion. "Ms. Wheeler, what's going on?"

With a calmness that made PJ rather proud of her, Sylvia asked, "Your Honor, may we approach?"

McPeak nodded and motioned for counsel to come forward.

"Your Honor, I know this is a bit unusual, but the victim's father has hired the firm of Wingate, Fogler, and Bush to assist the prosecution in this case."

"And why is that, Ms. Wheeler?"

Sylvia had prepared an answer to this question, "The victim's father wants to ensure that the prosecution presents its best case and has offered to pay all expenses associated with the law firm of Wingate, Fogler, and Bush to assist the prosecuting attorney's office in this case."

McPeak looked at PJ and uttered an ominous, "Ummm ... and is there any objection on the part of the defense?"

PJ likely could have objected for some obscure reason, but recalled that he had told Sylvia to use these guys if she thought they could help even though she was getting some help that she hadn't bargained for. "Uh, no objection, your honor," PJ said.

McPeak grabbed for his gavel and announced, "Court is adjourned for thirty minutes." In his chambers he frantically researched to see if there was precedent for such a thing, but could find none. When he returned to the courtroom, he looked at Myles and said, "For the record, Counselor, please identify who you are and what your interest is in this case."

"Certainly, Your Honor, I am Myles Wingate. My law firm, Wingate, Fogler, and Bush," Myles's arrogant tone rankled McPeak, but the judge hid that well, "has been retained by Mr. Paul McCall, the father of the victim in this case, to assist the prosecution."

McPeak harrumphed, "And your fee is paid entirely by Mr. McCall?"

"Your Honor, respectfully, I don't see ... "

"A matter of court record, Mr. Wingate. Please answer the question." McPeak impatiently interrupted.

Reluctantly Myles nodded and said, "It is, Your Honor."

The judge looked at Sylvia and asked, "Ms. Wheeler, you have approved of Mr. Wingate's assistance in this case?"

The judge was giving her one last chance to separate herself from Myles and Clipper. Myles's firm had been helpful, she had to admit, in preparing pretrial submissions and deposing potential witnesses, etc. However, Myles's uncalled-for and, really, unwanted critique of her opening remarks was, in her opinion, unfair. He'd ended it with, *Let me take this first witness. Listen and learn, young lady.* She was as infuriated as she was belittled, but she did not ever want to hear from Clipper that she hadn't let Myles *work his magic.* Blankly she said to McPeak, "I have, Your Honor."

"Very well, then. This is highly irregular, but I am unable to find any legal precedent that prohibits such assistance. You may proceed, Mr. Wingate."

Dupuy was sworn in; Sylvia glanced over at PJ and shrugged. He continued to feel sorry for the young litigator. They'd talked. They probably shouldn't have, but they had and that fact would never be known to either Myles or Clipper. PJ knew the dilemma she was wrestling with.

By the time Myles finished with Dupuy there was no doubt anywhere in the courtroom that it was David who had done the shooting. Artfully, with a smirk and an air of irreproachable authority, Myles turned to PJ and said, "Your witness, Counselor."

This wasn't the deputy that PJ wanted on the stand. He anticipated Myles's next witness, so he stood and demurely said, "No questions of this witness, Your Honor."

That stunned Myles, but he hid his surprise well. Myles then called Manistee County Sheriff's Deputy Jim Alter. As Alter stepped forward from behind the railing that separated the spectators from the trial's participants, he loomed large. He stood at least six feet, four inches tall. An immaculate uniform covered a rock-hard, flat belly and biceps that stretched the sleeves of his short-sleeved shirt to their max. In fact, PJ half expected the right sleeve to literally burst at its seams as the deputy raised his right arm to be sworn to tell the truth, the whole truth, and nothing but the truth.

Myles's questions were nearly the same as those asked

of Depuy, and Alter's answers were nearly the same as Dupuy's. PJ watched McPeak squirm slightly in his seat. He knew the judge detested unnecessary redundancy in his courtroom. But PJ wanted this witness. In fact, he would have called him as a defense witness, if the prosecution hadn't. PJ was chomping at the bit by the time Myles turned to him and said in a tone of overconfidence that was both annoying and belittling, "Your witness, Counselor."

PJ's first question of Alter was, "You have served in the military?"

"Yes."

"In what capacity?"

"Army staff sergeant. I was an assistant platoon sergeant."

"Did you serve in that capacity in combat?"

Myles decided he'd let this go on long enough. "Objection. Relevance, Your Honor."

The judge looked at PJ but before he could say anything, PJ, who'd anticipated Myles's objection, said, "Your Honor, my next question will get to the relevance of this line of questioning."

"Very well, Mr. Keller, but get to your point quickly. Proceed. Objection overruled."

"I served one tour in Afghanistan and one in Iraq. I was an assistant platoon sergeant during both tours."

"And in the period of time you were in the military did you ever have the occasion to observe someone suffering from PTSD?"

On his feet once again, Myles, more emphatically than the last time, said, "Objection, Your Honor. The witness isn't qualified to answer that question."

McPeak looked at the deputy on the witness stand and asked, "How many years were you in the military?"

"Eight, Your Honor."

"What units?"

"All with the 101st Air Assault Division, including both combat tours. I was a grunt, Your Honor."

The judge smiled, looked at the court recorder, and said, "Let the record reflect that a *grunt* is more correctly called an *infantryman.*" Then he turned to Myles and said, "Objection overruled. The witness may answer the question." Myles sat down slowly and shook his head.

"I've seen it a lot. Every one of them was a combat vet; some were still in theatre ... "

McPeak interrupted the witness, clarifying for the jury again, "By *theatre* I assume you mean that they were *still engaged in combat?*"

"Yes, Your Honor," the deputy said, turning toward the judge. Then, returning to PJ, he added, "They zone out. They are somewhere else, fighting some other fight. Not much you can do except hold them back ... keep them out of the action ... out of harm's way ... until they snap out of it. Sometimes that's just a few minutes and sometimes it can be hours, even days."

"And on the morning you pulled up on the crime scene what did you tell the other deputy with you?"

"I told him I recognized the shooter as David Keller. I was familiar with his war record from the coverage of his arrival back home in Onekama. We were trying to reason with him, but nothing was working. He didn't know us. He didn't trust us. Guys who are having flashbacks are like that. I told the other deputy I thought he was having a flashback and that is when I called the sheriff and asked him to have you come down to the boat ramp. You're his brother. He was going to trust you long before he'd trust either one of us. Turns out, I was right."

"Objection," Myles shouted. "Move to strike that last statement."

McPeak instructed the recorder to strike that last comment by the witness and then told the jury they were to disregard it. But both PJ and Myles knew it was too late. The jury had heard what they'd heard and there was no putting that genie back in the bottle.

Court was adjourned at noon after McPeak advised the jury that they weren't to discuss the case with anyone, including among themselves. They would reconvene at one thirty sharp. McPeak prided himself on punctuality. PJ watched Myles and Clipper leave, talking frantically together. Sylvia trailed behind them, excluded from the conversation until they were in the hallway outside the courtroom. "Gentlemen, I think we need to have a talk before we reconvene. How 'bout my office?"

Myles declined for the two men, but Sylvia calmly said to him, "That may have sounded like a question, Mr. Wingate, but it wasn't. Let me rephrase, 'my office, now.'" And she pointed in that direction.

Minutes later they sat around a conference table in Sylvia's office. She began the discussion, "You two seem to have forgotten that this case is being tried by the prosecuting attorney's office. So after what happened just now on the stand with that last witness, please tell me you're not going to call both of the fishermen to the stand this afternoon."

Incredulously Myles looked at her. "Of course we are. Both of them. He's charged with two counts of assault with a dangerous weapon with intent to kill. The jury needs to hear from both of the men he shot at."

"To what purpose?" Sylvia inquired.

Impatiently Myles replied, "Well, for one thing, it will further prove that David Keller was the shooter ... "

With equal impatience, Sylvia interrupted him, "Mr. Wingate, do you honestly believe that there is a single person who was in that courtroom this morning who doesn't already have it firmly in their mind that David Keller was the shooter? Did you not hear the defense admit in their opening remarks that David was the shooter? All you're doing is trying everyone's patience. Neither one of you know Judge McPeak like I do. I've watched him this morning. You are trying his patience."

Myles got up on his high horse. "Ms. Wheeler, you seem to forget that this is a trial by jury. I don't give a damn about trying the judge's patience. I want to impress upon the jury that David Keller was the shooter." Myles paused for a moment and then added, "I have much more experience with judges and juries than you. That is the primary reason Mr. McCall has asked for my assistance in this matter." He looked to Clipper for support.

Clipper wasn't bashful in giving it. "He's right, Ms. Wheeler. I want those two called this afternoon to testify and I would also like it if you would defer to Myles to do the questioning."

Sylvia was furious. She stood up, put her palms down on the table in front of her, and said, "I couldn't disagree more with both of you. It's a mistake, but it is also obvious to me that neither of you will recognize that fact until it is too late. Do what you will." And with that she turned on her heel and left both of them sitting there.

★ ★ ★ ★

McPeak reconvened right on time. Sylvia had arrived in the courtroom at 1:29 p.m. and took her seat, but said nothing to Myles or Clipper. "Will the prosecution please call your next witness," McPeak said. Stiffly, Sylvia turned her head to Myles, who stood and confidently announced, "Your Honor, we call Bert Chartwell to the stand."

It was familiar territory to Chartwell. During his days as a Manistee County sheriff's deputy, he'd testified plenty of times in court. He took the oath, sat down on the witness stand, and waited for the first question.

"Mr. Chartwell, please tell the court what happened to you on the morning of July 2 of this year."

"I was attempting to put my boat in at the Portage Lake public boat launch in the village of Onekama when we started to take fire. At first, I wasn't sure what was happening, but my fishing buddy came scrambling up to the truck and said someone was shooting at us. As soon as he got in, I hightailed it out of there. As soon as we got to what I thought was a safe distance, I called 911 and reported the incident."

PJ was distracted by McPeak squirming in his seat. He took the opportunity to interject, "Your Honor, in the interest of trying not to waste the court's time, if the prosecution is still attempting to prove that my client was the shooter, we are willing to concede that point."

McPeak turned his attention to Myles, who could feel Sylvia's eyes bearing down on him. "Mr. Wingate?"

"Your Honor, if the court pleases, just a few more questions of this witness."

"Very well, Mr. Wingate, but the defense's stipulation is a matter of court record now. Get on with your point in calling this witness."

Myles asked Chartwell, "Can you identify the shooter?" Myles had not done his homework; if he had, he would have known exactly how an experienced witness like Chartwell would answer that question.

Chartwell answered honestly. "Can't say that I saw him shooting at us. Me and Al were in too much of a hurry to get the hell out of there that morning. But later I saw the sheriff's deputies take the defendant into custody."

Myles was suddenly aware of McPeak's squirming in his chair. He made the decision to back off. "Your witness, Counselor."

PJ thought he might have an opening with Chartwell. It was risky. It was a rookie mistake to ask questions of a witness unless you had some idea about how they would answer them, but ... *what the hell* ... he decided to take it. "Mr. Chartwell, you are retired from the Manistee County sheriff's department, is that correct?"

"Yes, sir," Chartwell responded and then added, "I was a deputy for thirty years."

Myles didn't like him volunteering information like that, but could see no legal grounds for objection.

PJ, playing to the jury in an attempt to make this witness appear even more credible, said, "Thanks for your many years of service, Mr. Chartwell." He gave that just a second to set and then asked, "So, in that time, did you ever observe any of your colleagues whom you suspected might be suffering from PTSD?"

Myles jumped to his feet, "Objection, Your Honor. The witness was a deputy, not a psychiatrist. He isn't qualified to answer that question."

PJ added, "Your Honor, he was a deputy with a lot of experience in a dangerous profession, like my client's. If anything, because of his experience, he is as credible as Deputy Alter."

McPeak thought for a moment. Myles's objection had its point. However, he'd allowed Deputy Alter to testify about his experience in combat with PTSD, and he wanted to be fair but consistent. He rubbed his chin and said, "Overruled. The witness may answer the question."

Sylvia looked over at Myles and shook her head as he sat back down. Leaning in his direction, she advised, "You better not call the other fisherman." Myles did not respond to her, because Clipper was reaching across the rail from behind him and tapping his shoulder.

Chartwell rubbed his chin and confided that, indeed, he had suffered from it himself for a period of time after responding to a horrific traffic accident on US 31 just south of Bear Lake in which an entire family: mother, father, and four kids, had perished after being run off the road by a drunk driver. "My family was about the same age as those kids ... I just couldn't get that out of my mind and it made me angry, out of sorts, every time I pulled a motorist over. That anger carried over to my wife and kids at home."

PJ paused before asking his next question to let the dramatic testimony of the former deputy sink in with the jury. Then he asked, "What did you do, Mr. Chartwell?"

Myles piped up, "Objection, Your Honor. Relevance?"

PJ was quick to respond, "Your Honor, the witness's answer goes to the state of mind of my client after serving six combat tours in Iraq and Afghanistan."

McPeak thought for a moment and then said, "Sustained."

"But, Your Honor ... "

More forcefully this time, McPeak said, "Sustained, Mr. Keller. Rephrase or ask your next question."

PJ smiled at the witness. He'd made a point with the jury. He would have liked to have driven it home, but McPeak wasn't going to allow him to do that, so he looked at the judge and said, "No further questions, Your Honor."

"The witness is excused. Ms. Wheeler, Mr. Wingate, your next witness."

Myles's previous confidence seemed rocked to. He stuttered, "Uh ... uh ... Your Honor ... uh, if the court pleases ... uh ... may Ms. Wheeler and I have a moment to consult?"

"A moment or a brief recess?" McPeak inquired, impatience marking the question.

Myles looked at Sylvia, who appeared calm on the outside. Inside, however, she was feeling justified. Myles had been subdued. She turned to McPeak, "A moment, Your Honor, is all that we need." Sylvia, relishing the upper hand she now held with this jerk, asked her co-counsel, "Got any more bright ideas?" Myles shook his head. "Me neither," Sylvia said, the disgust evident in her voice. Al Harkness was not called to the stand. She said to Myles and Clipper, "Let me handle Dr. Effingham."

Clipper leaned over the rail. "What about this guy Sharp's ex-wives? Call them. This guy is a scum bag. They'll tell the jury that ... discredit him before he even has a chance to testify."

Sylvia looked at Myles and asked, "You haven't told him yet?" Myles just sat there. Sylvia shook her head and answered Clipper, "He might be a scum bag, but he's made a settlement that is satisfactory to the McComb County court. Besides, if you want a mistrial, just call one of the wives to the stand to discredit Sharp before he's even testified and I can guarantee PJ over there will ask for it and McPeak will likely give it to him." She looked at Myles and said, "Am I right, Counselor?" Reluctantly Myles nodded.

Clipper raised his voice, "Myles, dammit ... "

Sylvia saw McPeak raise his eyebrows. She put a hand on his arm, "Cool it, Clipper, or you'll get thrown out of here. Then she turned to McPeak and said, "The prosecution calls Dr. Frederick Effingham, Your Honor."

Sylvia, from the moment she'd met him, had little confidence in Dr. Effingham as an expert witness, but he had been the one that the state had hired to do the forensic competence evaluation on David Keller. His academic credentials were impeccable: undergraduate degree from Boston College; medical degree from Penn State; psychiatric residency at Massachusetts General Hospital. He'd practiced for over fifty years, but was now retired and contracted with the state of Michigan for these types of pro-forma exams as necessary. He was slow moving, requiring a cane to get to the witness stand, overweight, sloppy in appearance, and somewhat cranky. He slowly raised his hand, took the oath, and sat down heavily in the chair. Sylvia didn't want to waste any more of the court's time, so she quickly moved to her point. "Doctor Effingham, you examined Mr. David Keller at the Center for Forensic Psychiatry last month. Please tell the court your findings."

Effingham was equally to the point, "The defendant presents with a clarity of focus that indicates he is fully aware of his location and identity. He also has acute situational awareness. Questioning reveals that he is fully aware of the murder of Mr. Ray McCall, that he is aware of his role in that murder, and that he fully understands what is taking place in these legal proceedings."

Sylvia followed up on his comment. "In your expert opinion, do you believe situational awareness can be influenced by previous traumatic experiences?"

Dr. Effingham adjusted his posture to a more upright position in the witness chair, looked at the jury as if he were a bird about to preen its own feathers, and began, "If you are asking me if the defendant's behavior that evening could be influenced by his previous experiences in combat, I would say that I saw no such evidence presented during the approximately six hours I spent with Mr. Keller."

Sylvia asked him, "So, you have previous experience in dealing with clients who claim that their actions at some particular point in time were dictated by some previous traumatic experience?"

"I do. Over the last decade, which also happens to be that period of time when post-traumatic stress disorder has become a recognized mental disorder, I have worked with dozens of people who claim to suffer from it."

Sylvia responded, "*Claim* to suffer from it, Doctor? Is it safe for me to say that in your professional experience, many who *claim* to suffer from it, don't?"

PJ stood and said, "Objection, Your Honor. The prosecution is leading the witness and the jury away from my client's specific mental state, which is the only mental state this trial should be concerned with."

Sylvia countered, "Your Honor, I assure you that question is simply background. My next question will bring us back to the specifics of this case."

"Very well, Ms. Wheeler. Continue. Objection overruled. The witness will answer the question."

"My professional experience is ... " He glanced over at the jury again to be sure they were listening to him. "Many claim to suffer from PTSD, but most do not. In my professional opinion, it has become a trite excuse for erratic, socially unacceptable behavior."

"And is that what the defendant is doing? Is he trying to cover up the murder of Ray McCall by first claiming that he couldn't remember anything, but now suddenly claiming that while he can't remember pulling the trigger that fired the shot killing McCall, he can remember being threatened by him?"

"Your Honor, I object ... " PJ angrily pleaded.

McPeak interrupted him, "Overruled. The witness is a credentialed expert, Mr. Keller. He can answer that question."

PJ sat back down. If he was going to attack Dr. Effingham's credibility, it would have to be done during cross-examination.

Dr. Effingham was short and to the point, "Yes."

"What makes you so sure?"

"First of all, my experience is that partial recall of an incident is very rare. In fact, it is the first time a client has ever tried that trick with me. Second, Mr. Keller presents as very stable mentally. Thus, I conclude that he is trying to cover up his behavior by claiming to suffer from PTSD."

Sylvia turned to PJ and said, "No further questions. Your witness."

McPeak interrupted, "Counselors, it's four o'clock. Court is adjourned for today. We will resume again at nine tomorrow morning."

★ ★ ★ ★

PJ, Dr. Hightower, and David sat around the table at The Blue Fish Restaurant on River Street in Manistee, just a few blocks from the courthouse. PJ wanted to go over events as he saw them occurring the next day. "Jill, what's your take on Dr. Effingham?"

She shook her head. "Not good. Remember our conversation about *sometimes patients can fool us?*" PJ nodded.

"Well, Dr. Effingham is one of those shrinks that avoids being fooled by rarely committing to a diagnosis that can be elusive. PTSD is definitely one of those, but it was a recognized metal disorder in the DSM-IV and its criteria have been further defined in the DSM-V." She looked at David and said, "You have a legitimate case of PTSD. I will testify to that, and we have a corroborating deposition from Dr. Masters at Walter Reed. Between the two of us we have much more experience with the disorder than does Dr. Effingham, despite the way he presented himself to the court today. He is not the definitive expert on PTSD that he portrays himself as being."

Cocktails arrived and everyone relaxed for a minute and talked about the lovely view out of the window next to their table that overlooked the Manistee River about half a mile before it flowed into Lake Michigan. As dinner arrived, PJ said, "OK, here's the batting order tomorrow. I'm pretty sure Dr. Effingham is the prosecution's last witness. So, after I cross him in the morning, it's our turn. First will be Charley Sharp. That may take a while. They will try and attack his credibility, but, somehow, he's worked out a settlement with the McComb County Family Court. Bill LeVault at the Onekama Hardware Store has brought him back as a full-time employee and is allowing him to live upstairs above the store. And, here's perhaps the best point: Charley is attending Gamblers Anonymous meetings twice a week. He has a sponsor and everything. He's become a model citizen, believe it or not. They can try to get to him, but I can get all of this out first thing and maybe that will throw them off track. After Charley I'll call Rose Davenport, the waitress from Shirley's. She'll corroborate that Charley and Ray were meeting and Ray was giving him money. Then it's your turn, Jill." She nodded. PJ turned to David, "Then, I think you should take the stand ... " There was a long pause. David looked at Dr. Hightower, who nodded at him. The tenuous doctor-patient relationship between them had morphed into something better after the two had an honest conversation about Maggie's positive impact on his mental state.

"OK. If you think that's best."

PJ offered, "I do. I don't know if Sylvia will cross-examine you or if it will be Wingate. But you can handle whichever one of them takes you on." PJ put his hands on the edge of the table and leaned in his brother's direction, "David, you aren't crazy, but you do suffer from PTSD." David looked at Dr. Hightower, who, again, was nodding. "Don't be afraid to talk about that on the stand tomorrow. OK? I thought one of the best moments today was when the jury heard and saw how PTSD impacted Bert Chartwell. I'm convinced they are sympathetic to the disorder despite what Dr. Effingham had to say about it."

★ ★ ★ ★

The bailiff called the court to order promptly at nine o'clock the next morning. Judge McPeak took his seat, and as Dr. Effingham moved laboriously to the stand, he reminded him he was still under oath. When he plopped down in the chair, McPeak looked at PJ and said, "Your witness, Counselor."

"Thank you, Your Honor." PJ turned to Dr. Effingham and asked, "Doctor Effingham, please tell the jury what the DSM-V is."

The question seemed to surprise him, but after a few rather uncomfortable moments he began, "The DSM is a guide ... "

"Doctor," PJ interrupted, "please tell us what the letters DSM stand for."

"Uh ... uh ... well, you know I am so familiar with the book ... I reference it almost daily ... uh ... but, I'm not sure ... "

PJ thought, *some expert witness,* and then said,

"The Diagnostic and Statistical Manual of Mental Disorders ... DSM ... isn't that it?"

Dr. Effingham began to backtrack to cover up his embarrassment and inability to recall the exact full title. About thirty seconds into his answer, McPeak interrupted him and said, "Doctor, the question requires a simple *yes* or *no*. Please answer the question."

"Uh ... yes ... of course, your honor. Yes, that is what DSM stands for."

"And the Roman numeral V simply means that it is the fifth edition of the DSM?"

He nodded and that prompted McPeak to say, "Doctor Effingham, please *answer* the question."

"Yes, that's correct."

PJ continued, "You mentioned that you refer to it daily and you also mentioned that you have had dozens of patients who claim to be suffering from PTSD. So, let's begin with, is PTSD a mental disorder recognized in the DSM-V?"

"It is, yes."

"And of the dozens of patients you have dealt with, exactly how many of them have you actually diagnosed with PTSD?"

Myles stood up. Sylvia looked at him speculatively, but he persisted. "Objection, Your Honor. Relevance."

PJ shot back to Myles, "I have a series of questions, Your Honor, that, providing the witness answers honestly ... "

Myles objected again, "Your Honor, that comment is uncalled for. The witness is under oath."

"Sustained," Judge McPeak said and glared at PJ. "Be careful, Counselor. Sustained ... the jury will disregard the defense's remark about the witness's honesty. But, for the moment I will allow the defense to continue its line of questioning. Mr. Wingate, your first objection is overruled."

PJ turned back to the witness. "Thank you, Your Honor. So, Doctor Effingham, how many patients have you actually diagnosed with PTSD?"

He puffed himself up. "None. I have never diagnosed a patient with PTSD."

"Out of *dozens* of patients, you have never diagnosed a single case of PTSD?" PJ's inflection was one of incredulity.

"That is correct," Dr. Effingham announced confidently. "It is a complex disorder."

That part of his answer offered the perfect segue into PJ's next question. "Ah, yes, Doctor. Please tell the court exactly how many criteria must be considered when making a diagnosis of PTSD?"

"Well, without the DSM right here in front of me I can't be ... "

PJ interrupted him, "Come now, Doctor, if you've denied *dozens* of patients the diagnosis of PTSD, then surely you must know ... "

"Eight ... there are eight criteria to be considered in such a diagnosis," he interrupted back.

"And then for each criterion there is a list of ways, I believe they are called, by which the clinician may determine that a patient could meet any of the eight criteria. Is that right, Doctor?"

"Yes, that's correct. And all eight of the criteria must be met before PTSD can be confirmed as a diagnosis."

"So, it is as you have said, complex?"

"Very much so."

"And you said that you examined the defendant for a total of six hours?"

"Yes, that is correct."

"Is six hours sufficient time to make a clinical diagnosis of such a complex mental disorder?"

Myles jumped up again, and theatrically, plaintively this time said, "Objection, Your Honor. Dr. Effingham is a recognized expert. While the DSM-V may lay out the criteria for the diagnosis, if six hours is all Dr. Effingham needed to make his diagnosis, or in this case, lack of diagnosis, then the defense's question is moot."

PJ offered, "Your Honor, I'm trying to draw a comparison here between the time Dr. Effingham, in his capacity as an examiner for the state and as an expert witness in this trial, has spent with my client versus the amount of time Drs. Masters and Hightower have spent with him."

McPeak looked at Myles, shook his head and said, "Seems relevant to me, Mr. Wingate. Objection overruled. The witness will answer the question."

Dr. Effingham looked confused, so PJ asked again, "Is six hours a sufficient period of time to spend with a patient when making such a complex diagnosis like PTSD?"

"Yes, I believe it is, sir."

PJ turned to the jury and said, under his breath, but loud enough for everyone in the courtroom to hear, "Well, it's not."

Myles roared, "Judge ... "

McPeak interrupted Myles. With a scolding edge to his voice, the judge said, "Mr. Keller, do not do that again in this courtroom, or I will hold you in contempt of court. You know as well as I do that those kind of sidebar comments are inadmissible." He turned to the jury, "You will ignore Mr. Keller's assertion. Now, proceed, Mr. Keller."

Sheepishly, PJ looked first to the jury and then to the judge. "No further questions, Your Honor."

Sylvia announced, "The prosecution rests, Your Honor."

McPeak turned to PJ and said, "Call your first witness, Mr. Keller."

Charley Sharp took the stand. He was wearing a black suit. The trousers were a bit too long, the jacket was a little short in the sleeves, but both were neatly pressed. His shirt was a bit too large at the neck, but a solid red tie knotted in a perfect Windsor knot took attention away from the collar's ill fit. PJ had seen him in the courthouse hallway this morning before court resumed and complimented him on his appearance.

"Thanks, Mr. Keller," Charley had replied. "Mr. LeVault took me to the Goodwill store in Manistee yesterday and we got this suit." He reached up with one hand and slightly adjusted the knot in the tie. "Wallace Jackson gave me this tie to wear. It's the one he had on the night we first met." He looked down rather shamefully. "He tied the knot in it for me. I just slipped it over my head and pulled it tight. He told me it was for good luck. I can't remember the last time I had a suit and tie on. Feels kind of ... " Charley hesitated, looking for the right word, and then said, " ... feels kind of respectable." PJ had patted him on the shoulder and said, "*Respectable* is a good thing, Charley."

PJ wasted no time in getting the defense rolling. "Mr. Sharp, please tell the court about the work you did for Mr. Ray McCall in the immediate few months before his death."

The testimony was rehearsed. Charley knew what to say and had been coached on exactly how to say it and he delivered his testimony flawlessly ending with, "Ray McCall paid me to keep tabs on his ex-wife Maggie McCall. He wanted to know who was seeing her, how often ... things like that."

"Why did he want to know these things, Mr. Sharp?" PJ led him in the direction he wanted him to go.

"He was crazy jealous of her. He told me that they were just going through a rough patch. Now mind you he was telling me this after they'd already been divorced. When he told me about the Chicago lawyer that he'd almost killed ... "

"Elaborate on that, Mr. Sharp, if you would, please." And when Charley related what Ray had done, all hell broke out in the courtroom. From his seat in the gallery's first row, just behind Myles, Clipper jumped up and shouted, "You lyin' sonuvabitch ... "

McPeak slammed his gavel down and began shouting himself, "Sit down, Mr. McCall, or I will have you removed from this courtroom." The bailiff was already moving in Clipper's direction. Myles stood up and put his hands on his client's shoulders and pushed him back down. McPeak admonished, "Mr. Wingate, if your client does that one more time, I will have him ejected from the courtroom for the remainder of these proceedings. Is that clear?"

Myles nodded, "Yes, Your Honor." He then turned his attention to the still-distraught Clipper.

PJ continued, "Did Ray McCall confess to anything else that he had done in one of these apparent fits of jealous rage?"

"He told me he'd burned down the Webers' house."

That likely would have led to Clipper's ouster had not Myles still been ministering to a near-hysterical client. He continued to keep Clipper seated, but Clipper kept saying, "Myles, you can't let him get away with that. He's lying. He's a damned liar. Do something about him."

PJ was watching the jury focusing on Myles and Clipper. He wanted to be sure they heard what Charley had just said, so he waited until a modicum of order had been restored in the courtroom and then asked the question again. This time he was sure the jury heard Charley.

PJ continued to ask probing questions about the business arrangement between Charley and Ray. Several times PJ saw Myles put his hand on Clipper's arm and bear down. When PJ wasn't watching Clipper, he was watching the jury and it was his considered opinion that Charley was a credible witness and the case for self-defense was shaping up nicely. When Charley was finished, PJ turned to Sylvia and said, "Subject to redirect, the defense has no further questions of this witness."

Myles rose, walked toward the witness stand, buttoning his suit coat as if it was armor and he was preparing for war. He got as close to the low partition in front of the witness stand as he could, placed his hands on it, and leaned over to where his face was a scant foot from Charley's. PJ stood and objected, "Your Honor, Mr. Wingate is clearly trying to intimidate the witness."

McPeak looked at Myles. "Sustained. Mr. Wingate, please respect the witness's personal space." Myles harrumphed, but backed a few feet away and straightened up before he asked his first question, "Mr. Sharp, are you married?"

PJ predicted this would be the first thing the prosecution would try to attack in discrediting his witness. He barked, "Objection, Your Honor. Relevance?"

"The question goes to the witness's credibility, Your Honor," Myles shot back. "This first question is merely background."

McPeak was wary, but he gave Myles the benefit of the doubt. "Overruled. The witness will answer."

Charley had been prepared for this question. He and PJ had gone over his answer. "I am not currently married. I have been married twice before. Both wound up in divorce."

Smugly, Myles continued, "And do you have children by either of these marriages?"

"I have two children by each marriage." PJ was pleased that Charley was sticking to the script.

"And isn't it true that you have been charged with felony failure to pay child support?

"It is."

"And how is it, Mr. Sharp, that you are here today in this courtroom as a witness for the defense, rather than the defendant in a family court hearing in McComb County?"

"I have reached a settlement in both of those cases that is satisfactory to the McComb County prosecutor and to the court."

"Tell us exactly what that settlement is, if you would, Mr. Sharp."

PJ jumped to his feet this time. "Objection, Your Honor. Mr. Sharp is not on trial here. The settlement in McComb

County is a matter of public record. Mr. Wingate I'm sure already knows what it is. All he is doing is badgering the witness with this line of questioning."

"Your Honor," Myles smugly replied, "These questions go to the character of this witness."

McPeak looked at him and asked, "Mr. Keller has a good point about the witness not being the one on trial. Where are you going with this line of questioning, Mr. Wingate?"

"In his opening remarks, Mr. Keller said to the jury that they must decide guilt or innocence beyond a reasonable doubt. I believe Mr. Sharp's history casts reasonable doubt upon his credibility as a reliable witness, Your Honor, and these questions demonstrate that ... as long as the witness answers them honestly."

PJ immediately shouted, "Move to strike that last comment, Your Honor. The witness is under oath." But as had been when PJ used this ploy, the words were already out there and one thing was for sure, Charley did not have a sterling record of honesty and integrity.

McPeak immediately instructed the court recorder to strike the comment and cautioned the jury to disregard it, but then overruled PJ's earlier objection. "The witness will answer the question."

"I pay a monthly stipend to each of my ex-wives of three hundred dollars a month, plus an additional three hundred dollars a month until the six thousand I owe each has been brought up to date." He turned to McPeak and said, "I pay twelve hundred dollars a month, Your Honor. Mr. LeVault at the Onekama Hardware Store lets me live above the store rent-free in return for me keeping an eye on things when we're closed. He pays me fifteen hundred dollars a month for working there. That leaves me with three hundred dollars a month to live on. I can do it, Your Honor, as long as I stay away from the casino."

Myles seized on that. "Do you have a gambling problem, Mr. Sharp?"

"I do. I always will. I'm like an alcoholic, I guess. But I've joined Gamblers Anonymous ... "

Myles rudely interrupted him, not wanting the jury to get any ideas that the man might be at all credible. "Thank you, Mr. Sharp. Tell us, where did you get the money to pay off half of the arrears you owed your ex-wives?"

PJ rose again. "Objection, Your Honor. Relevance?"

"Your Honor, I have read the McComb County Family Court record. It discloses a payout of twelve thousand dollars, six thousand to each ex-wife, with a balance of six thousand dollars remaining to each of them, but it does not disclose the source of that twelve thousand dollars that has been paid. For all we know, Mr. Sharp has come by that money in some nefarious manner." Turning to PJ, Myles puffed himself up and offered, "I would certainly hope that the money is not in any way connected to defense counsel."

PJ, furious now, angrily replied, "Your Honor, that remark is slanderous."

McPeak, sensing the tension level between the opposing counsels was reaching a dangerous level, banged his gavel and ordered, "Approach." The two attorneys stepped toward the bench. "Do either of you know for sure where the defendant got that much money?" Both shook their heads and responded that they did not. "Well, then, Mr. Keller, the court would like to know." Myles offered, "Your Honor, I will rephrase the question." That made PJ immediately wary, but he sensed that he needed to deescalate. McPeak motioned for them to return to their places and then announced, "Restate your question to the witness, Mr. Wingate."

"Yes, Your Honor," Myles said, continuing, "Isn't it true that the twelve thousand dollars you received was in return for your testimony for the defense in this case?"

Charley looked at PJ with a deer-in-the-headlights look. PJ simply shrugged, because he didn't really know where the hell Charley had come up with that money either, even though it was something he should have known. Inwardly he was kicking himself in the ass. Charley turned to the judge and said, "Mr. LeVault gave it to me. It's an interest-free loan. I signed papers. He says I can pay him as much as I can each month, but that I can't miss any of the payments to my ex-wives. The loan papers also say that if I get caught gambling, whatever I might owe him at the time is due right then or else he will take me to court. I haven't started to make any payments yet on the loan, but I've started to look for a part-time job. I'll use those wages to help pay Mr. LeVault back. So, I can't screw up." Charley began to tear up.

Myles saw the jury react to the tears. He couldn't get Charley off the stand soon enough. "No further questions."

But PJ wasn't going to let the opportunity pass. He stood and said, "Redirect, Your Honor."

McPeak nodded and said, "Proceed, Mr. Keller."

"Mr. Sharp, it seems that you have turned to a new chapter in your life as a result of all of this, wouldn't you say?"

Myles roared, "Objection! Relevance?"

McPeak ruled, "Sustained."

PJ looked at Charley, who was wiping tears from his cheeks. He turned to the jury and gave a sly smile, "No further questions, Your Honor."

"Call your next witness, then, Mr. Keller."

"The defense calls Rose Davenport." Once again, Rose's testimony was well rehearsed and well delivered. She corroborated Charley's story that he would meet with Ray at Shirley's Restaurant. She testified that on one occasion she'd seen Ray give him money. No, she couldn't see how much, but it was multiple bills. On another occasion she'd seen Charley take an envelope from Ray. She assumed it also contained money. PJ asked her about anything else she'd seen that seemed odd to her. She told the court about seeing Ray slam his fist down on the table once as if he was angry at Charley and then offered to the court that she didn't like either of them very much. "Ray," she said, "wouldn't leave a decent tip if his life depended on it, and the other guy hit on me once." Myles objected on the grounds of relevance and McPeak sustained his objection, but, once again, no one could be sure how much the jury members would actually disregard as the judge instructed.

Myles's firm had hired a private investigator to take a good look at her. The guy had a "source" which, for the right price, even accessed Rose's bank accounts, but all they were able to find was that she was a single mom living barely above the poverty line and paycheck to paycheck. There was nothing to attack, so neither Sylvia nor Myles cross-examined Rose.

★ ★ ★ ★

PJ had to suppress a laugh as he watched McPeak, Myles, Clipper, and nearly every other male in the courtroom perk up as Dr. Jill Hightower stood and strode to the stand. Her long, blonde hair was pulled together in a ponytail that fell to just between her shoulder blades. Its color was the perfect complement to her suntan developed over the course of the summer playing in a local Ann Arbor women's beach-volleyball league. Dressed in a skirt that came to exactly the right length to appear both feminine and professional, a summer blouse that was both comfortable and colorful, and heels of a height that were high enough to accentuate her athletic look but not so high as to appear unprofessional, she took the stand. In the heels, PJ guessed she stood about six feet, six inches tall. Sitting down, she crossed her long legs and smiled at PJ.

He began by offering her qualifications as an expert witness. "Your Honor, if the court pleases, Dr. Hightower holds her undergraduate degree from the University of Notre Dame, her medical degree from the University of Michigan, and her residency in psychiatric medicine was at Riverside Medical Center, in Columbus, Ohio." Then, turning to her, he asked, "Doctor Hightower, you are now the chief of psychiatric medicine at the Veterans Hospital in Ann Arbor, Michigan, is that correct?"

"Yes, that's correct."

"And Mr. David Keller has been a patient of yours?"

"Mr. Keller *is* a patient of mine."

"Doctor Hightower, for the record you have treated him during his rehabilitation from the injury in which he lost his legs, and then, most recently, after the unfortunate incident involving him and Ray McCall in Onekama. Is that correct?"

"It is."

"Could you estimate for the court the number of hours you have devoted to his care during these two periods of time?"

"Yes, I would estimate that David and I have spent in excess of a hundred and fifty hours together over the last three or four months, talking about his mental state of mind."

"And have you conferred with other doctors who have treated him for the same mental disability as you?"

"I have talked extensively via phone and email with Dr. Philomena Goldstein, the chief of psychiatric medicine at Landsthul Regional Military Medical Center in Germany, and with Dr. Robert Masters, chief of psychiatric medicine at Walter Reed National Military Medical Center."

"Could you tell the court if you, Dr. Goldstein, or Dr. Masters have reached a diagnosis?"

"Yes. In light of what each of us has observed while David

was under our care, the three of us have each diagnosed him with post-traumatic stress disorder stemming from his involvement in combat operations in Iraq and Afghanistan."

"Could you tell the court what led you to this diagnosis?"

"Certainly. My diagnosis is based upon my observation of him following his referral to me by Dr. Masters. That diagnosis has been further reinforced after an incident that occurred during his most recent hospitalization following his involvement in the shooting of Ray McCall."

"Would you describe that incident to the court, please, Doctor?"

"A wheel came off of a medicine cart as it was being wheeled past his ward. The loud crash occurred in the middle of the night and it startled David, who had been sound asleep. The event caused him to flash back. Unexpected loud noises are a very common trigger among patients who suffer from PTSD."

"Are there other things that could serve as such a tripwire?"

"Yes, absolutely. One such thing could be being threatened by someone."

"Do you believe this could have happened to the defendant?"

"Objection," Myles blurted out without giving a reason for it.

McPeak looked at him quizzically, expecting to be given some reason for his objection and when none was forthcoming, the judge said, "Mr. Wingate, she *is* an expert witness and I am not a mind reader. Either give me a reason for your objection or withdraw it."

Resignedly, Myles sat down and said, "Withdrawn, Your Honor."

McPeak smiled at her, "Proceed, Dr. Hightower."

"As David was coming out of the flashback, I was seated next to his bedside. He suddenly turned his head toward me and said, 'I remember.' I asked, 'What do you remember, David?' and he replied, 'Ray McCall came at me. He threatened to throw me into the lake.' I delved a little deeper to see if he could remember the rest of what happened that night, but it all ended as he and Ray were apparently struggling and David was tipped out of his wheelchair."

"You heard Dr. Effingham testify that he has never seen partial recall of an event occur. Have you seen it before, Doctor Hightower?"

"I have not, but the next morning, after David's partial recall of the shooting incident, I spoke with Dr. Masters at Walter Reed. He told me it's rare, but he has seen it on several occasions."

"I see," PJ said. "Will you tell the court how many years of experience you have in dealing with veterans who may or may not be suffering with PTSD?"

"I have worked at the VA Hospital in Ann Arbor since completing my residency in psychiatry twelve years ago. In that time, I've worked with hundreds of veterans suffering from PTSD, some of it not even service-related. It's a legitimate mental disorder, and people who suffer from it lead diminished lives until they are able to get help."

PJ turned to McPeak and held up a document. "Your Honor, the defense requests that this trial deposition be entered into evidence as Defense Exhibit One."

McPeak looked at the prosecution's table. "You have a copy of this?"

Sylvia answered, "We do, Your Honor."

The judge looked at PJ, "Very well, Mr. Keller, so admitted."

PJ turned to the jury. "This trial deposition was obtained from Dr. Robert Masters of Walter Reed National Military Medical Center, in which Dr. Masters was examined and cross-examined by myself and an associate from Mr. Wingate's law firm. In it he discloses that he has been a military psychiatrist for nearly twenty years ... almost twice as long as Dr. Hightower. He measures the number of patients with PTSD that he has treated in the thousands and in this deposition, he advises that he has diagnosed my client as suffering with it.

"Doctor Hightower, please tell the court if you agree with Dr. Masters's diagnosis of my client."

"Dr. Masters is a recognized expert in the area of PTSD. I certainly agree with his diagnosis in this case."

PJ looked at the jury and then back to the witness stand. "No further questions of this witness, Your Honor, subject to redirect."

"Very well, Mr. Keller. Your witness, Ms. Wheeler, Mr. Wingate."

Myles stood, but with this witness he did not attempt intimidation. He stood at the prosecution's table and asked, "Doctor Hightower, were you aware that the defendant bought a gun at the Ann Arbor Gun and Knife Show last April, while he was under your care?"

"I was not aware of it at the time, no. But I am now aware that he in fact did do that."

"You are aware that he bought this gun illegally?"

"I am now, yes."

"Yet, you signed his release from the hospital in June."

"I did, yes."

"Would you have done that had you known about the gun?"

"Certainly not."

"So, would you admit that Mr. Keller rather fooled you into thinking that he was mentally ready to be released from your care last spring?"

Reluctantly, Dr. Hightower nodded and said, "Yes, unlike other medical fields, psychiatry isn't ... "

Myles didn't want to let her explain any further and rudely interrupted, "So could he not be fooling you with this partial recall and story about the deceased threatening him at the boat ramp?"

"He is not."

Myles smugly turned to the jury, his one and only seed of doubt planted exactly where he wanted it to be, as he announced, "He fooled you once, Doctor."

PJ was on his feet objecting. McPeak immediately sustained it. Myles, still smiling at the jury confidently, said, "No further questions. Thank you, Doctor Hightower."

★ ★ ★ ★

PJ did not sleep well the night before the trial's third and what he hoped would be its final day. On his mind was the witness he would put on the stand at nine o'clock, his brother, David. He knew David wasn't crazy and that he suffered from PTSD. He knew that Dr. Hightower was making progress with David. And he knew that David's and Maggie's relationship was beginning to blossom and that had had a very positive effect on David's mental state. So much so, in fact, that PJ honestly believed that any thoughts of suicide were no longer a part of David's thinking. His challenge tomorrow was going to be to present his brother as a man who was deeply wounded both inside and out as a result of his service to his country, as a man who was victimized by Ray McCall, and as a man who did not present any kind of threat to society no matter how violent his actions at the boat dock may have been. He wanted the jury to believe that David had done what he did in total self-defense, including the gunshots at the fishermen, because he thought he was shooting at approaching Taliban or Al Qaeda fighters. He'd gone over some of the questions he would ask his brother once he was on the witness stand. He'd used Natalie to play the roles of Sylvia and Myles. She'd asked David a series of questions PJ anticipated the prosecution would ask him during their cross-examination. But there was one series of questions that he had not gone over with his brother. He was holding them back, only to be used if necessary, and he earnestly hoped that would not be the case.

★ ★ ★ ★

"The defense calls retired Major David Keller to the stand." It was the first time in the trial that anyone referred to David using his rank. From the beginning of his testimony, PJ wanted David to be perceived by the jury as a man who'd served his country with courage and distinction. The witness stand, elevated about six inches above the floor of the courtroom, sat next to McPeak's bench and had no ramp for disabled access. The bailiff pointed to a spot on the floor directly in front of it. David positioned his wheelchair there facing the attorneys, raised his right hand at the direction of the bailiff, and was sworn in.

David also had not slept well the night before. He was confident at this point that the jury believed he had murdered Ray McCall in self-defense, but he wasn't at all sure that they were going to just simply forgive him for killing him. There was, in his mind, the matter of his obtaining the gun illegally, and neither he nor PJ could read the jury well on the importance of that in their minds. He also wasn't sure about the PTSD thing either. Dr. Hightower had been superb, but Myles had opened that shadow of a doubt right at the end of her testimony, that shadow about how he'd played her during his recuperation at the Ann Arbor VA. In the pit of his stomach he felt a jolt of adrenaline. There was a lot at stake with his testimony today.

PJ began, "Let's get right to the point here, Major Keller. Tell us what you remember about the night of July 1 and the morning of July 2 as it relates to the death of Ray McCall."

As they had rehearsed, David unflinchingly turned his

head toward the jury. Everything about him from the waist up spoke "leader." His jaw was rigidly square. His clean-shaven face was tan from his long-distance "rolls" around the highways and byways surrounding Onekama. His hair was neatly trimmed and the flecks of silver on the sides gave him a distinguished look. His shoulders were broad and square. His tanned hands were steady and his voice was an unwavering pitch somewhere between a deep baritone and base. "I had gone down to the public boat dock in Onekama around ten o'clock at night. It had become my habit. It's only about a hundred meters from my front door and it's the perfect spot to reflect and watch the sun set over Portage Lake, the channel, and Lake Michigan. I hadn't been there very long when I heard someone call to me from behind. I thought I was alone, so the sudden interruption startled me. I swung my chair around to see who it was. At first, I didn't recognize him, until he identified himself as Ray McCall. He babbled something about me trying to take Maggie, his ex-wife, away from him. None of it was making much sense. I thought he was drunk or on something; he said he wanted to see if I could swim, and then he lunged at me. From that point on, things happened quickly. I was sure if he got me into the water, he would make sure I wouldn't get out alive. We struggled. My wheelchair tipped over, but as I was fall-ing out, I managed to grab a handgun I had in the pouch on one of the handles. From the time the gun filled my hand, I have no memory of what happened after that ... until you showed up. I remember giving you the gun. I remember going to the hospital in Manistee, but during those first twenty-four hours after the shooting I was back and forth a lot ... in and out of the flashback."

"Tell us about your relationship with Ms. McCall."

"There's really nothing to tell. Maggie ... Ms. McCall ... and I are old friends. We were close once in high school ... " The secret of Jack never even came close to being revealed. "Then I left home to attend the military academy. The army became my life until ... " he swept his hands across the stumps of his legs, " ... until this happened. I came back to Onekama because that is where my family is. Yes, I've seen Maggie since I got back. We've talked, but it's just two old friends reconnecting. There was really nothing for Ray McCall to be jealous of. Besides, they were divorced. Maggie could do whatever she wanted to do."

Myles objected on the grounds that this was a personal opinion and should be struck from the record. Somewhat reluctantly, McPeak sustained and directed that the last remark be struck.

"So, Major, this happened at 10:00 p.m. on July 1. That boat ramp at the public park in Onekama is busy during that time of the year. There was no one around to see or hear what took place between you and Mr. McCall. Is that correct?"

"No one that I saw. I purposely waited until all the boat trailers were gone from the park before I went down to the dock. Like I said, I went down there to reflect. I really didn't want anyone around."

"The gunshot ... no one heard it?"

David looked at his brother and smiled, "Apparently not. Look, it's summer in Onekama. There are fireworks going off almost every night, but especially that close to the fourth of July. I'll be honest, they spooked me at first ... loud bangs just don't set well with guys like me that suffer from PTSD. I really had to talk myself down when I first settled into my place. So, I think anyone that might have heard the gunshot just thought it was a firecracker going off ... "

"Objection, Your Honor. Speculation," Myles interjected. "Move to strike."

PJ did not respond. The point had been made. "Sustained. Strike the witness's last remark. The jury will disregard."

PJ turned to Myles and said, "Your witness."

Again, Myles did not try intimidation. He knew it wouldn't work on this witness, and besides, he didn't want to be seen by the jury as trying to intimidate a person with a disability. Standing at the prosecution's table, Myles asked, "What prompted you to buy a gun at the Ann Arbor Gun and Knife Show?"

David gave only a half-truthful answer, "For the last twelve years, I've always had a gun at my side. It just made me feel more comfortable."

"Come now, Major. There must be another reason ... "

PJ rose to his feet and objected, "Your Honor, the witness answered the question."

"Your Honor, with respect, if the witness merely wanted the gun because it made him feel more comfortable, then why did he buy it illegally?" *Gotcha,* Myles thought.

McPeak looked at PJ and said, "The prosecution has a point. I'll allow the further questioning of motive."

David felt the adrenaline surge, but he couldn't bring himself to divulge the real reason he'd bought the gun ... not to this asshole ... not in this courtroom, no matter how high the stakes might be. "I was an in-patient at the VA Hospital. I couldn't bring the gun on the grounds of the hospital ... " It was weak and everyone in the courtroom knew it.

Turning to the jury, Myles moved in for the kill, "We know you bought the gun prior to your release from the hospital. Dr. Hightower has testified that she did not know about the purchase until your most recent hospitalization. If comfort was all you were seeking, why be so secretive; why so ... " he paused here for some dramatic effect, "why be so *devious?*" It was the way he said the word that raised the hackles on David's neck, and PJ's as well. There was an answer, but David would not divulge it. Myles had planted another important seed of doubt with this jury and there was only one way PJ knew that he could dig it out and end its potential growth. Theatrically, Myles waited just the right amount of time and then, when David didn't answer, Myles turned triumphantly to the jury and said, "Isn't it true you used guns for the last twelve years to kill people ... "

PJ shouted, "Objection ... "

McPeak didn't wait for a reason; he immediately cut Myles off. "Mr. Wingate, stop right there."

Myles shut up, but looked at the jury with his patented smug smirk. "No further questions, Your Honor."

McPeak turned to PJ and said, "Counselor."

"Your Honor, the defense would like to redirect."

McPeak nodded.

This was going to be one of the toughest things PJ had ever had to do in his entire life, but it needed to be done. "Major Keller, have you ever considered taking your own life in the wake of the tragic event that took your legs away from you?"

The physical effect of his brother's question was like getting hit in the stomach with a wrecking ball that he didn't see coming. David could hardly breathe. The mental effect was, *You are my brother. How could you betray me like this?*

PJ could read his brother's mind, but he knew what he had to do at this point. He steeled himself and asked the question, "Isn't it true you bought that gun illegally because you didn't want anyone to know that you had it because it was your intention to take your own life with it?"

An utter silence fell over the courtroom. David bent forward, raised his right hand, and cradled his head between thumb and index finger. The silence lingered as his head began to lightly bob as tears issued from his eyes and landed on his empty trouser legs. In the gallery, Dr. Hightower began to weep for her client. It was a minute or more before David looked at his brother.

PJ prodded, "David, why did you buy that gun?"

David's eyes were fiery red rings that seemed to burn with a loathing for what he was about to say and disgust for having to disclose it. His deep, confident voice cracked with emotion as he began, "I ... I bought that damned gun to kill myself. I dunno ... maybe I should have done it before I came back to Onekama. None of this would have happened if I'd done that ... just bought the gun, sat in some park in Ann Arbor on that rainy day, and just pulled the trigger. But I felt like I needed to set the record straight with you and Dad." He paused to wipe some tears away, to gather his thoughts. "But everyone welcomed me home like the prodigal son ... the parade, the house, the committee that organized all of it, you, Dad, Maggie ... "

In his peripheral vision, PJ saw Myles turn as if anticipating an outburst from Clipper, but it didn't come.

"Then there was the tape from Sergeant Vassiliack." PJ, David, and Dr. Hightower were the only ones in the courtroom who knew what that was about, but it didn't need further clarification. It was obviously something that had a great impact on any decision he might make regarding suicide. "I've made peace with the fact that I'm going to be bound to this wheelchair for the rest of my life. Everyone in Onekama has given me a life there that's worth every minute of living. Suicide is not an option now, but there was a time when ... when I thought it was my only option and that is why I bought that gun."

PJ, tears staining his cheeks, managed to say, "No further questions, Your Honor. The defense rests."

McPeak broke early for lunch. It had been an emotional morning. "Court will reconvene at one o'clock with summations."

★ ★ ★ ★

The prosecution's summation was short. The defendant was guilty of murder, maybe some lesser degree of murder than open murder, but guilty nonetheless. He was also guilty of two counts of felony assault with a dangerous weapon. The general good order of the community required the jury to find David Keller guilty of such.

PJ eloquently argued that the murder charge should be dropped completely because his brother had to act to save his own life that evening as an out-of-control Ray McCall assaulted him with intent to murder. As to the two counts of felony assault with a deadly weapon, his brother at the time was in some faraway war-torn country. The fishermen at the time weren't fishermen, but the enemy, and his brother was merely doing what he'd been trained to do. He concluded that it was a sad fact that there were many like his brother who suffered from the effects of PTSD because the country had been at war for too many years.

By two thirty on that third day of the trial, the case had been remanded to the jury.

PJ and David went to TJ's pub for a drink. From there, it was their plan to head home to Onekama. "Plans for the weekend?" PJ asked his brother as they sat at the bar, cold beers in front of them.

"Maggie has invited me over for dinner tomorrow night."

PJ was aware that his brother had been seeing a lot of Maggie since his return from Ann Arbor, but thus far, Dr. Hightower's theory that their relationship might jar David's memory into total recall hadn't panned out. Nonetheless, he knew seeing her made David better.

"Jack's going to be there," David said, trepidation evident in his voice.

PJ thought for a moment, clueless about Jack's paternal background, but certainly aware of his brother's role in Ray McCall's death. He said, "Yeah, I can see where that might be a little tough, but Emily Weber tells me Jack and his father really weren't that close. She says Jack knew how badly his father was treating Maggie and he didn't like it."

"Even so, PJ, I killed Ray and now we're all going to sit

down at the dinner table together and what ... act like that never happened?"

"Listen, big brother, Natalie's got a saying, *if it's mentionable, it's manageable.* The hard part is making it mentionable. Just a suggestion, but you might want to give it a few minutes tomorrow night and see how it goes. Maybe Jack will bring it up. From what I know of him, he's a pretty good kid ... good athlete, good student." PJ paused for a moment and then added, "He's a lot like you, David, if you stop and think about it."

David didn't respond, but the irony wasn't lost on him.

"Why don't you and Maggie join us for dinner on Sunday?" When David didn't respond, PJ said, "David? Hello. Are you there?"

"Sorry. I was thinking about what you said ... the *if it's mentionable, it's manageable* thing."

PJ repeated his invitation to dinner. David smiled at him, "Can't wait to find out how it all turns out, huh?"

PJ faked a hurt look. "No, that's not it. Natalie and I are just anxious to see Maggie again, that's all." He let that comment linger for just a moment and then added, "And, hell, yes, I'm dying to know how it turns out with Jack."

David was paying the bill for their beers when PJ's phone rang. It was four thirty. The clerk advised him that the jury was back and Judge McPeak had decided to reconvene court for the verdict.

"Geez, that's awfully quick, isn't it?" David asked.

"It is," he said, but he offered nothing more.

David persisted, "So what does it mean?"

"Big brother, if I knew the answer to that question, I'd be a true legal scholar. I honestly don't know. Let's go find out."

★ ★ ★ ★

Sylvia sat alone at the prosecution's table as PJ and David arrived back at the courtroom. Sylvia smiled at them and said, "And then there was only one."

"What happened? Where's all the hired help?" PJ inquired with a smile.

"Beats the hell out of me! Myles said he had to get back to Lansing. Clipper cursed him, then me, and stomped out of my office. So, I don't know, but honestly, I'm glad they're gone."

The door to the jury room opened and the jury filed in and took their seats. The bailiff called the court to order, McPeak entered, looked at the jury foreperson, and asked, "Has the jury reached a decision in the matter of the State of Michigan vs David Keller?"

"We have, Your Honor." The foreperson offered up a folded piece of paper to the bailiff, who brought it to McPeak.

He unfolded the paper and read it. When he was finished, he looked at David and then at PJ and nodded. Normally he would ask the defendant to rise, but that was not possible in this case. PJ stood beside his brother in his wheelchair. Looking at the foreperson, the judge said, "What is your verdict?"

"We, the jury, on the charge of open murder find the defendant not guilty."

Immediately there was a reflexive sigh of relief from both David and PJ. David immediately thought of Maggie. She had not been in the courtroom at all during the trial. They had discussed it but had decided that they didn't want to give the prosecution any speculative fodder. David, though he never mentioned it to Maggie, also feared that he would not have been able to face her had the verdict gone the other way.

Continuing, the foreperson said, "On the two counts of felony assault with a deadly weapon, we, the jury, find the defendant not guilty on both counts."

David reached up, PJ bent down, and they embraced. The judge polled each juror to confirm the verdict and once done with that technicality, declared "This court is adjourned."

Sylvia stopped at the defense table and said to PJ, "Well done, Counselor." Then, extending her hand to David, she said with the utmost sincerity, "Thanks for your service, Major. I'm glad this turned out the way it did."

34

OL' TOM KELLER

The day after his acquittal David and PJ pulled to a stop in front of the hardware store. They were there to thank Bill LeVault for the chance he'd given Charlie, who was at the cash register just completing a sale as they entered. "Good mornin', Charlie," PJ said to him. "Is Bill around?"

With an air of humility, Charlie acknowledged both men, smiled, pointed in the direction of the office and said, "He's in the back fillin' out orders on a couple of big jobs. Go right on back. I'm sure he'd appreciate bein' interrupted. He's been at it for I don't know how long. I opened at six this mornin' and he was here then."

The two found him with his head buried in a catalogue and the desk top covered with many more. "Good mornin', Bill," PJ said with a lilt to his voice.

Bill looked up, smiled as though he was ready to be interrupted, and said, "Well, good mornin' to you too, PJ ... Major Keller."

David looked at him and said, "How 'bout makin' that *David,* there, Bill."

"Sure thing ... David. Nice to see you both and congratulations on what happened in court. Everybody I've talked to thinks the scales of Lady Justice balanced perfectly yesterday. Either of you want a cup of coffee? Just made a fresh pot." Without waiting for an answer, he turned and retrieved two mugs from the rack on the credenza behind him, poured two fresh cups, and topped off his own. "Take anything with this? It's pretty strong stuff. I'm orderin' materials for the new Weber house. Been at it since about four this mornin' so I made this pot extra strong."

They took the mugs, declining sugar or cream. PJ pushed David to a spot in front of Bill's desk and then took a chair next to his brother. Bill continued, "So glad the Webers are going to stay here and rebuild. Chuck is my best customer, and Emily ... well, what can I say about Emily? You know she just sold that huge lakefront parcel just north of their property for a million two and Chuck thinks the buyers are going to contract with him to build their home. Those two are really vital to our economy here in Onekama. Don't know what we'd do without them."

PJ and David nodded in agreement and the three men took sips of their coffee. David began, "Listen, Bill, PJ and I wanted to stop by today and thank you for what you did for Charley out there." He pushed a thumb over his shoulder in the direction of the storefront.

"No need to thank me, Maj ... " Bill caught himself and said, " ... uh, David. I needed someone to replace old Mike, who's been itchin' to retire and spend more time huntin' and fishin'. Charley's a good man as long as he stays away from that casino and I think he's really workin' on that little flaw in his character. Hell, we all got 'em. Sometimes we just need help in managin' them. Speakin' of managin'," Bill opened the center desk drawer, removed an envelope, and handed it over to PJ, "would you mind passin' this to your dad? It'll save him a trip comin' to get it or me havin' to take it up to the house. It's Charley's first payment on the loan Tom made him."

PJ looked at David at the same time David turned to him, their faces full of confusion. David was the one who asked the question, "Dad loaned Charley the money for his back child support?"

Bill sensed their confusion and realized he'd unwittingly disclosed to them something that apparently neither man knew. "Uh ... Uh ... listen, boys. I'm sorry. I guess I wasn't supposed to tell you. I know Tom didn't want either of you to know about the loan while the trial was going on. But now that it's over ... " there was a long and awkward pause ... "well, I guess I just thought that maybe ol' Tom had told you what he'd done. He gave me the money. Sly ol' fox that your dad is, he just said that it was a loan and I could figure out the repayment plan ... said he didn't want Charley to know where the money had come from other than me ... and I haven't told Charley different ... and I never will. But I just figured that ol' Tom had told you two what he'd done. It ain't nothin' illegal or anythin' like that is it, PJ?" Bill's voice had a fearful edge to it.

PJ looked back to Bill, who could still sense confusion, but seemed to be relieved when PJ rather absently said, "No ... No, Bill, there's nothing illegal about what either you or Dad did. Technically, the money was given as a loan, no strings attached to the trial or his testimony. Right?"

Immediately Bill's head began bobbing like a bobble-head doll, "Uh, yeah, that's exactly right, PJ." He pointed to the envelope. "Uh, do you want me to take that back and just get it to Tom? I'm happy to do that."

PJ handed him back the envelope. "Uh, yeah, Bill, that might be best for now at least."

"I ... I hope I didn't screw up telling you about how I got the money to loan Charley. I just thought ... "

PJ interrupted to reassure him that he had done no harm and then added, "We appreciate what you've done for Charley. We surely needed him at trial and you're helping to make him a contributing citizen in this community, Bill. David and I are grateful." He looked over at David, who was nodding in complete agreement. Bill changed the subject by thumbing through a file on his desk. "By the way, Henry placed an order from the committee on some roofing work you need done at your house, David." He slowly thumbed through the order and gave them an update on its progress.

When, they'd finished their coffee they again thanked him and excused themselves.

On the street in front of the hardware store, as they headed back toward their car, PJ bent down and, in a whisper, asked his brother, "Still think Dad hates you?"

35

MANAGING EXPECTATIONS

He held the Silver Star, multiple awards of the Purple Heart, he'd faced the enemy in combat over and over again, but as he pulled his van into Maggie's driveway, he felt sick to his stomach. Methodically he lowered himself out of the van, unlocked his wheelchair from the hydraulically-driven platform, remotely returned the ramp into the van, and began to roll himself toward her front door, grateful that the entire process took the time that it did. Over and over in his head, the burden of the trial lifted from his shoulders and he played out various scenarios of how it might go tonight with Jack, his son. Only Jack, of course, had no idea that David was his birth father and he and Maggie, rightly or wrongly, had both decided that this was information that should not be shared with him, at least not tonight.

Maggie met him at the front door, smiling, dressed in black slacks that accentuated her long legs and a white blouse that plunged just enough at the neckline. Around her slender neck, a single strand of black pearls was the perfect complement to her simple but classically beautiful outfit. Her long, dark hair was pulled back in a ponytail and as he looked up at her, David thought she had never been more beautiful. Maggie gave him a quick peck on the cheek and whispered, "Nervous?"

"Almost to the point of being sick. He knows I'm coming,

right?" They'd discussed this a dozen times, but he needed the reassurance.

She stood back up and merely nodded her head.

"And?" he persisted.

"And, I'll be honest, he's not thrilled."

"Any suggestions on how we play this?" David asked.

"I don't know, David. I think it best if we just play it by ear and see where Jack is tonight. He has a date later, so it's really just dinner and then he's heading out. If he brings it up during dinner ... anything ... Ray ... you ... me ... us ... let's be honest with him."

"Us? If he asks about "us," what do we say?"

"Well, I don't know about you, but I'm going to say, 'We are old friends, high-school sweethearts who lost touch with one another for a lot of years, and now circumstances have brought us back together again.' A simple honest answer, David." She stepped behind him to push him up the temporary ramp she'd had Chuck Weber install just in time for their dinner tonight.

He reached over his shoulder and put his hand on hers. "OK, Mags, but do me a favor."

"What's that?" she inquired.

"Don't leave me alone with him?"

She laughed.

★ ★ ★ ★

Maggie walked to the bottom of the stairs and called up, "Jack, dinner's ready." Both of them were disappointed that he had not come downstairs earlier and that Maggie had had to call him to dinner. They took it as a sign that Jack was not looking forward to any of this, but, if both of them had to be honest with themselves, neither could blame him.

When he came to the dining room, Maggie did the

introductions. Jack shook David's hand when he'd offered it with the greeting, "Nice to meet you, Jack." Jack had offered nothing in return except a firm but abbreviated hand shake.

Awkwardly, Maggie said, "Let's sit down and eat before it gets cold." Cold, however, was exactly how Maggie would describe the mood in the room. Dinner was served in silence. Maggie tried to make small talk, but it fell flat.

David looked at Jack and said, "Your mom tells me you play three sports."

Jack didn't look up, just nodded.

"Got a favorite?"

Between bites, Jack offered, "Baseball."

"Yeah, I liked that, too, but I think football was my favorite when I was your age."

"Was that when you were dating Mom?" Jack asked, some derision in his voice.

The comment made Maggie and David look at one another. Maggie piped up, "Yes, that's exactly when it was. David was a senior, I was a junior. I was a cheerleader, he was captain of the football team ... "

Jack interrupted her and looked at David, "So, you got promoted, huh." The crack dripped with sarcasm, but David was somewhat impressed that he was aware of the progression of army rank from captain to major.

Maggie on the other hand knew her son and she certainly recognized his sarcasm. Now it was Maggie's turn to interrupt, "Jack, don't ... "

David looked at Maggie. "No, Maggie, it's OK." He turned his attention to Jack. David had mellowed considerably in the past eight or nine months. "Yep, Jack. That's pretty much the normal progression." There was no bitterness, no anger.

Jack looked over at his mother, "Mom, I don't know what you expect of me. I didn't like the way Dad treated you. He was a jerk. But as big a jerk as he was, he didn't deserve to die for it. Now I'm sitting here at dinner with you and the man that killed him." He let that hang there for just a moment and then concluded, "And it's just weird. I guess you can do it because you and he have a history. I don't."

"Jack ... " Maggie started to say. For a minute, David thought she was going to spill the beans about their paternal relationship.

"Maggie, let me have a crack at this." David turned to Jack, "Listen, this is as hard for me as it is for you. I'm truly sorry for what happened to your dad, Jack. If I could change anything that has happened in my life, it wouldn't be this ... " he pointed to his missing legs, "it would be that I killed your father. I only have a partial memory of that night, but I know that I did that and for that I am eternally sorry."

"So why are you here now?" Jack asked. The question wasn't fueled by inquisitiveness, but by anger. "You think you can just come back into my mom's life like nothing ever happened. My grandfather says that's what you're trying to do. You left Onekama once and hurt her badly. He told me so. Are you going to do that again? Is that your plan? Because if it is, I just wish you'd leave us alone. My mom doesn't deserve to be hurt again."

Maggie's heart ached for her son. She sat, unsure of what to say, unsure of how she would answer those same questions if put to her about David. Since he'd returned from Ann Arbor, they'd seen one another nearly every day. Their relationship had started to grow again, but this time it wasn't fueled so much by hormones as it had been all those years ago when they'd been in high school. It wasn't that the hormones had gone away. They hadn't. But, now there were deeper bonds, built out of years of being apart, but never really ever forgetting how each felt about the other. There were deep feelings of mutual respect.

David began to answer Jack, but Maggie, perhaps even more than her son, lingered on his every word. "Jack ... "

This was so hard for him because it was such a difficult thing to admit to the more profound mistakes in one's life. "Jack, sixteen years ago I was angry with my father. Maybe not the same kind of anger that you have for your father and what he did to your mother, but I was angry nonetheless. I knew what I wanted to do with my life. It was honorable, yet he would have nothing to do with it. So, I left him, this town, your mom ... I left everything behind. I thought I knew what I was doing. And then this happened." He waved his hand over his missing legs again. "Since coming back to Onekama, I've had to reevaluate everything ... several times over. I know I have little right to be sitting here with you tonight, especially after what I did to your father. I know I have little right to expect your mother's friendship, but it is one of the things that I am so very grateful for now. It's changed my thinking about a lot of things, including my will to live ... "

"What do you mean 'will to live'? You mean you were considering suicide?"

"Jack!" Maggie shrieked at her son.

David held up a hand in her direction, "No, Mags, it's OK." He turned his attention back to Jack. "Yeah, I would have to say, I was right there next door to it. That gun I had was meant to put a round through my head, not your father's."

"Yeah, well ... "

"Jack!" Maggie shrieked again.

David continued, "Your mom, more than anyone else, has turned that around. She made me realize just how selfish I had been ... how selfish I was being. I don't think that way anymore. I enjoy her company. I want to continue seeing her. I know that hurts you now, but, with time, I hope I can prove to you that I'm worthy of being called your friend."

Dinner was cold. Maggie was in tears. No one had much of an appetite, but expectations, if not perfectly clear, had been roughed in. Jack looked at his mother and asked, "May I be excused? I have to get ready."

Maggie nodded. As Jack got up to go to his room, she looked over at David and mouthed, "I'm sorry."

The two of them were in the kitchen cleaning up dishes when they heard Jack come downstairs and leave through the front door. They heard the Equinox start up and Maggie watched Jack leave through the kitchen window. Maggie put a hand on his shoulder and asked, "Do you think he's going to be all right with this ... with us?"

"Only time will tell, Mags, but I am not going to give up on him ... or us ... not now ... not ever."

★ ★ ★ ★

That evening on Maggie's sofa, they made love. It was awkward at first. David needed her help to get into position; pillows had to be rearranged on a trial-and-error basis. They laughed at their clumsiness. She cried at his gentleness. He wrapped his arms around her so tightly and told her he'd never really forgotten her touch, her scent. They weren't the kids they'd been sixteen years ago. Life had matured both, but the naturalness of their union, even without David's legs, was as it had always been. Instead of lingering over the lost years, they ended the evening talking about their future ... and how Jack might someday fit in.

AFTER THE SNOW HAD FLOWN

Maggie and David sat at the foot of the boat ramp in the chilly darkness of a moonless night. It was October 18. The sunset that evening had been obscured from view by the approaching storm. The temperature hovered just below the freezing point and snow was in the forecast. Maggie didn't see the first snowflake, rather, she felt it. It landed on her cheek and the warmth of her skin immediately turned it into water that ran down her face like a tear. Maggie grabbed his hand and squeezed it. With his other hand, David reached across and covered her hand with his. "It's been a helluva year, hasn't it, Mags?" She merely nodded and smiled at him. "Henry Hanratty came to see me today," he said to her.

"Really. What did Henry want?"

"Asked me if I'd ever considered a career in politics."

"You're kidding?"

"No. Seems as though Pat Kincaid is term-limited for the State House of Representatives. Henry wanted to know if I'd consider running in the Republican primary."

"What did you tell ... "

"No." He interrupted her.

"You know you'd be ... "

He pulled her over to him and kissed her gently, then said, "I told him I made you a promise."

"David, you shouldn't ... "

"No, Mags, I left you once, I'm sure as hell not going

to do that again. If I won, I'd have to be in Lansing too much ... away from you." He smiled broadly at her. "Besides, I've been thinking. I can't just lay around here not earning my keep. You've got the Yellow Dog. I need something to keep me busy. But state politics isn't the answer. I've looked into what I would need to do to get a teaching certificate. Looks like about twelve, maybe fifteen hours of course work and I could qualify as a math and science teacher. I talked with the principal at the high school. He says they can always find a job for me. Maybe even do a little coaching after school. So, what do you think?"

"I don't want you to shortchange yourself."

"C'mon, Mags. I'm not doin' that. Teaching right now really sounds like something I'd like to do. Politics ... not so much ... I wouldn't like that. Besides, I had a good recommendation for someone who would be great at that job."

"Who?"

"PJ."

She chuckled, "What did Henry say to that?"

"He thanked me and shook my hand. I saw him pull his phone out on his way to his car. A little later PJ called me and said Henry had just been there."

"And?"

"Looks like PJ's going to put his hat in the ring! Want to know something else even more astounding?"

"Wow! This is a lot to wrap my head around."

"You ain't heard nothing yet. Henry told PJ that he was on his way over to Clipper's house. He's going to ask Clipper to endorse PJ as the Republican nominee."

"Oh, my God. Henry had to know what kind of a buzz saw he'd be running into."

"PJ said he told Henry he'd better be ready for Clipper to come off the rails. Henry told PJ it didn't matter. Clipper needed to get over it or sit back and watch while the Manistee Republican Party Committee moved forward with PJ's nomination."

"What do you think Natalie thinks of all this?"

A sheepish look crossed David's face and then he gave her one of those smiles that said, *I know something you don't.* It was, to say the least, a bit disconcerting to her, as was his answer to her question. "Didn't think too much about it. I know she doesn't mind the big city ... "

Maggie laughed. "And how did you deduce that?"

"Well, you heard her the other night when we were in Traverse City with them. She said she wouldn't mind living up there."

Maggie remembered the brief conversation and didn't quite recall it the way David had. "Well, that's quite a leap. What she said was 'I love that house.' She was talking about a particular house that was for sale a couple of blocks south of Front Street, David. She didn't say she wanted to move there."

He shrugged his shoulders and nodded. "Yeah, I suppose you're right, but I don't think she minds the big city and once PJ's elected, there will be times when she needs to be in Lansing with him. That's something she'll need to get used to. She'll be spending more and more time in Lansing."

"You're quite confident he'll get elected, aren't you?"

"Yeah, Mags, I am. PJ's going to be governor of this great state one day and Natalie will be right there with him. And I will need to be right here to take over with Dad." He'd said that without ever thinking of all the ramifications of it. In the short time he'd been home, he'd not noticed any further decline in his father. All he knew was that his father was different than he remembered him.

Maggie reached over and took his hand in hers and said, "*We* will need to be right here to take over with Dad, is what you meant to say."

He looked at her as tears formed in both their eyes, perhaps from the brisk north wind that had just picked up, perhaps not, but David again knew she was right. That *was* what he'd meant to say, and he loved her for reassuring him. He felt Maggie shiver. "Let's go inside, it's getting cold out here."

She folded her chair and placed it across his lap and stepped behind the wheelchair to cover the short distance to David's house. As she pushed, she said, "OK, now it's my turn to share some unexpected news ... two pieces of it."

"Good news? Bad news?" he chuckled.

"I don't know, David. You're going to have to tell me."

"OK. Now you have my curiosity piqued."

This time it was Maggie's turn to chuckle as they reached the door to the house. The snow had intensified, huge flakes of the stuff coming down heavily and beginning to cover the grass in the park and around his house, but not on the warmer asphalt roads. There had already been half a dozen heavy frosts that chilled the earth, but the sun during the day was quicker to warm the roadbeds than the frozen ground. "OK, let's get inside. This all might come easier with a glass of wine," she said.

David turned on the gas-log fireplace as Maggie poured them each a glass of merlot. As she gave him his, he looked at her and said, "OK, the suspense is killing me. What's your news?"

Standing in front of the fire, she drew a deep breath and began, "Let's talk about Jack, first."

"OK," he said somewhat warily.

"He came home today from school with a scholarship application."

"Great! Where to?"

"Western Michigan University. They have, according to Jack, one of the top aviation schools in the country. He's thinking he wants to be a pilot."

David smiled broadly and rubbed his chin. "Well, he's certainly got the smarts for something like that. His eyes are good. He shouldn't have any difficulty with the physical or mental end of being a pilot."

"Uh, yeah ... that's what Jack said, too. Have you and he talked about this?"

"No. But I've known a few pilots in my time. Crazy dudes that drove army helicopters." He was trying to be humorous, but he could now sense that Maggie didn't want this conversation to be humorous. He shifted gears, "What is it, Maggie?"

"It's the scholarship application, David."

"What about it? That has to be an expensive program. I'm sure it's going to involve a lot of flight hours. Those are going to be some whopping lab fees ... "

Maggie cut him off. "It's an Army ROTC scholarship application, David. Jack wants to become an army helicopter pilot."

David's head dropped and his eyes focused on where his legs should have been. In an instant, his senior year of high school flashed in front of his eyes: all the dysfunction that the riff between him and his father had caused. He shook his head. "Oh, Maggie!"

"Yeah, I know. How ironic can things get."

"OK, let's talk about this. What was your first thought when he told you?"

Maggie looked at him. She was so very grateful she had him to talk to about this, but, at the same time, she was reluctant to bring up painful times in his past. Somewhat tentatively, she said, "What do you think?" The question was, of course, rhetorical; she knew intuitively his mind had gone to the same place hers had when she first learned about Jack's idea. "I went right to the trouble you and your father had in dealing with your appointment to West Point. I wouldn't blame you if you looked at this exactly the way your father thought about you joining up. I mean, my God, David, you were nearly killed."

He took a drink of the merlot. A long silence drew out between them. Each knew the other was trying desperately to work their way through all of this. Finally, David said to her, "Mags, listen, what happened to me was, pure and simple, an act of war. Sure, we can argue about whether the war is just or not. God knows, that certainly was the argument my father tried to make with me about Vietnam. I didn't listen to him then and if I were to take that same approach to this thing with Jack, I would devalue my ten years of service. I would devalue the sacrifices of everyone who has ever served this country, much less those who have died for it. My dad was drafted. He didn't have a choice. I did. No one made me go to the academy. No one made me stay in for as long as I did. And no one is forcing Jack to do this. It's his choice. It's an honorable choice. And I think we have to honor his right to make that choice."

She didn't respond. David had repositioned himself onto the sofa. She joined him there, snuggled close to him, and nuzzled her head against his shoulder. They sat there for a long time until finally David asked, "So, the second thing has to be easier. What's the second thing you wanted to tell me?"

Maggie lifted her head, stared into his eyes, and said, "I'm pregnant."

★ ★ ★ ★ *POSTLUDE* ★ ★ ★ ★

It was the spring of 1970 and I was a young army lieutenant when I answered the phone in my quarters early one morning. The staff duty officer told me there had been a death, probably a suicide. What we found was both gruesome and poignant. The soldier, a medic by training, had nineteen morphine syrettes stuck in his arm. Doctors who later examined the body said they didn't know how he remained conscious long enough to insert that many needles into himself. We also found a letter, not from the deceased, but from a girl back home. As the battalion's personnel officer, it was my job to begin the long notification process that would stretch from Germany all the way back to the Pentagon and then halfway across the US. The soldier's unsuspecting parents would be told by a next-of-kin notification officer what had happened to their son. Next-of-kin duty is truly one of the toughest things a service member can be assigned. There is no easy way to tell a loved one the tragic news and it is especially difficult when the cause of death is suicide.

What causes a person to believe that suicide is the only way out? The feeling of isolation must be overwhelming. They may feel completely bereft of any possible solution to their problem(s). They may feel that their burden is heavy beyond their ability to bear it and there is no one to help them take it on. They may feel overwhelming guilt about something in their life; perhaps even guilt over what they are contemplating. They may feel a deep and abiding sense of loss that drives them into the depths of depression. I've listened to Kevin Hines, a suicide survivor, who freely tells his story around the world in hopes of preventing someone else from doing what he tried to do. Suffering from bipolar disorder, he says he felt all of these things. He is passionate and poignant, making the point that in the split second between the time he jumped off the Golden Gate Bridge and the next instant when he hit the rough waters below, he felt a deep and abiding regret over what he'd just done.

Yet, his answer to the question of what can be done to prevent suicide is not difficult at all to grasp: TALK TO SOMEONE.

That solution sounds easy ... but it isn't. The critical thing is someone must take the first step. If you are the person contemplating the act, you have to overcome that overwhelming depression that is gripping you and reach out to someone. Hines tells the story of standing on the bridge with other pedestrians the day he jumped and hoping just one of them might say something to him, but no one did. Maybe if he'd reached out to one of them, his leap to the waters below would never have happened. Likewise, things might have been different if just one person on the bridge that day had gone over to him as he stood at the rail staring down into the bay and said *what?* I don't know for sure what I'd say, but it might be something like, *"It's a long way down there, isn't it?"* Or, perhaps, *"The water sure looks rough from up here, doesn't it?"* You might say something completely different. The point is, you've just become a much needed distraction and pulled their mind away from what they are thinking. A single simple question from a complete stranger could prove to be the difference between life and death.

It's important to realize that it's OK to feel inadequately prepared to help. Most of us aren't mental health professionals, but that person contemplating such a desperate act doesn't care about your credentials. You have been chosen by *who? Them? Someone else? Or maybe you were chosen by God.* All that really matters is that you have been chosen to be that precious Samaritan. You have become the barrier in someone else's struggle between life and death. First, just LISTEN. Then help them find professional help. Don't know where that help might come from?

The National Suicide Prevention Hotline Number is 1-800-273-8255.

If they won't call, then make the call for them. Lead them to help. No one should ever die like that soldier in my unit did all those many years ago. Likewise, neither you nor I should ever suffer the burden of guilt for not having helped when we could have ... when we should have.

ACKNOWLEDGMENTS

There is an almost overwhelming sense of accomplishment when an author finally gets to hold his or her book in their hands. It is the culmination of endless hours of thought, writing, rewriting, more thought, and then more rewriting. It is easy for us to sit there and dote on what we have just finished.

However, those of us who take this art form seriously understand that, unlike other art forms, writing is one that very seldom is made best when only one person is involved in its creation. I certainly am not an exception to this rule. So, I gloat only momentarily over my accomplishment and then realize that there are many people to thank for the book that I hold in my hand, and hopefully, the book you either will read or have just finished reading.

Let me begin with my wife, Diane. She is my ultimate beta reader...my editor-in-chief...and my biggest fan. She is always supportive, even when she is being critical, and, I hasten to add, she is almost always right. I could not do this sort of thing without her and, in the case of this book, I have relied upon her expertise as a licensed professional counselor.

My daughter, Brynn, still a true military brat after all these years, told me she thought this was the best book I've written. That kept me going and made me want to make it even better.

I have two "go-to" beta-readers, Marie Showers and Dr. Rolla Baumgartner. Both of them are voracious readers...

fiction, nonfiction, romance, thriller, memoir, historical fiction...it doesn't matter. They are two of the most well-read people I know and I have come to trust their comments about my work. In the case of this book, they saw the weaknesses, provided feedback, offered gentle suggestions, and then followed up with a reread. Many, many thanks to the both of them.

I am indebted to long-time friend and retired judge Al Garbrecht. The trial scenes in the book are important and my experience there is largely limited to what I watch on TV. Al helped me keep it real. The same is true for Dr. Jay Sewick and Captain Emilee Johnson, Army Nurse Corps, when it came to the medical details. How blessed I am to have these three experts to fall back on and to be able to call each of them *friend*.

I want to give credit to my writers group. We call ourselves the Manistee Writers' Group, a collection of a dozen or so folks who take writing seriously for a huge variety of reasons. Their comments have helped me immensely. I can't thank these folks enough!

Finally, there is *my* team at Mission Point Press. Now, let me say that they aren't *just my team*. They are every author's team that works with Mission Point Press. But during the process of my three collaborations with them, I have always felt like I was the only one they were working for. I thank Anne Stanton, Doug Weaver, Heather Shaw, and Tanya Muzumdar for another great experience and for helping me make *Before the Snow Flies* the best it can be.

ABOUT THE AUTHOR

John Wemlinger is a retired U.S. Army colonel with 27 years of service. The author of three novels, he lives now in Onekama, Michigan, with his wife, Diane, close to the Lake Michigan shore. When he and their border collie, Sydney, aren't roaming the beaches or nearby hiking trails, he is playing golf, working on his next novel, creating an unusual piece of original art from the driftwood, rocks, and beach glass that he finds along the shoreline, or is working on becoming conversationally proficient in the German language. One of the true joys of his life is talking with people about his books and his art. He can be contacted at www.johnwemlinger.com, or follow him on Facebook.

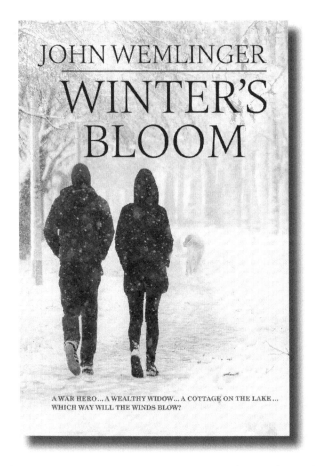

FOR OVER THREE DECADES, Rock Graham has carried the physical and emotional scars from a tour in Vietnam. He is a decorated war hero, but guilt from what happened one dark night in a steaming Southeast Asia jungle is always lying in ambush, waiting for an unguarded moment to set his demons free. When he tries to find solitude at a cottage on Lake Michigan in the dead of winter, a chance encounter on the desolate, frozen shoreline changes his life forever.

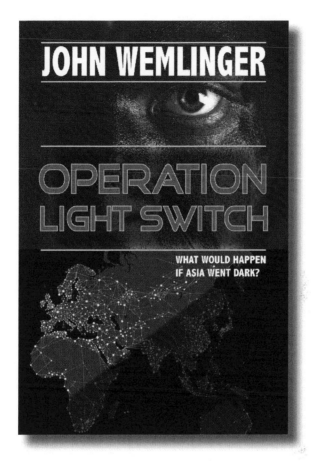

CLEVELAND SPIRES, A RESPECTED AND HIGHLY DECORATED SOLDIER, lost his career, his family, and much of his pride when he was sent to prison for a crime he did not commit. Now he's out, and after returning to his hometown, he stumbles onto a clue that might prove his innocence. That clue leads him to Bangkok, Thailand, where he finds himself thrust into the middle of an international conspiracy that will rock the global economy. What he does next will take all of his courage and an unflinching faith in a system that once failed him.

41968831R00189

Made in the USA
Middletown, DE
14 April 2019